**TOR ROMANCE BOOKS BY CONSTANCE O'DAY-FLANNERY**

*Shifting Love*
*Colliding Forces*
*Best Laid Plans*
*Twice in a Lifetime\**
*Old Friends\**

\*forthcoming

# Best
## Laid Plans

# Best Laid Plans

## CONSTANCE
## O'DAY-FLANNERY

tor romance

A TOM DOHERTY ASSOCIATES BOOK
NEW YORK

BEST LAID PLANS

Edited by Anna Genoese

A Tor Book
Published by Tom Doherty Associates, LLC
175 Fifth Avenue
New York, NY 10010

Tor® is a registered trademark of Tom Doherty Associates, LLC.

ISBN-10: 0-7394-6788-3
ISBN-13: 978-0-7394-6788-6

Printed in the United States of America

This is for the one who really
believes it's all an adventure

# Chapter

## I

WASN'T SHE A LUCKY WOMAN?

Well, maybe not lucky. Fortunate.

Luck implied chance, and it was not chance. More of a blessing.

*Yes, you are a fortunate woman, Cristine Dobbins, blessed with a wonderful life,* she thought, maneuvering her way through rush-hour traffic. Even the weather seemed to be smiling down on her as a warm breeze played with the tendrils of her hair. She quickly looked into the rearview mirror at a red light and decided her hair would have to do, but she could use some lip gloss. Checking the traffic light, Cristine reached into her purse and fumbled through the mess until her fingers felt the little pot. She quickly unscrewed the lid and dipped her pinky inside. Spreading the goo on her bottom lip, she pressed her lips together and thought of the note Charlie had left this morning by the coffeepot.

*Don't make plans tonight.*

She dropped the gloss back into her purse and grinned. Charlie . . . just thinking about him brought a smile and a warm cozy feeling. She looked at her left hand on the steering wheel as the last of the sun's rays caught the diamonds in her wedding band, tiny, perfectly cut diamonds channel-set into wide gold. It wasn't a true wedding band, not really. She and Charlie weren't so provincial as to get married. Seven years ago they had fallen in love and within three months had moved in together. Bliss. Well, mostly bliss. She tried not to think about the challenging times. It was a pretty darn good relationship in a world where over fifty percent of marriages ended in divorce. She and Charlie had stayed together, working their way over little hiccups along the way. Nothing ever serious.

As she pulled away from the light, she was excited to arrive home. Maybe he was taking her out to dinner, or maybe he had made dinner for them. He didn't do it often, but when he did she felt like a pampered woman. In her mind, she pictured the last time . . . months ago, when she had arrived home in the dark to find the door open, soft music playing, candles lit, and the table set on the patio. It had been an unusually warm autumn evening and so romantic. Charlie knew how to do romance when the urge hit him. Too bad they had consumed so much wine during the evening that they'd both fallen asleep while attempting to make love.

Her eyes narrowed at that thought. With both of them so busy with work and the remodeling of the kitchen, it had been a while since they'd made love. Excuses. A frantic life got in the way of romance. But now Charlie was making it a priority. One of them always brought the relationship back into the center again. A little flutter of excitement began in her stomach and she was glad she'd washed her hair this morning in the shower. Shoulder length, it needed to be trimmed and she might also treat herself to having it colored, streaking the brown with some blond highlights for the summer.

Charlie would like that.

Again she smiled as the diamonds in her ring glittered in the sun. Charlie had one just like it. They introduced each other to strangers as husband or wife, since it was easier than trying to explain their partnership after seven years together. She and Charlie thought alike, truly believing that marriage was an obsolete institution. Really, who in their right mind would want to live in an institution? Wasn't it better for two people, two relatively sane adults, who loved each other to remain together for just that . . . love? Wasn't it far healthier to be together because you truly wanted to be with that person? It was much more civilized to have a renewable contract every seven years. If you knew your contract was up for renewal, you wouldn't take your partner for granted. You would communicate and resolve issues. And if you didn't want to renew, the parting was spelled out without all the high drama of conventional split-ups. It was the only sane thing to do, she thought as she turned onto their street.

Feeling very happy and more than a little sexy, she tried to suppress a giggle of anticipation as she continued the rest of the way home. She loved their house with its wide wraparound porch. Actually, it was her house, her first house, and she had seen the possibilities in remodeling it herself. And then Charlie had come along and had taken over. The kitchen was the last and most expensive room, and that should be done within a few months. Then they would be settled, and she almost laughed when she thought how Charlie would cringe at describing them with such a boring term. But they were comfortable with each other, accepting of each other, and she trusted him with her life. Most importantly, they loved each other and they were a good team. Together, they had accomplished so much. Pulling the car into the driveway, she noticed Charlie's SUV in the garage and it looked full.

Grinning, she wondered what he had bought now. Maybe something for the kitchen, she thought as she turned off the car engine and grabbed her purse. She'd have to remind him the garage door was open. He probably just forgot. Again, she smiled, anxious to see what surprise he had in store for her.

She unlocked the front door, walked inside, and dropped her keys onto the foyer table. From some distant corner of her mind, she had the sensation that something was not right, something was different . . . missing. The sculpture she and Charlie had bought together on their trip to Europe was gone. Blinking, Cristine turned her head toward the living room and her jaw dropped. More than half the books were missing from the built-in shelves around the fireplace. Everything looked different, as though someone had gone through all their belongings, removing certain things and disrupting the flow of the room. "Charlie?" Even to her, her voice sounded tiny, scared. Had they been robbed? "Charlie!"

"I'm right here."

She spun around at the sound of his voice. "What happened?" she demanded, rushing to him and clasping his forearm. "Were we robbed?"

He shook his head. "No, Cristine. Sit down."

"I don't understand," she muttered as he led her into the living room where she perched on the edge of the sofa. Her stomach muscles tightened and she suddenly felt sick to her stomach. Something terrible was coming. She just knew it, as she stared up into Charlie's serious expression. "What's going on?"

He sat opposite her, on the edge of the square coffee table. Blowing his breath out roughly, he ran his hand through his hair. "Cristine, there's no easy way to say this."

"Say what?" she demanded, feeling her heart begin to race. Had someone died? But then why was the house looking like this and—

"We need to talk," Charlie said, looking very uncomfortable as he interrupted her thoughts.

"Okay," she said slowly, feeling as if she had stepped into someone else's life.

"I . . . I don't know how to begin this, Cristine."

He looked so forlorn that she reached out and touched his hand. "Just tell me, Charlie. We can talk about anything."

"I'm leaving," he said, pulling his hand back from her fingers. "It's what we agreed to. Seven years. The contract. I don't want to renew. It's over, Cristine."

She stared at him as he rattled off his short, clipped sentences, stared at his tall lanky frame, those long fingers that had so lovingly caressed her body; his sandy hair that gray strands were weaving through, his brown eyes behind his rimless glasses, that Ralph Lauren pale blue shirt she had bought him last year. It was as though time stood still as seven years of love flashed across the expressway of her mind. This couldn't be happening. She couldn't have heard him correctly. "What?" she asked in a shocked voice.

"I'm leaving."

Just two words, yet their impact made her feel as if she had been shot under the center of her breasts. Instinctively, her hand pressed up against her solar plexus, as though to protect it from further assault. "Why?" she whispered, still unable to grasp the reality of his words. It didn't seem real. He didn't seem real. She felt as though she were falling into an alien world where nothing made sense.

"C'mon, Cristine, things haven't been right for months now."

"What hasn't been right?" she asked, hating that her voice was beginning to tremble. "I've been under pressure at work and exhausted when I come home and I haven't given you the attention you need? Is that what hasn't been right?"

He got up and began pacing in front of the coffee table. "I'm not going to do this. We had a contract. I've fulfilled it. Seven years. Now I'm moving on."

"Why, Charlie?" she demanded, no longer able to stop

the tears from sliding down her cheeks. "I deserve to know why. What have I done? We don't argue. You're my best friend, and I thought I was yours. Why are you doing this to us?" This was insanity. It couldn't be happening. Not to them! Everyone thought they were the perfect couple . . .

He shook his head. "You don't get it, do you?" He looked away from her to the darkened television. "I've met someone else and I want to explore that relationship. I have the right to explore it."

She lost her ability to respond. She didn't even know if she was breathing. She could only stare up at him as the truth finally was revealed and she felt the bile rising in her throat. He was forty-six years old and he was talking like some young kid who didn't know about commitment, who thought seven years of love could so easily be flushed down the toilet. "I . . . I . . . don't understand," she said stupidly. Of course she understood. He was dumping her for another woman! She just didn't want to believe it.

"I'm leaving, Cristine," he answered more forcefully. "I took the day off to pack and I'll be back sometime this weekend for the rest of my things."

She knew she must look like a wounded deer because she felt as if she'd just been run over by a Mack truck. "Where are you going?" she asked incredulously, still not accepting his words.

"I have a place."

"A place?" She gulped, finding that shock was robbing her of her ability to communicate in anything but questions.

He nodded, jamming his hands into his pockets.

Her eyes narrowed as her brain started to kick in. Wait a minute . . . "Who is this woman? How long have you been seeing her? Are you going to her now?" Okay, so she was still asking questions, but now they were the important ones.

"You don't know her," Charlie said, looking out to the foyer, as though he couldn't bear to see what he was doing.

"So you've been cheating on me? For how long?"

"Do we have to go through this?"

She rose to her feet, a little surprised that they actually held her upright. "Yes, we do," she stated in a stronger voice, hating that tears were brimming in her eyes and blurring her vision. "You didn't communicate before, so yes, *now* would be a good time!" Shock was quickly segueing into something far more powerful. "How long, Charlie?"

"I met her before Christmas."

She knew her mouth had dropped open like a dead fish, yet all she could see in her mind's eye was Charlie on Christmas Eve, asking whether she minded if he went to his office Christmas party with a few of the guys from work. He'd acted as if it were a chore he'd had to perform for his coworkers. He'd even bought himself a new outfit, and she had complimented him, telling him how great he looked and wishing him a good time. He'd said he was only making an appearance, yet hadn't come home until almost midnight. She remembered sitting on the sofa at ten o'clock, feeling a little hurt that he was leaving her alone on Christmas Eve, her first real day off after months of working overtime. He had been with *her,* and now she knew it in every cell of her body.

What an actor he was, deceiving her so easily . . .

"You bastard," she spat at him. "You liar, deceiver. So for months now you've been cheating on me, plotting behind my back, and now, *now* you've decided you can communicate?"

"I knew you were going to make this ugly," he said, and walked out of the room into the kitchen.

"It *is* ugly!" she nearly screamed as she followed him. "And you broke our contract! I trusted you with my life, and you could do this, *like this*? As a done deal? I don't have any say in the matter, except to accept it? Who are you? You're like this stranger, this ugly, manipulative stranger."

"Well, then you should be glad to be rid of me," he said, picking up a square brown box and carrying it toward the laundry room door that led into the garage.

"Get the hell out of my house," she said in a deadly quiet voice. Thank God the knives were behind her in the kitchen because her fingers were itching to hurt him, to rip at him the way his words were slicing away at her heart, her dignity, her very soul . . .

"As you can see, Cristine, that is exactly what I'm attempting to do." He threw the box onto the passenger seat and got into the driver's. "I'll call you in a few days after you've calmed down and we can discuss me finishing up here."

She watched him throw the car into reverse and back out of her garage, out of her house, out of her life. Just like that, she thought, gripping the door molding to keep herself upright.

Charlie was gone.

Wasn't it only minutes ago she was patting herself on the back, telling herself she was a fortunate woman?

She had no idea how long she spent at the laundry room doorway, staring out to the parking space that always had been Charlie's. It was the pain in her feet that broke through her shock. Blinking, she touched the button to automatically close the garage door and backed up into the laundry room. She closed the interior door, removing one high heel and then the other. She felt like a ghost as she carried her shoes through the house, through the half-finished kitchen, the foyer, and up the stairs.

She didn't want to go into the bedroom, afraid of what she'd see, but it was almost as though something else or someone else was pushing her down the hallway, past the guest bathroom and into the place where she had shared all her intimacy with a man who had turned into a cruel stranger. She dropped her heels onto the rug and walked up to his closet. She watched her hand shakily open the door.

Empty.

She knew his dresser drawers would also be cleaned out so she didn't put herself through that slice of pain. It was enough to see his matching ring placed in the center of the wooden top, discarded, just like her. Instead, she slipped off her skirt, stepped out of it, and sat on the edge of her bed, slowly unbuttoning her suit jacket. She pulled the sleeves off and dropped it to the foot of the bed, then attempted to unbutton her blouse, but her fingers wouldn't stop shaking so she gave up and crawled up to her pillow.

Sinking onto the mattress, she reached out and grabbed Charlie's pillow and clasped it to her chest, hearing the raw wail of agony bubbling up in her throat and choking her.

How unfair of him, she cried, gasping for air, for sanity.

He had taken everything, and left his damned scent on the pillow.

She glanced at the clock in the kitchen and sighed deeply as she reached for the bottle of red wine. At least the bastard hadn't touched the wine collection. And if he thought he deserved any he was truly crazy, she thought as she poured herself another glass. Sipping the Merlot, she tried not to think about missing work again. So what? She deserved a few days off, didn't she? After all, the man she'd trusted with her life had just betrayed her and she hadn't the energy to continue with life as normal. Nothing ever again in her life was going to be normal.

How could she have been so wrong? Why hadn't she seen this coming?

*Because you loved him and trusted him and never would have believed he was capable of such deception,* her mind screamed back at her.

She felt so foolish as she glanced at the telephone, silent for the last two days. He hadn't even called to find out how she was, if she'd slit her wrists or . . . no, he knew she wouldn't do anything to herself. She was the strong one. He was weak and needy. His damned allergies to dust mites or anything else that might upset his delicate immune system had ruled their lives, but it was a trade-off, right? No one was perfect. Charlie had come with his own matching set of baggage, but the love they'd shared had offset that near-anal obsession of his with dust. At least that was the deal she'd been telling herself for the last seven fucking years of catering to his every need . . . and boy, did he have a lot of needs. He was as close to a hypochondriac as she ever wanted to know, always prone to colds and upper respiratory diseases. How many times had she nursed him through bronchitis? Or ear infections, or some other ailment that demanded her attention? Talk about high maintenance. She'd run her life around him, what was best for him, what was healthy for him, denying herself to keep him happy and healthy and . . .

Damn, had she given up her identity for him?

No, no, she had loved him unconditionally, connecting to his soul, forging a new kind of relationship based on respect . . .

What kind of respect had he shown toward her when he'd first decided to betray her with another woman?

Charlie didn't respect her. He'd used her, as his personal nursemaid, until he'd found someone else who maybe wasn't as tired of his litany of complaints.

Someone else.

Another blow that felt like a baseball bat to the side of her head.

Who the hell was he, then? Who had she devoted seven years of her life to? Someone who could so easily deceive and betray her?

She was a fool.

She was the only one who had loved unconditionally and now that was—

The sudden ringing of the phone halted her introspection and she raced over to the kitchen wall to pick it up. It was him. Finally, he was calling. He had said a few days to calm down. Maybe he'd calmed down too and realized how irrational his behavior was and—"Hello?" she asked with hope in her voice.

"Cristine? How are you?"

She felt her entire body sag with disappointment. "Tina. Hi."

"So how are you, girl? This is day two of what? A virus? A bug? Do not tell me you've got spring fever, because I just know you would not leave me hanging here at the office to rest on your laurels while my own laurels are in a permanent state of numbed attachment to this desk chair."

"I'm sorry, Tina. I . . . I just can't . . ."

"Can't what? *What* is wrong with you? You never miss work."

Cristine gulped down the lump of emotion and just said it. "Charlie left me."

"What?"

"You heard me. He's gone."

"Gone where? Holy shit, Cris, when did this go down?"

"Two days ago when I came home from work and he was already packed. He's got another woman, has had her since Christmas."

"Oh, my God. I'm so sorry," Tina whispered with sincerity. "This is unbelievable. I thought you two were fine, so happy and . . ."

"Yeah, me too," Cristine said, sniffling. "I thought we were so damned enlightened, you know? Two spirits soaring together and pioneering a new age of relationship. What crap, huh? The only thing lightened is my bank balance and the contents of my home."

"Oh, God . . . I am so sorry, Cristine." There was a pause. "Does anyone else know?"

"Know what? That I've been dumped by the person I trusted with my life? I don't think so, Tina. In fact, I'd appreciate it if you kept this to yourself."

"Why? You need friends right now."

Cristine looked down at her pajama bottoms. She'd worn them for two days and the cotton material was sagging at the knees, distancing itself from her unwashed body. She was pathetic, deservedly pathetic. "Look, Tina. Maybe this is just a midlife crisis for Charlie, you know? Men have them all the time, screw up their lives, and then they eventually come to their senses. I don't want to make a big deal of this to everyone and then no one will forget what a dog he was to me and nothing will ever again be the same."

"Now, you listen to me, you fool. Nothing *will* ever be the same again. Ever. Don't you get that? He's deceived you. How are you gonna trust him again? You want to be his warden if he comes back? What kind of life is that, for either of you? His choices, his actions, have destroyed what you had. Maybe something different can replace that someday if he has deep therapy or a lobotomy, but what you had is altered, gone, kiddo, and the sooner you face that the better off you're gonna be."

Cristine felt the tears well up again and her throat tighten. "Don't say that, Tina. I don't know how to go on without him. It's like slicing off my own arm. I don't know how to do it."

She heard Tina's loud sigh.

"Okay, look, I'll cover for you until Friday, but then

you are simply going to have to pull yourself together and get back to work next week. This is a business, *our* business, remember?"

"I don't know how to pull my life back together," Cristine whimpered, feeling helpless and hopeless and abandoned, and seeing herself as the righteous victim of cruel circumstances.

"Well, I do," Tina declared. "With a little help from your friends, that's how."

"Tina—"

"Shut up. I'm calling an emergency meeting of the Yellow Brick Road Gang. Friday night. Your place. Be prepared." She then hung up the phone.

Cristine blinked. Sniffling loudly, she replaced the receiver onto the wall.

Damn it, damn it, damn it. As if things weren't bad enough, she thought while reaching for her wine glass and gulping the remaining Merlot. Damn it all to hell and back. Now the real torture was going to begin.

The Yellow Brick Road Gang.

There would be no stopping them.

FRIDAY SEEMED TO SPEED TOWARD HER WITH THE force of a bullet aimed at her head, and Cristine knew ducking to avoid impact wouldn't save her. She would've had to leave the country to get away from the gang and what she knew was coming.

She'd taken a shower, had even dressed in jeans and a cotton sweater. Somehow, she'd pulled her act together enough to make a vegetable dip and a pan of brownies. She had already figured out that when Tina called the group and told them her news they would descend upon her with more food than she could consume in a month. And none of them had called. Not a good sign. That meant they were saving themselves for tonight, for a frontal charge. Lighting a sandalwood candle, Cristine thought of the women who would walk through her front door and, despite her dread, found herself smiling. Through thick and thin, good times and bad, tragedies and victories, they had remained friends, as close as family, maybe closer in her case.

They had thought of calling themselves Metaphysical Misadventurers in the Search for Enlightenment, but everyone agreed it was too long and too difficult to say. Then Isabel had come up with the Yellow Brick Road Gang and all had approved.

Cristine pictured each one as she took down six wine glasses, preparing for their arrival. Isabel, the oldest, was a well-respected clinical hypnotherapist specializing in children's learning disabilities who had lost her extraordinary husband seven years ago and was still a hippie at heart. Claire, a financial adviser, fascinated by the stock market and legal affairs, as evidenced by her spectacular divorce settlement and her uncanny ability to pick and sell off stocks, would be the hardest on her tonight. There was Kelly, a computer sales rep who claimed to be the world's most powerful loser magnet with a teenage daughter approaching puberty, and who had a soft heart for the underdogs in life. And then there was Paula, the anthropologist turned housewife, with a wild tribe of five kids and a work-obsessed husband. All of them came together eight years ago as a book club and began a spiritual Oprah-like search. They had explored Eastern and Western religions, as well as the goddess culture. They had discovered tarot cards, the Kabbalah, Tantric sex, crystals, channeling. You name it; they had delved into it in some form or another.

Throughout the eight years they had become close friends, and each woman, with her own timing, had arrived at the realization that after all their searching for knowledge and guidance they had come full circle. The only constant is change and the only thing they knew for certain was that they actually knew nothing for certain. Anything is possible at any time, any moment. Thus the group's name. After all their misadventures along the road of philosophy and self-help . . . they had become women without rules and believed the answers inevitably are in your own backyard. All you have to do is pay attention.

Hah! She certainly hadn't been paying attention to her own backyard. Wait till the women got a hold of her tonight. One of them was sure to point that out.

Each one of them had bought a pair of red high heels to click and she knew the gang would show up in them tonight. Her own were by the front door. No sense in torturing her feet until she had to. She was pouring herself a second glass of a decent Chilean wine when the doorbell rang, causing her to jump with fear.

Sighing deeply, Cristine gently put the wine bottle back on the counter and walked toward the front of her house. Before she opened the door, she slipped her feet into her red high heels to which she had glued glitter on the toes years ago. Oh, if she could only click her heels now and vanish for the next twenty-four hours. Instead, she took another deep steadying breath and reached for the doorknob. There would be no escape for her.

"Cristine!" Red-haired, as tall and skinny as a Calvin Klein model, Kelly threw an arm around Cristine and whispered, "I am so sorry, honey. Don't you worry. We're going to fix you right up."

Cristine nodded as she allowed Kelly to enter the house, and was immediately wrapped in Paula's embrace. "You poor thing," Paula said, patting Cristine's back in sympathy.

Cristine inhaled the distinctive aroma of baked cookies mixed with Chloe perfume surrounding Paula. The perfume had probably been applied right before she left her wild brood with her husband. She stroked Paula's back, touching her long braid of dark brown hair. "I'm okay," she lied, pulling back. "Come in, come in . . ."

Paula looked deeply into her eyes and Cristine found it hard to hold the other woman's stare. Paula's brown eyes probed deeper. "You are not okay. You are devastated by this. Any woman would be. But not to worry. The gang's all here."

If Paula only knew how that last statement was twisting her stomach muscles into a painful knot.

Tina arrived next, looking dark and furious as she

handed over a casserole of chicken and rice, her favorite dish for an emergency, full of carbs. "I hope the bastard's dick becomes a mass of sores and it has to be cut off."

Cristine closed her eyes and let out her breath. "No you don't," she said, opening her eyes and smiling at her good friend, who was covering for her at work. Tina's clear, perfect chocolate-brown skin softened around her mouth.

"You're right, there's karma to consider. Maybe if he just gets herpes from her that will be enough. A lifetime reminder of his cheating ass."

Shaking her head, Cristine nodded to the foyer. "Get in here and join the rest of them. Where's Isabel and Claire?"

Tina passed her and entered the house. "Claire is picking up Isabel and they'll be here soon. Where's the wine?"

"In the kitchen," Cristine called back, just as Claire's BMW pulled in behind Paula's SUV. She watched as Isabel exited the car. Dear, dependable Isabel who would speak her mind without censure and not let her feel an ounce of pity for herself. Isabel carried herself with the regal air of a queen. Her hair was almost pure white, but it framed a youthful face that didn't show her age. At forty-nine, Isabel looked ten years younger, and even though the woman stood almost six feet tall, she wasn't imposing . . . unless you tended to find solace in denial. Isabel also wasn't going to pull any punches tonight.

Claire followed up the driveway, her red designer shoes looking pretty good with her dark gray business suit. Claire was the prettiest of them all, a perfect specimen of womanhood . . . fit, firm, smart, funny, intelligent, and needing no man to uphold her self-esteem. Claire was going to be ruthless. She'd start off nice, but given a few glasses of wine, the woman would tell the truth even if it hurt to hear it.

So much for tea and sympathy.

Tonight was going to be intense. She knew it in every fiber of her being.

"Isabel, thanks for coming. Sorry about this, but Tina wouldn't be talked out of it."

Hugging her, Cristine felt Isabel's maternal energy wash over her, which was odd since Isabel never could have children of her own. Maybe that's why she had devoted her working life to helping kids where she could.

"Now, you know you couldn't keep us away, Cristine. In time of need we're going to show up, whether you like it or not. You were there for me when Chuck died, remember? Now it's my turn with you."

Cristine shook her head. "Please, Issy. Chuck was a saint and my loss could never compare with yours. Charlie's just crazy, going through a midlife crisis, or something."

Isabel pulled back and gazed seriously into her eyes. "Sometimes what you're going through is harder than death. At least with death there is a finality, a closure. This mess is going to take time to heal. But I'm glad he's gone," she stated, shifting the bowl of salad in her arm. "Truth be told, he sucked the very life force from you. He was too needy. You deserve better. Far better."

Cristine blinked. "I thought you liked him."

Shrugging, Isabel said, "You liked him, so we liked him because we love you. But we all saw him for who he was. He used you, dear. I think you're seeing the true Charlie now."

Christ, but this was going to be depressing. Resisting the urge to defend the man she loved . . . which was crazy in itself since how could she love someone who had been lying to her for months? . . . Cristine shrugged noncommittally to Issy's statement and turned to Claire.

Gorgeous, blond, movie-star-charismatic Claire could play with the big boys in the financial world and yet she had a heart of shimmering gold, which every one of the group had experienced, along with a dynamic skill for salesmanship when she wanted to sell them on an idea.

"So the SOB finally showed his true colors, huh? Sorry, kid. I know it was a shock for you," Claire added as she held up a plastic bag. "Not to worry. Ben and Jerry's chocolate chip cookie dough ice cream. The *big* container. I know you don't see this as a good thing yet, but I promise you will." She kissed Cristine's cheek as she entered, making her way toward the women who were already pouring themselves glasses of wine. "C'mon, Cristine. Tonight, we're gonna raise the roof."

She was already tired, almost exhausted, just at the thought of what was coming. Women without rules could be very dangerous to one's sense of righteous self-pity. She wanted to wallow for a while yet. But these dames were gonna mess with her head until she saw the silver lining in her dark cloud.

She wasn't ready for the silver lining.

She was still grieving.

Two hours later, after dinner and five bottles of wine, the women had retired to the living room, each finding a spot surrounding Cristine who sat on the sofa with Paula on one side of her and Kelly on the other.

"Okay, let's get down to business," Tina declared from her cross-legged position on the floor. "If you haven't already, kick off your heels."

Only Claire still had hers on, so she did as ordered, and grinned. "Now comes the down and dirty," she murmured, lifting her wine glass to Cristine. "Truth time."

Cristine's stomach twisted painfully, reminding her that nervous eating and drinking don't mix well. She tried to steel herself for what was coming next.

"Cristine, you know we're here for you because we love you," Isabel, who was sitting on the fireplace hearth, stated in a gentle voice. "You know that when one door closes, another opens. The universe has a plan for you, and it doesn't include Charlie. You were traveling parallel paths for seven years, but now he's veered off onto another, and you are walking your own path alone. I know how scary and painful that can be, but you must believe it's part of the big plan. Something wondrous is waiting for you."

Cristine's shoulders sagged and she felt those damned tears welling up in her eyes. "Rationally, Issy, I know you're right, but I *miss* him terribly. It's like something vital has been cut away from my body and I don't know how to function."

"What do you miss about him?" Tina asked matter-of-factly.

She blinked. "I miss his company, his . . ." She knew immediately she shouldn't have hesitated.

Tina pounced on her. "His company? Get yourself a dog. Look, I thought you guys were so happy, and then after our phone call I really started thinking about your perfect little relationship. Do you know how much of your life revolved around that man? How many things you put off because of him and his needs? Damn it, Cris, he was passive-aggressive, neurotic, and a hypochondriac. It was like the only time he felt good was when you were around him and he could suck your energy. These past six months you were working overtime and couldn't give him as much attention. He caved, couldn't take being asked to act like a grown-up and take care of himself during a bump in the road, and so some predator saw his weakness and struck, giving him his fix. He was a damn energy junkie. Doesn't it say anything to you about how weak he is, what low self-esteem he has? I don't think I ever met a male who was so damn needy and over seven years of age. And now we know he's also a liar and a betrayer. C'mon, tell me what else you miss about him."

Each statement struck her mind like a sword, slicing away her illusions. "I thought you all liked him."

"He was a user," Claire called out. "You practically supported him for six years."

That one struck deep. "But he was working on the house."

"Yeah, he was real handy," Kelly muttered. "He could fix anything, except himself. Great diversion, huh?"

Cristine was silent as their words sank in. Even though in some deep dark corner of her mind she already knew everything they were saying, she hadn't wanted to deal with the reality of losing respect for the man she loved. Love was a trade-off, right? You got someone else's baggage too. Now that it was being put into words, out there to be examined, Charlie's baggage looked like a ship container that needed to be lifted with a crane.

Paula patted her thigh in sympathy. "So maybe you miss the intimacy of a partner."

"Yeah," Tina called out, "so how was the sex, Cristine?"

"You people are cruel," Cristine muttered, crossing her arms over her chest for protection.

"Honey, everyone here loves you," Kelly said, wrapping her arm around Cris's shoulders. "And everyone here knows what a loser magnet I am when it comes to men, so I'm the expert on this subject. I know you don't want to hear this, but Charlie really was a loser. Did he, or did he not, nearly fall apart when he got that job, when he had to take some responsibility for himself? Didn't you tell me he was constantly sick, screwing up on the job and worried he might be fired? Cris, he was a front end manager at a retail store, for God's sake, and not even the head manager. That's not rocket science. Follow the directives and deal with customers. And he wasn't even good at that. Don't you get it? He *wants* someone to take care of him, because he's too weak to do it himself."

"You dodged a major bullet," Claire called out. "That person would have sucked you dry and then moved on to the next woman. At least this way you've still got something of yourself left."

Cristine finished the last of her wine and Paula immediately picked up the bottle from the coffee table and refilled the glass.

"So I'm still waiting," Tina said. "How was the sex?"

Cristine blew her breath out in a frustrated rush. Tina knew exactly how the sex was, or wasn't, and now this so-called friend was going to make her tell the truth. Truth. Seemed like she'd had her head buried in the sand of delusion for years. "You know the answer to that one, Tina."

"*I* know. I think *you* need to say it out loud and make it real."

Cristine gulped her wine and then blurted what she knew they'd drag out of her anyway. "It was great in the beginning, but it was nearly nonexistent at the end. Truth was, I just wasn't attracted to him like that for months. The last time we tried, I drank too much wine and fell asleep. All his whining and complaining and negativity just turned something off inside of me. I mean, I loved him, but—"

"But he had turned into the worst kind of woman, and you don't go that way, honey. Of course he turned you off. How can you make love to someone you can't respect anymore? Someone who doesn't even respect himself?" Tina asked with a sympathetic smile.

"Okay, so there was no sex, no respect, no equal partnership, because you were always the stronger one, Cristine, and now he's lied to you, betrayed you, manipulated your emotions, and was, quite frankly, using you until he finalized his plans to leave you. What about all that do you miss?" Isabel asked gently. "Because that is who he is, dear friend. You hold a romantic view of the man. We don't. And that's why the truth is so important tonight."

"Then why do I miss him so much?" Cristine demanded as the tears broke over her cheeks and ran down her face. "Why do I feel like something so vital has been ripped away from me? I know everything you're saying is the truth," she mumbled as she gulped for air. "Christ, I've known it for months now. Yes, he was weak and neurotic, but I loved him! Everyone's forgetting that. I still love him!"

"What do you love, honey?" Paula asked in a gentle voice. "Not the person he is now, today. You still love a liar? A cheat? Someone who plotted behind your back, instead of being truthful with you, not even communicating something this important to you? Maybe you love who you thought he was, not the reality of him."

"And maybe what you love, Cristine," Isabel murmured, "is the familiar. None of us likes change. We want things to remain the same, until the same becomes too painful. When are you going to surrender? How much more pain are you going to allow, because it is you making that decision. Charlie's already done his damage and now you know the truth about him, who he really is. This isn't a midlife crisis. This is *in* him, the capability to lie and deceive and manipulate always was a part of him. You're just seeing it for yourself now. He's been lying and deceiving probably his whole life, acting for others, trying to give them what they expect, because down deep he must believe who he is isn't good enough or will never be accepted. He lives a life of pain and sickness, inflicting it upon himself and letting the runoff spill onto those who have loved him. I think Claire's right. You dodged a major bullet, Cristine."

They all remained silent as the residue of Isabel's words filled their minds.

It was Claire who broke the silence.

"You know what they say, don't you? The best way to get over a man is to get another one under you."

Laughter erupted, bringing them all back to the present.

"Easier said than done," Kelly pronounced. "Believe me, I should know."

Tina waved her hand at Kelly. "Oh, you're looking for Mr. Right, and what Cristine needs is Mr. Right Now. If he's got the equipment, he's got the job."

"A one-night stand?" Paula asked, shaking her head. "Maybe we should plan a holiday someplace exotic and just see what happens."

"What the woman needs is a few nights of great sex to wipe the feckless, dickless Charlie from her mind and let her know exactly what she's been missing," Claire declared amid chuckles from the others.

"What I would really like is some time alone to grieve and get over things. The very last thing I need right now is another man."

"Face it," Tina said, giving Cristine a stern look. "You need to get laid. It will recharge your batteries and resuscitate your life force."

"You know," Paula muttered, "in such cases the women of some tribes in Africa would offer their husbands as a special gift to their sister-in-need."

Shaking her head, Cristine covered her eyes and groaned. "Since you're the only one of us with a husband, Paula, I think I'll pass, but thanks anyway."

The others laughed.

Still chuckling, Kelly added, "Nice gesture, Paula."

"Well, it's true," Paula insisted, sounding a little hurt by their laughter.

"I've got the perfect solution," Claire pronounced, and got everyone's attention. "Men with money have always been serviced by high-priced prostitutes, beautiful women who are intelligent, cultured, charming, and safe."

"Yeah, so? Where's a place like that for women, 'cause it would sure take all the torment out of dating," Kelly said with sigh.

"Right," Tina agreed. "There isn't such a service for women. We're not supposed to have sexual needs. For God's sake, sex is one of our greatest gifts and women are supposed to wait until some male thinks we're pretty enough or sexy enough for him to gift us with his penis? No wonder vibrators are such huge sellers now."

"Listen, listen," Claire ordered, getting up and sitting next to Isabel on the hearth to close the group around Cristine. "There is such a place . . . for women with money and the right contacts."

That got everyone's attention.

"I had a client last week who recently came back from Paradise Island in the Bahamas looking ten years younger with a smile of dangerous kilowattage. No emotional attachment. No worrying over body parts or if you're good enough or firm enough. Just three days of impeccable attention and mind-blowing sex. And all available from a very, very discreet enterprise with an exclusive clientele."

"Wow," Kelly whispered, almost in awe.

"Yeah, wow," Tina agreed. "How much?"

Claire sipped her wine, then said, "I didn't ask, but I will." She had that look.

"What about the romance?" Paula asked. "Sex for just the sake of sex?"

"Why the hell not?" Tina demanded. "Cristine's not looking for commitment or marriage. Just some mind-blowing sex to recharge her batt—"

"Hold it," Cristine interrupted. "How did *I* get put into this scenario?"

"Well, honey, this is about you," Tina answered. "You ready for romance and dating?"

"No, that's the point," Cristine stated. "I'm still grieving Charlie's loss and—"

"I thought you realized you weren't grieving Charlie. You're grieving the loss of the familiar, what you were addicted to, those emotions. You were codependant with him for seven years. Okay, so it was because of love, but did he ever get any better? Look at him. He's like an addict who needs his energy fix. He's just running to a fresh dealer, that's all." Tina dared her to challenge her words.

After a few moments of silence, Cristine said, "Well, I'm not going to Paradise Island to meet a male prostitute."

"Secretly she wants the romance," Paula insisted. "Charlie was good with the romance, wasn't he?"

Cristine nodded. "In the beginning and then every once in a while . . ."

"How do you think he got her hooked into being codependent?" Tina asked Paula. "Oh, I heard it all. Charlie bringing her the morning coffee with a fresh-picked flower. The candlelit dinners. The soft music. Charlie fixing her house. What did he use to say, Cris? You think it up and I'll make it? What he couldn't make was a whole man, a decent human being with a conscience and a life of his own. He's always got to move in and borrow someone else's life and then suck the life force right out of it."

"Oh, for heaven's sake," Claire interrupted. "Haven't we had this discussion before? Didn't we all agree that romance isn't real; it's the carrot that's dangled in front of your nose to get you into a relationship? It's like a form of insanity where you make insane decisions and lose your own identity and then find yourself living with a stranger when it wears off and reality hits. So let's get real here. What Cristine needs is for her body to wake up to desire again. Right now she's closed down, physically and emotionally. The only males she's going to attract will be ones with the same issues she's trying to heal. We know this stuff. We know how it works. Our thoughts create our reality."

Claire turned to Cristine. "Look at it this way. Your energy, what's left of it after dickless Charlie, is blocked.

It's not flowing. You need to get it flowing again. Not to find another partner, but to get back to the business of why you came here to this planet. To *live*. Fully. Wholly. No rules. And gather your rewards."

"I can't do that," Cristine whispered. "I can't meet a strange man in a strange place and have sex with him. Sex that's paid for . . ."

"Why not?" Isabel asked in a gentle voice. "I find all this very interesting. What Claire says is true. I can hypnotize you later tonight and have you accept the loss you are feeling and also help you open to whatever the universe has waiting to replace it. I'd go," Isabel said with a grin. "You've already lost, Cristine. Accept that and move on to what's waiting for you. The longer you spend grieving something that was in reality very unhealthy for you, the longer you put off living. Does it feel like living now? Or are you just waiting? Thinking Charlie will come to his senses? Dear friend, right now Charlie has no senses, except to save himself and, as Tina said, find a fresh dealer. Could you ever trust him again?"

Cristine thought about it, seeing a future of questioning and worrying. "No, I don't think I could."

"Then it's over, isn't it?"

That anguish in her solar plexus became heavier and hotter and more painful. The tears rolled down her cheeks and she wanted to curl up in a ball and die. Just disappear and leave this misery behind her.

"Isn't it?" Isabel asked again, this time in a whisper Cristine couldn't ignore.

She nodded, wiping her cheek with the sleeve of her sweater.

"Say it out loud," Kelly whispered, stroking Cris's hair with compassion.

"It's over," Cristine cried out between sobs of grief. "Over. Done."

They all reached out to her at the same time, placing

their hands on her face, her back, her arms, her knees, touching, stroking, in a way only females can do with each other. Their already strong bond deepened even more as they each looked into the other's eyes with soft smiles of compassion for a precious soul who'd taken a powerful hit of reality. No one broke the connection as they continued to surround their friend with their energy.

It was Cristine who sniffled and muttered, "But I'm still not going to Paradise Island!"

Claire wiped Cristine's cheek with her fingers and leaned in to kiss her red nose. "We'll see about that. Listen, I've made a bundle on Google stock in the last few months. It will be a treat from me to you. The only contingency is you have to give us all a full report when you get back so we can live it vicariously."

"Do it," Tina said, squeezing Cristine's knee.

Cristine sniffled and looked at them as though they had suddenly lost their natural minds. "I can't!" she insisted.

"Yes you can," Kelly declared.

Paula gently pushed Cristine's hair behind her ear. "Claire's right. You are blocked. Reawaken your desire and get your life force back."

"But a gigolo? A man who is paid to be with me?" She shuddered and dropped her head as she shook it.

Isabel touched Cristine's chin and lifted it so she could see into her eyes. "Stop being prejudiced. That's not like you. Why don't you just try to live your life for yourself for a change? You've given it away for seven years, why not begin with desire? You know it leads to everything else, health, wealth, happiness. You get desire back and there's no stopping you."

Cristine merely blinked, knowing Isabel was speaking the truth. Without desire there couldn't be creation. Without creativity, everything remained static. She shook her head. "Oh, I don't think I could. It's just not me."

"Who *are* you, Cristine?" Isabel asked gently. "Do you

know anymore? Who are *you,* without someone else to define you? Now is the time to find out."

"Here," Claire said, handing Cristine her glass of wine. "Drink up. By the time this night is over, you're going to begin to find your way back."

Accepting the wine, she said, "You're still not going to talk me into going to Paradise Island. That's just insanity."

Claire stood and her Cheshire cat grin was back. "We'll see. Now, who's up for chocolate chip cookie dough ice cream?"

"Me!"

"Me, too."

"Me, three . . ."

After they had stuffed themselves with ice cream, one by one the women started to drift off to sleep. The combination of wine, carbs, and emotion had exhausted them. They camped out on whatever flat surface they could find, doubling up in the bedrooms. Claire had insisted she take the sofa. She waited until the rest of them went upstairs and then walked into the half-finished kitchen, ignored the mess of unwashed dishes, and flipped open her cell phone. Within minutes she ended her call and then sat at Cristine's computer.

So what if Cristine had agreed because she was drunk? She'd agreed and said what the hell. As far as Claire was concerned, that was good enough.

Now to make the airline reservations and have the tickets delivered by private courier on Sunday morning. So what if that cost more money? Dickless Charlie would probably show up on Sunday to get the rest of his things and Claire wanted Cristine to have a plan so she wouldn't cave in his presence.

Cristine was going to have the time of her life, get back her desire, and then tell them all the exquisite, juicy details. If it turned out well, she might go for it herself.

What was money for, if not to help others when you could? And this was such a delicious way. Some gorgeous man catering to Cristine's every wish, bringing her life force back and having a hell of a good time to boot. Who's to say it was wrong?

After all, they were women without rules, weren't they?

# Chapter

# 3

Paradise island.

Cristine smiled nervously as she rode in the golf cart to her cottage. She tried to listen to the friendly hotel employee as he described the many amenities available to her, yet her heart felt as if a lead weight were attached to it. What in the world was she doing here? And how the hell had she allowed herself to be talked into it?

She knew, of course, the moment she had surrendered.

It was last Sunday when Charlie had come back for the rest of his things. He had obviously moved on and had left her behind. Discarded, that's how she had felt. All the love of the last seven years had meant nothing to him. She was un-thought-of. And it had hurt more than she could have imagined. So when the courier had delivered the tickets right in front of Charlie, she had acted thrilled to be getting away to the islands, wanting to hurt him in return, to show him she, too, was moving on.

Because of pride she was now plunged into this madness, though as a soft tropical breeze caressed her she felt her spirit lifting. It was a gorgeous treat, or perhaps it was simply a well-deserved retreat from the harsh reality of her life.

"And your cottage overlooks the ocean," the man sitting next to her announced in his lyrical island voice.

"How lovely," Cristine answered with a smile as he drove her around exquisitely manicured gardens with lush colorful flowers blooming everywhere. This was a secluded property with private cottages nestled into the landscape, unlike the big resorts with their almost Disney-like attractions. In spite of her hesitation, she couldn't help but be impressed and grateful to be spending a few days in paradise.

The ocean came to her first with its scent carried on the breeze, then she caught her breath as her eyes took in the gorgeous mixture of color ranging from pale blue to deeper cobalt. It was beautiful and her guide drove right to a lovely pale pink cottage with a white porch surrounded by palm trees shaped by the wind blowing in from the ocean.

"Here we are. The Alyanna Cottage."

"Alyanna?" she asked as her driver pulled up to the steps and stopped the golf cart.

"Yes. All our cottages have tropical names. The original owners of the property spent years in Hawaii."

Cristine smiled with anticipation as she looked at the wide porch with potted plants and cushioned wicker furniture. She couldn't wait to take off her traveling clothes and just veg on that chaise longue. Maybe this wasn't such a terrible idea after all. And then she thought of the real reason she was here and that tight, painful knot twisted in her belly again.

Maybe she could somehow cancel the whole thing and use this time to heal. It was the perfect setting.

She opened her purse as her driver picked up her luggage. Taking out a twenty, she followed him up the stairs to the front door. He unlocked it and led her inside.

Inhaling deeply with appreciation, Cristine certainly felt pampered.

A huge bed, beautifully dressed in a subdued tropical print, dominated the room and was draped with a sheer netting. In front of the bed was the sitting area, a sofa and two chairs, and off to the side was a small square kitchen.

"The kitchen is stocked, but if you should desire anything we've missed just call the main office. The menu is on the desk to order your meals. Just allow us thirty minutes to bring it to you."

Cristine glanced at the desk against the wall. A large bouquet of flowers in cellophane was lying on top of it. "You mean room service? You bring the food all the way out here?"

"Yes, madam. If you should wish to eat at our restaurant, just call and someone will come and get you."

"So I'm out here . . . all alone?"

"It is perfectly safe. This is a private property with a private beach. There is security all day and all night. And there are other cottages on the beach. Eighteen in all."

She simply nodded.

"Here is your television," he said, opening an armoire for her to see and then closing the double doors. "Your bath is right through this door."

Again, she nodded, a bit overwhelmed by the quiet elegance of the place.

"Do you wish a maid to help you unpack?"

"No, no, I can do it. Thank you." She handed him the tip.

"If you need anything, madam, my name is John." He accepted the money and added with a brilliant smile, "Thank you and I hope you enjoy your stay with us."

"Thank you, John," she answered, "I'm sure I will."

A lie. If she could cancel a strange man showing up with the intention of having sex with her, she actually would enjoy this retreat from the madness of her life.

When John left, Cristine looked around and exhaled loudly. Then her eyes settled on the flowers on the desk. Claire and the girls had probably sent them. She dropped her purse onto a chair and walked over to them, seeing the riot of color from the many tropical flowers. Opening the card, she stared at the masculine script.

*Welcome to Paradise Island, Cristine.*
*May I suggest dinner tonight on your porch? I shall*
*arrange everything.*
*Seven o'clock.*
*Simon.*

Her jaw dropped. Simon? Dear God. It was starting. Tonight. Dinner. Here!

The card left her fingers and landed on the desk.

She couldn't do this!

It was crazy. Perhaps she would just talk to the man and let him know he'd still get paid, but they didn't need to have sex. Yes. That was it. He might even be relieved. Then she could just relax and enjoy this minivacation and come back and tell the group that the sex was fantastic. No one would be the wiser, and she would be off the hook.

Feeling better now that she had a plan, Cristine took the flowers into the kitchen and found a large glass vase. This would be all right after all, she thought with relief. She couldn't be the first woman to have backed out of such an arrangement. What did it matter if the man still got paid? Everyone would be happy.

Especially her.

She put the arrangement on the long glass top of the coffee table and lifted her suitcase onto the bed. Opening it, she carefully unpacked and put everything away in the dresser. There wasn't that much since she was only here until Monday. She left out a pair of khaki shorts and a white T-shirt and began undressing. Hanging up her slacks and blouse, she decided to dress for the warmer climate and go exploring. Walk on the beach. Breathe the ocean air. And maybe, just maybe, before she left this island she could let go of the weight that still pulled on her heart.

In spite of everything, she still felt love in her heart for a person who had cruelly abused it. She just didn't know how to turn it off. Even her anger didn't last long before thoughts of good times began sneaking in and making her long for what was lost. She felt sick. Lovesick. As real a disease of the heart and mind as any disorder known to man. Somehow, she had to heal herself.

Dressed, she looked at herself in the long mirror attached to the bathroom door. Good Lord but she was white, she thought, and shook her head. In a land where everyone else appeared dark and healthy, she looked like the soft underbelly of a dead fish. Sun. She needed to go out and get some sun; then she would look more healthy, more vibrant. Cristine pressed her palms against her upper thighs as though it might magically make them appear thinner. Sitting at a desk working overtime hadn't helped her figure, which had never been model-thin. How could she allow a strange man to touch her? She had felt safe with Charlie, accepted, and immediately felt that knot tighten with pain again.

Damn him.

Why was it that he seemed to haunt her when he was obviously going on with his life and she seemed stuck in the past? She had to remind herself that she had been sleeping with the enemy, someone who had plotted behind her back, who had deceived her, manipulated her, and then discarded her when something more useful came along.

Angry with herself for letting thoughts of Charlie ruin the moment, she grabbed her sunglasses and the key to the cottage and left.

She stood on the porch and breathed deeply, pulling the fresh air into her lungs, and then headed for the beach. Walking past a grove of red hibiscus, she was tempted to pick one and slip it into her hair. She let the temptation pass. No point in going island just yet. At the beach, she took off her sandals and held them before stepping onto the warm sand. For a moment, she simply stood still, feeling the rays from the sun penetrate her pores and relax her as she stared out to the gorgeous water and the waves lapping the shoreline. A cooling breeze came off the water, played with her hair and it fell back from her face.

For a timeless moment she was filled with peace. No thoughts. Simply being in the moment, absorbing the beauty that surrounded her, she felt her heart begin to soften and open up to nature. She moved closer to the waves, wanting to feel the water.

She stood at the shoreline, letting the foamy soft water tickle her ankles. When it receded she almost felt dizzy with happiness as her feet sank into the sand. It was heavenly. She kept standing in the same spot, staring out to the ocean, opening herself to whatever the universe had in store for her, like Isabel had said. She was a strong woman. A smart woman, if not in love than at least in business. She and Tina had opened a real estate office together after both had been brokers for years. They had combined forces two years ago and within the last ten months had hired three more agents. It was hard work and time-consuming, but both of them knew it had been the right time to take advantage of low interest rates and the soaring prices of homes. Sometimes it amazed her what people were willing to pay for a house, to move up in a market that just kept growing. She knew the market would burst eventually, but for now the profits were there for anyone with ambition.

She'd had ambition, so much of it that it had ruined her relationship.

She blinked and then shook her head as she stared once more at the ocean.

It wasn't her fault. She had never betrayed Charlie. He simply needed constant attention to bolster his own lack of self-esteem. God, but she was tired of being a cheerleader for other people. When was it going to be her turn? Who was her cheerleader? Sadly, the faces of her group danced across her mind's eye. Could she ever trust a man again? Could she trust herself to make a sane decision about a man, any man?

"You'll burn if you stay here like that."

She turned her head and saw a good-looking man smiling at her. He was tall, well built, wearing tan shorts and a tropical cotton shirt. And he had a great smile, so she smiled back. "You're probably right," she answered, pulling her feet up from being buried in the sand. "It's just so lovely here."

"Yes, it is. You looked lost in time."

She straightened her back. "Lost in the past. A foolish exercise for anyone, and especially me."

He placed his hands in the pockets of his shorts and looked out to the water. A breeze lifted the ends of his short dark hair. "And why especially you, if I might ask?"

He was still smiling, so she shrugged her shoulders. "Coming out of a bad relationship. Didn't realize how bad until it was over."

Nodding, he said, "Well, you picked paradise to recover in, so you must be a survivor."

She played with that word in her mind. "You know, for years I kept telling myself I didn't want to just survive. I wanted to thrive. Then I fooled myself into thinking I was doing just that." She paused. "Truth is, I am a survivor. And I don't know how happy I am by the admission."

"Why?" he asked, looking at her.

She wished she could see beyond his sunglasses. Was he married? She didn't see a ring, but who else besides a dumped woman would be here in paradise alone? Only one set up by her well-intentioned friends. Shrugging, she said, "It's just that I've been really foolish and in denial about certain things in my life. It's tough when reality hits . . . and I don't know why I'm telling a perfect stranger about it," she added with an embarrassed laugh.

He smiled again. "Sometimes, I think, talking to a stranger can be very therapeutic. There's no history and you can say whatever you want."

"Well, what I want right now is to go exploring. Are you staying here?" Couldn't hurt to ask.

"I am." He pointed to the left. "There's a nice cove beyond that rock."

"I'll check it out, thanks. See you around," she added, holding up her hand in a wave as she walked away.

"Have fun."

She was still smiling as she headed toward the jutting rock formation. Now that was a nice encounter with a stranger. No pressure. No trying to impress. Just natural and . . . nice. And she wasn't in such a deep funk that she couldn't recognize a good-looking man. He had to be married, here with his wife, and was simply being friendly. Now that's what she would love to find. A normal man. A committed man. Someone without a hidden agenda who didn't want to suck the life force out of her and then abandon her for a newer model.

And maybe she was asking for a miracle.

She had thought Charlie was that man, but once again she had been disappointed. She really wasn't asking for the extraordinary, was she? Was a man capable of being truly committed? Happy and committed? She remembered once talking to a married broker who had admitted men are always looking for greener pastures, for something or someone better, prettier, younger, or for a more advantageous arrangement. He had said that instinct was inbred into men and at the time she had thought he was a jerk. But what if he was right? What if this whole insane relationship thing was doomed from the start? She tried to think of one truly happy relationship. Unfortunately, her and Charlie's had been the closest. How many couples were pretending, putting on a happy face, when in reality they were indifferent or miserable and separation was always a possibility lurking right there on the edge of the greener pastures?

She had to wade into the water to go around the rocks and she wondered if America had become such a disposable society that instead of working to keep a relationship together, couples now considered it normal to run away from a crisis. What had happened to commitment, to seeing things through, holding on to each other over the rough bumps in life, working together *for* the relationship?

The whole thing was hopeless, she thought, and then her breath caught in her throat as she came upon a secluded cove with wading pools and wild flowers in bloom. She sat on a rock and dangled her feet in the shallow warm water.

A feeling of intense sadness washed over her, wishing she could share this beauty with another. Her reality slammed her in the face, demanded recognition. No more denial, or wishful thinking. She was alone now. A single woman . . . again. Why wasn't that enough for her? Why did she think she needed another to validate this experience?

Maybe that's what this time was all about now.

Maybe she needed to love herself again. She'd loved herself before Charlie had invaded her life, sweeping her off her feet with his attention. Then she'd had a reflection, someone to validate her. Now there was no one, save herself.

Somehow, she thought as she gazed into the water, somehow she had to get herself back again if she was going to not only survive this, but learn once again how to thrive.

And she *would* survive Charlie and his lies.

She had to. Like it or not, she was now a survivor.

§

At twenty minutes after six three hotel employees arrived just as she came out of the shower. They were busy in the kitchen and on the porch, so Cristine shut herself in the bathroom and looked in the mirror, wanting to make sure it wasn't as bad as she thought.

It was. And even worse since the shower.

She looked like a lobster, one with an odd shading of red around her eyes, her face, her lower arms, and her legs. Who would have thought such a short time in the sun could have caused this? It was so uneven that she wouldn't be able to wear the gorgeous sundress Claire had lent her. She would look like a fool with white shoulders and burned forearms. Now what? If she had this Simon's phone number she would have called and canceled the whole evening. As it was she now had an authentic excuse to refrain from his romantic overtures. She would play up the sunburn and he would understand. He simply had to understand. She'd make him understand.

Feeling a bit better, she soothed lotion onto her sensitive skin and decided she might as well be comfortable. It really didn't matter what the man thought of her. She wasn't out to impress him . . . which would be a difficult task, considering the state of her body and her neon-red skin. She brushed her teeth, applied a little eye makeup, and let her hair dry naturally, not exactly her best look. Going into the bedroom, she opened a drawer and took out a leather headband. She slipped it onto her head and then pulled it forward a bit. Using her fingers to separate the strands, she let her hair fall to her shoulders. It would have to do. There wasn't any way she was using a hot hair dryer with a sunburned face. Next, she took her underwear into the bathroom along with her clothes. Minutes later she emerged dressed in pale gray silky cropped pants and a cream-colored poet's blouse with a soft ruffle at the cuffs. She looked in the bedroom mirror and was satisfied. The silk material was light enough on her sunburn not to bother her and her matching cream camisole meant she didn't have to wear a bra. She would have added earrings, but even her earlobes were sunburned, along with her wrists, so a bracelet was out. Tonight she was going to be comfortable; well, at least as comfortable as she could manage when meeting a stranger who thought he was taking her to bed.

Cripes . . . who would have thought she would get herself into such an insane situation?

Only the Yellow Brick Road Gang could come up with something like this. Women without rules. Fine. But some things just weren't done, right? Who had ever even heard of women paying to be serviced by . . . what was this Simon, a gigolo? Was that the right term? It sounded so old-fashioned and indecent.

But then again what had decency gotten her so far?

Lying, neurotic Charlie.

She inhaled the aroma of food cooking and realized she was very hungry. Starved, to be more accurate, since she hadn't eaten anything save a small container of yogurt this morning before leaving her home.

Taking a deep breath, she looked at her reflection in the mirror.

"Just be yourself tonight," she whispered. She wasn't going to worry what any man thought of her.

"Miss?"

Embarrassed to be caught talking to herself in the mirror, she turned to one of the women who had been busy with preparations. "Yes?"

"We are finished. Would you like to check?"

"Sure," she answered with a smile, and left the bedroom. "What are we having?"

"Robert will remain to serve you and your guest," the woman said, indicating the kitchen where a man was busy at the counter chopping something. "I believe it is fish. Here we are," she added, holding open the door to the porch. "I hope it meets with your approval."

Cristine followed the woman outside and drew in her breath with appreciation. The porch had been transformed into an intimate dining room with a round table covered to the floor in white linen. Fine china and crystal and silver adorned the place settings and white tapers were enclosed in glass on either side of a low arrangement of colorful trailing orchids. "It's exquisite!" she breathed, completely in awe. "Did you bring these chairs?" She ran her hand over the side of a wicker fan-back chair with a thick seat cushion.

"Yes. So much more comfortable for an evening such as tonight."

Cristine stared at the woman, scared she might know of her ridiculous arrangement. What if this Simon was well-known around here as the resident gigolo? What if everyone knew how lonely and desperate she had become? She wanted to tell the woman all this was arranged by her crazy friends and to spread the word that she had no intention of having sex with the man, but she knew any explanation would only make it worse. Instead, she gathered up what was left of her courage and responded. "Tonight?"

The woman nodded and waved a graceful hand out to the ocean. "The sunset this evening should be beautiful."

"Oh, yes . . ." Cristine murmured in relief and noticed that both chairs were angled toward the west. "Everything is just wonderful. Thank you."

"There are frozen daiquiris in the refrigerator with an extra bottle of rum. Now we will meet Robert? And he will tell you about your dinner?"

Cristine nodded and followed the woman back into the cottage. Everyone was so polite here. It would be hard to disagree with anything.

Robert stopped his preparations when they entered the small kitchen.

"Hello," Cristine said, wondering if she should shake his hand. She'd never had a private chef before. "Whatever you're cooking, Robert, smells heavenly."

"Good evening, miss." The man pointed his knife to the counter. "Spiced shrimp skewered on sugar cane with a mango-cilantro mojo, followed by medallions of butter-poached lobster on a sweet corn pancake with fresh tomato coulis. For dessert there are tartlets of pear or Key lime, along with banana-lime galettes. I hope this meets with your approval. The menu was selected earlier."

"My mouth is watering with anticipation," she said with a smile, and she wasn't kidding.

"Would you like a daiquiri, miss?" the woman next to her asked.

"Yes, I think I would," Cristine answered, marveling at how organized the staff was, and she had to give this Simon fellow credit for selecting a terrific menu.

She accepted the banana daiquiri and sipped greedily through a slender straw. The iced slush hit the roof of her mouth and she experienced a painful brain freeze.

"Slowly, miss," the woman said with a slight laugh.

"Right," Cristine answered, pressing her thumb between her eyebrows to stop the pain. "I'll try to remember that."

A knock sounded at the front door and Cristine immediately became as frozen as her daiquiri as the moment she had been dreading was upon her.

"Would you like me to answer?"

Cristine shook her head to the kind woman. "No, thanks. I'll get it."

Taking a deep breath and praying for strength, she forced her legs to move out of the kitchen.

He stood at the open door.

The guy from the beach.

Great. Now she had to get rid of him before her gigolo arrived. God, she had to find a better term for this Simon person. She could call him her date . . . in the loosest way.

"Hello," her beach friend said, looking very handsome in tan linen trousers and a peach-colored linen shirt with the sleeves rolled up. Without his sunglasses, his brown eyes seemed to sparkle with friendliness.

Just her luck. What if he wasn't married and was making a social call? What if he wanted to ask her to join him for dinner?

"Hi," she answered with a grin, wishing she could run off down the beach with him and forget this crazy evening. But then she smelled the food cooking and it brought her to her senses.

"This looks inviting," he said, glancing at the table.

She had to get rid of him, damn it.

"I'm sorry. I'm . . . well, I'm expecting someone," she blurted out. "I wish I could ask you to join us, but I'm afraid I don't really know this person very well and—"

"And I think it's time we introduced ourselves," he interrupted with a grin of his own. "My name is Simon, and I hope you are expecting me."

Her mouth dropped open. "You? You're Simon?"

He nodded. "And you should have used sunblock, Cristine. Does it hurt?"

"What?" She still couldn't make the switch in her head from cute beach guy to paid sex companion.

"Does your sunburn hurt?" he repeated.

"Yes . . . no . . . why didn't you tell me your name on the beach this afternoon?" Cute beach guy was her Simon? Well, not her Simon, but *the* Simon, the one she had been dreading meeting since she'd arrived!

"I would have introduced myself if we had spoken any longer, but you made it clear you wanted to go exploring." He smiled again, this time with gentleness. "I feared you were going to get burned."

Overwhelmed, she thoughtlessly sipped her drink and again was hit with a powerful pain in her forehead. She tried to stop herself from wincing and screwing up her face.

"Brain freeze?" he asked with sympathy.

She grimaced. "In more ways than one. I can't believe *you're* Simon."

"Well, now that we know who we are, can we sit down? You don't want to miss the sunset. It's supposed to be especially good tonight."

"Sure, of course," she answered, now totally embarrassed. Simon, who she thought was a committed married man, had turned into her companion tonight and for the next two days. "Oh, would you like a drink?" she thought to ask, realizing she should become the hostess now. She'd deal with her true brain freeze later.

"You sit and relax, Cristine. I'll get it."

She sat down in the large chair and leaned her head back against the wicker. This was beyond embarrassing. She had been attracted to him on the beach and he was even better looking all dressed up without the sunglasses. Suddenly she wished she had taken a few more minutes in front of the mirror. She sipped her daiquiri slowly, continuously, until her sucking made a very impolite slurping sound at the bottom of the glass. Who cared? No one heard her. And she wanted another, perhaps several.

Her paid companion had arrived.

And she was attracted to him.

How unfair was that?

Still, she had to make clear that sex was not going to be part of the equation for this weekend. As a companion,

Simon just might be fun. Companion she could do. Lover, she couldn't. And he wouldn't be her lover. That would imply one would actually have to know the person a little before love could even enter into it. This didn't have anything to do with love. This was about sex. Pure and primal.

Fucking, she thought, and cringed at the crudity of it.

"Oh, you need another drink. Here, take mine."

His voice interrupted her thoughts, and embarrassed to be thinking about sex, she smiled her thanks. "They are very good."

"Enjoy yourself, Cristine. I'll be right back to join you."

She nodded and he returned to the kitchen. Running her hand over her forehead with nervousness, Cristine sipped the drink slowly. She was going to have to watch herself or these delicious daiquiris would hit her fast, and she needed her wits about her now. Somehow, she had to have a serious discussion with Simon and let him know his attentions, his sexual prowess, would not be needed this weekend.

She looked out to the ocean and the sunset and sighed deeply. It was so romantic, and as if to torture her even more, her traitorous thoughts flashed a mental picture of her and Charlie sitting together at this table. In love. Happy. Grateful for each other. She shook her head, as if to shake out the stupid thought. How long was the past going to sabotage her like that? She simply had to stay in the present. And in the present Charlie was busy setting up housekeeping with a woman who had trespassed. Men are so weak, but a woman should know better than to stray into another woman's relationship. There was an unwritten code, understood by women. You don't trespass. What you give out you will experience in one way or another. Life just does that to you.

So what had she ever done in her life to be sitting here

in paradise with a gorgeous man who was being paid to have sex with her?

Her brain simply couldn't compute it.

Was it a reward, or a humiliating punishment?

# Chapter

## 4

THEY GOT THROUGH DINNER WITH POLITE SMALL talk about the island, the food, the sunset. Nothing really personal, about either one of them. Maybe that was part of the deal, no details. Cristine kept looking at him, curious to know why someone so polished and intelligent would choose to make a living by servicing lonely women. Why wasn't he a banker or an entrepreneur? Anything besides a male escort? She'd also had four more banana daiquiris and knew she was getting tipsy because she almost didn't care that he was being paid to be with her. She just liked looking at him, listening to his voice. So much more handsome than frail and sickly Charlie, more handsome and funny and cultured and . . . and . . . what the hell had she been doing for the last seven years with a man whose main concern was the state of dust mites in his life? Maybe she was the one who had lost her senses to have put up with Charlie and his selfishness all those years.

"What are you thinking, Cristine?" Simon asked with a sexy grin.

Startled out of her reverie, she sat up straighter. "Nothing. I'm just so relaxed." She turned her head to the ocean. "The sunset truly was beautiful."

"It was. And, if you don't mind me saying this, so are you."

Her head turned sharply back to him. "Please. There's no need to flatter me with false compliments just because you are—"

"Excuse me," he interrupted, staring deeply into her eyes. "Am I not allowed my opinion?"

"Look, Simon," she answered softly, trying to smile. "I know who I am. And I'm not beautiful. With some help from Lancôme I can be presentable, but beautiful? I don't think so."

He leaned his arms on the table and asked, "Who has done this to you? How could you not see your own beauty?"

Suddenly her chest tightened with emotion and her eyes began to fill with tears. She did not need him being this nice and she had no intention of talking about Charlie. "The story is too long . . . and I don't want to ruin a perfectly lovely evening." There. That should shut him up.

It didn't.

"When I first saw you on the beach this afternoon, standing there in the surf, staring out to the ocean, I thought you looked beautiful. At one with your surroundings."

She smiled sadly. "I don't want to appear pathetic, but Simon, you are being paid to give me compliments."

"I wouldn't have said it if I wasn't sincere."

She figured the time was right. Dessert had been served. They were watching the stars come out. "I've never done this before. I've never even heard of this . . . this arrangement before. You, all of this"—she waved her hand at the tropical setting—"was a gift from my friends. They thought I needed it. I'm not so sure."

Simon sat back and nodded. "So this wasn't your idea."

She half laughed. "No."

"But you're here now, Cristine. Why don't you enjoy yourself?"

"Well, first of all, I'm sunburned, so that leaves out the more intimate part of the arrangement. And secondly, I'm not really comfortable being with someone who's being paid to be with me." It sounded harsh, but at least she was being truthful. The quantity of alcohol she had consumed didn't hurt, either.

Simon again nodded. "You think you are unique? That it's only wealthy women who require such services?"

She laughed. She couldn't help it. "Unique? Hardly." Okay, so she was heading toward being drunk, but now that the conversation was veering in the right direction she might as well continue. "What woman wouldn't find you attractive, Simon, wealthy or poor? It's just that I've never done anything remotely like this before."

"Does that make it wrong?" he asked, picking up his drink. "Simply because it's beyond your previous experiences?"

She shook her head. "I'm not judging it. It's just so foreign to me."

"So you've never had fun for the sake of fun? No commitment, no agenda, no intention of anything beyond the present moment?" Again he leaned into the table and rested his elbows as he stared into her eyes. "Why can't you simply let go and relax and see what happens? I find you attractive, Cristine. Nothing will happen you don't want to happen."

"Why do you do this, Simon?" she asked, knowing the rum had given her the courage to pry into his life, something she never would have done sober. She'd be too embarrassed, and it was bordering on rude. "I mean, you seem so intelligent and cultured."

He chuckled. "This isn't my profession, Cristine."

"It isn't?"

He shook his head. "I do it because powerful women turn me on. I'm attracted to intelligence first."

"But I'm not powerful," she protested. "And my level of intelligence has been severely tested, considering the choices I've made in the last few years. Hell, I can barely figure out my life as it is."

"That's not true. Nobody forced you to come here. You made a choice for yourself, and I respect that. Do you have any idea how many women, self-made women, are alone today? How most men find them intimidating? How lonely it can be for a smart, independent woman, when those same characteristics are admired in a man?"

He grinned at her. "I find them sexy as all hell. I love being with a woman who's not afraid to be herself and state what she wants. There's nothing better, Cristine, than being with an equal."

She sat back and her mouth dropped open. He had her there. In a flash she saw that she hadn't been with her equal. Not ever. All of her relationships had been with men she'd had to take care of by cheering them on when their self-esteem plummeted or nursing their fragile egos. She'd cooked for them, babysat them, washed their clothes, figured out their finances, taken them to doctors. She'd been their mother, their sister, their therapist and confidant, their lover . . . but had she ever been herself? How many times had she just wanted to tell Charlie to shut up, to stop complaining and get on with life, however it presented itself? That people weren't sabotaging him. He was sabotaging himself with his constant litany of misery. But she hadn't. Not once. All those things she had thought were part of being in a relationship now seemed false. She had felt needed and had somehow equated neediness with love. But neediness *wasn't* love. Neediness was like being trapped by a vampire that sucked the life force right out of you. She'd been addicted to energy vampires!

Damn . . . it was as though dawn was breaking through years of a dark delusion.

"Wow, Simon," she murmured. "You just said something very profound, at least for me. I just realized I've never been with my equal."

His grin was slow and sexy. "Maybe before you get on the plane home, you will."

She smiled back, suddenly feeling more free than she had in years. "Maybe I will," she stated, holding up her drink. "But not tonight. My sunburn . . ."

"I could always put lotion on you to soothe away the sting."

She looked at him in the soft lights from the candles, now that it was dark. Dear Lord, but he was handsome and charming and sexy and just about everything any woman could ask of such an encounter. Still, she didn't want to be in pain or half drunk. If she did this, she wanted to experience it for real. "Thank you, but I'm really tired. The flight, the sun, the expectation of you . . . and now these banana daiquiris . . . I think I would just like to crawl into bed and sleep. Alone."

He nodded. "Do you need help?"

She smiled. "No, thanks."

"Then I will leave you to your rest. Would you like to go exploring tomorrow? We could take a catamaran and a lunch and I'll show you the island."

"That sounds terrific. What time?"

He rose. "I'll come back at eleven?"

Cristine looked up at him and grinned. "This was very nice tonight, Simon. Thank you for arranging it."

He leaned down and looked into her eyes. "You are worth every moment of it, Cristine."

And then he kissed her.

Softly, slowly, grazing his lips over hers with the promise of a controlled passion. When the kiss ended, he smiled. "Sleep well."

She simply nodded and watched him walk down from the porch. He turned once and waved and she waved back, wondering when she would be capable of speech again.

That kiss!

Cristine hadn't expected it, hadn't expected to enjoy it so much, nor want it to go on or deepen, or feel his lips open or any of the other crazy emotions and thoughts that were racing through her brain and body.

Banana daiquiris or not . . . Cristine knew before her time on this island was up, she was going to wind up in bed with the man. And she didn't care what anyone thought. Something inside of her was saying she deserved it. She deserved him . . . if only for one night.

Simon was an expert with the catamaran and Cristine was becoming adept at scrambling from one side to the other as the sail was repositioned for the wind. It was glorious, sitting in her navy one-piece bathing suit with a T-shirt over it, her knees drawn up to her chin, the wind blowing her hair back, gliding over gorgeous water of ever-changing shades of turquoise. Even her morning headache had disappeared. And to see Simon grinning like a kid, master of his destiny and the cat, only added to her good mood. The man was nearly impossible to refuse with his love-of-life attitude.

*I want to remember this,* Cristine thought. She wanted to memorize every detail to recall later, back home, when she was all alone and dealing with her life. For a few days in paradise she had been happy simply by being herself. She didn't worry about looking windblown or that the cellulite in her legs might just make her back thighs re- semble dimpled oranges left in the bottom drawer of the refrigerator. None of it mattered. Not the way she looked, or what she thought. She didn't have to worry with Simon.

Crawling to the other side of the cat as the sail was turned, Cristine thought even if she never again experienced this kind of freedom with a man, she would cherish this memory, and a part of her heart seemed to slowly defrost in the tropical sun. She was grateful to Claire, to all the girls, for urging her to come to Paradise Island. And she was grateful to Simon for his patience and his understanding. Plus, he appeared to be having even more fun than her as the cat skipped over the water, gaining speed.

He pointed to a hidden cove. "Let's stop there," he called out and used the rudder to turn the cat.

Cristine nodded and quickly grabbed the edge to keep from sliding across. She balanced herself until the cat evened out and then watched as Simon expertly brought the small craft into the cove. She helped him gather up the sail and then they were gently brought closer to the shore with the tide.

"This is so beautiful," Cristine breathed, taking in the pristine beach, the palm trees, the wild display of flowers. "Why do we live in crowded cities and suburbs when paradise is right here?"

Simon laughed. "Because most people can't make a living on an island. We need people, and we'd probably take it for granted if we saw it every day."

Cristine sighed. "I don't think I would. How can I go back to Pennsylvania after *this*?"

Simon reached out and patted her shoulder. "Don't think about Pennsylvania, Cristine. Enjoy this."

She nodded and then inhaled the scent of the sea as she absorbed the natural beauty of her surroundings. "I so needed this. I didn't realize how much until just now."

"So shall we eat lunch or swim?"

Cristine giggled. "I have a choice?"

"Whatever you desire," Simon stated, wrapping the sail and lowering the boom. "This is your weekend."

"They say you shouldn't eat and swim," Cristine answered, pulling her T-shirt off. "And I can't wait any longer." She perched on the side of the cat and then slipped into the pale blue silky water of the Caribbean. It was heavenly and seemed designed to fulfill all her expectations. She swam toward the shore, watching as Simon pulled the cat up onto the sand. He then stood with his hands on his hips and watched her with a big grin on his face.

"Come in," she called out, treading water. "It's wonderful!"

He pulled off his shirt and Cristine was treated to a well-defined six-pack above a pale blue boxer-short bathing suit that rode low on his hips.

"My, my, my . . ." she whispered, treading water even more slowly while watching as he entered the surf. Something was stirring within her, something she hadn't felt in a long time.

Desire.

She desired him. But then again, what woman wouldn't? He swam toward her smoothly, cutting the water with expert strokes, and Cristine couldn't help but wonder if he did everything with such expertise. Here was a man that liked women, strong women. He was turned on by their intelligence and will. And he was funny, gracious, and fabulous looking. He also must be damn good in bed, so how much more perfect could he get?

Watching him close the distance between them, she wondered if she could treat this weekend as playtime? Was it so wrong to have a playmate, one she would never see again? And could she actually go through with it?

He came up to her, treading water, grinning, and Cristine marveled at the sunlight sparkling all around him, bouncing off the water, how it made his eyelashes spike into damp points and his skin glow with . . . with more than health. It was like he oozed those pheromones she'd read about, that powerful chemical substance that influences the physiology or behavior of others of the same species. And in that moment his influence was potent, far stronger than she had expected.

"It's a shame we didn't bring snorkeling gear with us," he said, coming closer.

She couldn't stop staring at him and grinning back.

"Maybe tomorrow?" he asked.

She knew she should say something, anything, yet it all felt like a dream, or a scene in a romantic movie where the lovers embrace in the water and become entangled. But if she tried that, she was sure they'd both go under, so instead, she replied, "I'd like that."

"Good, then after breakfast."

She simply nodded and swam backward, away from him. He followed.

"You're a good swimmer," he said, his head bobbing up and down as he pushed the water out of his way.

"So are you."

"Swim team."

"High school?"

He nodded. "What about you?"

"Just always loved the water. Someone claimed I was part fish. I never wanted to get out."

"A primal instinct, then."

"That's me. Part dolphin, part woman."

"A mermaid."

She laughed, sputtering seawater, and had to tread water again until her throat cleared.

"You okay?" he asked with concern, coming very close to her.

She nodded. "Should have remembered not to laugh and swallow water at the same time."

He touched her arm, letting his fingers glide over her skin. "How does the sunburn feel?"

"Great, now that I'm in the water." When goose bumps appeared on her flesh where he was touching, she pulled her arm away in embarrassment. Even her skin was betraying her.

"Why don't we have lunch and then rest for a bit. We can take another swim before we leave."

"Sounds good."

"Hey, Cristine . . ."

"What?" she asked, seeing his grin.

"I'll race you to the shore."

Okay, he liked a strong woman and wasn't afraid of competition, so she couldn't back down. But it had been years since she'd done anything more than swim a few laps in Claire's backyard pool. Taking a few deep breaths, she said, "You're on. Last one there has to serve lunch to the other."

He seemed to like that wager. "So when do we start?"

"I already have," she called out over her shoulder, leaving him behind.

She really didn't expect to win, since Simon was in great shape, so after she had served him delicious chicken sandwiches on thin crusty bread, fruit salad, and a glass of chilled wine, Cristine was sated and lying on the canvas catamaran, soaking up the sun.

It had been a long time since she'd had a perfect day, and this one was certainly in the running. Her tummy was full. The wine was giving her a pleasant buzz. The sun bathed her in warmth while the breeze offset it by cooling her damp bathing suit. Birds were chirping somewhere on the island and her eyes were closed as she listened to the soft lap of the surf rocking her gently.

"I am in heaven," she whispered with a contented sigh.

"Just make sure you don't burn in heaven," Simon, lying next to her, whispered back.

She shielded her eyes and turned her head to look at him. Good God, he was so handsome. His profile showed a slight smile. His eyes were closed and he looked just like she felt. Happy and contented. Again, desire welled up inside of her. Her fingers itched to touch his skin, the tiny golden hairs on his arm reflecting the light from the sun. That's it, she thought dreamily. He was golden, kissed by the sun with an even tan. She couldn't help wondering what he did back in the real world, but knew that was off limits.

How very odd to be attracted to someone like this. She also wondered how many other women had looked at him and felt the same thing.

"What are you thinking?"

He startled her and she laughed nervously. "I was just thinking how perfect everything is right now in this moment." Okay, only a part lie. She wasn't about to admit her desire.

He turned his face, opened his eyes, and smiled. "It's almost perfect."

She grinned. "Almost?" she asked in disbelief. "What more could you want?"

He chuckled. "A very leading question."

Extremely glad her face was sunburned, Cristine tried not to betray her blush or her embarrassment. Well, he liked bold women, didn't he? Women who stated what they wanted? Now was not the time to be shy or coy. Why *couldn't* she be herself, how she felt right now, staring into his eyes? She found her lips answering his sexy grin. "So answer it. What more could you want?"

His smile deepened. "How about you? For a memorable dessert."

She half laughed. "You had a delicious fruit salad for dessert."

"I'm still hungry. I've been staring at your mouth for two days now." He reached out and stroked a drying stray tendril of hair behind her ear. "I'll settle for a kiss."

She felt mesmerized by his eyes, his touch, and she watched in amazement as he leaned closer to her, his mouth inches from her own. She need to say something. He was waiting for her permission. He said he wouldn't do anything she didn't want. And what she wanted right now was for him to close the space between their mouths. She didn't care if she had sworn earlier that nothing was going to happen between them. She couldn't even think about the consequences of what she was about to do. Nothing seemed to exist, save that sweet electricity between them. Mere inches would make the connection.

"I would never deny a hungry man sustenance," she whispered, feeling his breath on her chin as she stared at his mouth, into his eyes, and then back at his mouth.

That was all he needed to hear.

His lips came down on hers gently, almost sweetly, grazing across her mouth with tenderness. Cristine had to hold herself back from moaning with pleasure; she had an intense desire for more. He seemed to sense her need and obliged, deepening his kiss until their mouths were open, both of them hungrily devouring the other. He rolled over her, leaning up on his elbows as they continued to kiss. His fingers were entwined in her damp hair and he held her, pulling her in closer.

Cristine stifled a surprised gasp and her entire body stiffened as she felt his erection against her belly. This couldn't be happening. Could it? He really did want her. She wasn't about to have sex out in the open with a man she hardly knew! Or was she? Because his hands were sliding down to the straps of her bathing suit and soon her breasts were exposed to the sun, the wind, and his glorious mouth. Tilting her head back with pleasure as he captured one nipple, she decided she would be crazy to deny herself whatever came next. This was beyond anything she could have imagined.

It happened so quickly, yet later, when she thought

about it, it was as if it were in slow motion . . . Simon was sliding her bathing suit down her body slowly, kissing the skin he exposed. She had only wanted to help him to get the damn wet suit off, to feel his skin on her own, so when she slid up the cat as he pulled the suit down she hadn't expected the sharp spasm of pain to seize her lower back and race down her leg.

"Arrggghhhhh . . ." Honestly, she couldn't have swallowed that yell even if it did mean the end to probably the best sex of her life. The pain was so sharp, so crippling that she was frozen in fear. Actually, panting in fear.

"Cristine! What's wrong?"

"I . . . I don't know," she gasped, trying not to cry, yet feeling her eyes water anyway. "I . . . can't . . . move."

"What do you mean you can't move?" Simon demanded, sounding fearful.

"I mean I can't move!" She tried to roll to her side, but the pain seized her right butt cheek and raced down her right leg. God, she was paralyzed with her bathing suit tightly rolled down to her doughy belly, only making it appear even more huge and disgusting! Somehow she had to get it up and—

"What can I do?" Simon interrupted, touching her shoulder and looking a little wild with fear.

He wasn't alone in fighting panic.

Cristine gasped as the pain became a spasm every time she moved. "I don't know what to do!" she answered, starting to get really scared. "We need to get back to the cottage and call a doctor."

Simon immediately began assembling the boom. He then jumped off the cat, pushed it completely off the sand, and jumped back, causing the craft to sway and Cristine to cry out in pain as she held on to the edge with one hand.

"I'm sorry, I'm sorry," Simon muttered, adjusting the sail.

"Simon," she called out.

He turned to her.

"You have to help me get this suit back up," she whimpered. If she was going to be carted back to the hotel with one side frozen in pain, at least she wasn't going to arrive half-naked like the catch of the day.

He crawled back to her, kneeling at her side. "What should I do?"

"Pull it up . . . gently," she called out as each movement caused a fresh spasm.

He worked with determination and Cristine bit the inside of her lip each time he tugged the wet material up her body. Wasn't it only moments ago that everything had seemed so perfect? Now she would need a doctor or a chiropractor or a miracle worker just to get off the catamaran.

"Okay, here we go," Simon declared when her suit at least covered her breasts. "I'll try to take it slow and gentle," he added, raising the sail.

Cristine groaned and it wasn't just from the pain.

Slow and gentle.

A few minutes ago those words had such a different meaning.

# Chapter

## 5

"THE SYMPTOMS DO INDICATE SCIATICA, NEURAL-gia along the sciatic nerve." The kindly doctor smiled down at her as she lay on her side in bed. "I believe you have a pinched sciatic nerve, miss," he added, to clarify.

She panted through the pain and blinked away the moisture at her eyes. "Sciatica? Isn't that what old people get?"

Again the doctor smiled. "It can affect anyone. Have you had lower back pain before?"

"Nothing like this."

He nodded. "I am going to give you a prescription for Flexeril, a muscle relaxant. It will help to ease the spasms and the pain will lessen."

"Thank you," she said with gratitude, too scared to try and shake his hand as every movement only brought on the excruciating spasms that felt like painful electrical shocks racing from her butt cheek down her leg.

"I will give the prescription to your husband and he can get it filled at a local pharmacy."

She thought about Simon, waiting on the porch. "He's not my husband," Cristine whispered. "He's a . . . a friend," she added. She didn't have a husband, or a partner, or anyone in her life who could take care of her. She was alone. The thought only made her feel more miserable.

"The Flexeril may make you tired, but rest can only help now. When do you leave for home?"

"Tomorrow morning."

"How long is the flight?"

"About an hour and a half. How will I be able to make the plane? I can't even walk on my own." All she wanted was to get home, to be in her own bed.

"It should ease enough for you to sit for a short plane ride. I will speak to your friend about buying you an inflatable cushion ring to sit on to take the pressure off your lower spine. Now the best thing you can do is rest. Call me if you need me."

"Thank you again, Doctor," she said, feeling truly miserable and hating that she was causing all this fuss . . . But really, she literally couldn't move without shooting pain taking her breath away.

He patted her shoulder. "You'll be fine. When you get back home, go to your own doctor for a reevaluation."

"I will," she promised.

"Now I will talk to your friend and soon you will feel some relief."

She nodded and watched as he left the cottage. Closing her eyes, she sighed in disbelief. How the hell had this happened to her? Was there some curse on her? Ever since Charlie had made his little speech about leaving, her world had turned upside down. If she wasn't afraid that it would hurt her, she would have cringed, thinking how her back had given out just as she had surrendered to Simon. And then there had been that ordeal of getting her bathing suit back up her body, which she was still wearing and somehow needed to get off. During the trip back to the cottage, poor Simon had seemed frantic and she couldn't blame him. She had tried not to shout out her pain every time the sail was repositioned. When they finally had arrived at the resort, how painfully humiliating it was to have been rolled over onto a surfboard and, with the help of another man, carried into the cottage.

Talk about making lasting impressions!

She'd be lucky if Simon came back from his errand and didn't run for the hills to get away from her. But she prayed that he wait until he returned from the pharmacy, as the only thing she was holding on to at the moment was the promise of drugs.

Twenty minutes later Simon entered the cottage carrying a white and blue plastic bag. "I have your pills and the cushion."

"Thank you so much." She motioned to the drawer. "Go in my purse and get the money."

"Don't be silly, Cristine. It hardly cost anything and I feel responsible," he answered, opening the bag and taking out a bottle. "I'll get you a glass of water and you can take your pill."

She nodded and closed her eyes in weary relief. Finally, something to work on the pain.

When she heard him shaking out a pill, she opened her eyes in gratitude. "You've been very kind, Simon. I don't imagine you have many women literally spasing out on you like this."

He smiled and held out his hand with the pill. "I told you, you were memorable."

She wanted to laugh, but was afraid of the internal movement. Instead, she gingerly moved her arm and took the pill from him. Lifting her head, she popped the pill into her mouth and sipped some water. "Just one?"

Simon looked at the bottle and nodded. "One every six hours."

"Two would be better, right?"

"Why don't we try the one and see how it works?"

What she really wanted was to zonk out, retreat into oblivion where she wouldn't feel pain or have to remember just what an embarrassing mess she had made of the afternoon. Defeated, she rested her head against the pillow that was scrunched in her arm. "You don't have to stay here with me. Believe me, I'm not good company."

He stroked the hair back from her forehead. "You poor thing."

"And don't be sweet to me, or I may just show you I'm inches away from becoming a blubbering mess."

He pulled a chair to the side of the bed and sat down. "Is there anything at all I can do to make you more comfortable?"

She felt the tears burning her eyes again. "You've been my hero, Simon. Really. Thank you for everything."

"So what about that bathing suit? Wouldn't you be more comfortable in a nightgown, something soft? Especially if you fall asleep?"

She sighed deeply. "I know I have to get up and get it off. I'm just dreading it."

"I can help."

She closed her eyes and shook her head. "I've already embarrassed myself enough in front of you and you've been really great about it, but that would be going beyond the call of duty."

"Who said anything about duty? Jesus, Cristine, part of the reason you're in this position is because of me. Let me help you get into your nightgown."

"Now see . . . you're being sweet," she murmured, "and I'm going to start blubbering and—"

"Well, before you start blubbering, let's try to get you upright," he interrupted, pulling the light cotton blanket back. "You hold on to my shoulder and I'll slide your legs toward the edge of the mattress."

"It's gonna hurt," she stated, but reached for his shoulder. She gasped through the pain yet soon found herself in a sitting position. "Hurry, before I lose courage," she muttered, letting Simon pull her upright as she put all her weight on her left leg.

Standing, holding on to Simon's arms, she felt like she had run a marathon. It seemed as if there were a heavy weight attached to her right lower back, pressing on a nerve and causing intense pain to shoot up her back and down her leg. "The bathroom," she gasped. "Help me to get there."

Together they made it into the smaller room. "My nightgowns are in the first drawer of the dresser," she said, transferring her weight from Simon's arm to the sink vanity. "There's a white cotton one, with tiny straps and stitched pleats in the front."

"I'll get it."

She looked at herself in the mirror over the sink and groaned. Her hair was a wild, frizzy mess from swimming, sticking out at all angles like an exploded firecracker. Her sunburned face was devoid of makeup and dark circles were starting to form under her eyes. God, what a mess! Who cares? she thought, hanging her head in defeat. It wasn't like either Simon or she had any notion of a continuing liaison. It had always been a dumb decision, right from the start. She wasn't one of those sophisticated women who take charge of their lives, get their sexual needs met by a handsome stranger, and then walk away with a smile of . . . what did Claire say? Dangerous kilowattage? She blew her breath out in derision. Hell, her only kilowattage was the painful surges of pain from sciatica. *Sciatica!*

It *was* an old person's complaint.

She might be past her prime, but she wasn't old yet, was she?

Cripes, old *and* alone. All she needed now was the six or seven cats to complete the picture.

"Is this the one?" Simon held the nightgown out to her.

She lifted her head and tried to smile. "That's it. Thanks." She put the nightgown on the vanity and said, "Would you close the door for a minute, please?"

"Sure. No problem." Simon slowly closed the bathroom door and added, "I'll be right here if you need me."

What a sweetie, she thought as the door clicked shut. He really was a decent man, despite his island sideline. And who was she to judge? She'd agreed to come here. Shaking her head, she gently pulled the bathing suit down her body, trying to ignore the pain it was causing, especially when it came to her right hip. When she got it to her knees, she just shook her legs, trying to make it slide to her feet. But the rolled spandex stuck there at her knees, and when she attempted to bend down to push it her right butt cheek exploded in a fresh wave of electrical pain.

"Owwwww . . ."

"Are you okay in there?"

She sniffled. "Wait a second." And she grabbed the nightgown and pulled it over her. "I . . . I think I need your help, Simon."

The door opened. "What can I do?" he asked with concern.

She looked down and wanted to burst into tears. How much more humiliating was this going to get? "I can't get my bathing suit off. I can't bend in any direction."

He stared at her nightgown.

"It's stuck. At my knees."

He seemed relieved. "Oh." Bending down, he lifted the hem of her nightgown and pulled the suit to her feet.

Cristine lifted one leg and then had to shift her weight to lift the other . . . as if she were an invalid. "Thanks," she said, gulping down fresh emotion. "Now I think I'll try to use the bathroom before getting back into bed. I don't want to make this trip again."

He simply nodded, taking her suit and closing the door.

Yeah, she was memorable, all right. The woman who threw her back out trying to have sex and then needed his services as a nurse to get through the night. Cristine hoped he was being paid *very* well. He deserved it.

Minutes later she knew she should never have asked how much more humiliating it was going to get, for the level rose several notches. If she had any pride left, sitting on the toilet, unable to wipe herself, that shred of pride was ripped away. The tears came and she couldn't stop them. She was stuck on the damn toilet! No matter what arm she used, the pain in her back, her hip, and her leg seemed attached to the movement.

She would not!

She could not!

"Fuck this," she whispered, beyond shame or pain. A woman had to retain some shred of dignity! Taking a deep breath, she worked through the pain and refreshed herself before collapsing back onto the toilet seat with a grunt of effort and a sheen of sweat. She didn't care what the doctor said. She was taking another pill and then she hoped she slept until morning when she could get on a plane and end this nightmare.

"Cristine?"

She cringed. She couldn't get up! She was stuck! On the damn toilet seat! She tried using the closest wall. The vanity was too far. There was nothing to support her. This couldn't be happening. How cruel was this? All because she had wanted to get laid!

"Cristine, do you need help?"

That's when the blubbering began in full force.

"Yes . . . I'm so sorry . . . I can't believe this . . . please . . . just close your eyes and come in . . . I'm so . . . so . . . sorry . . . Nothing like this . . . ever . . . in my life . . . *Please close your eyes!*"

She couldn't even look at him as he pulled her into an upright position and her nightgown fell down to cover her body.

She was definitely now beyond memorable.

Poor Simon looked rattled by this new turn of events. Cristine bet his job description didn't include hauling a near-hysterical woman off the toilet! She was a nightmare that would probably haunt him for the rest of his life. He might never have sex again.

Great.

She had ruined the island stud.

## Another day in paradise, lost somewhere inside your eyes

Huh? Cristine thought she heard the words and techno music somewhere inside her head, but her brain was foggy and all she wanted was to get back to oblivion.

## Strong enough to live

*A life without you by my side*
*'Cause now I know just who I am*

Oh, for heaven's sake! Cristine licked her dry lips and fought the urge to tell whoever was trying to wake her to shut up, stop singing, and leave her alone.

## It took a little time to see

*That all I really need is me*
*And now I know it's been there all along*

As those words echoed inside her head, Cristine blinked, trying to gain her bearings. Where was she, and why was someone singing words that seemed to resonate with her soul, waking her and making her pay attention?

*"It took a little time to see that all I really need is me"?*

This time she opened her eyes fully and saw Simon sitting in a chair reading a magazine. It all came rushing back to her. The sailing trip on the catamaran, her back going out, the return trip, the doctor, the bathroom . . . the *bathroom*!

She closed her eyes and cringed with embarrassment.

"Are you awake?"

His whisper was gentle and she nodded. "Barely. What time is it?"

"You've been sleeping for seven hours. It's late. I just wanted to be here to make sure you took your next pill."

Her shoulders sagged. He was so sweet. "You shouldn't be here babysitting me."

"I wanted to be here, Cristine. How do you feel?"

"Sleepy," she murmured. "Who is that singing?"

"Oh, Amala," he said, looking at the CD player in the armoire. "You ever hear of him?"

She shook her head.

"He's big in Europe and just now getting known in the States. Funny thing is, he's an American."

"Nice voice," she murmured. "What was that song a few minutes ago? Something about only needing yourself?"

Simon got up and picked up the CD as he shut off the player. "It's called 'Strong.' Do you want to hear it again?"

"Maybe later. Really, Simon, you should get some rest. You don't have to stay here."

He put the CD jacket back and pulled the chair closer to her. Sitting down, he said, "I will, but before I go I want you to eat something and take your next pill."

"Why are you so nice? After . . . well, everything."

He laughed. "Because I feel responsible for you."

"I hope you get a bonus for this, then," she mumbled. "You've really gone beyond the call of duty."

"I know what it's like to be alone, Cristine. And alone

and sick can be scary. I just wanted to be here, to let you know somebody was aware and concerned."

"You're going to make me blubber again." She sniffled and then tested her back. It was still sore and sensitive to any movement. "I bet all your women fall in love with you."

"Not the way you think. The women I see know this isn't about forever. This is about enjoying each other for a short while, that's all."

Nodding, Cristine said, "I'm dying to know what you do in real life, away from all this."

He paused, staring at the floor, and then looked up at her. "I'm a teacher."

She was stunned. "A teacher?" she repeated stupidly.

"A professor of philosophy at a university."

"Really?" She couldn't compute it. "Then why . . . this?"

"I told you. I'm turned on by powerful women, women who have risen above the programming society has placed on them. Independent women who know what they want and know they are any man's equal." He shrugged. "I was approached a few years ago after a lecture, so three or four times a year I get to come to paradise. I've met some extraordinary women here. Now," he added while rising, "there's a dinner plate in the kitchen waiting for you, but first . . . your pill."

He shook one out and handed it to her, while reaching for the glass on the night table.

Swallowing the pill, Cristine touched his hand as he took back the glass. "Thank you, Simon . . . for everything."

He simply smiled and walked into the kitchen.

# Chapter

# 6

"OH, YOU POOR WOMAN!" ISABEL EXCLAIMED, HUGging Cristine, who was finally in her own bed in Pennsylvania.

This was accomplished after a plane ride where she was escorted on and off the aircraft in a wheelchair. After Claire had first seen her at the airport, she had immediately called Isabel to meet them at Cristine's home.

"I'm really so much better now that I'm back. Besides, the muscle relaxants do their work and it's not nearly as bad as when it first happened."

"How *did* it happen?" Isabel asked, sitting on the edge of the mattress.

"Oh, wait till you hear this!" Claire pronounced with a laugh as she entered the bedroom and put a tray on the night table. "I laughed the entire way back from the airport. Only Cristine could have orchestrated this kind of disaster to get out of sex."

"Claire! I did not orchestrate this! Are you crazy?" She looked at Isabel for support. Isabel, dressed in jeans and her husband's blue shirt with the tails tied at her waist, looked sympathetic. Even after all these years, she was still wearing Chuck's clothing for comfort. "I was about to have sex when it happened."

"On a catamaran," Claire added, handing Cristine and Isabel a cup of herbal tea. "With the gorgeous and sexy Simon, who wound up nursing her and putting her on the plane."

"So you threw your back out having sex?" Isabel asked gently, trying not to show her amusement.

"No, not *having* sex," Cristine answered in her defense. "Trying. See, we'd been swimming in this lovely cove and my suit was still wet, and well, trying to get it down on a swaying catamaran, I must have pulled something and . . . and it's not funny!" she scolded, as Claire and Issy burst into laughter.

Issy put her hand over her mouth. "I'm sorry, Cristine, but it is funny!"

Cristine shrugged. "It's not funny if it's happening to you. It's humiliating. I felt paralyzed. Poor Simon had to get the suit back up my body, get us back to the cottage, and then find help to cart me off on a surfboard . . . like I was a beached whale. And then the bathroom . . ."

Claire and Isabel were now beyond trying to hide their laughter.

"I haven't heard this," Claire managed to get out. "What about the bathroom?"

Cristine could see why they were laughing, but the memory still held the sting of humiliation. "I was stuck. On the toilet."

"Oh, no," Issy whispered.

"And Simon had to help me get up."

"From the toilet?" Claire demanded, nearly spitting out her tea.

Cristine relented a little bit and grinned. "I know. Could anything be more humiliating? And he was so sweet about it all."

Issy was shaking her head. "Obviously, this was not the right path to take, or everything wouldn't have fallen apart on you. We need to find a more local solution."

Cristine held up a hand in protest. "No more solutions. *Please!* The next one might kill me!"

Claire laughed. "Oh, c'mon, Cristine. If your back hadn't gone out, you know you would have had a great time."

"But it did! Can't you see I'm meant to be alone? A couple of years and a couple of cats and I'll be the strange lady who lives alone. The only way you know she's alive is because you see smoke coming out of her chimney."

"This is what we should do," Issy said, as though Cristine's protest hadn't even been uttered. "We should make a list of all the attributes we want in a man and focus on the universe bringing him to her, instead of the other way around."

"You aren't listening to me. I need to heal. My body and my heart. None of this is going to go away overnight."

Claire propped herself on the edge of the mattress, leaning her head against the wooden post. "So what would you want in a man if you could design him? Tall, handsome, virile . . ."

"Compassionate," Issy added. "And with a sense of humor."

Cristine sighed. It was no use. They weren't listening.

"Healthy," Claire declared. "Not allergic to dust mites."

Surrendering, Cristine laughed. "Healthy would be nice."

"Intelligent. Someone who's already gone through their midlife crisis and knows the importance of self-discovery."

"Right," Claire said, holding her cup between her hands as she thought. "Someone you can depend on, who won't bolt at the first signs of taking responsibility."

"Someone who's gentle and sexy and kind and . . . who are we kidding?" Cristine asked. "If this man exists, he's already taken. I mean, look at us, the three of us. We're all those things we want in a man, and we're alone."

"By choice," Claire answered.

"Yes. Since Chuck, by choice." Issy's chin lifted as she added her statement.

"Well, it wasn't my choice," Cristine said. "Though I'm starting to see it was the best choice for me. I heard this song down there. What I remember about it was something like 'It took a little time to see that all I really need is me. And now I know it's been there all along.' That's the place I want to get to."

"I agree," Claire murmured. "You don't need a man to complete you. You are already complete. But it might be nice to want a man every now and then."

"Did you want this Simon?" Issy asked.

"I certainly did. Not the first day—I was too scared—but most definitely that afternoon in the cove."

"Then you accomplished the goal of the trip, to regain your desire. It doesn't matter whether you had actual sex. You felt desire again. Now you can begin creating the life you want."

"I don't know what I want, except to get healthy again and heal my back. Tina is going to be furious with me if I miss any more time at the office."

"We'll take care of Tina," Claire said. "You concentrate on healing yourself. Do you want one of us to stay with you tonight?"

She shook her head. "No. These pills are easing the spasms and I think I can make it to the bathroom and back by myself now."

Grinning, Issy came forward and tenderly kissed Cristine's forehead. "I know how embarrassed you must have been by that. Sometimes all we have to learn is that we're human and drop the pretense of being anything more."

"I didn't have a choice."

Isabel straightened and smiled down at her. "If you need anything, you'll call?"

"I promise. Thanks for rushing over here to hear my tale of humiliation."

"I wouldn't have missed it for anything. Besides, if we haven't learned yet how to laugh at ourselves, then we're in serious trouble. I'll call you tomorrow."

She watched Issy leave the room and looked at Claire. "You can go too. I know you're busy."

"I'll stay the night if you want."

"Go home. You've done enough."

Claire slid off the bed and picked up the small bottle of pills. "Take another one now. It's only fifteen minutes early. Once you do, I'll leave."

After she'd swallowed the pill, she looked up at her dear friend. Claire never looked flustered, always had it together. Even her pale yellow slacks that matched her blouse looked ironed. "Thanks for everything. I mean it. Even if it didn't turn out exactly like we thought, it was lovely to be there in paradise. I really had some great moments."

Claire kissed her cheek. "Good. Now I'm just a phone call away. If I don't hear from you, I'll call in the morning and I'll stop by after work. You're not hungry?"

"Claire, I'm fine. Really. Go home. Besides, in twenty minutes I'm going to be out like a light. I'll see you tomorrow if you have time."

"I'll be here. Don't hesitate to call if you get . . . stuck, or anything."

Cristine grinned. "I'm beyond being stuck, but thank you. Now go!"

"I'll lock the front door on my way out," she called out from the hallway.

"Thank you, Claire," she called back. "For everything."

"You'd do the same for me."

Cristine listened as Claire went out the front door, and knew she would do whatever she could, for any of the gang. They always had . . . right from the beginning. Claire had already unpacked her suitcase and had brought up a sandwich she'd bought at a local deli. There really was nothing to do but wait for the meds to take effect.

Closing her eyes, she thought of Claire and Issy laughing. She figured it was funny—to them. Soon she'd see the humor in it, but for now it was just like the rest of her life. Screwed up. Oh, she supposed it would be wonderful to order a man up, like Issy said. A more local solution.

First, he couldn't be crazy. She'd had enough of crazy with neurotic, hypochondriacal, lying, cheating, what-the-hell-was-I-doing-with-him charlie. No more crazy, needy people who wanted to be saved. She was no one's messiah and was definitely down off the cross. As the saying goes . . . someone else always needs the wood. The woman whose life he had just invaded, for example. No, if there ever was a next time, the man would have to be self-sufficient. Gentle, intelligent, kind, healthy, sexy with a sense of humor . . . and it would be a huge bonus if he didn't look like a troll. For a moment, just a simple drug-induced moment, Cristine caved into Isabel's suggestion and let herself believe with her whole heart and soul, because she knew she deserved it. She did. She deserved someone truly wonderful to love her . . . and maybe one day, way out there in her future, he would make an appearance. And then again, maybe not.

Her eyes began to feel heavy, along with her limbs, as she sensed she was sinking into the mattress. Why was it when she knew better than to believe in romance, she still wanted it? Those looks, those touches, that anticipation? It was Simon's fault. He had awakened desire in her again, and what was the point, when she would probably live out the rest of her life alone . . . no children, no husband, only cats. Dragging a grocery cart behind her and not shaving her legs anymore. Warts on her chin with hairs growing out of it, and saving newspapers to make paths through her home. Scaring children who thought she was crazy . . . and . . .

Time seemed to faded away as the Flexeril took effect. She let herself be cradled with relief and felt as if she were falling into a cloud, obscuring reality. Now she would sleep, she thought, blinking even more slowly, waiting for the moment of oblivion.

Okay, it was a dream.

It had to be.

Only she wasn't supposed to dream . . .

Cristine fought the effects of the medication and tried to open her heavy lids.

There were lights . . . beautiful *dancing lights* around the bottom of her bed!

She couldn't make sense of it. The blinds were closed. The only mirror was on the back of the bathroom door, and that was facing the wall. They continued to dance, mesmerizing her with their spectacular show of rainbow colors, and Cristine inhaled with awe as they slowly came around the side of the bed, closer to her.

She really didn't think. There was no time, or time didn't exist, as the lights began to encircle her, swirling around her . . . and she felt a surge of something so pleasurable, so intensely sexual, gushing through her, making her back arch with gratification as she seemed to swell into them and the fantastic colors nearly blinded her, blocking out all else.

"Oh, God . . ." she murmured, as the feeling built and built, wiping out all thought. Nothing existed, save absorbing the intensity of it. The pleasure became nearly unbearable and she didn't know how to contain it until she felt herself exploding. Disintegrating. She yelled out in exquisite pleasure as she climaxed over and over and over again. Nothing existed in that timelessness, save feeling herself separate into tiny pieces and shoot out of the room, her house, the sky, beyond the stars into nothingness . . .

And then . . . just as unexpectedly . . . she was back, gasping for breath, clutching the sheets, trying to separate reality from fantasy.

She was still gasping, completely awake, staring out into her bedroom.

No lights.

Everything seemed the same. Normal. Save for the residual tingling in her body, her rapid heartbeat, her raspy breath, her confused state of mind.

What in the name of all that's sane had happened to her?

Did she just have a stroke, or something? But she was sure having an unbelievable orgasm wasn't a reported symptom. She would have remembered that!

And this was not some ordinary orgasm either.

This was . . . an out-of-this-world kind of orgasm.

A blow your mind, body, and soul kind.

And what was with those lights?

It wasn't a dream. It couldn't have been. It was all too real. Sure, she was on drugs, but a muscle relaxant didn't induce hallucinations. Did it? It wasn't a mind drug. She wished she could get on her computer downstairs and look up Flexeril to find out. 'Cause if it had produced *that* hallucination, then she was getting the prescription renewed tomorrow! Filled with a strange mixture of joy

and confusion, she giggled nervously, seeing herself
hooked on that tiny yellow pill, going from doctor to
doctor, trying to score more. She would gladly live alone,
with the cats and the grocery cart and all the rest of it, to
experience *that* again!

Hell, who needed a man?

That, whatever it was, was beyond anything a mere
mortal had ever done!

It was . . . almost supernatural.

Her flesh tingled with goose bumps at the thought.

And that's when Cristine decided she couldn't wait until morning to get on the computer. She simply had to find
out what the reported reactions were to the medication.
She'd just take it slow and be careful. Moving her legs to
the side of the bed, she was surprised not to feel pain. She
slowly rolled over into a sitting position, pushing her
torso upright. No pain.

Hmm. That was odd. Usually she felt twinges, even
with the Flexeril.

She held on to her night table and pushed herself up
onto her feet.

No pain!

Gingerly, she let go of the night table and stood with
no support. There was no accompanying pain. Totally
bizarre. She took a step, and then another, and another,
then stopped and touched her lower back.

*No crippling pain!*

It was gone. Completely.

Testing, she lifted her right leg easily, then bent down
from the waist, something she hadn't been able to do in
days.

"Oh, my God!" she whispered in amazement. It was
like a miracle!

*That orgasm had cured her?*

No one was going to believe this. She walked to the
door and felt no ill effects. Giggling, Cristine made her

way to the stairs. This would be the hardest test. Facing a staircase had seemed like climbing Mount Everest. There was always pain and it took forever.

She descended one step, and then another. Amazed, she slowly walked down the remaining ones until she was downstairs. It was a miracle. She didn't care what anyone thought. Something *had* happened to her up there in her bedroom, something beyond understanding. Tingling with excitement, she let go of the handrail.

In the darkness, she walked into the kitchen and turned on her computer. Even when she sat down there was no pressure on her lower back. It was as though she were cured. Returned to her old self. No, not her old self, she thought as she waited for her desktop to appear. She was different. Changed. Altered.

Nothing in her life was ever going to be the same after . . . whatever had happened to her in her bedroom.

Within minutes she was online and typing in "Flexeril." She read the information provided, but not a single line mentioned hallucinations, or visions of lights, or orgasms.

It wasn't the medication.

So then what was it?

And would it ever come back?

She was too awed to even check her e-mail, so she shut off the computer and stared at the screen until it turned dark. Something had happened to her. Something extraordinary. It was as if she had been visited by those lights. They came out of nowhere, encircled her with intense pleasure, and then disappeared.

She knew what she had experienced was real, more real than anything else in her life had ever been. She hadn't been dreaming. Dreams don't cure you, throw your back into alignment, and leave you gasping with intense pleasure. At least no dream she or anyone else ever had did. Surely, if this were a common occurrence, she would have heard about it.

It was extraordinary, that's what it was.

And she felt awed by the experience.

So now what?

Would they return?

Dear God, she hoped so!

※

"You're back!"

Cristine walked up to Tina and hugged her, feeling renewed with energy, like she'd had a special vitamin shot and her body was still tingling with health. She had barely slept last night and had decided to come back to work and get on with her life. No need for the Flexeril either. This was simply pure happiness surging through her veins.

"I'm back," she declared. "And ready to get to work."

Tina stared at her. "Wow, I can't wait to hear all about it. You're . . . *radiating,* girl! Must have been some trip."

Laughing, Cristine nodded. "Oh, it was, believe me, but not in the way you're thinking. I'll tell you about it at lunch. Now, what's on my agenda?"

Tina scrambled through the papers on her desk. "Thank God you're back. I have the Maxwells' settlement at ten and the Campbells are scheduled to see the Rice house at eleven. I was about to cancel the showing when—"

"No need. I'll take it. What else?"

"Well, there's this list I was working on . . ."

"Hand it over."

Impressed, Tina sat back. "What exactly happened to you on that island?"

Cristine grinned. "I'll tell you the whole story at lunch." She really hadn't been able to stop smiling since she woke up after a few hours' sleep, and she was itching now to get back her life.

"I don't know if I can wait for lunch. And do they bottle the stuff? 'Cause I sure as hell can use some."

Relenting, Cristine leaned down and said, "This is what I got from the island, Tina." She paused. "It took a little time to see that all I really need is me. And now I know it's been there all along."

"You learned how to rhyme?"

Cristine laughed. "It's the lyrics of a song I heard."

"Island rap?"

"No. It's from a song called 'Strong,' by Amala. But the whole point is that I got me back. The me I lost when I surrendered my identity to another."

"Okay. I don't know if I'll be out of settlement by lunch, but I'm definitely coming over tonight to hear everything."

"All right. I'll make dinner."

"Deal. And by the way, you look fabulous."

Cristine's grin widened. "I feel fabulous."

"You're over Charlie then? So quickly?"

She looked down at the papers in her hand and then back at her friend. "Charlie who?"

"All right!" Tina exclaimed with a laugh. "Now I'm dying to hear everything."

"Tonight, then," Cristine called out, heading for her office.

She was back. *Really* back.

And better than ever.

Two hours later she was showing the Campbells around the Rice home. "As you can imagine, the views of the city are spectacular at night." She opened the wide double glass doors and they walked out to the flagstone patio. "And your own spa to relax in after work," she added, waving to what looked like a small swimming pool with seats. It was cement and right now bubbling in invitation. She'd made sure the Rices turned it on for the viewing before they left. "There's a semiprivate stream running along the property line and a meditation garden that's really lovely."

Anna Campbell turned to her husband. "I like this one. Really like it. Two master bedrooms. One for the kids when they come to visit."

"But it's fifteen years old," Nate Campbell complained. "And white carpeting throughout the whole place. It looks like it hasn't been decorated since the eighties."

They were an older couple, in their late fifties, and looking for a retirement home outside the city. Cristine knew Anna had fallen in love with the Mediterranean house, before they even entered. The exterior and the landscaping were quite breathtaking, but the inside needed some TLC.

"Why don't we go back inside for a moment?" Cristine suggested. When they were standing in the great room, she said, "You could replace the carpeting with wood, or tile. Large travertine tile would really make this space look huge. And there's central vacuuming so cleaning either would be a breeze. I know this place needs a little work, but you have to admit it's got great bones and you could make it spectacular."

"I don't want the work," Nate stated. "I wanted to move in and put our things away."

"Then we should be looking at new homes under construction, because if you want this neighborhood bordering the golf course, I'm afraid you're going to have to deal with someone else's taste. This is a premium house in a gated community on the ninth hole and, yes, it is fifteen years old. It wouldn't take much effort to bring it up to your taste. If you decide on this, we can always start our initial bid sixty thousand less, which would more than cover any renovations you might do. The owners know the house needs some work. So we play for a little while."

"And the kitchen's outdated," Nate countered.

Cristine smiled. Mr. Campbell was warming to the idea. "You're right. New tile in there and refacing the cabinets."

"Bid seventy-five thousand less."

Her smile disappeared. She so disliked greedy. "Nate, let me be frank with you. In today's market, with the baby boomers retiring, the owners might very well get lucky and have someone accept their asking price. This house has only been on the market for nineteen days. Granted, the list price is high, which gives us some room to play, but you don't want a flat-out refusal. The owners know they're probably going to have to come down in their asking price, but they also know houses on this golf course don't come up very often. What I'm hoping for is that we settle with sufficient money to renovate."

Mrs. Campbell looked pleadingly at her husband.

He sighed deeply and looked out the windows to the view of the golf course and the city farther down the hill. "So go in with a bid of six twenty."

Christine flipped open her cell phone.

Damn right, she was back.

*Chapter*

7

DINNER WAS CHINESE TAKEOUT AND CLAIRE joined her and Tina. They were sitting in the living room, casually eating, as Cristine told her island story yet again for Tina's sake, and she was starting to see the humor in it. For some reason, even though she had ample opportunity, Cristine was hesitant to mention what had happened to her last night. Not that she thought her friends might ridicule her . . . it just seemed too personal, too new, almost pure, and she didn't want to taint it just yet with anyone else's opinion.

"So how did this happen?" Claire asked, motioning toward Cristine. "You should have seen her yesterday, Tina. She could barely walk without pain."

Cristine shrugged. "I got out of bed last night and . . . and the pain was gone. Something must have slipped back into place."

"Well, you should have seen her today at work, Claire. She was a dynamo. I told her I wanted some of whatever magic she got in the Bahamas. Doesn't she look great?"

Claire stared at Cristine closely. "She looks totally different from last night. What kind of miracle really happened here?"

"I am totally different from last night. I'm pain free!"

"Nah." Claire slowly shook her head. "It's more than that. You look almost rejuvenated."

Cristine laughed a little nervously. "It's like what Isabel said last night. I got my desire back. And the first thing I desire is to get my life in order. Charlie's gone. That's a fact, and as time goes on, I'm also seeing what a blessing it's turned into."

"You don't think you're a little manic right now?" Tina asked. "I mean, less than two weeks and you're over him?"

"I know it seems fast and maybe a little unnatural, but so much has become clear to me. I really didn't have anyone to compare him with, especially not someone as terrific as Simon."

"But Simon's fantasy," Tina countered. "Most men would come up short when compared to him."

"It doesn't matter," Cristine answered. "He exists. Simon. Therefore, a real man, a secure man, compared to Charlie showed me how little I'd settled for. And that I so deserve better, even if it turns out I'm living alone for the rest of my life. Alone would be better than being with a lying manipulator. Charlie betrayed me in a horrible way, but I was thinking . . . was it any worse than how I have been betraying myself for years by living with him and all his demands, his litany of complaints? My so-called blind love didn't serve either one of us."

"You really are over him, aren't you?" Claire asked with a little bit of awe.

"I've moved on to me for a change, Claire."

"That's new," Tina stated.

"I know, and I'm thinking it's about time."

"I just can't get over the change in you, Cristine," Claire said, before plopping a dumpling into her mouth. "It's like you're a new person."

"Now we need to get Kelly some of that island magic," Tina said. "As long as she thinks she's a loser magnet, she will be."

"Haven't you gotten it yet, Tina?" Claire asked. "Kelly says she wants the right man to come along, but does she? It probably won't happen until Colleen goes off to college. How do you reclaim your life when you have a demanding, temperamental, teenage daughter living with you?" Claire used her chopsticks to make her point. "It's part of the price you pay for parenthood. You give up your own needs for the sake of your child's. Maybe that's why I never wanted kids. Too selfish."

"Claire, if you met the right man you would have his children," Cristine said, as she helped herself to fried rice. "Wouldn't you?"

Claire hesitated. "Why? I'm forty-two. What do I have to prove at my age? Some women aren't meant to live the Donna Reed life."

Tina laughed. "Claire, no one, ever, would think of comparing you to Donna Reed. I can't even imagine you in domestic tranquility."

"I don't think there is such a thing as domestic tranquility today. How many women do you know who even stay at home anymore to raise their children? For most Americans it takes two parents working, two incomes, just to live decently in this country. Do you know in some countries in Europe they pay mothers a monthly allowance to stay home with their kids? Makes more sense than sending them off to strangers to be raised."

"Well, let's all be glad right now we aren't pregnant," Tina stated. "If we were, we wouldn't be successful businesswomen. I know I'm taking a chance waiting until I'm financially secure, but I figure if it doesn't work, I'll adopt. Plenty of kids, especially minority kids, who need a good home." Raising her glass of wine, she added, "To

us then. Women who aren't afraid to take risks and follow
their own path."

Cristine raised her glass, but wondered if it wasn't too
late for her. There was a part of her that wanted the whole
family-unit thing, father, mother, two point five kids, the
white picket fence . . . hadn't that been what she was
working toward with the renovation of the house? When
the kitchen was completed, she had planned on bringing
up the subject to Charlie.

Thank heavens she never did.

Why in the world would she want to pass on his weaknesses to a child?

Still, the thought didn't leave her, and she couldn't wait
to get into bed tonight and wait for the lights to return.

"You're lost in thought," Claire accused. "Where are
you?"

Cristine grinned sheepishly. "Wandering thoughts, I
guess. I was just thinking about how I'm going to get that
kitchen finished on my own. It's the last room. Maybe I
could get a second mortgage."

"If that's the route you want to go, let me know and I'll
make some calls for you," Claire said.

"Maybe I will," Cristine answered. Claire was well-
known in the financial world and would guide her to the
best contacts.

A second mortgage. The thought terrified her, but she
wanted her home completed. It was almost like a mission
now, without Charlie. She could work harder at the office,
putting in even more hours now that she didn't have to
take care of anyone. This was her chance to prove herself
and create the life she wanted. Maybe she'd cut her hair
too. A fresh start. Since a man wasn't on her agenda for
quite some time, if ever, why not make life more simple?
Why waste a half hour of precious time each morning
slathering products on her hair and then blowing it dry

section by section to have sleek straight hair when her natural hair was curly?

A sense of freedom surged through her body.

She really *could* create her life any way she wanted now.

Maybe she needed to take some time to figure out exactly what it was she did want. The only thing that came to her mind was another visitation by those lights, those wondrous, glorious lights . . .

It didn't matter how hard she concentrated or meditated, how hard she wished or prayed, how open she tried to be, her nights were solitary. The lights never returned. And that was depressing and a little scary. As much as she told herself they were real, as time went on she began to wonder about the whole incredible evening. Surely something like that didn't just happen once in a lifetime. There should be some confirmation, so a person didn't start to question their sanity. For three weeks she tried to invite them back into her life during the night and during the day she worked hard for her client base and sold four houses. She had her hair cut into a cap of curls that everyone seemed to like and said she looked younger. She got the second mortgage approved and had contacted a building contractor who was sending out someone to give her an estimate on finishing her kitchen.

She was getting her house in order, figuratively and literally.

All in all life was pretty good, except she felt abandoned. Not by Charlie. Charlie was thing of the past, save for his messages on her machine that she never returned and his emails when he was, in his words, *touching base*. She simply wrote back and told him he should be touching base where he lived and she had nothing more to say to him. No, she felt abandoned by something unexplainable. Sometimes she wished she'd never experienced that miraculous night, as everything since seemed so mundane.

It was like glimpsing the extraordinary, the possibility of bliss, being transported from the ordinary into the sublime . . . and then dropped forever back into cold, hard reality where, in comparison, life had lost its shine.

Glancing at her watch, Cristine tapped her fingernails against the sample piece of granite on her old countertop. If this guy didn't show up in the next ten minutes, she was going to be late for her appointment and it wasn't one she could postpone. Mamie Pitcairn was looking for a house for her mother. One floor, gated community, clubhouse, maintenance free. Cristine had three to show her. Bless the Rices for recommending her to one of the best-known matrons of Philly suburbs society. While Cristine lived in a good neighborhood of Haverton, Mamie Pitcairn lived in *the* neighborhood. Hell, her home was just about the whole neighborhood, set so far back off the road in a parklike setting no one she associated with had ever seen the place, save for the rare picture in the newspaper.

She had dressed in her best business suit and her good Prada heels with an Hermès scarf casually draped over her shoulders and she was nervous enough without being delayed by a handyman who should have shown up fifteen minutes ago.

"'Bout time," she muttered when she heard the doorbell ring, and headed toward the front of the house. Now she was going to have to simply brief him and leave.

"You're late," she said, opening the door and seeing a man dressed in jeans and a blue shirt. "I can only give you five minutes and then I have to run."

"You are running?" he asked, looking at her designer suit and heels.

"I mean I'll have to run to an appointment." She held the door open wider. "Come in. The kitchen is in the back of the house."

She heard him following her and in her mind she pictured him. Tall, nice looking, dirty blond hair, blue eyes.

Didn't look like a contractor, but he was recommended and he'd have to do since she didn't have the time to conduct a proper interview. When she entered the kitchen she said, "As you can see, the kitchen is only partly finished. This granite needs to be laid on the counters and backsplash, and there's the new sink and the stove top is in those boxes. Do you think you can handle it?"

She waited, not too patiently, as he looked around the room.

"I really am running late," she prodded.

"You want me to do this?"

Her eyes widened. "Ah . . . yeah. Isn't that why you're here? To help me get this finished?" She moved closer to him and showed him the page she'd ripped out of a magazine almost a year ago. "See. I want it like that, but instead of one long sheet of granite, you're going to cut the tiles to fit."

He stuck his hands into the pockets of his jeans, leaned over the picture for a moment, and then said, "I believe I can help you."

She let her breath out and grabbed her purse. "Great. So you'll get started today? There's an extra set of house keys on the hook by the garage. Just lock up when you leave, if I'm not back, okay?"

"Okay."

"Oh, and I'm Cristine, no *h*. Cristine Dobbins." She stuck out her hand. "But you already knew that, right? And you are . . . ?"

He extended his hand with an amused expression. "Daniel Burns. What does that mean? No *h*?"

She shook his hand and then dropped it. "Oh, just that my name is spelled without it. So you'll be fine here? Because I really have to run. We can talk about your estimate later. Call me if you're gone when I get back and don't forget to leave your card." She looked around. "Are your tools outside? Because there's some in the garage if you need them."

She was already heading toward the garage and her car.

If she drove a little over the speed limit she'd be right on time for Mamie.

Mamie Pitcairn was fifty-nine years old, though she looked at least ten years younger, and she had married into one of the oldest families in the Delaware Valley which insured that even if she wasn't filthy rich, the name alone would have given her entrance anywhere she wanted to be received. Cristine was quickly learning that Mamie was no one's fool. The woman was dressed in tailored slacks, probably designer, and a leather jacket, also designer. She wore little makeup and her white hair was pulled back into a tight knot that actually complemented her finely sculpted face.

"Here's what I want," Mamie stated, as she dropped her sunglasses into her purse, which had the designer's initials at the clasp. "My mother is aging and she needs to live on one floor, no stairs, but not in one of those depressing adult communities where the emergency vehicles cart away your dying neighbors on a weekly basis. It has to be gated for her peace of mind, but it should have people of all ages, even children. But with enough property that she wouldn't have to be bothered by them. The children, I mean. I firmly believe that if you think young, you stay young. So I want young people around her."

"All right." Cristine was taking notes, writing down everything Mamie was saying. She didn't remind the woman she had already given her this speech over the phone when they made the appointment.

"And there should be a guest cottage or servant's quarters, for her companion who happens to be a registered nurse."

Cristine nodded, knowing how important it was to make Mamie happy. The woman could have gone to any of the exclusive agencies that specialized in estate homes, but was taking the Rices' recommendation for a more personal approach from a smaller firm. It also was in her favor that the Campbells had bought the Rice home after negotiating a more fair price.

Sitting back in her chair at the conference table, Cristine put her notebook aside and opened a black leather portfolio. "I have selected three homes for us to see today that I think may meet your requirements. All are in gated communities and—"

"A pool!" Mamie interrupted. "She does her exercises in a pool. Heated, of course."

"Of course," Cristine murmured, taking one of the home brochures out of her portfolio and setting it aside. It would have been nice to know a pool, a heated pool, was a requirement. "If you'd like to take a look at these two homes, I'll just be a minute. I want to go back onto the computer and see if I can pull up any more properties with a heated pool."

Mamie didn't say a word as she took the portfolio and began reading.

"Excuse me, I'll be right back," Cristine said, pushing her chair away from the table and walking out of the room.

She had gone no farther than five feet when Tina pounced on her. "How's it going? Does she seemed pleased?"

"Jesus, Tina, how should I know?" Cristine muttered, grabbing her friend's arm and pulling her into Tina's office. "She doesn't give much away. Listen, I need help and fast! I need a heated swimming pool. Get on the computer and look. All the same requirements, one floor, gated community, and she wants a guest cottage or servant's quarters. I'm going to my office and between the two of us we'd better come up with something quick!"

"Oh, God," Tina muttered, plopping into her chair and swinging it toward her computer. "We've gotta get this sale, Cristine. It'll make our name. It'll be like taking out a full-page advertisement in *Philadelphia Magazine*."

"Then find me the place!" Cristine nearly hissed and hurried into her own office.

An hour later, she and Mamie walked into a sprawling one-floor home with a grand master suite off the living room that was as big as the combined space in her own kitchen and living room. The gorgeous bathroom was as big as her bedroom, and all of it had been decorated with simple good taste. She let Mamie walk through the house ahead of her, noting the woman's subdued interest. But it was interest. The house was listed with Sotheby's, and if Mamie decided on it, Cristine's fee would be split, but the sale alone would turn heads and overnight they would make their name in an upscale market.

It was best not to push Mamie, Cristine thought as they left the master bath and reentered the bedroom. "You can see the guest cottage beyond the pool," Cristine offered, walking to the double French doors that opened onto a covered patio that ran the long length of the house.

Mamie opened a door and went outside. Cristine followed. "Is there an intercom system?"

Cristine looked at the slick four-page brochure loaded with pictures and details. Sotheby's had done a nice job of putting it together. She scanned the list of amenities. "Yes, there's an intercom in the house and it also works in the guest cottage. The home security system is wired to the local police department and emergency services."

"Let's see the guest cottage."

They walked around the pool that looked so inviting Cristine had to glance away from the temptation to plunge into it. Maybe she should have a pool installed in her backyard. It would be heavenly in the summer to get home and jump into cool water. But first she needed to get the kitchen finished with the late-arriving Daniel Burns. He had better have at least started her countertop by the time she got home if he intended to stay on the job.

Turning her attention back to Mamie and her own job, she opened the door to the cottage and inhaled with appreciation. It was lovely. Whitewashed floors with overstuffed furniture and chintz curtains in shades of blue and yellow welcomed them. Fresh flowers scented the room and Cristine thought she'd be happy just to live in the guest quarters.

"One bedroom?" Mamie asked, walking into the small kitchen.

Cristine checked her fact sheet. "Yes. One bedroom, wired for cable and broadband. It's quite lovely, isn't it?"

Mamie peeked into the bedroom. "It will do."

Good news. An admission. Cristine asked, "Would you like to walk the grounds? There's a small peach orchard that separates the property from the neighbors and a—"

Mamie waved her hand. "Heavens no. Why don't you meet with my mother tomorrow and show her this place. If she feels like taking a tour you can do it with her."

Nodding, Cristine said, "Certainly. What time?"

Satisfied with what she had seen, Mamie was walking toward the door. "I'll call you after I speak with her."

Outside, walking back toward the main house, Cristine asked, "Would you like to see the other properties now?"

"Not really."

Was that a good sign? It seemed like a good sign. She wanted her mother to see the place. Had she made up her mind already?

Sighing, Mamie stopped walking when they hit the patio. "Look, when I see something that's right, I know it. And this house is what I'm looking for. If my mother agrees, then we can begin negotiations. Are you up to negotiating with Sotheby's? If they know who the buyer is it'll be much more difficult."

"Of course I'm up to negotiating with them," Cristine said firmly, though her heart leaped inside her chest. "You just tell me where to begin."

"It's two point three million. Start at one point eight, but wait until my mother approves of the place. I'll go two million, but that's it. And, since you'll split your fee with Sotheby's, I assume your percentage points are negotiable."

Cristine tried to keep her face composed. Joe Nobody buying a home wouldn't even consider asking to negotiate her commission, but Mamie Pitcairn was used to getting discounts for everything from clothes to houses. It never made sense to her that those who could well afford it never paid full price. She supposed that's why they remained rich. "Why don't we first see if your mother likes the house," Cristine replied with a smile. "Then we'll go from there." She opened the French doors that led back into the house. "Would you like to stop for coffee, or something to drink?"

"No, just take me back to my car. I'll call you later this afternoon with the time to expect my mother."

Following Mamie, Cristine didn't take offense at the woman's brusque tone. Cristine wasn't her peer. She was simply a working stiff who had better negotiate the best deal possible if she wanted to keep her as a client. And, even though her cut of the commission would really help out the agency, she would take less if it meant closing the deal.

It would be an investment in their future. Even Tina would have to agree.

Three hours later, after trying to calm down Tina and the rest of the staff who seemed to think the deal was in the bag, Cristine was driving home, wondering what she should wear for her meeting with Mamie's mother. She would be meeting Lillian Brooker and her companion/nurse at eleven the next morning for a walk-through of the property. Cristine felt drained from the pressure and stress of the day, and she wished so much didn't depend on her successful completion of this deal. What if she failed? What if Lillian didn't like the color of the house? What if the guest cottage was too far from the master bedroom? There were so many variables that had to fall into place before she could make the first call to the other agency and begin negotiations.

She stopped at a light, and for a moment, she remembered the last time she was at the same light and lost in thought. Then she had been excited to get home to Charlie, who was waiting to dump her and spin her life around a hundred and eighty degrees. How simple life had seemed then. Now her life was filled with uncertainty, each day different from the one before, never knowing what to expect.

Taking her foot off the brake, she continued through the green light and headed for her house. God, she hoped that man had at least started on her countertop. After viewing the house today with Mamie, so pristine and put-together, she was going to find it hard to face the bedlam of her kitchen. Soon, she told herself as she turned onto her street. Just one more room to go and then the house would be finished. If this Daniel Burns didn't work out, then she'd hire someone else fast. And hopefully, she'd collect a decent commission and be ahead of the game financially to repay her second mortgage. She *had* to repay that as quickly as possible, for it was like an ax over her head waiting to fall. She wondered what it was like to never worry about money, but simply use it as a tool as Mamie had done. Mamie wasn't even talking about a mortgage. This would be a cash transaction or more probably a wire transfer through the ethers, words and figures representing actual money. That's how the wealthy did it.

Her driveway was empty. Great. So the contractor was gone.

She pulled up and pushed the remote garage opener on her visor. Come to think of it, she hadn't seen his truck or van when she'd left. But she'd been so rushed that wasn't surprising. She pulled into the garage, shut off her car, and closed the double door. Grabbing her purse, Cristine got out of the car and headed for the main house while again mentally going through her closet and wondering what she should wear tomorrow.

She entered the laundry room, slipped out of her heels, and headed to the kitchen fully prepared to pick up the phone and complain. Instead, she found herself frozen in place, her lower jaw hanging in shock.

The countertop was done.

Completed.

Beautifully completed. Just like in the magazine.

Her brain felt fried. How could he possibly have finished it in a few hours? Cutting granite was precision work. That's why Charlie hadn't even attempted it. She looked around for any debris, dust, anything that would indicate extensive work had taken place. There was nothing except her gorgeous shiny new granite countertop.

"Amazing," she whispered, finally moving closer and running her hand over the smooth dark stone. "This guy's good. *Real* good."

She suddenly felt giggly, as if she'd just been given the best present. And then she stopped giggling when she realized she'd never gotten an estimate. He must charge a small fortune.

God . . . she simply *had* to sell Lillian Brooker on that house tomorrow!

The money from the second mortgage was going to be eaten up fast, and she was going to have to replace it with the same speed as Daniel Burns worked. Which only left her with more stress and pressure.

When would this end? When would she be able to breathe easily again?

"Don't think about it," she told herself as she again admired her new countertop. "Day by day." And then she wondered if talking out loud to herself was a sign she should be worrying about.

Hell, at least she hadn't gotten a cat yet and she still recycled her newspapers.

She had tomorrow with Lillian Brooker to worry about.

*Chapter*

# 8

LILLIAN BROOKER DIDN'T LOOK LIKE ANYONE'S grandmother Cristine had ever met. The woman was in her early eighties, wore Capri pants and a tight pink sweater that showed off an ample bustline. Her thinning, bleached hair was fashioned into an intricate upsweep you could actually see through to her scalp, with tight tendrils expertly curled at her temples. Without the heavy makeup, she still looked like she could be Dolly Parton's aged aunt.

Cristine felt decidedly overdressed in her business suit as she extended her hand in greeting. "It's a pleasure to meet you, Mrs. Brooker."

A jeweled hand that looked too fragile to support the many diamonds shook hers with a surprisingly firm grip. "Nice to meet you too. So you have the perfect house to show us."

"I certainly hope you think so," she answered with a smile. Cristine held out her hand to the serious-looking older woman behind Mrs. Brooker. "Hello, I'm Cristine Dobbins. I'm glad you'll be joining us."

"This is Maxine Carter, my companion."

Cristine's smile remained fixed. Maxine was dressed in denim, from head to toe, actually open-toed denim espadrilles. Her short straight hair was dyed a very odd shade of red that bordered on purple. The woman also shook Cristine's hand firmly. "Hello."

Not getting much of a reading from Maxine, Cristine turned her attention back to Lillian. "Yes, your daughter thought you might like this house. It has everything you want . . . one floor, gated community, a heated pool."

"Then let's take a look at it," Lillian said. "Maxine will drive. She always drives."

"All right, just let me get my purse and we'll take off," Cristine answered. "Excuse me for a moment."

She walked back into her office where Tina was waiting.

"*That's* Mamie Pitcairn's mother?" Tina's brown eyes were wide with shock.

"It appears so," Cristine murmured, grabbing her purse and her portfolio.

"It's like looking at *Absolutely Fabulous,* the senior edition."

Shaking her head and trying not to laugh, Cristine said, "See, another lesson about expectations being blown away. Who were we expecting? The Queen Mum?" She stared at her friend and business partner. "And her companion wants to drive, so I'm at their mercy. Wish me well."

Tina clasped her hands together at her heart. "I'll do more than wish you well. I'm gonna have the whole office chanting for this sale."

Taking a deep steadying breath, Cristine nodded and rejoined Lillian and Maxine. It was already turning into an adventure.

First of all, Maxine drifted . . .

Seated in the back seat, giving directions, Cristine gulped down her apprehension as the older Maxine drifted in her driving. Cristine wanted to point out that the white lines were Maxine's friends and, like when

Maxine was a child and coloring, to try and stay within them. But she shut up. This sale meant too much to become a lecturing back seat driver, even if all their lives were held precariously in the woman's hands. Several times she shut her eyes as the older woman crossed over into the oncoming lane or drifted off onto the gravelly shoulder of the road. It was only when Lillian yelled "Fly Right!" that Maxine would quickly swerve into her own lane again. And *this* was the nurse and companion that was watching out for Lillian?

Dear God, she'd be lucky if they made it to the house alive.

Cristine was sweating with nervousness, praying they didn't get into an accident, praying every other driver on the road was alert and defensive. She could just picture an outraged Mamie blaming her for trusting her mother's well-being to an unprofessional. When they finally reached Skyline Country Estates, Cristine almost wept with gratitude. Rolling down the window, she showed the guard at the gate her ID and the Sotheby's brochure to gain admittance into the exclusive community.

"As you can see, it's almost like a natural reserve," Cristine said, trying to keep her voice steady as she began her sales pitch. "The homeowners' association maintains the grounds and, of course, you'd have full access to the clubhouse. Do either of you play golf?"

"Maxine did, years ago," Lillian remarked, looking out her window with interest.

"Turn left at the next street. It's the first driveway."

Maxine managed to get them to the house and Cristine exhaled with relief. Now to sell Lillian that this would be the perfect place to live. She got out of the car and opened Lillian's door for her.

"Big place," she remarked, looking at the exterior.

"Who's going to keep it up?" Maxine asked, joining them.

"I'm sure you could find a good landscaper. I could look into it for you."

"You do that, honey, after I see if I want to live here." Lillian and Maxine walked together toward the front door. Cristine gave them space and she could see they were chatting together, pointing out different features. It seemed Maxine's opinion was very important to Lillian, and Cristine made a mental note not to exclude her in the showing.

She opened the lockbox and took out the key for the front door. Handing Maxine a brochure, she invited them inside. She let them explore on their own and hung back. If they had any questions they would most certainly ask. Neither one of them seemed hesitant about speaking their minds.

They really were characters, she thought, watching them together in the kitchen. They moved almost as one, reaching for the oven door at the same time and then, as though by silent communication, one would hold back and allow the other to open it.

When they walked into the master bedroom, Lillian turned around to Cristine. "It's huge, isn't it?"

"It sure is. Quite spectacular."

"I'll give Mamie credit," Maxine said. "She isn't stingy."

"Not like that asshole she married," Lillian muttered. "I do believe the man was born with a pole up his behind."

Cristine merely blinked and turned her attention to the French doors. She probably shouldn't have overheard that conversation. "There's a wraparound covered patio that leads to the pool and the guesthouse. You'll probably want to check that out, Maxine. I saw it yesterday and it's quite lovely."

"Why wouldn't I be interested in it too?" Lillian asked as they walked outside.

Cristine was taken aback by not only the question, but Lillian's tone. She seemed a bit annoyed. "Of course you would, Mrs. Brooker. I'm sorry, I didn't mean to exclude you. It's just that your daughter mentioned your need for a guesthouse for your companion and nurse. I just assumed that was Maxine."

"Well, Maxine *is* my companion. Has been for over thirty-two years."

They were all staring at each other and Cristine was sure somehow, in some way, she might just have squelched the sale . . . but she wasn't sure how.

Lillian closed her eyes briefly, as though for patience. "Let's just get this out in the open, since it's obvious Mamie didn't make things clear. Maxine and I have been together for thirty-two years as companions and lovers and nurses and friends, and that's longer than all three of my daughter's marriages. The last one got her where she wanted to be, the wife of a real stuffed shirt, but I say if it makes her happy to be the center of attention and live with a passionless man, that's her business. Unfortunately, it doesn't work both ways. When my heart began to give me trouble, old stuffed shirt Pitcairn didn't want us living in their guesthouse so he sent Mamie out to find us a place. To get rid of us, you might say. We are an embarrassment to him and his kind."

"I see," Cristine murmured, and she did. Now it made sense why Mamie had picked a small agency without ties to her social tier.

"Do you have a problem with us too?" Maxine asked, standing closer to Lillian.

Her smile was quick and sincere. "Not at all. As a matter of fact, I recently came out a long relationship, so you have my admiration. Thirty-two years. That's some accomplishment."

Lillian reached for Maxine's hand. "It sure is. There's something to be said for making it through all those bumps in the road and still holding hands as friends as you walk together down the last miles."

Cristine nodded. "You know what? I think that's what everyone wants. Congratulations in making it so far together."

"All right, so now that's settled." Lillian looked around the property. "So far I like this place. It's private, has everything we want and more. Let me and Maxine walk around for a bit by ourselves and then we can make up our minds."

"Sure. Absolutely. I'll just sit here on the patio and you two feel free to explore wherever you want." Cristine sat down at the wrought-iron table and watched as the two older women slowly walked around the pool to the guesthouse. She felt a lump in her throat and her eyes began to burn as she saw Maxine's deep concern for Lillian, holding her elbow and gently leading her around. What was so different about them, except at their age they simply didn't care any longer what anyone thought? Two old souls had found each other and were in it for the long haul.

She didn't have that. Never had. Charlie obviously hadn't been in it for better or worse. Their bump in the road became a fatal crash. Why was it that she still wanted what Lillian and Maxine had? A soul mate, someone who would be there through thick and thin, who would be holding her hand during the last of life's journey.

Sniffling, Cristine told herself she was just being sentimental.

What those two old women had was rare. It was too easy in today's society to walk away. Everybody thought if it didn't work out, they'd find someone new. But what if that wasn't true? What if we walked away too soon? Even though she was glad Charlie was out of her life, she had felt he'd walked away too soon. He hadn't even discussed it with her. How could she trust another man?

Did anyone today really have commitment when things got rough? In a disposable society, were relationships like toasters? Great while they worked, but too much trouble to fix them?

And still, knowing how precarious relationships were, why was it her heart yearned to connect intimately with another soul? Hadn't she learned her lesson, or were these old women and their devotion to each other simply relics of another time and place?

And then again, maybe she should be focused on her job, instead of her heart.

Just look where her heart had brought her.

Two hours later she was hot into negotiations with Sotheby's agent, Lorraine MacIreney.

"Your client has to realize this property hasn't even been on the market for a week yet. My clients can still get their selling price if they wait."

"Lorraine, let's not play these games, all right? Your clients want to sell. I have a buyer. Let's come to a compromise. The longer it takes to sell that house the faster the list price drops, and we both know it."

"Cristine, you've got to come up from one point eight. Do you realize you're asking me to go back to my people with an offer for half a million less?"

"It's overpriced. The last property that sold in Skyline went for one point nine."

"That house didn't include a pool or a guest cottage."

"And a pool, not a large pool at that, and a guest cottage is worth half a million? I've got a contractor doing work for me right now that could do both for less than two hundred thousand. Five hundred thousand would buy a three-thousand-square foot house in a different neighborhood."

"But it is Skyline Country Estates, prime real estate."

"Lorraine, Lorraine . . ." Cristine closed her eyes briefly and tried to summon more patience. "My buyer

has the money, cash, right now. This is an easy sale for
both of us. Don't make me go into Bryn Athan. I have
two other houses under consideration."

There was a pause. "I'll go to my clients for two million."

Cristine paused. "One point nine."

"Two million."

"One point nine five and that's my final. My client
knows that property isn't worth two million and won't
pay it. You still get the highest selling price in the neighborhood and all the prestige. How greedy does this have
to get? Are you willing to lose an immediate cash sale
because we're quibbling over fifty thousand?"

A period of silence followed Cristine's statement and
her heart thudded almost painfully against her chest wall.
Had she gone too far? So much depended on this sale that
she felt sick to her stomach.

"You've got chutzpah, I'll give you that," Lorraine finally said. "I'll call you back."

She let her breath out as she hung up the phone. *Please,
please, please,* she prayed, *let this work out.* The split
commission from this sale would mean that she could repay her second mortgage and put the rest back into the
business. Her office door was closed and she didn't want
to open it. Tina would be on her like a flea, making her
more nervous, and she needed to focus, seeing Maxine
and Lillian in that house, pruning the rosebushes together, eating dinner on the back patio, doing their exercises in the pool. She needed to know this was the right
deal for everyone involved. The only variable was the
sellers. They had to know they were shooting for the moon
with two point three million. She would have done it herself if she were the listing agent, but she would have cautioned them not to depend on getting it, that they'd be
lucky to walk away with two million. How smart was
Lorraine? Did she have a college tuition that needed to be

paid? Did she need a new car, or to repay her own second mortgage? She might work for Sotheby's, but that didn't mean anything. She still worked for a living.

Thinking of her second mortgage, she wondered if Daniel Burns had shown up and left an estimate. She had a feeling he was going to be very expensive. Still, if she made this sale, she'd be able to have her kitchen finished and be out of debt, well, major debt anyway. She still had the credit cards that Charlie had helped to max out, and her car payments for the next year and a half, but she would almost own her home again. Just five more years and her mortgage would be cleared, or it would have been five years if she hadn't been forced to get the second mortgage. She'd spent years doubling, sometimes tripling her mortgage payments whenever she sold a house just so she could shorten her debt, and not simply rent it from a bank for thirty years of interest. She'd seen too many people go under in this business. Jobs were no longer secure, with outsourcing taking more every week. How many countless families bought the house of their dreams when interest rates dropped and prices soared, only to find themselves selling out before the bank foreclosed? Nobody really talked about that in the news, but Cristine had held the hands of sellers who never could have predicted the economy would fall and they would be the ones to crash.

It was very important to her to own, really, wholly own, her own home. And she was so close.

She rarely talked about her childhood to anyone, not even to Charlie or the gang. Only once had she mentioned that she'd been an orphan and Isabel's eyes had softened with compassion. She had made it clear it wasn't under discussion, so no one asked her about it and she was grateful. There was no point in living in the past, she knew that, but she also knew the past can affect every choice made in the present.

And she knew why getting that second mortgage had filled her with dread.

She'd been alone, growing up in foster homes. Her single mother had been alive somewhere, probably in some commune in California, stoned out of her mind. A hippie—at least that's what the caseworker had told her as a child. And later, after giving up all hope that her mother would come and rescue her, she'd been determined to follow all the rules, give no one reason to hit her or abuse her, make good use of the one thing all her own, her brain, to get a scholarship and find her own way in the world. She had been a ward of the state, shuffling from one home to another, and she swore one day she would own her own home where no one would have the right to tell her she had to leave.

And she was close . . . so very close to achieving that dream.

All she needed was to get back on schedule and—

Her phone rang and all thoughts were cut short, along with her breath. Her heart again began thudding with nervousness as she answered it. "Cristine Dobbins."

"Cristine, it's Lorraine."

"Lorraine . . ." She left the woman's name hanging, not willing to ask if the offer was rejected yet.

"Well, you're one lucky woman. Or did you somehow know my clients are going through a nasty divorce and just want out of the house?"

Cristine couldn't help giggling and she covered the mouthpiece of the phone to hide it. Bringing herself under control, she said, "That's wonderful, Lorraine. Not the divorce, but the sale. I'll put together an agreement and maybe we could meet for lunch to celebrate."

"You're taking this casually. I would think this is a megasale for you. Puts you in a different league. By the way, what's the client's name?"

Cristine decided to ignore the first remarks. "Mrs. Brooker. Lillian Brooker. She's an elderly woman who wants one-floor living. And, since I now know the sellers want out of the house ASAP, I'm sure we can arrange a quick settlement."

"All the better, all around."

"Let me call my client, Lorraine, and give her the good news, and then I'll get back to you and we'll schedule lunch."

"Right," Lorraine answered. "And congratulations."

"Congratulations to you too, Lorraine. It was great working with you."

She hung up the phone and just stared at all the papers on her desk, without really seeing anything. It was done. She got the house for under two million. She wanted to jump up and scream out for Tina or start dancing on top of her desk. But she didn't. She was still in shock and she had yet to call Mamie Pitcairn.

It was like asking to speak with a head of state when she called the Pitcairn residence. Cristine had to give so many details just to be put through to the woman.

"Cristine. What news do you have?"

"Congratulations, Mamie. I got the house for one point nine five. Under two million."

"Well done, Cristine. My mother will be pleased." There was a pause. "Now about your percentage points . . ."

"Mamie, my percentage points will remain unchanged. I got that house for fifty thousand less than you expected to pay. Let's just call it even, and your mother and Maxine can move in ASAP, as the sellers are going through a divorce. Lillian did say it was important that they find a new place quickly. She mentioned you and your husband were quite clear about that. This deal serves everyone's needs, and it was achieved in two days."

"Yes," Mamie said hesitantly. "It appears it does."

Cristine could tell the woman was wondering just how much Lillian had told her. "And I told the agent from Sotheby's that my client was Mrs. Brooker. I assume the house will be in your mother's name?"

"Yes. That was my intention."

"Fine. I'll be with her throughout settlement and walk her each step of the way so she won't be lost. If you have a lawyer you'd like me to go over everything with, then—"

"No, no . . . you seem quite competent. I . . . trust you."

"Thank you, Mamie. So you'll inform your mother of the good news? Or would you like me to call her?"

"I'll tell her."

"I will need a down payment, a show of good intention, and there are some papers Lillian needs to sign."

"Can't you do that for her?"

"Not really. Would you like me to messenger them over?"

"Yes, please. And I'll have them returned with a certified check."

"Great. There's some tedious things that are standard, like a home inspection, things for the state, but once the papers are signed and we have the down payment in escrow, then everything should proceed smoothly. After that, we'll be in contact as soon as I learn the date of settlement."

"Thank you, Cristine. I must write Patricia Rice a note and tell her how professional you are."

"Well, thank you, Mamie, and be sure to give Lillian and Maxine my congratulations. I just know they'll be happy there."

"Yes, yes . . . well, I must run. Send those papers."

"Good evening, Mamie. Thank you for choosing me."

"Good evening."

Cristine hung up the phone and stared once more at her desk. Slowly, she rose from the chair, as though in a dream. Only then did she realize she had called *the* Mrs. Pitcairn by her given name without permission. Mamie. Like she'd known her for years. And Mamie had surrendered her fight to lower the percentage points when she'd stopped her at the attempt. Just like that. Cristine felt like she was sleepwalking as she made her way to the door and deliberately opened it.

Only then did she allow herself to lose it.

*"Tina! Tina! We did it! We just played ball in the major leagues and hit a home run! Hell, a grand slam! Where are you, girl? It's time to celebrate!"*

Four hours later, Cristine walked into her kitchen, dropped her purse onto the beautiful new countertop, and was about to turn away when she stopped and stared at the big double stainless steel sink that had been installed with the polished nickel faucet.

She had gone out with Tina to celebrate the sale and suddenly felt the effects of three glasses of wine. How in the hell had Daniel Burns done it again?

It was like being in the middle of a fairy tale, like the shoemaker and the elves. She goes away and the work somehow magically gets done!

Reaching out to the faucet, she turned on the cold water and watched a steady stream come out of the tall metal. She pulled on the nozzle and a coiled steel hose was released for spraying.

"Amazing," she murmured, remembering how expensive the faucet had been when she and Charlie had bought it almost a year ago. She'd almost forgotten about it.

She sprayed the sink, then replaced it and looked underneath to the new garbage disposal unit. Everything had been put back in perfect order. No mess. Closing the cabinet door, she looked around the kitchen. It was almost finished. Just the stovetop needed to be installed.

Cristine looked around the room, trying to see if he'd left an estimate.

Nothing. Everything was neatly in place.

Daniel Burns was a dedicated craftsman, but he was going to cost her. She just knew she was going to pay dearly for him.

*Chapter*

# 9

SHE WALKED INTO TINA'S OFFICE AND SAT DOWN opposite her desk. "I'm going to take off early, okay? I need to catch that contractor before he leaves again."

Tina sat back in her chair. "Lady, you sold two houses this week and you have no appointments for the weekend. Take tomorrow off and make it a long one."

"Maybe I will. I just need to get together with this guy and get an estimate. I'm afraid he's going to cost me a small fortune."

"Before you go, take a look at this ad I'm putting together. I thought we should invest in ourselves and put us in *Philadelphia Magazine* with the rest of the big hitters. Not big, just tasteful." She turned her computer monitor around.

Leaning over Tina's desk, Cristine read, "'When you're ready to make one of the most important purchases of a lifetime, you want the perfect balance of design, value, and service . . . the right combination of style and quality, in the very best locations. A home that fits your comfort zone.'

"That's great, Tina." Cristine sat back. "What else?"

Looking pleased, Tina said, "Then I'll just add an invitation to visit us, very properlike, and make it look like our business card. It'll be cheaper that way, without the color."

"Terrific idea. Really. Who knew you could write ads?"

Tina laced her long fingers together. "You know what I think, Cristine? I think the universe just handed us a fabulous opportunity to expand into a new market. You and I both know this isn't going to last forever. Someday the bottom is going to fall out of the market, but before it does I say we take advantage of this opportunity and see what it brings. You've got to spend money to make money."

"You're the business end of this place, Tina. I trust you know what you're doing."

"And when the bottom does fall out, you and I can retire to the islands and see if that Simon fella has friends. Sort of a *How Stella Got Her Groove Back* kind of thing."

Cristine laughed. "*You* can retire there. I just want to pay off my house and figure out the next phase of my life. Speaking of which, I'm going to take off. I don't want that Burns fella to disappear again. I swear, he's like the elves that come in the night and then vanish."

"Go get your man. I'll call you tomorrow. We're fully staffed this weekend, so don't even think about this place."

"Thanks, Tina."

"No, the thanks go to you and whatever magic you performed to get that property for under two million *and* save your percentage points with Mamie Pitcairn. Seems like whatever happened to you down in the Bahamas brought good luck with it."

Shrugging, Cristine stood up and simply said, "It wasn't the Bahamas, but whatever it was, I hope it continues." She couldn't tell Tina since those lights had visited her, her luck had seemed to change . . . for the better. Anyway, who would believe her? As more time went by even she was starting to doubt what had really happened.

She got in her car and began the drive home while looking forward to a free weekend. Home. If anything gave her pleasure it was that she was back on track financially with the house. The remodeling was almost finished and soon she could clear the second mortgage. If Tina was right and they brought in a more upscale clientele, then she'd be able to knock the remaining five years on the first mortgage down to a year or two.

And then she would think about a family. She so wanted at least one child, to give it a home, a real home, and lavish it with love. There were so many options open to her. Normal parenthood if by some miracle the right man came into her life . . . but she wasn't counting on that. Single parenthood was just as acceptable. At her age most men were interested in younger woman, and did she really want to put up with someone's baggage again? Then there was in vitro fertilization or even adoption.

After Charlie left she had been so miserable she had pictured herself with cats, but now with everything back on track, she could let her mind return to her original dream of a family. She knew in a side corner of her mind that she was trying to fix her own childhood. Hell, with all the studying the gang had done over the years, she'd have to be totally ignorant not to get that one. But she didn't care. She couldn't change her past, but she damn sure could create her future. And that's what she thought about as she drove the rest of the way home, a bright sunny future.

"Shit!" The expletive shot out of her mouth when she pulled into her driveway and didn't see a truck. She'd missed him again! Her good mood and her feeling of everything falling into place vanished. This time he had better have left a business card. She'd written a note this morning and taped it right to the new faucet so he couldn't miss it. Now she was going to have to call him and negotiate over the phone.

Well, if she could successfully negotiate with Mamie Pitcairn than surely she could do the same with the mysterious Daniel Burns. She left the car in the driveway since she would be going out later to the grocery store. A rare weekend off meant she'd have the time to restock her kitchen, and maybe she'd invite the gang to dinner on Saturday to celebrate her good fortune.

She opened the front door, slipped off her heels, and walked back to the kitchen.

And that's when she saw the most remarkable thing.

*The lights! They were back! In the daytime!*

Those glorious dancing lights were hovering over her new stovetop.

Cristine's body became rigid with shock and she gasped in awe as it seemed the lights instantly encircled her. One moment they were across the room and in the next they were swirling around her, infusing her with such joy that her mouth opened but no sound could come out. Instead, she seemed to be enveloped by such intense pleasure that she felt the beginning of an orgasm building and building, and before she could control or contain it she sensed herself disintegrating again, breaking up into a million ecstatic pieces that seemed to shoot out into the universe . . .

It came as no surprise that whatever part of her remained knew she was fainting, dropping to the floor of her kitchen and into oblivion.

"Cristine! Open your eyes."

She heard the voice, but it sounded as if it were coming from the far end of a tunnel.

"Open your eyes!"

This time she didn't dare disobey. Something about the voice commanded her attention. It was the contractor, Daniel Burns, who was kneeling at her side. And she was lying on the kitchen floor! "What? What happened to me?"

"I believe you lost consciousness. Let me help you up."

He held out his hand to her and her own was shaking as she reached for it. "I . . . don't understand . . . how?" And then their hands touched and she felt a frizzle of electricity pass into her. "The lights!" she exclaimed, suddenly remembering. "Did you see them, Mr. Burns? Tell me you saw them!"

"Lights?"

"They were over there," she said, sitting up and pointing to the stove. "And then they came to me. You must have seen them. It couldn't have been long, just seconds ago . . . but I don't know how long I was . . . out."

"Let me help you up," he answered, wrapping his arm around her waist and assisting her to stand. He led her into the living room and gently placed her on the sofa. "Should I get you something cool to drink?"

She rested her shaky hands on her thighs, wondering if she were having a nervous breakdown. Surely Daniel Burns should have seen them. "Yes," she murmured. "Cold water would be wonderful, thank you."

He left her and she rolled over to lay her head against the pillows on the arm of the sofa. Dragging her feet up, she simply stared ahead while trying not to think of anything. It was best to keep her mind clear until she was alone. But they had come back! And fainting for the first time in her life certainly was some kind of proof something had happened.

"Here. Drink this." Daniel handed her a full glass of water.

"Thank you." She sipped and then held the bottom of the glass to her forehead. She had such a headache. Maybe she had hit her head and . . .

"Can I get anything else for you?"

She opened her eyes and looked at him. He appeared

really concerned and she was embarrassed for he had found her passed out on the floor. "No, nothing. You've been very kind. Did you just get here?"

He stared back at her with those deep blue eyes and blinked. "I beg your pardon?"

"You weren't here before, were you? I mean, I didn't see you in the kitchen."

"I was here."

"And you didn't see any lights?' she asked desperately, bringing the glass down from her forehead. "If you were here you had to have seen them."

"What did they look like?" His expression was kind, not condescending.

"They looked like . . . lights . . . fairy lights . . . dancing. And they were beautiful."

"Have you ever seen them before?"

"Look, I'm not crazy." She put the glass onto the coffee table. "I have seen them before. Once. This is the second time."

"I didn't mean to imply you were . . . unbalanced," he said, adding the last word with care. "I was simply interested in your opinion of them."

Sighing, she let her shoulders drop in defeat. "I'm sorry. I shouldn't have snapped at you. It's just I've never fainted before. You've been very nice and you're a terrific worker . . ." She lifted her shoulders. "Which brings me to the reason I came home early today. I really do need your estimate."

"My estimate?"

Why did he keep repeating everything she said? "Yes, didn't you read my note?"

"Yes. I'm afraid I didn't understand it." Again, his expression showed kindness.

Cristine was beginning to feel like one of them was an idiot, and she wasn't sure which of them it was. "I asked that you give me an estimate on the work you've been doing in the kitchen. I really do need to know how much money it's going to cost."

"Oh, money." Mr. Burns seemed to finally get her point and grinned.

A very nice grin, Cristine noted, even though she was dreading the amount he was going to quote.

"I don't need money."

She blinked. "I'm sorry? You don't need money?"

He shook his head. "No."

"But how am I supposed to pay you?" Okay, she now knew she wasn't the idiot. Something must be wrong with him. Maybe he was a mechanical savant, or—

"I didn't ask for payment," he said, still staring at her with those magnetic eyes.

"But you said . . . you said you would do the work. Didn't Glen Kennedy send you?"

"No, no one sent me, Cristine with no *h*. I came because you called out to me."

Okay, so the guy was good-looking, maybe even great-looking, and he was a near genius as a handyman in the kitchen, but he was now starting to scare her.

"You asked me if I could do the work in your kitchen. I said yes. And I've been doing it. I never asked for payment from you."

"But I thought . . . I mean, you came here when I was expecting a contractor from Glen Kennedy's crew and—"

"And I told him the job was taken when he came after you left. You were in such a rush I wasn't able to talk to you then." He sat down at the other end of the sofa. "It's good we can talk now."

She pulled her legs away from him and sat up herself. Her headache was becoming even more intense with this nonsense. "I don't understand, Mr. Burns. You say no one sent you and yet you've put together my kitchen and—"

"You still have pain in your head, don't you?"

She stared at him. What was he, a mind reader too? "I'll get something in a minute, but first we really need to settle just what the hell is going on here."

"Shh," he murmured. "Your thoughts are chaotic. You need to rest your mind and allow your neuropeptides to flow."

"My *what*?" Okay, enough was enough. She didn't care how good a craftsman he was, this was getting ridiculous. Attempting to rise, Cristine was shocked to see his hand come out and clasp the top of her head.

"Just relax, Cristine," he said calmly. "There's nothing to fear."

She sat back down automatically, as though he somehow controlled her muscles, and within moments, she felt a pleasant sensation begin at the crown of her head. She rested her head back against the sofa and just concentrated on what she was feeling. It was like warm honey that seemed to flow down from her crown to her temples, relaxing her mind, her jaw, her shoulders . . . all the way to her feet.

"Now, please listen to me," he said.

His voice sounded so calming that she didn't even consider interrupting. Besides, her headache had disappeared. And, truth be told, she was afraid to move her muscles in case he'd paralyzed her or something. What kind of magic hands did this guy have? Because she was so relaxed that she felt her eyes closing.

"I have not come here to harm you. Quite the opposite. Don't be afraid of what you don't understand yet. Just relax and allow your body to heal."

She waited for more words, but nothing came. After a few moments she forced her eyelids up and was stunned to find herself alone. She looked around the living room.

"Mr. Burns?" she called out softly.

Silence.

Where could he have gone so quickly and silently?

Maybe he was back in the kitchen. "Mr. Burns? Are you still here?"

When she didn't get an answer, she slowly rose from the sofa and walked back into the kitchen. It was deserted, but her new stovetop was in place and her note was attached.

Below the words she had written to him was a very precise script.

## I'll be back

Good God, who *was* that man? The good terminator?

It would be too easy to dismiss the whole thing as a figment of her imagination. There was no great-looking man who picked her off the floor and healed her headache and made her relax and then disappeared . . . oh, yeah, and who didn't want any money for all the work he had done for her!

Something had happened, and she was, for the first time of her life, seriously questioning her sanity.

Since Charlie had left her nothing had been the same. There was no normal. But then that was saying Charlie was normal, and he most certainly wasn't, unless normal is a neurotic liar who plots behind your back to abandon you. Okay, so Charlie wasn't normal, but her life had seemed like it was. Now nothing made sense. She went to the Bahamas, threw out her back in the midst of sex, saw lights in her bedroom that gave her the most outrageous orgasm—which also healed her back—and then she cut her hair, took out a second mortgage, became manic in creating a new life for herself, and finally sold two houses in a week, one of them to Mamie Pitcairn's mother, who happens to be a lesbian.

No wonder she was rattled and questioning reality. She had wanted those lights to come back so much that she'd rushed home and, upon seeing her kitchen completed, she'd simply fainted and then made up the rest about Mr. Burns. She hadn't eaten lunch, and a blueberry muffin and coffee were obviously not enough to sustain a quick drop in her sugar level. There. That was a reasonable explanation. She wasn't having a nervous breakdown. She wouldn't allow it. She didn't have time for it.

*Just don't think about it anymore,* she told herself as she opened the refrigerator and took out a plastic container with mandarin chicken inside. Using her fingers, she greedily ate two pieces. She needed to get changed and go grocery shopping for good food, healthy food. It was obviously time to take care of herself.

Imagine . . . fainting. How totally bizarre!

But she still wondered how she had wound up on the sofa.

*Don't think about it,* she mentally commanded.

There was no reasonable explanation for any of it.

She woke up Friday morning with a surge of energy and determination. After shopping last night, her kitchen was fully stocked again and today she was going to tackle the rest of it. For almost a year, she had been storing things in the garage, like her good Cuisinart coffeemaker, her espresso machine, her good china and flatware. It was finally time to dust them off and put them back in place.

For breakfast she had two soft-boiled eggs on twelve-grain toast, juice, and, for the last time, instant coffee. Then she began to unwrap her treasures. With each object, she felt a surge of pleasure as she put it into its proper place. Something wonderful had been accomplished. Her house was done. Finally finished. Now all she had to do was stay aggressive at work and soon it would be paid off. Then the next phase could begin.

When the doorbell rang, she was grateful for the interruption. Hopefully, it was Daniel Burns, coming to be paid. And thinking of the remarkable man, she ran her fingers through her short hair before she opened the door.

"Hello, Cristine."

Her heart dropped, actually sank. "Charlie. What are you doing here?"

"I like your hair."

He looked thinner, with dark circles under his eyes, but she steeled herself against falling back into the role of caretaker. He was someone else's problem now. Not hers. "You didn't answer me. Why are you here?"

His smile was weak. "I can't stop by to say hello?"

"Hello. Is there anything else?"

"I thought, maybe, we could talk for a few minutes."

Sighing, she said, "I can't imagine what we would have to talk about."

"I called your office, but Tina said you were off today. I thought she might be putting me off, but figured I'd take a chance you'd be here."

"As you can see, I am."

"Can I come in for a cup of coffee?"

And then she pictured the kitchen. Okay, so it wasn't exactly graciousness when she opened the door wider and waved her hand back into the house. She was allowed a little gloating.

She was behind him when he stopped at the kitchen entrance.

"Wow."

Thank heavens she had gotten up early and the kitchen was almost finished. Even fresh-brewed coffee was still warm on the Cuisinart. She walked over to it and opened the cabinet above for a mug. He didn't deserve her good china. She poured him a cup as he came fully into the room and ran his hand over the shiny countertop.

"How did you get it done so fast?"

She could hear the amazement in his voice. "I met a wonderful man," she answered, and left it at that as she put a small white serviette on the counter and placed his mug on top. "Your coffee."

He picked up the mug and held it at his chest as he continued to look around the kitchen he, himself, couldn't finish. "It looks great, Cristine."

Gazing around the kitchen, she nodded. "Daniel . . . he's quite a man."

"Are you . . . seeing him?"

"Seeing him? I don't believe that's any of your business, Charlie. How are you and the little woman doing?"

"Fine. It's just that . . . well, she isn't you, Cristine."

She couldn't help it. She threw back her head and laughed. Hard. "Ahh . . . wasn't that the point, Charlie, when you made your decision to go exploring?"

"I know, I know." His expression looked tortured. "It's just that she's . . . sometimes coarse and—"

The doorbell rang.

"Hold that thought," she said, rushing to the front of her house. This was just too good. Charlie standing in her finished kitchen saying the woman he left her for was coarse. What could be better?

She had her answer when she opened her front door.

"Daniel! I'm so glad you're here. Come in, come in," she nearly ordered, taking his shirt sleeve and pulling him into her house. "The kitchen is fabulous. I'm spending the morning putting it back together. Would you like a cup of coffee?"

"No, thank you," he answered, walking into the kitchen and seeing Charlie standing there.

"Let me make the introductions. Daniel, this is Charlie. Charlie, this is the remarkable Daniel who finished my kitchen in record time." There had to be a god somewhere to have arranged all this so perfectly.

"How do you do?" Daniel asked, almost formally, as he held out his hand.

Charlie appeared disappointed, maybe even annoyed, as he shook Daniel's hand and said a bland, "Hi."

"Well, now, you were saying, Charlie? Something about being coarse?"

He definitely looked annoyed now and Cristine had to bite the inside of her lower lip not to smile.

"I'll come back another time," he announced, putting his untouched coffee back on the tiny napkin.

"Oh, all right. You know your way out," she said to his back. "I have to discuss something with Daniel."

"Good-bye, Cristine."

"Good-bye Charlie," she answered, almost too gaily, and turned to Daniel, who was staring at her. "Listen, I'm real sorry about that. That was my ex, and I'm afraid I didn't come right out and say you were only my kitchen contractor."

"Did you enjoy that? Seeing him suffer?"

Cristine felt as though someone had just thrown cold water into her face, taking away her high of retribution. "I'm sorry?"

"Why did you want him to suffer?"

She felt the muscles in her shoulders stiffen. "Not that it's any of your business, but he happens to have made me suffer far more than that little discussion."

"And so that gives you the right to even the score?"

"Like I said, I don't think this is any of your business. Now I hope you've come this morning to give me an estimate. I'll write you a check and then you won't have to judge me or my behavior any longer." Sheesh, who did he think he was?

"I wasn't judging you. I was asking you a question. And we've already discussed this estimate you keep talking and writing about. I don't want your money."

Oh, no . . . it was back. *He* was back. That horrible instability was slamming into her brain with the force of a Vulcan mind meld.

*"Who the hell are you?"*

# 10

DANIEL BURNS WAS NOT AN ORDINARY MAN. IN fact, he wouldn't be termed a human at all. He was an advanced form of energy and information that had picked up on Cristine's sincerity and her yearning for intimacy. Attracted by her genuineness, he was drawn into her presence the night she had returned home in pain. Once he had mingled his energy with hers, he knew he had found what he had been searching for. After he attained maturity through study and practical usage, it was now his mission to serve. Complicated, fear-driven, intelligent, compassionate, and beautiful, Cristine Dobbins was the perfect assignment.

"I asked, who the hell are you?" She was holding on to the edge of the granite as though it were supporting her.

"It's a complicated answer. Perhaps you might wish to sit down."

"Tell me. What do you know about those lights? You saw them, didn't you?"

He paused and smiled with tenderness. "I am them, Cristine."

She stared at him, her eyes open wide in fear. "What?"

"I know you heard me correctly. Please, let us go into the next room where you can sit."

"I don't want to sit. I want answers. What do you mean, *you* are those lights?"

He sensed her intense fear and wanted to calm her. She would never hear what he had to say if she remained in such chaos. "I will answer all your questions if we both can sit down and discuss them rationally."

*"Rationally?"* She laughed with great nervousness as she moved a step back from him. "Nothing you are saying is rational! How can *you* be those lights?"

He didn't want to exert his will over hers, but she simply wasn't listening. He took her wrist before she created more distance between them. Concentrating his energy and allowing it to flow down his arm and into hers, he felt her muscles loosening, her heartbeat slowing as her blood began to flow more easily. "Now, please come with me. I promise I will answer whatever you ask."

He led her into the larger room where they had sat previously. She sat down on the sofa and he sat in a chair a few feet away. "You may begin to ask your questions."

She stared at him with fear still in her eyes. "Who are you?"

"At the present moment I am using this body suit and calling myself Daniel Burns to make contact with you in a tangible way you can understand. Who I am in reality is more complex. I am an advanced form of energy and information that you have been calling your dancing lights." He paused and smiled. "I very much like that phrase."

She was shaking her head in denial. "I don't know what you're talking about. What you're saying can't be true or . . . or real. How can that be?"

"How can it not be, Cristine? You have seen me in this body suit several times and also in my true form. Your science today has something they call string theory. Contained within the physics of string theory is the belief of parallel universes, eleven dimensions or elegant universes composed of energy strings, a grand cosmic symphony, if you will, vibrating at the heart of reality. Sometimes you, yourself, experience this as déjà vu, the sensation of being in two dimensions. Now if your science is considering parallel universes, is it such a far leap in thought to imagine one of these universes, far more advanced than your own, has always been watching out for humanity and making rare appearances that sometimes have been recorded as angelic?"

"I don't understand half of what you just said, but are you actually telling me you're an . . . an *angel*?"

He could hear her near-hysterical disbelief. He wanted to calm her again, but thought perhaps it would be best if she got all her fears out now so they could begin work that much sooner. "I never said I am an angel. Remember, that word is simply a label, though others like me who have come into the lives of humans have been termed angelic. You may think of me as simply Daniel."

"Well, simply Daniel, I think you might just be nuts and in need of a clinical expert in . . . in crazy people who claim to be from another planet!"

"I am not from another planet. I am from another dimension. There is a difference, and I am not crazy, as you put it. I am here because of you, Cristine."

"Because *I'm* crazy? This is all a delusion, right?"

"You're not crazy. You're simply filled with fear and it's altering your state of mind to understand the importance of this discussion."

"Why me, then? Huh? Out of all the people in the world, why crash-land into my life? Tell me that."

"With pleasure . . . Because that night you put your desire out into the universe I picked up on it. Because beyond all your fears and doubts and contradictions, you have the most beautiful soul. And I resonated with it. Spectacular. Wondrous. Those are the words you might use. For me, it was the beauty of unity. You and I became one, Cristine. And you invited me back, many times. You can no more stop this than stop the earth from revolving around your sun. You, my frightened one, put all this into motion."

He stood up and smiled down into the stunned expression on her face. "And now you must excuse me. Later I will inform you of the difficulty in maintaining this body suit. We will meet again. Soon. Keep this knowledge to yourself, for your own protection."

And with those words, he released the particles and swirled into his natural form.

§

She sat, her mouth open, limbs frozen in fear, as she watched a man disappear into tiny lights and evaporate right out of her living room.

She was having a nervous breakdown. It didn't matter that she wouldn't allow it or didn't have time for one. It was happening anyway, right now, in her living room!

Cristine had no idea how long she sat on the sofa, staring out, yet not focusing on anything. It simply couldn't have happened. Daniel Burns *did not* just tell her he was her dancing lights! She had not called him to her and then . . . became one with him because . . . because if she did, then she had been falling in love with . . . something out of this world! Something that wasn't even real! Something bizarre!

She would not have it!

She couldn't!

She had a plan to follow. And it didn't include some . . . some dimension traveler who had given her the very best orgasm of her life!

*Get up!* she commanded herself. Just get up and get back into the kitchen.

None of it had happened. It simply couldn't have.

She stood up and mentally shook off the feeling of losing her mind. She would not allow this to happen. Walking back into her kitchen, she was still talking herself out of the delusion when her eyes spotted Charlie's untouched coffee mug on the counter.

Charlie had been here!

He'd seen Daniel Burns!

Her heart began racing and she felt panic-stricken. Charlie had seen him, right? So what did that mean? She was either having a nervous breakdown or Daniel Burns was real. She so wanted to find Charlie and ask him if he'd seen Daniel, but that would mean tracking him down, and her pride wouldn't allow her to need Charlie for anything, ever again.

No, she had to figure this out alone.

She looked about her kitchen. *That's* how he had done everything so quickly!

Daniel Burns had some kind of advanced, space-age magic. He was like Samantha on *Bewitched*. He could just wrinkle his nose or . . . or whatever, and *ta dah*! The granite was cut and her countertop completed. The same with the sink and the stovetop. Hadn't she walked in and caught him in the act over her stove?

But that meant he was real!

No, no . . . he couldn't be real, because if he was then her world and everything she knew about reality was turned upside down.

An angel! Hah, and where were his wings?

But he didn't claim to be an angel. He said others like him had been termed angelic. What were angels? Messengers, right? What the hell kind of message did Daniel Burns think he was delivering to *her*?

"I don't want this!" she yelled to the ceiling of her kitchen. "Do you hear me, Daniel Burns? Whatever you think you have to do, forget it. I . . . I release you! Go away!"

Silence.

Okay, maybe he heard that, and maybe he didn't. But it wouldn't do for her to go around shouting into empty space. If anyone overheard her, she'd be carted away. No, she had to be firm in her resolve. She didn't care how great their *unity* had been. It wasn't worth her sanity or messing up her plan, especially now that she was back on track.

Cristine picked up the phone.

She'd call the gang together. That's what she should do.

"Love the kitchen, Cristine, and congratulations. Tina told me about your great week at work."

"Thanks, Claire," Cristine answered, checking the salmon in the oven. "I hope this plum sauce doesn't burn."

"You really have gone all out. Good china, silverware." She held up her wine glass. "Crystal. And dinner smells fabulous. It's a shame Paula's missing it."

"Paula couldn't get a sitter, and it was last-minute. Besides, weekends never were good for her. She's got a husband."

"Right."

"She calls it her bonding time with Hank."

"Or more likely, her babysitting time with Hank."

Cristine grinned. "You are cynical, Claire," she remarked while placing fresh baby spinach in the center of the five plates on her new counter.

"I'm not cynical. I'm a realist. Paula is so Mother Earth that she spends her weekend nurturing Hank, just like the rest of her brood. She should get some sexy nightgowns and take him away for the weekend so someone can nurture her for a change."

"Maybe nurturing is the reason she's still the married one in the group. Besides," Cristine added with a chuckle, "knowing Paula, she'd come back pregnant."

"Oh, God, you're right," Claire answered with a laugh. "So tell me, why are you acting so nervous?"

"Nervous?" Cristine was trying her best to play the perfect hostess. She didn't want to get into anything until they were seated in the dining room.

"Look, I know you too well. Something's up. Now out with it."

Cristine's brain scrambled. She simply couldn't blurt out the real reason. Even though Claire loved her, she would be the first to cart her off to a shrink. "Charlie showed up yesterday." That was a good save, she thought, and congratulated herself for coming up with it so quickly.

Claire put her wine glass on the counter. "Do not tell me you are even considering taking that loser back."

Shaking her head, Cristine said, "No, no. Not at all. He said the woman he's with is coarse, whatever that means."

"It was poor-me victim Charlie making a pitch for you to save him, that's what that means. Coarse, huh? Well, it looks like he's met his equal."

"He was amazed how the kitchen was finished in record time. I have to admit to a certain degree of gloating when he saw it."

"So there was no . . . spark of anything?"

She shook her head. "None. Kind of surprising. I mean, after seven years."

"Thank heavens!" Claire said, picking up her wine again. "Everyone is so glad he's out of your life. It's like you've . . . blossomed, I guess."

Cristine checked the salmon. It was done. Taking out the long glass dish, she set it on the stovetop and picked up the large pot of tarragon rice. "Well, no need to worry. He's not coming back," she said, spooning out the rice over the spinach on each of the plates.

"Oh, he'd come back, I think, if you'd even consider it. He's had time to see what a mess he's made of his life, and it looks like he was testing the water."

"Well, I think he found it to be extremely cold," Cristine answered, putting the pot back onto the stove and bringing over the salmon. That was what was so wonderful about granite. No need for a trivet. *Don't think about the counter and how it got there now,* she thought, and forced herself to concentrate on the task before her. She portioned the salmon into five filets and carefully placed each on top of the rice, then took the plum sauce and drizzled it over the entire entrée.

"Wow, will you look at you," Claire said in amazement. "The green of the spinach, the white rice, and the pink salmon with that sauce over it looks like you've turned into a five-star chef. See, that's what I mean about you blossoming."

Cristine picked up a plate and handed it to Claire with a smile. "Let's wait to see how it tastes. Would you help me take these into the dining room and call the others? Tell them dinner is ready."

Claire did her bidding and Cristine picked up two more plates. She walked into the dining room to find her friends gathering around the table and complimenting her on everything. "Let me get the last two plates and

then we can eat," she said, rushing back to the kitchen.
Picking up the plates, she took a deep breath. Okay, now
to somehow pick the brains of her friends. Surely, between five fairly intelligent women, they could come up
with a reasonable explanation for the unexplainable.

Seated at the head of the table, Cristine smiled with
satisfaction as she watched her dear friends enjoy her efforts. Isabel was on her left, with Tina seated next to her,
and Claire was on her right, with Kelly next to her. She
felt surrounded by love, good humor, and intelligence.
She grinned when Tina told the others the Mamie Pitcairn story and described Lillian and Maxine. She hadn't
told anyone, not even Tina, about their real relationship
as it would feel like a betrayal of something special she
had witnessed. Besides, it really wasn't anyone's business
how one loved for thirty-two years. What was important
was that love survived for such a long time.

They were nearly finished when Cristine said, "Does
anyone know anything about string theory?"

That brought all conversation to an end. In the silence
that ensued, she added, "I was just wondering."

"That's physics," Tina said. "Beyond my scope."

"Does anyone know anything about it?"

"Not me," Kelly admitted. "I'm still trying to get my
head around E equals mc squared."

Isabel sat back and looked at her plate in concentration. "What I can remember is that it's about strings of
energy that can't be predicted. It seems crazy. Particles
can pass through solid objects, like doors. And then they
won't. It's like the world is a game of chance. You can't
know the outcome. Uncertainty rules."

Well, that sounded like her life, Cristine thought. "So
not much is really known by science about it?"

Isabel shrugged. "You have to remember that all results
in science are influenced by the observer, the person doing
the experiment. That's the big news. You can't separate the

experiment and the observer. Kelly, if you're still having trouble with Einstein's theory of relativity, I've just about given up on his theory of everything."

"What's that?" Tina asked.

"Einstein sought a single theory to explain everything, the unification of all theories. First there was Newton's apple, force pulling the apple to the ground, and we've got the law of gravity. Then in the nineteen hundreds we get the theory of general relativity. The velocity of light is a kind of cosmic speed limit. Nothing can go faster than the speed of light. Like it takes eight minutes for the sun's rays to hit the earth and gravity doesn't exceed the speed of light. It was unifying gravity and the speed of light. Then we come to electromagnetism. Electricity and magnets produce dots and dashes and we have the telegraph, and why the tops of mountains during lightning can turn a compass around, because electromagnetism is stronger than gravity. Einstein was trying to unify gravity and electromagnetism and come up with a theory to understand and encompass all the laws of the universe. The theory of everything."

"And did he?" Claire asked, now as interested as the rest of them.

"No. He died before he could."

"But what about dimensions, parallel universes? Did he say anything about those?"

Everyone turned their attention to her and she could see the bewilderment in their expressions. "I just want to know," Cristine added.

"What's up, Cristine?" Kelly asked. "You've been . . . I don't know . . . your energy is a little frazzled."

"Yeah, I picked up on that too," Tina said, looking closely at her hostess. "What's going on?"

"Nothing," Cristine lied. "I was just interested in what Isabel was telling us. You know, we've studied so many philosophies and religions and even the tarot, but not really science. And I was thinking that might be the next subject we could tackle."

"Oh, let's do the tarot tonight," Kelly said with enthusiasm. "I want to see how long it's going to take this new guy to land into the loser category."

Cristine's shoulders sank. Nobody was going to explain string theory, because it sounded unexplainable even to scientists. It was only a radical theory. "What about angels?" she blurted out.

"What about them?" Tina asked.

Feeling like she was an exhibit at her own dinner party, Cristine tried to smile into the inquiring faces. "I don't know. I was just thinking about them. You know, how they show up in all religions."

"Messengers," Claire, said, picking up her wine glass. "Angels are supposed to be messengers. Bringers of good news."

"What about Lot then? Sodom and Gomorrah? How good was that news?" Tina asked.

"Well, it was good news for Lot. He got out."

"Tell that to Lot's wife," Tina countered, and Kelly laughed.

"The point I'm trying to make," Claire said, "is that the angel warned Lot ahead of time to clear out. Now me, I'd take that as good news."

"Okay, okay," Cristine intervened. "So they're messengers. We've got that. But we've always had images of angels with wings. Do we know that for a fact? That they have to have wings?"

Isabel chuckled. "Fact? None of this is fact. It's mythology that's appeared in all the ancient writings to explain things before science tried it. All the stories passed down to us are like religion's theory of everything, how the universe came to be and how it works. Which one do you want to believe? Strings of light that can't be explained, or angels with wings? Besides, if angels are actually real, I think the observer gave them wings to explain defying the laws of gravity."

"Right, and for their own sanity," Claire added. "Can you imagine an ordinary human being approached by something cosmic? You'd have to think you were losing your mind. So you try and explain it by saying it moved with wings." Claire looked at Tina. "And Lot's wife got the good news too, but she didn't believe it and looked back and that's when she turned into a pillar of salt."

Tina shook her head. "I still say destroying a place isn't good news."

Cristine was staring at her near-empty plate. What Daniel had told her was sort of making sense. What if others from his dimension had come to this time to bring messages and the person, the observer, couldn't explain them and their astonishing abilities? "And if they were surrounded by light, the observer would give them a halo and think they were holy or something."

She didn't realize her whispered comment was heard by the rest of them until she felt their gaze, hard and penetrating.

It was Isabel who spoke. "Cristine, what exactly is going on? Why this interest in string theory and angels?"

She laughed. Okay, nervously, but she did laugh. "Nothing, really. Just mental mastication, as we used to call it. It's simply something that got into my head yesterday and I wanted some feedback." She pasted a bright smile on her face. "Now what about dessert? Followed by the tarot? Isabel, you were always the best reader. Will you give Kelly a reading?"

"I'd rather give one to you," Isabel answered, looking directly at her.

Cristine averted her eyes. If anyone could see through her, it would be Issy, and she wasn't ready to share what was happening in her life yet. She still needed to figure it out for herself. "Who's going to help me clear?" she asked, picking up her plate.

"We all will," Kelly said. "That way we get to the tarot sooner."

Okay, so maybe she needed to have Daniel Burns come back one more time, to really explain himself and what he was doing in her life.

But that was it.

Just one more time.

Just so she knew she wasn't losing her mind.

"CALLING DANIEL BURNS . . . EARTH TO DANIEL." She shook her head in dismay, and then laughed as she looked up to the ceiling of her living room. "Come in, please!"

Okay, she felt stupid doing it, but how the hell else was she supposed to contact him? It was Sunday and she had one day to figure this thing out and then send him out of her life for good. But she wanted answers first.

And then she'd tell the gang when it was over. That way, whether they believed her or not, she wouldn't still *be* in the delusion. She'd have dealt with it and moved beyond it.

"C'mon, Daniel . . . show yourself." She closed her eyes and concentrated, picturing him with his lean frame, his sandy hair, his wonderful blue eyes, his sexy smile and—She shook the image out of her head. Really, how come he had to be good-looking? Couldn't she have been visited by someone who was old and balding and . . . looked like Yoda from *Star Wars?* She opened her eyes, and jumped with fright.

He was seated across from her!

"You scared me!" she exclaimed, catching her breath. "You can't just keep coming into and out of a person's life like this!"

"But you invited me, Cristine."

Her heartbeat slowed a little and she took a deep, steadying breath. "I know, but you could have waited until I opened my eyes."

"Hello," he said with a smile, as though this were an ordinary visit. "Are you better now that you've had time to think about all of this?"

"Look, it doesn't matter how much time I take to think about it. This is *crazy*. I don't know why you picked me for this, but I think you've got the wrong person."

He was still smiling. "And why is that?"

"Because I'm ordinary. Very ordinary. I don't have plans to form a new religion or save the world—no great life mission."

"What is your life mission?"

She stared at him. "I don't know . . . to just get through it."

"Now that would be a waste, especially for you."

"Why especially me?"

"Because you are meant for greater things."

She felt her heartbeat speeding up again. "I'm not. Really. I'm not. You've got the wrong person."

"That's impossible."

"You don't make mistakes? That's sort of arrogant, isn't it?" Good heavens, she was having a conversation with someone who just popped into her life, like he was some guy off the street!

"It's impossible because I've already attained unity with you, Cristine. I would not have entered your life had I not read your soul."

"I really don't want you in my life. Don't take it personally," she added, trying to make her point. "I just don't want anything crazy like this, no matter who it comes from."

"I wish you would stop thinking of this as being crazy. To me, your term *crazy* implies irrational thinking. And the only irrational thinking is the arrogance to believe you know everything and have nothing to learn."

"So you're a . . . a teacher?"

"If you like that term."

"It feels better than an angel. See, that stuff scares me," she admitted. "Angels and religion. A teacher I can at least deal with." She nodded and stared down at her hands, clasped together tightly in her lap. Just like when she was in school. She released her hands and nervously ran them down the front of her jeans to her knees. "So what is it you have to teach me?" She couldn't believe she was doing this! But how else to get him to leave her alone? Maybe if he told her his news, he'd leave her be.

"First of all, you have nothing to be afraid of, Cristine. You are not losing your mind or having a nervous breakdown. This isn't only happening to you. Your dimension, this dimension, is preparing to evolve. Surely, you have felt it, the quickening of time, the heaviness of the energy around your world. It is like labor pains, and this is the beginning of the transition part, the hardest part before something new is born."

She lifted her head. "What do you expect me to do? I'm just an ordinary person."

"Midwife it in. Help. That's what I am here to do."

"I don't understand."

"I know you don't. And you are not alone. Humanity seems to be caught in a net. You are only using a small portion of your brain and that is what's making this transition so hard. You have to rewire your brain, Cristine."

"Rewire?" That sounded frightening. "I like my brain."

"You would like it even better if you used more of it. Look, I told you I come from a different dimension, or level of consciousness. Using earth's magnetics, humans in this dimension vibrate at eight hertz, but what would you say if I told you that sitting in your midst another may be vibrating at a hundred hertz? In the same room, occupying the same space, save their time is faster than this time? And the reason you can't see them is because they are vibrating at a much higher frequency than you? In order for you to see them, they have to slow down their vibration, to shrink their expanded energy into a much smaller form. And it is not easy to maintain for a great length of time."

"That's you?" The words were whispered in awe, in disbelief and in fear, all mixed together.

"That's me," he answered simply.

"Then the real you is the lights?"

"That's closer to the real me. The field that exists between us you aren't open to see. It is momentum, moving as a wave of energy. When you let all so-called rational thought go, when you clear your mind as you did that first night in your bedroom, you begin to see lights, which actually is that energy wave collapsing into a particle with an orbital light—your science has called it an electron. You aren't afraid of the lights; you welcomed them. But when I use this body suit to communicate with you, you are filled with fear. Why is that? I thought this would be more comforting for you."

She was shaking her head. "The lights . . ." she began, trying not to show her embarrassment, "they were magical, glorious. I felt . . . I don't know . . ."

"At one with everything, all creation?" He was smiling.

She only nodded, unable to describe the feeling of breaking apart, disintegrating into nameless, timeless ecstasy.

"That, Cristine, is your natural state too. That is what you are evolving toward. All of humanity is, but the birthing process seems to take an eternity and you have made it so painful."

She lifted her head, near tears. "It *is* painful! Life is about suffering. Just when you think everything is falling into place, and you get comfortable, it explodes all around you."

"Rejoice then. For you are dismantling your own creation and beginning the process of creating something new. Energy cannot be destroyed. That much your science has gotten right. The energy that held those forms in place is still there, to be used for something new. What happens when you get comfortable?"

"I'm happy, that's what."

"You stop being creative. You want to hold life still, but life, all life, everywhere in the universe, is about creativity, and all creativity is about expansion. When you stop being creative, when you become static, you might as well give up your body suit and then try it all over again."

"Why do you call this a body suit? It's not a suit. I can't take it off."

"Of course you can, and you do. Over and over again. When you sleep, when you dream, when you die. But the you who is eternal, the one you became conscious of when you were an infant, is always there. It always has been, and it always will be. You, Cristine, cannot die. The concept of death is what has caught humanity in that net. Death is what holds religions and governments together, why humanity gave up the power to evolve. Why you are stuck in this dimension. Do you know that the mind is more powerful than any machine science will ever invent? Rewire and access more of your brain and your mind will evolve."

"My mind?" She almost laughed. "Right now my mind is blown away! I have this man, who's not really a man but some form of energy, sitting across from me, and he claims to be from another dimension. And he wants to teach me how to evolve so I can vibrate at a faster speed and then create something to help humanity. Oh, and I shouldn't be afraid of death because that's what's holding me back, in the thrall of religions and governments. Have I got it right?"

"Exactly! There is much more, but that is an excellent

beginning." He looked so pleased, she wanted to laugh even more.

"You know what, Daniel? We're both crazy!"

His pleased expression disappeared. "Why are you fighting this? Does it not make more sense to accept what I am telling you than to live the rest of this lifetime in denial?"

"Now there's a good word. Denial. It helps me retain my sanity."

"Perhaps you've had enough information for today and I should leave."

"No, wait. Really. I want to hear more."

"Why, if you don't believe it?"

"It's a good story, and I have nothing better to do with my Sunday afternoon."

"You've missed everything, Cristine, if you have not understood the importance of belief."

"But see, Daniel, belief would begin in the mind, and that's mine. My choice is to allow you to mess with it, or not."

"How can you think what I am telling you is messing up your mind? I am trying to assist you in opening your mind. I'm attempting to help you see your possibilities."

"I know what my possibilities are. I have a plan, and *that's* what you're messing with." He had no idea how important her plan was, and had been since she was a young girl. It was bad enough when Charlie screwed it up, but now some entity from another dimension wanted to mess with her life?

"Your concept of your possibilities is a limiting one. There is an infinite sea of possibilities that surrounds you, and yet you are unaware of them. Instead, you are so conditioned to the way you create your daily life that you allow into your consciousness the belief you have no control over it. That circumstances beyond your control shape the direction of your life. That is false thinking, Cristine." He paused and looked at her with compassion.

"Just as punishing Charlie and making him suffer is false thinking."

Her jaw dropped. How dare he bring up Charlie? "You know nothing about it."

"I don't have to. Making someone into the villain and you into the martyr is always false thinking. And it sets up a vicious circle of cause and effect that only makes life harder."

"You have no idea how much suffering he caused me."

"I don't have to. You, Cristine, somewhere in your consciousness, were ready to dismantle your own creation, or it wouldn't have happened. But you did nothing. You chose to remain static. You had gained everything you could from the relationship and gave what you could to it. It no longer served you, but you weren't ready to see that yet. Would you blame someone who pulled you back from an oncoming vehicle? Your arm might be bruised because of the physiology of your body suit, but you were saved from a potentially fatal circumstance. If you had stayed with Charlie, he would have drained your life energy, and you knew that, even if it hurt to admit you had allowed it."

"How do you know this? Were you spying on me before that night in my bedroom?" God, what else had he seen!

"I can read it in your energy. You have made too many decisions using only your heart. I would like to teach you to also use your head, more precisely your brain, which produces thought. Combine that with the energy of consciousness and you have your mind."

She thought for a moment. He was right. She had mainly used her heart when making decisions, and look where it had brought her. Alone, with a second mortgage and talking to a space man, or whatever he was. "So you're going to teach me to use my mind, and that's the good news you're bringing me?"

"Yes! Now you're getting it!" His eyes seemed to dance with pleasure.

She couldn't help grinning. Maybe she could learn something from him, but there had to be rules. "Okay, listen, Daniel. *If* I will allow this, it has to be on my terms."

He sat patiently, waiting.

"First, there will be no mind reading or barging into my life. No invasion of privacy."

"I can't help but read your energy. It's a part of you, like the color of your eyes."

She closed her eyes in exasperation. "Try to keep it to yourself then. I don't want to know you know everything about me."

"I only know your past that you keep carrying around with you. I don't know your future because you haven't created it yet."

"Well, forget my past and—"

"I wish you could do that," he interrupted. "It would help immensely."

"Do what? Forget my past?"

"Yes."

"It's who I am, what made me who I am."

"Do you really believe that?"

"Of course. Every decision I've made in my past has brought me to this present moment." She'd learned that much in all her studying with the gang.

"But it isn't who you are, Cristine. That is so limiting. You've been conditioned to believe that the external world is more real than the internal one. What if it's just the opposite? What if what's happening within you will create what's happening outside you? What if your firm belief that you are the past is why you keep re-creating the same reality over and over again? The same relationships? The same jobs? What if you knew, beyond any doubt, that you are extraordinary, and you could create a life that is extraordinary? Would you then be willing to let go of your past?"

"See, that's what you can't get, Daniel. I am not extraordinary. I am very ordinary. Like six billion others out there, just trying to get through it all, day by day."

"Someone has to evolve, Cristine. If one can do it, all can. And many already have."

"And so we come back to my original question. Why me?"

His expression softened, as his eyes peered into her own. "Because I attained unity with you. We are one now, you and I. I know you, the real you that you call your soul. And I will help you in this any way I can, for when you evolve, so will I."

To cover her embarrassment when he used the word *unity,* which to her meant orgasm, she grinned. "Ah, now we're getting somewhere. There's something in it for you."

"Of course," he answered matter-of-factly. "I give and in return I receive. It is the way of the universe. Always has been."

"So where will you go if I do this? Onto some higher plane of existence? A higher dimension?"

"Yes. That is what I desire."

"And to do that you need to pass some test? Like helping humanity?"

"I wouldn't call it a test. There is nothing to prove. What is, simply *is*. It is already in motion. Humanity *will* evolve, or cease to exist . . . for this lower level of density is affecting not just this universe, but all of creation."

"So let me get this right." She thought for a moment, no longer frightened of him, but not liking what he had just said about ceasing to exist. "You're like a big brother who's come back to this lower dimension to tell us to get our act together, because Daddy is coming home and getting pissed because we keep messing everything up?"

He laughed. "Only I would have said, Mother is coming home and she's in labor and you're making it take an eternity for her to give birth. So yes, she's getting annoyed with your tardiness."

She sat up straighter and grinned back at him. "Mother, huh? I like that."

"I thought you would. It is time for the female to assume her true role. We have tried the male, and he is too . . ." He was searching for a word.

"Too stubborn?" she supplied. "Too arrogant? Too selfish? Too warlike? Too greedy?" Let him take his pick.

"It is not entirely his fault, you must understand. Females gave males their power, and, too, perhaps more importantly, it is what your science calls genetics."

"Genetics? Men aren't wired for peace or evolving?"

"Genetically speaking, if you've met one male, you've met them all. They are quite predictable. Women are different from one another."

"So men *are* from Mars?" she asked with a laugh. "And women are from Venus?" When he looked at her in puzzlement, she added, "That's a current reference to distinguish the differences between the sexes."

He closed his eyes briefly, as if accessing something. "Then, as one of your scientists recently put it, you should say men are from Mars and women are from Venus and Pluto and Jupiter and who knows what other planets. They are creatures of an infinite variety. Men have forty-five chromosomes to evolve and their forty-sixth is the Y chromosome, which has only a few genes. And those few genes are centered on their reproductive organs. Women, on the other hand, have the full forty-six chromosomes to evolve and the forty-sixth is the second X chromosome, which is working at levels greater than your science has yet to comprehend. While men in the Y chromosome only have a few active genes, women have hundreds active in the X chromosome, giving women a significant increase in gene expression over men. Men are uncomplicated, predictable, made of just a single kind of cell. Women, on the other hand, are made up of two different kinds of cells. Women's cells have more complexity, more unpredictability. The Y chromosome has been shedding genes for millions of years and is now a fraction of the size of the X chromosome. So does it not make more sense to look to women now to midwife this new dimension? They are wired for it."

"Wow, is all that true?" she asked, amazed at what he had just told her.

"Of course it's true, and your present science can verify it, but there is so much more to discover. It is time for women to understand themselves, their extraordinary abilities, and to assume their natural place on this planet."

"Or it will cease to exist?" she asked in whisper.

He stared into her eyes, deeply, compassionately. "The planet will continue."

"But we won't?" she asked with dread.

"That is for humanity to decide. Do you know that your indigenous people here in this land made their decisions by keeping the seventh generation in mind? How many decisions were made like that by those who took their land? There are consequences to every choice. Humanity, in general, calls the earth a female, a mother, a giver of life. What kind of son poisons his mother, rapes her, takes away her lungs, and throws garbage in her veins? That son is thinking only of himself and instant gratification. He isn't thinking that his son will learn from him and continue his prejudice and pass it on to his son. The belief that the female will take abuse and continue to sacrifice herself is a false one, be it the earth or any woman subjugated by a male's arrogance."

"So the universe is angry with men?" She hated to admit, there were plenty of reasons. Especially today with war, famine, pollution, epidemics, corruption at all the highest levels.

"I didn't say that."

"But hasn't there always been war and famine and corruption?"

"In recorded history, yes. But do you actually believe there has never been a time on your planet when there was peace, when the earth was respected? Believe me, Cristine, there was. It didn't last very long."

"And then men came into power?"

"I am merely pointing out to you that men are predictable. Unfortunately, that means their behavior isn't about to change without a strong influence by the female. Women on your planet have held back, believing you were not equal. You are not only equal, you are, genetically speaking, far better equipped. That is why this new energy is coming mainly through the female this time. Through women like you. And you aren't alone. How did you put it? Your life exploded? I would rather say that old patterns are being challenged and when they cannot withstand the new energy those forms fall away, allowing something new to take its place. You are not the only one who thought their life was set, comfortable, and then find every aspect of it challenged. You are being asked to think of yourself differently."

"All of this is fascinating, Daniel, but I can't think of myself as extraordinary. I feel very ordinary." She paused and then smiled. "With maybe a few moments of magic."

He smiled back. "This isn't magic, Cristine. This is reality."

When he smiled at her she felt something deep within her open up to him. It was more than simple attraction. Any woman would be attracted to him. It was more like . . . oh, God, like that *unity* he kept talking about. She held up her hand. "Stop reading me!" she commanded. "I hate this, that everything I think or feel is so obvious to you."

His smile turned a little more sexy, or maybe that was just her imagination.

"What just happened is your energy field became more radiant. Very beautiful."

"So you don't know *what* I'm thinking, just how it's affecting my energy field?"

"I can make a good guess."

"Okay, that's the part that you have to stop. No guessing. Because you could be wrong. I have to have some privacy in this . . . whatever this is."

"I don't mean to intrude."

She laughed. Okay, partly in nervousness. "Daniel, you *have* already intruded into a very normal life."

"That can be extraordinary," he countered. "With some effort on your part."

"Fine. I'll put in the effort, as you call it, and you now can answer all my questions."

"Certainly. I told you I would."

"Okay. So you aren't really an angel?"

"*Angel* is a human term."

"Well, it's just that angels, in the stories I've read, don't simply sit down and have lengthy conversations like regular people. They usually have momentous things to impart. Like, 'Behold, I bring you good news,' or, 'Find a few good men and clear out.'"

He actually laughed. Laughed!

"I believe I have brought you good news. Would you have accepted it more easily if I had used an antiquated form of your language? I am trying to appeal to you, Cristine, the individual you in this dimension, any way I can."

She certainly didn't want him to know just how many ways he was appealing to her. "No, that's not what I mean. If you had come with wings and talking like that I probably would have checked myself into a mental hospital."

"You mentioned a key word. *Stories.* You have been studying these stories of history and spirituality for some time. Stories were the way people communicated ideas. Some of those ideas have been altered to suit the story or the storytellers. I came to you like this because you knew that already. I will say or do whatever it takes to help you accept who you really are."

"Okay. So how long can you stay like you are right now?"

"It is becoming more difficult as we communicate."

"Then I'll make my questions short. Do you eat when you're like this?"

His eyes brightened. "Oh, yes. I very much like tomatoes and avocados and ice cream. Chocolate ice cream is very good, is it not?"

She laughed. "Ah, yeah . . . more than a few people can blame their waistlines on it. Mine included."

He seemed puzzled again. "What is wrong with your waistline? Am I not understanding you correctly? Your energy field just dimmed slightly."

"That would be self-deprecating humor, Daniel. Get used to it."

"I think you look very lovely . . . Ah, yes, there it is. Your field just brightened again."

She didn't know how to stop it, so she blurted out, "Well, thanks, but I think you should go now." And then she said it, without much thought at all. "Come back tomorrow after I get home from work. I'll make you dinner and we can continue."

He stood and his energy seemed to encompass the entire living room as he did that disintegration thing. "Thank you. I will be here."

And then he was gone.
She looked at the brass clock on the fireplace mantel.
Three hours had gone by.
Time really was speeding up!

# Chapter

## 12

"CRISTINE, YOU'RE ACTING LIKE YOU HAVE A HOT date. What's with the rush to get out of here?"

Clearing her desk, she looked at Tina and shrugged. "I just want to get home and finish my kitchen. I've waited so long for it to be completed." She never would have kept something so important from her dear friend, but this—*Daniel*—wasn't something she was ready to share. How could she share him, when he was like some mysterious force that had swept into her life? And he wasn't a hot date. Really. He was . . . a teacher. He had things to impart to her and . . . Who was she kidding? Tonight was *the* hottest dinner date she'd ever had!

An hour and a half later, she'd taken a shower, wondering if *he* was aware of her. He had agreed to give her privacy, but she'd still wrapped a long bath sheet around her before exiting the tub. She'd prepared a salad of baby lettuce and loaded it with tomatoes and avocados and buttered croutons. She had also made her own balsamic dressing. And for dessert, chocolate ice cream, along with a scrumptious-looking chocolate cake she had picked up at a bakery on the way home. Healthy meal and sinful desserts. When she set the table, she put out two wine glasses, not sure if he would want any.

"Okay," she called out, as she straightened her starched white napkin to align perfectly with her good china. "I'm ready whenever you are." She fussed with her black top and then smoothed the front of her straight linen skirt. Why was she so nervous?

It occurred to her how silly it was to call out to him, but they hadn't set an exact time. Anyone observing her would be rolling their eyes at the ridiculous arrangement. But, somehow, in some strange way, she was getting used to it. Almost liking it, looking forward to it.

The doorbell rang.

Please, don't let it be anyone else, she prayed as she walked to the front of the house. Not Charlie or any of the gang. She opened the door and was surprised to see Daniel in slacks and a white shirt, holding a bouquet of late spring flowers and looking very handsome. "Hi."

"Good evening, Cristine," he answered, his eyes lighting with pleasure. "I believe it is appropriate in this dimension to bring a gift when invited to share a meal." He extended the flowers.

"Thank you. They're lovely," she murmured, taking the bouquet and noticing that it didn't seem to come from a florist. Good heavens, she hoped he hadn't taken the flowers from someone's garden. "Come in. Everything is ready."

"I didn't wish to frighten you again, so I used the doorway," he said when they were inside.

"Well, thank you for that. I never know what to expect from you."

"Is that so bad, to be unpredictable?"

"It keeps me on my toes," she answered, walking past the living room and into the kitchen. "Just let me put these into a vase and we can sit down."

"But you are not on your toes," he remarked.

She laughed. "It's just an expression. It means to keep vigilant. Do you know what *vigilant* means?"

"I do. To be aware. A very good word, *aware*."

She felt him watching her as she pulled out a crystal vase, put water into it, and arranged the flowers. "I think we'll use these on the table," she said, bringing the flowers with her into the dining room and replacing the centerpiece she had used for her dinner party on Saturday. "There," she said, standing back and admiring them. She put the older flowers on the buffet and added, "If you'd like to sit down, I'll serve."

"Allow me," he said, pulling out the chair at the head of the table.

Grinning, she sat down. As she placed her napkin on her lap and watched as he seated himself, she asked, "Did you study the manners of this time?"

"Oh, yes," he answered, taking his napkin and very properly placing it on his right thigh. "Much research took place before I even attempted to enter this dimension."

"Well, you must have aced all your exams because you seem to fit right in."

"Thank you, but there weren't any examinations. I knew when I was ready."

She nodded. "If you'd hand me your plate, I'll serve."

She filled his plate with the salad. "I didn't know exactly what you could eat, except for those things you mentioned. Ordinarily, I would have served this with broiled strips of chicken, but I thought perhaps you might be a vegetarian."

"Thank you."

"So you are a vegetarian?" she asked, handing him his plate.

"My choice is not to ingest body parts of an animal that was filled with fear. Fear spikes chemically altered hormone levels throughout the animal's body before its death. It would make my mission more difficult."

Cristine was glad she hadn't cooked the chicken, even

for herself. In fact, she didn't know if she'd ever look at the meat or poultry section of a supermarket the same again, thanks to him. Shoving the image out of her mind, she served herself.

"I've made a balsamic dressing, if you want to try it. It's very good on a salad."

"Thank you for being so thoughtful, Cristine. This is very nice . . . to share a meal with you."

She nodded and poured some dressing on her salad and felt him watching her again. She then handed the glass cruet to him. He followed her example perfectly, moving the cruet around exactly as she had done. When he finished, he put it back into the small silver container and picked up his fork.

He looked at her.

"Go ahead. Taste it."

"I am waiting for you to eat first. Is that not the proper way?"

She chuckled. "I think you're right." Picking up her fork, she stabbed a piece of avocado and some lettuce and brought it to her mouth. He did the same.

"It is most curious. A new taste, this balsamic, and quite delicious."

Swallowing, she said, "Good, I'm glad you enjoy it. Now, do you drink wine?"

"Wine? No, I have not yet tasted it. Is it also as good?"

She laughed. "I don't know about as good, but it's certainly a different taste." She raised the opened bottle of Chardonnay. "Would you like to try it?"

He held up his wine glass and she poured for them both.

"Now we earth humans sometimes make a toast, a . . . a good wish, before we drink." Earth humans? She was starting to speak like him!

"Why is that?"

"I really don't know. Just a tradition." She held up her

glass to him. "To an entertaining evening with good company."

He repeated her words.

"And now we drink," she stated, bringing her glass to her mouth.

She took a sip. He nearly finished his glass until she reached for his arm. "Whoa, there! Don't gulp it. Just sip."

He put his glass on the table and licked his lower lip. "It is a very different taste. Very . . . earthy."

She giggled. "That's one way to put it. It's made from grapes, a fruit that grows on vines."

"Yes, and the fruit ferments. I have learned this. It is a social beverage."

"It can be very social if you gulp it. But let me ask you something, if I may."

"Certainly, Cristine," he answered, concentrating on his salad again.

It was time to begin getting some answers. "Where you're from, your dimension, is it very different from this one?"

"Very different, and yet some things are the same. The moon, the sun are the same. The stars are different. There are more to be seen."

"So it's the same planet, but a different dimension?"

"It's the same universe, but a different dimension."

"Then you aren't . . . well, related to humans on some level?"

"Everything in the universe is related. At the most basic molecular level we are all one."

"But why Earth then? Why come here to help humanity evolve?"

"In this universe, if you could see how immense this universe is, you would see that Earth is far removed from the center, if a center could be found. But since all is one, what affects Earth produces a chain reaction, if you will, throughout all of creation. Allow me to say that in this time your people have become even more destructive. Your science has developed powerful forces, atomic forces they are called, and to many observers it is like watching a child playing with a very dangerous toy."

"So you've come to save humanity from blowing itself up?"

"No. Only humanity can save itself from itself. And only by assisting that child to evolve into an adult with responsibility. I do so like the taste of avocados with this balsamic. You are a very good meal maker, Cristine."

She had to do a bit of mental juggling to keep up with his abrupt change of subject. "Thank you, Daniel. I'm glad you are enjoying it."

"Oh, I am indeed," he answered, grinning broadly. "May I sip the wine again?"

She shook her head while chuckling. "You don't have to ask me every time you want to drink the wine. Just don't gulp it all at once."

"Very good." He picked up his wine glass and sipped, then held it for a few moments and sipped again.

He was getting the hang of drinking all right, she thought, sipping her own wine. And she hated to admit that not only did he look even more handsome out of his usual attire of jeans and blue shirt, but he was a very charming dinner companion. Something inside of her, probably something primitive and unevolved, made her ask, "Daniel, do you have a family?" Like a wife, or a lover? She didn't ask that part. Didn't have the courage.

"Oh, yes, an immense one," he answered, returning to his meal.

"Immense?"

He nodded. "Countless members. You may not understand because you are still wearing a body suit, but you also have an immense family. The same one, actually."

"Really?" She put her fork down. "You and I are related?"

"Of course. You and everyone are related. We all come from the same Source and are on a journey back to that Source."

"Source? You mean . . . like God?"

"That's your label. The best I can translate mine is, the Source of all that is, an exquisite intelligence."

"And this source . . . does it have a personality, like we think God has one?"

"If you mean does the Source mete out rewards and punishments, making judgments, then the answer is no. Every reward or punishment you have experienced, Cristine, can be directly traced back to your own state of mind and your choices. When you believe without a shadow of a doubt that you deserve whatever you desire, you shall have it. When you believe with an unhealed mind that you are unworthy, then you will experience what you have termed punishment. It is all very simple, but you humans tend to complicate it."

"Wait a minute. So you're saying that if I believe I'm worthy I can have anything I desire?"

"Absolutely. And that is how you must believe. Absolutely, without a trace of doubt."

"So I could, like . . . win the lottery if I wanted?"

"You could, if that is your desire."

Hmm . . . now that was very interesting. She ate a few more forkfuls of her salad and again put down her fork. "So how would I go about that then?" She couldn't help it. She had to ask.

Daniel put down his fork, and she noticed that every tomato and avocado piece was eaten.

"Are you ready then to begin work?"

"Work? How hard is it going to be? Remember, I have a job too."

He finished his wine and Cristine poured him a second glass.

"Only you can answer how hard it will be, Cristine. I

can only give you the information. What you do with it is your choice."

"Okay, how do I begin?"

"By getting to know your true self."

"My true self?"

"Yes. Who are you?"

She blinked. "I'm me. Cristine Dobbins."

"Cristine Dobbins is the name given to you. Who are you? Who have you always been before anyone assigned you a name? Before you entered this planet through the womb of your mother?"

"When I was unborn?" He was confusing her.

"Before that spark of energy divided the united cell of your parents to produce the physiology that became your body suit."

"Are you talking about a soul?"

"I am talking about what is termed consciousness. You, the real you, has always existed. You may not remember right now because you chose to forget in order to survive in this dimension, but you will soon. No one was there to remind you and so you forgot. When you remember how very extraordinary you are, extraordinary things will happen and become your ordinary."

"So how do I do that?"

He sat back and smiled. "You remember you. In some ways you are already doing it. That voice inside of you . . . has it changed so much as you aged? Is it not the same familiar voice as when you were a child? It may have a larger vocabulary, but is not the *feeling* still the same?"

She thought about it. "Yes."

"That comes closer to who you really are. Let me ask you this. Why do you see this world, this dimension, as real if the self that is determining that world is intangible?"

She didn't answer him. She couldn't find an answer.

"Your science has looked everywhere for that *self*. It has explored every part of the body suit, especially the brain, but its search has come up empty. It cannot be found. Yet you know for yourself that it is real. It has been with you from the moment you realized you existed and became self-conscious. It is the observer within."

"The observer," she repeated. "The one who sees."

"And observes. But allow me to ask who sees then? Is it the brain? The eyes?"

"Both?" She really felt like she was in school now. Out of her depth and desperate to understand.

"If one sees and then afterward imagines the same image, your science, through what is called a PET scan, has shown that the very same parts of the brain will light up with the experience of seeing and also by only using the imagination. Both produce the same result. So what is reality then? What you see with your brain, or what you see with your eyes?"

"I don't know," she answered truthfully. He was telling her things she had never heard of before.

"The brain truly does not know the difference between what it sees in its environment and what it remembers, because the same, identical neurons fire. You allow huge amounts of information into your consciousness that are processed through your sense organs, those bits that are most self-serving, about your body, your surroundings. Now if your brain processes four hundred billion bits of information a second, but you are only aware of perhaps two thousand of those, that means true reality is happening in the brain all the time. It is receiving all the information, but you haven't integrated it yet. Right now your brain is wired so you only see what you believe is possible. That is why I came to you using this body suit. Had I remained as beautiful dancing lights, we couldn't have communicated beyond our times of unity."

His smile was very nice, almost sexy, as though he were remembering their "times of unity."

She didn't know what to say. Her mind was filled to capacity with everything he had told her. "Daniel, it's going to take time to understand all this."

"I know that."

"You won't get impatient with me?"

"Never. Time is an illusion. At least for me."

"All right. If you're finished, I'll remove the plates and bring out dessert."

He handed her his plate. "It was very good, Cristine. A new experience to be appreciated."

She laughed. "Ah, Daniel . . . just you wait for the next experience, dessert. I think you'll find it even more enjoyable."

He looked well pleased. "I am very excited."

And Cristine thought she could see it in his eyes.

They actually sparkled, like those tiny dancing lights!

She cleared her throat. "Okay, well, I'll be right back. Just relax. Have more wine."

She left the dining room and took the plates to the sink. Good heavens, what was happening to her? Her whole body felt as if it were vibrating with . . . with something that wasn't entirely unwelcome. In fact, it felt downright pleasurable, but not quite appropriate for a dinner with an angel, or whatever he was. Maybe that was it, she thought as she scraped the remains into the garbage disposal. She didn't know exactly *who* she was dealing with, or even what.

Opening the cake box, she cut two pieces. It certainly was beyond foolish to feel like this about someone she hardly knew, especially since that someone did not even belong in this dimension. Was she simply setting herself up for a major fall when he left? How could she ever be satisfied with an ordinary man again? Taking out the ice cream, she opened the box and scooped out two servings, one much larger than the other. She was ruined. No man on this planet would ever compare to what she'd had with Daniel. That's what was going to happen. She was going to wind up evolved and still be alone and raising cats. Just so long as her crazy hats didn't resemble space helmets, she might just be left in peace.

But maybe, if everything Daniel said was true . . . maybe she could be rich. Really rich. Wealthy rich. Like Mamie Pitcairn rich. That would make up for being alone and being surrounded by cats.

She deserved to win the lottery.

It was the quickest way to find out if Daniel's theories worked.

She brought the plates into the dining room and placed one in front of Daniel. "Now this should be a treat," she said, sitting down.

"Chocolate ice cream!" He looked like a child whose wish had come true.

"*And* chocolate cake," she added. "Try it with the ice cream."

She watched as he brought the combination to his mouth and then grinned as he closed his eyes in appreciation and murmured, "This is . . . exquisite."

"A true chocoholic," she answered with a giggle, and she dug into her own dessert.

"I do not understand that word," he said, going back for more.

"Just someone who loves chocolate."

"I do love chocolate."

"Yes, I can see.

"You know, chocolate is said to produce endorphins, chemicals in the body that give you a feeling of well-being."

"Perhaps that is part of the reason. But it *tastes* wonderful too."

"It does," she answered, pleased by his unabashed pleasure. Okay, she had plied him with food and wine and chocolate. He should be in a good mood. "So, how do I go about believing in myself, Daniel? Is there any way I can test this?"

He finished swallowing and looked at her. "Begin by letting go of your past. It is as if you are putting out a request to the Source and you want that to be clear, not clouded or muddied by emotions that no longer serve you."

"How do I let go of my past?"

"You forgive everyone, for everything. And you do it for yourself, because you know you don't deserve to carry it around any longer. You know it no longer serves you in any positive way."

"Forgive?" Oh, she knew the importance of forgiveness. She just never liked the idea that those who harmed another got away scot-free. "That's not always easy, you know."

He nodded. "I know."

"It doesn't seem fair. There's no justice in it."

He put his fork on his plate and looked into her eyes. "You hold resentment, waiting for justice. Don't you know that holding resentment is like drinking poison and waiting for the other person to die?"

She sat speechless, staring back at him. Dessert was forgotten.

"The lower, dense emotions, like resentment, can kill you, Cristine. They change the biology of your cells. When you love yourself more than you love your addiction to those emotions, you can forgive everyone for everything. And when you know that the universal law of cause and effect works not just in your life, but everywhere in creation, you no longer have to judge another or wait to see justice for satisfaction. You may never see or know what truly goes on in another's life experience."

She felt her chest tighten with emotion. This wasn't going the way she thought. She wanted to talk about winning the lottery and he was making her think about her past. "My mother abandoned me, deserted me," she blurted out, and was shocked by her words. She never, ever, talked about that.

"I know," he said with compassion. "I have read it in your energy. That is the main issue you have not dealt with. Survival. Trust me, Cristine, you share that with most of humanity. You are stuck at survival. Perhaps you can begin by forgiving your mother." He touched her arm and she felt a frizzle of electricity rush up to her shoulders.

"But I could never understand how she could have left me and not even visit, or check up on me. She left me behind."

"Like Charlie."

She jerked her head up and glared at him. "Yes! Like Charlie!"

"Do you think, perhaps, just perhaps, that your mother couldn't care for you? That her mind was altered by chemicals and she realized her own life was precarious? That it was because she loved you she put you somewhere she thought would be safe?"

"But it wasn't safe and I never even heard from her."

"You couldn't."

"Why? She could have at least written to Children's Welfare."

"She was no longer in this dimension, Cristine. Your mother died shortly after placing you. Don't you see, for all those years you were resenting someone who was no longer alive, and your resentment only affected yourself."

She was silent for a few moments, then the tears came and she covered her face with her hands. "I'm sorry," she mumbled. "This is so embarrassing."

Daniel stroked her arm, sending even more electricity

to buzz through her. "Tell yourself you are sorry, Cristine, and mean it. Let go of that heavy piece of your past."

Even though the news of her mother's death had rattled her, she felt calmer. Sniffling, she brought her napkin up to her face. "Well, that certainly wasn't how I thought the evening would go," she said, trying to make a joke of her emotional display as she dabbed at her tears.

Daniel smiled. "You had expectations?"

"I thought it would be a bit more enjoyable than *that*."

"But that needed to happen. And Charlie's leaving you served also, in bringing that issue of abandonment to the surface again. Soon, when you think about it, you will be able to forgive." He resumed eating his cake, for the remaining ice cream had melted. When he swallowed, he added, "Why don't we begin by creating something small?"

She sniffled. "Small?"

"Yes, something you don't see ordinarily every day."

"There are lots of things I don't see every day. Like you, for example."

"Besides me."

Thinking, she said, "I don't see spaceships or monkeys or snowmen in spring or plenty of things. I don't know what to pick." She paused. "So you're telling me the lottery is out of the question?"

He grinned. "For now. When you wake up tomorrow morning, think of those things you just mentioned and see what happens."

"So I'm going to see spaceships?" she asked with a laugh, then became more serious. "*Are* there really spaceships?"

He laughed. "Are there really snowmen in spring?"

"You're not going to tell me."

"I'm going to allow you the experience. It is the best way to learn."

"Well, first I'm going to clear the table. Would you like

coffee, or . . . anything else?" She rose while picking up her plate.

Daniel also rose, a bit unsteady on his feet. "No, I am very satisfied, thank youuuuuuuu . . ."

Cristine watched in amazement as Daniel seemed to stumble toward her and then disintegrate into tiny particles of light that swirled, surrounding her. She gasped in awe, feeling him, the exquisite unity of his mingling with every cell of her body. And then just as quickly, it was over.

He was gone.

After closing her mouth, she began to giggle nervously as she leaned on the table for balance. Well, that wasn't the full, mind-blowing orgasm of before, and Daniel didn't exactly appear to be himself as he left.

Her giggle became louder.

It must have been the wine.

Who would have thought . . . a drunken angel.

Or whatever he was.

## Chapter

## 13

SHE WAS PUTTING HER COFFEE MUG INTO THE dishwasher when she heard the morning newscaster say, "It isn't the first time strange lights have been spotted in the Arizona sky. Last night hundreds of people called their local police. And our Phoenix affiliate, WCUA, logged eighty-six calls, everyone wondering what exactly were those lights hovering above the city. Was it the government testing ultrasecret aircraft? Or were they spaceships, moving in perfect formation for over one minute? Stay tuned after this break for actual footage, shot by eyewitnesses."

She closed the dishwasher and leaned against the counter, watching the commercial but not really paying attention. Instead, she was asking herself if it was lack of sleep that was making her think Daniel had something to do with those lights. She closed her eyes briefly, trying to summon the strength to get through the morning. Having an appointment at ten-thirty, Cristine knew she had better pull her act together by that time. It was important that she get the listing, and having spent the majority of last night either thinking or crying didn't exactly help. She had gone to bed exhausted after dinner with Daniel, yet no sooner had her head hit the pillow than she had thought of her mother. She had no picture, no image to mourn. Instead, it had been like grieving an empty space where the person who had given her life had disappeared. All those years spent in anger and resentment seemed futile, and so in the end she had cried for herself, for the lonely child, the resentful teenager, and the angry woman. And she forgave her lost mother. Now she was working on forgiving herself.

She listened to the news report, watched the shaky amateur video, and had to admit it didn't look like any kind of airplane lights she had ever seen, but then again she wasn't an expert. And she had only been interested because of what Daniel had said about a lesson in creating. She'd said she hadn't seen spaceships, and then the news used that term and it had caught her attention.

That's all it was.

Cristine picked up the remote and silenced the television. Then she picked up her suit jacket and slipped her arms into it. Time to get to work, she thought, grabbing the handles of her briefcase. Just in case she didn't win the lottery.

She put a call in to Tina from the car, telling her she was on her way to her appointment. Tina asked if she wanted to meet for lunch with Isabel, and Cristine said she'd try to drop in and made a note of the restaurant. As she drove through Haverton, she thought of everything she had discussed with Daniel the night before. He certainly was making her think and question reality . . . which wasn't at all comfortable. She had liked reality, well, most of it. She had liked knowing she could count on certain things. Like her state of mind. Since Daniel's arrival that was most certainly in question.

Stopped at a light, Cristine was lost in thought when a large white truck crossed the road in front of her and waited to make a left-hand turn. She blinked several times and then her eyes focused on a red snow cone painted on the side.

### Frosty Snow Cones

### Available at Your Local Supermarket
### Now in New JUMBO Size

And waving right at her, and at every other motorist on the road, was a huge cheery snowman painted in white and black and red.

She stared at the truck as it made its turn and drove away.

What was next? Monkeys running wild in the streets?

Shaking her head, she drove to her appointment.

Alice Shandell was a single mother and a doctor in private practice. Today was her day off, but Cristine knew all time was of the essence to such a busy woman.

"I dread showing the place," she said, leading Cristine into her kitchen. "My son is a genuine slob and this is going to be a trial in patience for both of us."

"Most buyers understand people actually live in the homes they view. Just watch out for clutter. That really puts them off."

"Great. Brian's room looks like his hamper exploded. Besides the magazines, the CDs, and the computer equipment."

"Well, the kitchen is lovely," Cristine remarked, noting the custom drapery at the breakfast nook that matched the tasteful wallpaper border at the ceiling. "This is a four-bedroom home, right?"

"That's right. There's a guest room, and I use the fourth bedroom for my office. I want to move into the new condos they're building by the park. It's closer to work and Brian's school and it has a first-floor office."

"Those are lovely, and quite large. Almost three thousand square feet."

"I know. I drove by on my way home one day and couldn't resist stopping. Of course when I did, I fell in love with the layout." They were now in the living room and Dr. Shandell looked around it. "It's time for a change."

Cristine nodded while making her notes for the listing. Brick fireplace. Built-in cabinetry. "How long have you lived here?"

"Twelve years. Brian was one when we moved in. Nice neighborhood to raise a child."

"It is. And good schools."

"Brian's going into the regional high school in September, so I thought it would be the right time for a change. He'd still keep the same friends."

Dr. Shandell led Cristine through the rest of the house and Cristine was fast writing down any feature that she could use to entice buyers. The place was around twenty years old, but in good condition and nicely decorated.

Upstairs, after viewing the large master bedroom, Cristine asked, "Would you object to having a photographer come out and take a few pictures? No matter how well we try to describe a house, interior pictures do a far better job and buyers love them. We'll include them in your brochure and, of course, on our Web site."

"Sure. Just not Brian's room, which I might as well show you next. It's a good thing I'm a cardiologist, just in case . . ." And she opened the door that had a poster attached, saying ENTER AT YOUR OWN RISK, with a skull and crossbones to indicate danger.

"Well . . ." Cristine murmured, taking in the mess. It was a teenage boy's room, cluttered, a sea of discarded clothes, magazines thrown on the floor, and posters of female rap stars. She laughed. "You weren't kidding."

"I'm afraid not."

"Okay, you really are going to have to work out a compromise with Brian. The posters have to go, not because of their subject matter, but there are so many of them that they make the room look smaller and closed in. Maybe you could buy him a larger hamper, and he could use it for the next month or so. Bribe him, if you have to."

"You don't think I've tried?"

Cristine chuckled. "Look, he's a teenager. You just have to find the right bribe. There must be something he's nagging you to get him."

"He wants to upgrade his computer."

"There you are. Tell him when the house sells, he'll get his upgrade. That way you're both working for what you want. Sounds like a compromise to me."

Dr. Shandell looked at her. "You *are* a clever woman. Lillian Brooker said I wouldn't be disappointed. Do you have children of your own? You seem to have some pretty good suggestions."

"No. No children. I didn't know Lillian had recommended me. I thought you just picked us from the Yellow Pages or got our number from one of our lawn signs."

"Let's close this door and I'll show you my office right next door." Dr. Shandell led her into a much more orderly room. "Lillian is a patient of mine and I saw her on Friday. She was thrilled with finding her new home so quickly."

"Lillian is quite a woman," Cristine said, taking more notes. "I think she'll be happy in her new place."

"Yes, she is quite a women, a real character, and Maxine keeps me on my toes. It's not easy when the partner of your patient has medical training. Maxine is always questioning me, but I like her—I like them both. They make me laugh."

"I like them too. And I have to say I admire them," Cristine added. Not wanting to get into a personal discussion about her client, Cristine asked, "Isn't there a fourth bedroom?"

Dr. Shandell nodded. "Down at the end of the hall. I call it the guest bedroom. Brian calls it the jungle. Follow me."

The doctor opened the door and Cristine stared in shock at the room decorated in an East Indian theme . . . with monkeys in the silk bed linens swinging from vines, monkeys holding up the lamp shades, monkeys lying on the night tables cradling candles.

"I think I went a little overboard with the monkeys," Alice Shandell admitted. "Don't worry, nothing is permanent and it's all going with me when I move."

Cristine burst out laughing. "I love it!" she exclaimed and, suddenly, she was filled with the unpredictable, unexplainable magic of life. Spaceships. A snowman. And now monkeys.

Lots of monkeys!

"So?" Tina asked as Cristine slid into the booth. "Did you get it?"

Cristine blew Isabel a kiss and sighed as she settled across from them. "Yes. The agreement is signed. You can process it all this afternoon. Hi, Issy."

"You look wonderful, Cristine," Isabel remarked, leaning her elbows on the edge of the wooden table. "What are you doing different?"

Cristine smiled. "Nothing, really. Just enjoying life a bit more, I think."

"She should spread some of it around, don't you think?" Tina asked no one in particular. "What do you want to drink? Wine?"

"No. I'll just have a glass of still water."

"Now she's getting healthy too."

Cristine grinned at Tina. "I can't just be thirsty?"

"So what price have you set?" Tina asked, ignoring her question.

"We'll list it at four ninety-nine. She'll be happy with four seventy. She bought it at two seventy, so it's a very good profit. She's buying a condo at Mystic Glen down by the park." Cristine unbuttoned her suit jacket. "Oh, and guess who recommended us?"

"Who?"

"Lillian Brooker, Mamie Pitcairn's mother."

Tina looked pleased. "No kidding. See, I told you that sale was going to bring us business. It's happening already."

Cristine nodded. "The seller's Lillian's doctor."

"Life is certainly full of surprises for you, Cristine, since Charlie left, don't you think?" Isabel asked with a smile. "Things seem to be falling into place for you."

"You could say that," Cristine answered. "Have you two ordered yet?"

"We have," Tina said, lifting her hand for the waitress.

Cristine ordered a caesar salad and water and sat back. "So what's new with you, Isabel?" she asked, to get the attention off herself. "How's the practice?"

Isabel sat back and sighed. "Actually, I'm a little scared."

"Why?" Both Tina and Cristine asked the question at once.

"It's just that I seem to really be making progress with these autistic children."

"That's great, Issy!" Cristine exclaimed. "Why are you scared?"

"Because I don't know what's happening. I don't know why it seems to be working. And the kids don't seem to be the problem. It's the parents."

"What do you mean?" Tina asked.

"Okay, take this one child as an example. When his parents brought him to me he was totally disconnected. Didn't speak. Didn't interact with anyone. His mother was sobbing, at her wit's end, saying if only he would look at her and say mommy she'd be thrilled. Well, he's not only saying mommy, he's actually interacting with his family."

"Isabel, that's incredible progress," Cristine said. "What did you do?"

Issy shook her head. "That's just it. I'm not sure. I spent a lot of time with him, getting on the floor with him, just waiting for that split second where he would recognize me. When he finally did, only for a moment, I knew I could get in there and help him. So I made CDs for him, well, for his parents to play when he goes to sleep. I tell him a story, using his family as characters and things I've learned from his parents about his life and I tell it like an induction into hypnosis. I don't know why, but I'm convinced that connecting with the subconscious is an open route for these kids, to actually reach them. So now that he's improved, the mother who only wanted him to say her name and connect with her is trying to mainstream him into regular school."

"What's so wrong with that?" Tina asked. "Any parent would want to keep up the improvement, right?"

"I know," Isabel answered. "But these aren't kids you can put under that kind of pressure. Two months ago he didn't speak, and now she's put him into the system where he's always going to be labeled as slow. And putting him back on medication has been suggested by the school psychologist. I wouldn't be surprised if he fell back into silence."

No one spoke until their food was delivered.

"And it's such a shame because now he has a vocabulary of almost two hundred words," Isabel said. "And he's such a sweet boy."

Cristine reached out and touched Issy's hand. "Obviously, you tried talking to the mother."

Isabel nodded. "She's listening to the school now and has new dreams of her child being normal. I don't know if he'll ever be considered normal, but at least he could function in the world."

"Kinda breaks your heart, doesn't it?" Tina asked.

"And he's not the only one. I just wish the parents would back off for a little while and give it a chance. I know it's done out of love, but . . ."

"But you can't stop them from dreaming," Tina offered. "You know what you should do?"

Isabel looked up. "What?"

"Write a book about it. You've got the credentials. How many of these kids have you worked with?"

Thinking, Isabel said, "About twenty right now."

"And they've all improved?"

"In different degrees."

"Then write about it. Get this out there."

"Tina's right, Issy," Cristine said. "You should do it."

"I would need more case studies."

"Then think about it." Tina said, picking up a French fry.

"You have something to contribute, and there are parents all over the world who may want to listen." Cristine looked at her dear friend. "You are such a remarkable woman, Isabel. And you have an extraordinary gift. Write the book. Go to those psychology seminars you used to attend every year and speak your truth."

"I'll think about it," she answered, picking up her fork and studying her curry.

Cristine smiled across the table. Isabel would think about it, but she probably wouldn't do it. Dear, dear Issy liked to remain in the shadows, to blend into the background. She didn't want the spotlight to shine on her. Instead, she dressed in browns or blacks or her husband's old shirts or jackets with the sleeves rolled up. Isabel was tall and regal with her white hair and could pull it off, but since Chuck had died she'd retreated from life . . . and she really did have so much to offer the world.

If Daniel had come into *Issy's* life it would have made so much more sense. Isabel was intelligent, spiritual, a truly good soul who was already using her gift to help humanity. Isabel wouldn't question everything and make things harder. Isabel had faith, real faith.

Not like her.

But it was weird today seeing those things she had mentioned to Daniel. Was that taking a tiny step in creating her reality? She'd have to ask him the next time he popped back into her life.

And thinking of that, she still had the makings for another salad, with leftover cake and ice cream.

Hmm, she wondered what he was doing tonight.

Yeah, right . . . like he was a regular guy she was seeing. But that's how it was beginning to feel, like he was a guy, a man who had come into her life. A strange man who spoke of things that seemed to resonate within her soul, an unbelievable man whose very nearness seemed to make her body tingle with desire, a male energy that at any moment could disintegrate right out of her life. The trouble was, she was now looking forward to his visits while this was simply some kind of job for him.

She didn't want to be anyone's job.

Truth be told, she wanted him to want her, at least want to be with her as much as she wanted to be with him.

And that was a really foolish and dangerous place to be.

*Chapter*

# 14

HE WAS HOLDING A BOWL OF CHOCOLATE ICE cream and grinning from ear to ear.

Cristine was putting their dinner plates into the dishwasher, and relating her day. "And when she opened the guest bedroom door I just stood there, taking in all the monkeys. I couldn't believe it. Monkeys everywhere!"

"So creating your reality proved to be fun?"

"Well, if that's all it takes . . ."

"That was focusing on something and then releasing it. Almost everyone has had that experience, thinking about someone and then you see them or they contact you. Looking for something you can't find and then releasing it and it shows up. There is so much more."

"Like the lottery, Daniel. How would I go about winning that?"

"Why do you want to win it?"

She finished the dishes and picked up their wine glasses. "Let's go outside and sit on the patio. It's a nice night."

He followed and sat next to her on the metal love seat. Cristine leaned back against the thick cushions and sighed as she looked up at the stars. "I want to win the lottery so I'll never have to worry about money again."

"Your survival issues."

She shrugged. "I don't care what you call it. Everyone has survival issues."

"And that's what keeps them at a lower level of energy. They never get past it."

"Because most people struggle every day just to survive, only to wake up and do the whole thing all over again. It's a trap."

"I agree," he said, setting his empty bowl on the table at his side. "So you believe that if you resolved your survival issues by winning the lottery, you could evolve quicker?"

"Oh, I do, Daniel," she said earnestly. Maybe he would fix it for her. She didn't care how she won. If he could put together her kitchen, he could easily make the right numbers come up. "It would make everything so much easier."

"And what would you do with the money?"

"I would pay off all my bills and . . . and help people."

"How would you help people?"

She crossed her arms and then ran her hands up and down the sleeves of her silk blouse. "I don't know yet. I really haven't thought about it, because it seemed like such a long shot."

"Now see, there is your problem. You think, if I am interpreting your phrase 'long shot' correctly, that it is almost impossible for you to win."

She laughed. "Well, the odds are very high against it. I don't even play because of that."

"If you don't play, how can you win?"

"I don't know . . . I was waiting for you to tell me how."

It was his turn to laugh. "You are such a delightfully complicated creature, Cristine." He picked up his wine glass and sipped. "It comes down to belief. Absolute belief. No-hesitation belief. Not anywhere, not in any part of you."

She didn't say anything for a few moments. "Can't you just like . . . I don't know, twitch your nose or wave your hands or whatever you did to finish my kitchen?"

"You want *me* to do it?" he asked with another laugh.

"Well, I don't see how *I* can."

"Listen to me. What you call money is just another form of energy, of power. You had a train of thought about a snowman, a spaceship, and monkeys and you brought them forth into your reality. You used your power in a very light way. You saw today the possibilities of your mind. Now you want to expand that to winning the lottery. Let me ask you if you think you were worthy of seeing those things today."

She blinked. "Sure."

"You knew that answer without much thought, correct?"

"Yes."

"Do you also think you are worthy of winning the lottery?"

"Of course. I'm as worthy as anyone else."

"Are you more worthy than a single mother who is working two jobs to feed and house her children? A man who cannot have a lifesaving operation performed for his dying son? An elderly woman who forgoes eating her nightly meal so she can buy her husband's medication?"

Cristine sighed. "Maybe not. You're right."

"And *that,* Cristine Dobbins, is why you believe you cannot win the lottery. In your subconscious mind you do not believe you are worthy."

She turned to him. He was staring up at the stars. "But those others are more needy."

"That's guilt. You do not have a healthy relationship with money. You look at it as whether or not you are more deserving of great abundance. I will tell you this . . . you are as deserving as anyone else on this planet, no more and no less. You know what you want and yet you analyze it, and while you are analyzing it, nothing happens because your desire is stuck in your judgments of guilt. You will create and win the lottery when you know—without a single cell of your body doubting, that you are worthy of it."

"That might take forever," she complained.

He grinned and sipped his wine. "Or it might take you buying a ticket."

She stared at him. "Are you making a joke?"

He looked at her and his smile increased. "Not at all. In order for you to win, don't you have to purchase a ticket? Is that not the way it works?"

"Yes, but the way you said it . . ." She was staring at his mouth, curved so nicely into a smile. He was so close, if she leaned in a little . . .

"Your energy is getting brighter," he murmured, staring into her eyes.

She blinked. "Do you have someone, Daniel? Someone in your dimension?"

"What does that mean, have someone?"

"Someone special. A . . . a lover." She really wanted to know because her body was nearly vibrating with desire for him, and if he said yes she was going to jump up from the love seat, run into the house and stick her head under the kitchen sink to cool down.

"If you mean do I have a partner, as you do in this dimension, then the answer is no. I have chosen to focus on my personal advancement."

"But how can you advance if you've never experienced love?" There. She said it. And it was out there hanging in the small space between them. "Isn't love important to evolution?"

"Love is everything," he murmured, now staring at her mouth. "There are . . . all kinds of love."

"Yes," she agreed. "Our unity. That was exquisite." Dear God, she was flirting with him! And it appeared to be working!

"Yes . . . I . . . I think I should leave."

"Why? Aren't you here to experience too? Like the chocolate ice cream?"

"It was very good." His voice sounded a bit shaky and he seemed to lean into her even more, as though drawn.

Cristine leaned in too, and then she turned her head slightly and brought her lips to his in a soft kiss. It was wonderful, heavenly, and . . . *over*?

She stared in disbelief as he turned into his dancing lights and swirled into the night sky to vanish.

When she caught her breath, Cristine looked up at the stars and grinned.

Maybe she had something she could teach Daniel.

The next day she walked into the QuickMart and bought a lottery ticket. Sitting in her car, she looked at the random numbers the machine had picked and whispered over and over, "I deserve to win. I so deserve to win. I am as worthy as anyone else who bought a ticket. I deserve to win!"

She didn't.

She threw away the ticket that evening while watching different numbers roll out of the machine on the nightly telecast.

The next day she bought another and repeated her mantra. "I deserve to win. I am deserving of winning. This is my winning ticket. I am so worthy of winning."

Someone else won. In fact, three other people won.

She was determined for the rest of the week. She even got to know the clerk at the QuickMart. Abrahim.

"So, today is your lucky day, yes?" he asked in his accented voice.

Holding her cup of coffee, she shrugged, not wanting to give away her secret strategy. "Who knows? I think I'll take two." She handed him the money.

"A woman such as you should be pampered with wealth."

It wasn't the first time Abrahim had flirted with her, so she just smiled while waiting for the machine to spit out her winning tickets. As far as she could tell, Abrahim flirted with every female customer. She took her tickets and held out a dollar bill for her coffee.

Abrahim held up his hand. "No, you a good customer. Take it. Go. My treat." He held his finger up to his lips. "Shh."

It was supposed to be their little secret? She shook her head. "No, really, I'd rather pay." Putting the bill on the counter, she smiled and added, "But thanks anyway." As she walked to the car, she thought that if she didn't win tonight then maybe she would buy her tickets someplace else. Maybe Abrahim's energy was messing with her own.

To hell with that, she thought. She had a right to an abundant life, damn it. As much as anyone else who bought a ticket anywhere in the state.

Daniel didn't come back for days and she didn't call him. She wanted to several times, but held herself back. He probably knew what she was doing anyway. And maybe he was embarrassed because of that kiss, that is, if he could be embarrassed.

Still, you would think he'd want some chocolate ice cream, if nothing else.

Cristine stopped just as she was about to open her car door. He'd gotten ice cream before. He'd tasted it somewhere else. It had never occurred to her that he might be seeing others. And with that thought, her stomach twisted painfully in the very human emotion of jealousy.

She realized she didn't want to share Daniel.

Opening her car, she got inside and sat for a moment.

She was falling for him. And that could prove to be really stupid. Somehow, she had to put Daniel Burns out of her mind . . . at least for now.

Cristine was into her winning mantra, repeating that

she deserved to win, seeing herself holding the check in her hands, paying off her bills, holding the deed to her house, when she suddenly had a strange sensation, as though a frizzle of electricity passed through her. And she realized she felt wealthy already. She had a terrific job that was really taking off. She was healthy. Her home was almost paid for. She had great friends. And she had a man in her life who was, literally, out of this world. In some respects she was as wealthy as Bill Gates or Mamie Pitcairn. Energy was energy, right?

It was already a pretty good life, she thought while dropping the tickets into her purse.

Turning on the car, she was about to pull out of the parking lot when her cell phone rang. She opened her purse and flipped open the phone. "Cristine Dobbins."

"Thank God, I caught you," Tina said, her voice sounding frightened.

"What's wrong?"

"Paula had an accident this morning."

"Oh, my God, is she all right?"

"She's okay. She called me from the hospital and they think she's got fractured ribs. The baby was with her."

Cristine's heart dropped to her stomach. "And . . ."

"And he's fine. You know Paula, good mother, he was in his car seat in the back. Some jerk ran a stop sign. Thank God she was on her way home or the car would have been full."

"What do you need me to do?"

"Can you pick up Paula and Conor from St. Mary's? Hank's on a business trip. She called him and he's catching the first plane home, but he's in California and he won't be back until eight tonight."

"Sure, I'll get her. Should I go now?"

"Yeah. I'll hold down the fort here and switch your afternoon appointment to later in the week. Don't worry about anything here at the office."

"Right. Do I go to the emergency room entrance?"

"I think so. Call me when you get her home and I'll come by on my lunch hour."

"Okay, let me go. I'll call you."

Cristine closed the phone and dropped it back into her purse. Even though it sounded as though Paula and Conor were all right, her hands were shaking as she placed them on the steering wheel.

Life was so fragile.

She pulled out into the morning traffic with more care than usual. Really, what control did a person actually have in their life if someone who's distracted or in a hurry can run a stop sign and ram your car? Thank heavens, it wasn't serious. For an instant she pictured Paula's five children without their mother and quickly shook the horror out of her head as she headed for the hospital. "Delete, delete," she murmured, replacing fear with gratitude. Paula and Conor were okay.

She walked into the emergency room and asked for Paula. She could hear a child crying loudly beyond the double doors leading to the examining rooms. Don't let that be Conor, she prayed, picturing the three-year-old frightened by his surroundings.

"Come with me," the nurse instructed.

Cristine walked through the double doors and her stomach tightened with dread as they passed another long desk. To the right was a larger room with curtains separating hospital beds. She could see the feet of those attending and hear the moans of patients. It had to be Conor crying because the nurse was leading her toward the source of that commotion.

"Here we are," the nurse said, drawing back the curtain.

Poor Paula was sitting on the side of the bed, trying to comfort Conor who was standing up in a high metal crib, reaching out for his mother and trying to climb out.

"Paula, thank God you're all right."

Paula turned her head and began crying. "Oh, Cristine . . ."

Cristine walked past the nurse who was closing the curtain and wrapped Paula in a very light hug. She kissed the top of her braided hair. "It's all right, Paula. You and Conor are all right." Reaching out to the frightened child with her hand, she added, "What a brave little guy you are."

Conor slapped her hand away and clawed at the empty space between himself and his mother. "Mama, mama, maaaaaaaaa . . ."

"What do we have to do to get you both out of here? Tina said it's just fractured ribs, not that a fractured anything is to be taken lightly, but—"

Paula sniffled and finished her thought. "But it could have been so much worse."

"So can you be released?"

Paula nodded. "I just need to get dressed. They've written out a prescription for me. Thank God, Conor is unharmed." She reached out and let him clutch her hand again. "The nurse said it's actually good that's he's crying like that, lessens the chance of a . . . a concussion." And she started crying again which only frightened Conor more and his crying became louder.

"Then let's get you dressed, okay? The sooner we get you both home, the better." Cristine picked up Paula's jeans from a chair and said, "I'll help you." She knelt down and held open the jeans as Paula put one leg and then the other into them.

Cristine slid them up Paula's hips as Paula held up the hospital gown and then she pulled up the zipper as far as she could. Paula tried to suck in her belly, then moaned in pain.

"Oh, jeez," she cried with fresh tears. "Now I can't get them closed. I . . . I mean . . . I know they're tight, but if I sucked in and pulled and . . ."

"Oh, who gives a shit?" Cristine asked, giving up the

struggle. "So leave them undone. Wear your top over it and no one will see. Now let me help you get that gown off." Cristine untied the gown in the back and Paula slid it down her arms. She was naked from the waist up. Cristine quickly turned back to the chair and handed Paula her top.

"What about my bra?"

"Do you think you can wear it, with the ribs?"

Paula, trying to hide herself with the front of the gown, was also trying to calm down her son. She looked like she was about to lose it again.

"Listen, Paula, just put the top on. Let's not even try for the bra, okay? Why put yourself through it?"

"But my boobs . . ." she muttered in misery. "They become part of my waistline without the bra."

"For God's sake, Paula, you've had five children and breast-fed each one of them. Where did you think they'd be? Up around your earlobes?"

Paula stopped crying. "Don't make me laugh. It hurts. Okay, give me the top. You're right—what do I care?"

"That's my girl," Cristine said soothingly, pulling the top over her head and stretching it as wide as the material allowed to get Paula's arms into it. Each time Paula tried to raise them, she cried out in pain, doubled over, and clutched her side. "This isn't going to work," Cristine declared. "Let me think."

"Why couldn't I have worn something with buttons this morning?" Paula murmured, her top gathered in the stretched circle around her neck as she once more tried to comfort Conor.

"Okay, I've got it," Cristine said, pulling off her suit jacket. "You'll wear my blouse."

"Oh, Cristine, I couldn't."

"Yes you can," Cristine answered, already unbuttoning her white pleated blouse.

"But you're much smaller than I am in the chest."

"Thanks for reminding me," she said with a grin as she slid her arms out of it. "Besides, it's that stretchy cotton. We'll make it fit."

Conor's cries lessened to pitiful whimpers as he watched the women in front of him disrobe once again.

"See, I told you it would be too small."

Cristine blew her breath out as she viewed Paula's breasts crushed behind the buttons that looked like they might pop off at any moment. "Put my jacket on to cover it," she said holding out the sleeves.

"But what will you wear?"

"I'll wear your top. Let's just do this, Paula, and get out of here."

Paula sniffled back fresh emotion as she allowed Cristine to help her into the jacket. "I'm so sorry, Cristine, to pull you into this. I know you're busy."

"Hey," Cristine called out as she easily brought Paula's yellow and white striped top over her head. "Stop being sorry about anything. Don't you know I want to be here for you? We're part of the Yellow Brick Road Gang. Where else would I be but with you?" She smoothed the cotton top down the front of her chest, noticing a fairly large stain under her breasts.

"Pancake syrup," Paula muttered. "Molly had an accident at breakfast. We were running late and I thought no one would see me."

Cristine grinned. "So can you stand now, or do we get a wheelchair?"

"I don't know," Paula answered.

"Fine, I'll go ask a nurse." Cristine opened the curtain and marched out to the long desk with nurses running back and forth. They looked at her strangely when she asked if Paula and Conor could be released, looked specifically at her new stained top. What did she care? As long as she got Paula and her baby home safely, they could take her picture and post it on the hospital's Web site under "emergency room wackos." A lifetime ago she'd dated an intern and the stories of what he'd seen people doing to themselves had been very entertaining. Black humor was big in emergency rooms.

Five minutes later she was holding the crying Conor and walking beside the wheelchair containing Paula. Conor, who didn't acknowledge the grateful good-byes from the staff, was twisting in her arms to get down. She'd just bet their fast exit was due to him and his strong lungs.

Outside, Cristine said, "I'll bring the car up here." She didn't know what to do with Conor.

"Come stand by Mommy and hold my hand," Paula said to her son.

Cristine put him down on the sidewalk and he immediately tried to climb up on his mother's lap.

"No, no, honey," Paula said, painfully keeping her child at bay. "Mommy's hurt and can't hold you. You wait here with me like a good boy until Cristine brings her car and then we'll go for a ride, okay?"

Conor sniffled and rubbed his eyes, looking rejected. "I want McDonald's. You said McDonald's."

"I'll hurry," Cristine promised, and took off into the parking lot at full speed.

The ride to Paula's house was a lesson in patience. With no car seat, Conor sat in the back with Paula and kept getting out of the adult seat belt. Then Cristine had to stop at a pharmacy and pick up Paula's prescription of painkillers and then McDonald's to shut up Conor. By the time they parked in Paula's driveway, Cristine felt like she had put in a full day's work.

And it was only twelve-thirty.

She held the objecting Conor's hand as Paula leaned on her to get up the steps to her front door. Just a few more feet and then they all could relax.

"Thank you for everything, Cristine," Paula said, almost out of breath with the effort. "I know I've ruined your day."

"Nonsense. This was a light day for me. And I already told you this is where I'd want to be, so let's just get inside and then you can lie down."

Paula had her door key ready and she handed it to Cristine. "It's a mess."

"Who cares?" Cristine answered, opening the door and finally letting Conor run into his home. She turned to Paula. "How's the pain?"

"Not as bad as childbirth," Paula answered with a grimace as she stepped inside her sprawling rancher. "At least this time I've got the painkillers."

"So let's get you to bed and then you can take them." She helped Paula through the hallway, hearing Conor turn on the television, and Cristine tried not to look at the chaos inside each bedroom they passed. At the end of the hall was Paula's.

The bed was unmade, clothes were piled high on a rocker in the corner. Toys were scattered on the floor. Paula's night table was littered with papers, bottles of lotion, a brush, a box of Band-Aids, and a collection of Barbie hair accessories, bobby pins, and rubber bands. She led Paula to the bed.

Paula sat down and exhaled deeply. "I told you it was a mess. I just didn't have time with the children and . . ."

She heard Paula sniffle.

"Who cares, Paula? You're home again. You're safe. None of this matters, does it?" She stroked the top of her friend's head. "Let's get you into something more comfortable and then you can take your medication."

Paula nodded, seeming to be in shock now that it was all over. "There's a clean nightgown in that pile on the rocking chair. I just haven't had time to fold anything yet.

Today Ana's biology project was due and I had to help with Alan's book report on Rudyard Kipling and . . ."

Cristine found a wrinkled but clean white cotton nightshirt and brought it over to Paula. "Honey, why don't you let someone take care of you for a change? Let's get you to bed."

Sniffling, Paula nodded. "You're such a good friend."

"So are you, now let me help you get the jacket off." She undressed Paula, noticing the stretch marks on her belly that looked like it was beginning to drop with gravity. As she pulled the soft nightshirt over Paula's head she saw silver threads among the brown. On Hank's night table was a brass picture frame showing him and Paula as a young couple, before they'd had children. Paula looked so alive, so happy and full of life, and Cristine found herself filling with tears at the transformation motherhood had brought to her dear friend. "Okay, now let me help you into bed. How do you want the pillows? Do you want to lie flat or propped up?"

"Maybe propped up for now."

She tenderly helped Paula get situated and then said, "Okay, now let me get you some water and you can take your pills."

"Thank you, Cristine," Paula murmured, closing her eyes briefly.

"Just rest. I'll be right back." She left Paula and hurried into the kitchen. The table held the remnants of that morning's breakfast. The dishwasher was open and full of clean dishes that hadn't been put away, so Cristine took a glass from it and filled it with water. On her way back to Paula, she noticed out of the corner of her eye little Conor standing by the wall in the cluttered family room.

Some instinct made her stop. "Conor, what are you doing?" she asked sweetly as she turned and made her way toward him. He didn't answer her, but the closer she got

the worse the whole scene began to look. On the wall was
a mural of scribble in red crayon! "Don't do that!" she
said, taking the crayon out of his hand. "You can't write
on the walls!" She looked around and spotted a coloring
book lying open on the rug by the television. She picked
it up and put it on the littered coffee table. "Here, use
this."

"No."

"What?"

"No, you're not my mommy." His chin was raised and
his mouth was screwed up with defiance.

"I know I'm not your mommy, but Mommy is sick and
we have to take care of her now. Would Mommy like you
writing on her walls? I don't think so."

"I want my mommy!"

Cristine sighed. His vocabulary had certainly increased now that he was home. "We have to let Mommy
rest. She needs to take a nap," she answered, trying to reason with him. Damn, how was she going to get crayon off
the wall?

*"I want my mommy!"*

"Conor, come see Mommy!" Paula called out from her
bedroom, and off he went, running.

Cristine bit her bottom lip in frustration. She knew she
should be more patient with the child. He'd just gone
through a trauma with the accident and seeing his mother
hurt. But still, when was it going to be Paula's turn? She
felt protective of her friend, who seemed to allow everyone in her life to suck the energy right from her. Coming
into the bedroom, she saw Conor up on the bed, cuddling
into Paula's side as she stroked his back. He looked like a
little cherub and her heart softened.

"Here's your pill," Cristine offered, holding out her
hand and the glass of water.

"What did he do?" Paula asked, her eyes looking
strained.

"Just a little mess. I'll take care of it. Take your pill."

She watched as Paula swallowed and hoped the pill was full of good strong drugs that would knock her out so she'd finally be able to get some peace.

"Don't worry about it, Cristine. I'll get it later . . ." And her head returned to the pillow with a sigh.

"You will not. Maybe the two of you can nap together."

"I'll keep him here with me. It's past his naptime."

Cristine nodded and backed out of the room. "Is there anything else I can get you?"

Paula shook her head. "Just the kids need to be picked up at three-thirty. Alan gets the bus with Molly, so you don't have to worry about them. I'm so sorry to use you like this, Cristine."

"Shut up, will you? That's why I'm here."

"She said a bad word, Mommy," Conor murmured, then rubbed his eyes.

"I'm sorry," Cristine whispered and gently closed the door.

Now what? She walked down the hall to the family room and exhaled with exhaustion. How did Paula do it? No wonder her house looked like this. Kicking off her heels, she proceeded into the kitchen and decided to start there.

She had just cleared the table when she heard a knock on the door.

Hurrying to answer it, afraid that Conor might hear and get up, Cristine opened the door and saw Tina standing there with a bouquet of flowers. "Thank God, you're here!"

"Why, what's wrong? Is it more than the ribs?"

She pulled Tina's suit jacket to get her into the house. "You have to help me. I can't do all this alone."

"Do what? And why are you wearing that top with that skirt?"

Cristine placed her hands on Tina's shoulders and turned her toward the family room. "See for yourself.

And . . . and young Conor Picasso left us a masterpiece on the wall that somehow has to be removed."

"Oh, my God . . ."

"Exactly. There's laundry all over the place that has to be folded and put away. But be quiet. Conor is napping with Paula and we'll never get anything done if he's up."

"*We.* I'm only here for my lunch hour."

"Then take an extended one, Tina, because this is more than a one-woman job."

Tina walked over to the masterpiece. "My mother would have whooped my behind for that."

"Paula doesn't know about it and she's not up to whoopin' anything right now. I hope she sleeps until tomorrow."

Tina turned back to her. "How is she?"

Shrugging, Cristine said, "I think, now that she's home, it's really hitting her. She was probably just holding it all together at the hospital." She jerked her head to the right. "Come in the kitchen. I'm starting in there."

Together they cleaned and talked.

"You know, I'm more than a little ticked at Hank. He's always working and Paula is left alone with all this. Obviously she's overwhelmed, raising five kids by herself."

Now that the dishes were put away, the dishwasher reloaded, Tina was wiping down the counter as Cristine swept the floor. "You don't know this family dynamic, Cristine. Maybe it's what Hank and Paula agreed to."

"Well, Paula needs help. No wonder she always loved getting together with the gang. It must feel like escaping prison to her."

"Maybe it's the only time she can be herself," Tina countered. "Not mommy or wife or PTA mother or soccer mom or chauffeur. Hard to believe sometimes she's a thesis away from her master's in anthropology. You'd think she'd be able to apply some tribal structure in this house."

"Did you call Claire and the rest of them?"

"They'll be over after work. They wanted to know what they could do. I should have told Claire to call Merry Maids to run through the place."

Cristine stopped sweeping and looked at Tina. "You know, maybe that's what we can do for Paula, until the ribs heal. Why don't we all pitch in and get her a cleaning service?"

Tina rinsed out her sponge. "Not a bad idea. But would Paula agree?"

"Look, did I really agree to go to the Bahamas? I was drunk. But you guys made me go. It'll be a done deal and she'll have to go with it."

Tina held the dustpan for Cristine. "She would never want someone in here like this."

"I know. That's why we're all going to clean this place today and then talk to the older kids about keeping it that way. And then I'm going to have a talk with Hank. This is an emergency and he's going to have to adjust to helping out." Putting the broom away, Cristine sighed. "C'mon, let's tackle the family room next. And you should call Claire and tell her to pick up a slew of pizzas for dinner tonight. No one is going to mess up that kitchen, if I have anything to say about it."

Tina laughed. "You'd be a tough mom."

Cristine looked at the crayon on the wall. "Are you kidding me? Spending a day here is like aversion camp. Who wants kids? I don't think I have the strength for it."

"Sure you do," Tina said with a laugh. "Just don't have five."

"What about you?"

Tina sighed as she gathered the crayons and put them back into their box. "I grew up with five brothers and a sister. Being the second to the oldest and a girl, I feel like I've already raised my kids, thank you. Even now, whenever

I cook, I still find myself making enough to feed a family of nine. I'm not in any hurry, if ever."

Cristine nodded, understanding Tina's hesitancy. "So, since you're the expert, do you know how to get crayon off a painted wall?"

Kids . . . she was starting to rethink her plan.

Maybe she was too old, too impatient, too tired.

# Chapter

# 15

CRISTINE CRAWLED INTO BED WITHOUT TAKING A shower to wash off the grime, the cleaning products, the pizza, the dirty bathwater, or the blue Magic Marker that had leaked onto her thumb . . . let alone her makeup, or whatever was left of it. She could smell her armpits, having worked herself into a sweat more times than she could count while getting Paula's house in order. She'd picked up the two kids in grade school, allowed them to peek in on their mother, fed them, supervised homework while folding the rest of the laundry, and waited for reinforcements to arrive. Then the older ones came running loudly into the house and she'd had to sit them down and explain everything again, while Alan raided the refrigerator and Molly began crying. She'd calmed Molly down, then took Alan to his baseball practice while Molly watched the younger children. She was into her third load of laundry when she had to leave and pick up Alan and when they returned, she supervised the lot of them in cleaning up their rooms amid playing and protests. It had never ended, even when Claire and Isabel and Tina and Kelly had come with food and help with the baths.

She'd talked to the gang about the cleaning service and everyone had agreed to pitch in for Paula. Then she had left Claire with instructions to talk to Hank when he came home around nine. Claire would be the person best suited for that job.

It was only nine-thirty and she was too tired to get up and clean herself. How did Paula do it? Day after day, every day? Lying in her clean bed, in her clean house, Cristine felt like crying. And not just from exhaustion. All she could picture was that photograph of Paula, young, hopeful, happy. She wished she had never seen it. Was that what happens? Did a woman give away her identity, her dreams, her life force, to raise a family? Cristine knew she couldn't have done it. There was Paula, once so close to getting her master's degree, now overwhelmed with a big family and the unending chores of keeping them all intact. It was beyond thankless.

She wondered if the love Paula felt from her family balanced that out.

It would have to, just to keep her getting up each morning.

And then she thought of her mother again. She pictured some faceless hippie flower child, living in a commune, pregnant by someone, deciding she couldn't take care of her. She better understood the sacrifice now, and the blame she'd always assigned her mother lessened. Maybe she was more like her mother than she had ever wanted to admit.

Maybe she wasn't cut out for the sacrifices of motherhood.

That possibility depressed her and the tears continued to fall.

This wasn't easy, this business of life. Especially the motherhood part. Forget about the commercials or the movies or the greeting cards touting the merits of mother and child.

Maybe she should just get a dog.

But no cats. Not yet, anyway.

Cristine awoke the next morning feeling like she had a hangover. And she was late, so she had to rush through her morning routine. She drove straight to Paula's to check up on her and was pleased to see the house was still in relative order and Paula was doing better. Then she made it to the office just in time to get the call from the title company that the settlement was scheduled for Lillian's home next week. That was superfast, even for a cash deal. She phoned Mamie with the information and then played phone tag with the agent from Sotheby's. She was showing Alice Shandell's house in less than an hour, so she rushed through the remaining paperwork on her desk and barely had time to find Tina and let her know she was leaving.

She was meeting the prospective buyers at the house and she hoped that Alice's son had cleared out his room. Maybe she should prepare the clients, just in case. When she turned onto the doctor's street, she saw an SUV parked in front of the property. She pulled up behind it, checked the name in her appointment book, picked up her portfolio and got out.

A woman left the van and met her.

"Nancy? Hi, I'm Cristine Dobbins."

They shook hands.

"Hi, I'm really excited to see this house. I've wanted to live in this neighborhood for years." She was in her mid-thirties and grinning broadly as she glanced at the home.

"Your husband isn't with you today?" It was always better to show a house to a couple, rather than just one.

"He's working. We can bring him back later, can't we, if it's everything I hope it is?"

Cristine smiled at the woman, dressed in an attractive pantsuit. "Of course. How did you hear about us?"

"Oh, I drive by this neighborhood all the time, and when I saw your sign yesterday on the lawn, I just knew I had to call to see it."

"Well, why don't we do that?" Cristine asked, opening her portfolio. "And here's a brochure listing all the amenities you'll find."

Together they walked up to the front door and Cristine mentioned the in-ground sprinkler system, the mature trees. She unlocked the front door and allowed Nancy to explore on her own. Good for Alice, Cristine thought as she looked about the place. Clutter was gone and scented plug-ins were in light sockets.

Since she was not the one who'd made the appointment, Cristine looked down at her information sheet. "How long have you lived in the area, Nancy?"

The woman turned from examining the kitchen. "Oh, I grew up in Haverton."

"So you have a house now?"

"Yes. Not this big. This has four bedrooms, right?"

"It does. Is your home on the market?"

"Not yet. I wanted to find the right place first."

"Actually, Nancy, that might not always be the safest route. This home just went on the market a few days ago, but in today's market it could be sold within the week for all we know." She saw the look of disappointment on the woman's face. "I'm not pressuring you. I just want you to know that if you're seriously looking, you might want to think about listing your house. With the interest rates so low right now, houses don't stay unsold for long. That's good news for the seller, but not always for the potential buyer."

"Has someone else been looking at this house?"

"I think you're the first. But don't do anything until you know you're ready. We're just looking today."

"But I already know I love it. Unless the roof is falling in, this is my dream home. I can see my kids playing in the backyard. It has a great school system. It's everything I want."

Cristine smiled. "And now comes the big question, and

I don't mean to appear rude. Can you afford it? It's listed at four hundred and ninety-nine thousand."

Nancy's face lost it's hopefulness. "I know. Half a million. I never thought I'd be looking at a house in that price range. You think the owners would come down?"

"My first obligation is to represent the owners and get the best price for them. You might want to contact another agency to represent you, but I will tell you that real estate, residential real estate, today is about compromise. Where's your house?"

"Over in Glen Oakes. We bought it nine years ago. It's our first home."

"Did you refinance when the interest rates dropped?"

"No, we kept saying we should, but never did."

"What's your rate now?"

Nancy thought about it. "I think it's eight, or eight and a half."

Cristine pictured the very nice town houses in Glen Oakes. "Nancy, you could sell your house, use that money as a down payment, and with a new mortgage at a much lower interest rate and with some creative financing you might be paying slightly more than you're paying right now in Glen Oakes. Those town houses are going for three hundred thousand."

Her face transformed. "Really? You mean, this isn't completely hopeless?"

"Nothing is completely hopeless, Nancy. C'mon, let's take a look upstairs. Besides the master, there's three other bedrooms. One's being used as an office and the other . . . it's a really fun guest bedroom." Cristine pictured the monkey room and grinned. "At least I love it, but it's not everyone's taste."

Cristine led the woman up the stairs and Nancy said from behind her, "This would be so simple if I was the lucky one who won the lottery, but I have to work for my money, I guess."

Cristine's ears perked up. "The lucky one?" she asked as she reached the top of the stairs.

"Didn't you hear? It was on the news this morning. Someone in Haverton won the lottery, and the state said they tracked the winning ticket to that QuickMart on Westover."

Cristine felt her mouth go dry. Lots of people bought lottery tickets there. It didn't mean anything. Swallowing hard to bring moisture back into her mouth, she said, "Really? How much was it? The lottery . . ."

Nancy was already heading to the master bedroom. "I think they said thirty-six million. Oh, my, would you look at the size of this room! Do you think they'd leave the window treatments? It's really such a lovely material and I . . ."

Cristine didn't actually hear the rest of Nancy's statement. Her head was starting to spin. Even though everything in her experience told her the odds were against her, she had the oddest feeling rushing through her body, like when she'd entered the guest room down the hall. Leaving Nancy to her explorations, Cristine walked toward the room. She stood inside the doorway and stared at the monkeys holding the candles and the light fixtures, the ones in the silky bedspread swinging from vines.

It would be too bizarre, and she had a moment out of time, seeing how it all fit together. She'd met Mamie Pitcairn, a very wealthy woman who got her thinking about money, real wealth kind of money. Through Mamie she met Lillian who told her cardiologist, Alice Shandell, about finding her house. Through listing Alice Shandell's house she'd seen the power of her mind in creating her reality, and now, as if by chance, in showing Alice's house she'd heard about someone in Haverton winning the damn lottery! At the same store where she had bought two tickets right before getting that phone call about Paula's accident!

Good God, could it be *her*?

"Wow, this is a wild room," Nancy remarked, walking ahead of her into the bedroom. "But somehow it works, doesn't it?" The woman turned her head, waiting for a response. "Are you okay? Your face looks . . . pale."

Cristine blinked, bringing herself back to the present. "I'm sorry. I'm fine. Yes, yes, it does work."

"I love the monkeys! It takes real decorating courage to do this and pull it off."

"I love them too," Cristine murmured, swearing if she had, by some miracle of the universe, won the lottery, she would help Nancy get her dream home.

And it took every ounce of willpower to complete the viewing and not bolt out of the house to check the winning numbers.

She waited until Nancy drove away before opening her purse and searching for the tickets she had thrown in yesterday. The receipt for Paula's medication. The paper with her shopping list and . . . there they were, stuffed at the bottom. Her hands were shaking as she brought them out. She turned over one ticket and read in small print the telephone number to call. Reaching for her cell phone, she flipped it open.

A recording told her everything she wanted to know.

A half hour later she calmly walked into her house, stepped out of her heels and took off her suit jacket. She carried her purse into the kitchen and placed it carefully on the counter. Opening her refrigerator, she did something she hadn't done in days.

"Daniel? Are you there?" Her voice was low and controlled.

She took out a half-finished bottle of wine and two glasses. Pouring the wine into both, she waited.

"Are you happy?"

This time she didn't even jump when she heard his

voice behind her. Slowly, she turned to him. He was beaming, as though very satisfied with himself.

"Did you do it?"

"Did I do what?"

"Did you fix the lottery so I would win?"

He came closer to her. "I thought you would be extremely pleased, yet your energy shows confusion."

"I need to know, Daniel, if you fixed the numbers."

"Cristine, *you* did it. You set your intention and, finally, you released it to the universe to work out how it came to you." He tilted his head. "You should be very pleased with yourself. I am very pleased with your effort."

"You didn't do this?"

"Why are you doubting yourself now, when you have manifested exactly what you wanted?"

She took a deep breath. "Because it's so . . . so *unbelievable,* that's why!"

He laughed. "Let me give you the next lesson. If you want to keep what you have manifested, believe that it is yours and you deserve it totally and completely, or it will disappear to someone whose intent is stronger. Besides, you don't own it."

"I don't?"

He shook his head. "You don't own anything material, in true reality. But you may play with it for as long as you know you are worthy of it and it serves you to evolve. You *are* the creator of your life. Now you will not only believe it, but also know it in every cell of your body. You did this, not me."

"But I don't know how . . ." She was too shocked to fully understand his meaning.

"Drink your wine and we shall sit down and I will explain it in more detail."

Cristine nodded and handed him his glass. She followed him into the living room and sat down stiffly on the sofa like a doll that had been bent at the waist and placed on the cushion.

"Take a sip, Cristine," Daniel advised.

She did as he directed, still attempting to deal with the shock of it all.

Daniel sat next to her, holding his glass in both hands. "When you bought those tickets and you believed, really and truly believed, that you had a right to an abundant life, you sent your desire out into the invisible worlds of the universe. Then your friend needed you and so you didn't pick at your desire with your doubts or your lack of self-worth. You had no time to focus on yourself and worry it away, as you had been doing the times before that. You didn't even think about the lottery because you were so busy giving of yourself without thought of any return. You just gave because it felt right for you to do so. That was unconditional love and love, like any commodity of energy, will seek to find a return circuit. For you, it was through your most recent and strongest desire. To win the lottery."

She stared into her wine glass. "So I won because I was so preoccupied with Paula I didn't sabotage myself like I usually do?"

Daniel chuckled. "I suppose you could say that. You got out of your own way and allowed the energy of the universe to work for you."

Blinking, Cristine still couldn't believe it and she knew she had to, or it might all go away. "So the old saying is true? I'm my own worst enemy?"

"And your own best friend. The trick is to find the right balance in censoring those thoughts that don't serve you and nurturing the ones that do."

She finally brought the wine glass up to her mouth.

"Don't gulp!" Daniel warned.

She gulped. "This is a time for gulping," she muttered.

"Really, there is such a time?"

Oh, he was so innocent, Cristine thought, and grinned for the first time since she'd left her client. "There is. Most definitely. And this is it."

She watched as Daniel gulped his wine.

"I won the lottery, Daniel," she said softly, feeling like she might explode at any moment.

"I know, Cristine. Well done."

"Daniel?"

"Yes?"

"I won."

"Yes, I know."

"I mean I won! *Really, really won!*"

He laughed. "Actually, you manifested the winning part of it. You didn't really win anything."

"Daniel Burns, I don't care how you rationalize it, I *won* thirty-six million dollars!" She was staring at him in amazement. *"Thirty-six million! Dollars!"*

"Yes, Cristine. I know that."

"This is a big deal. A really big deal, Daniel. Of course, after taxes it's probably going to be half that, but still . . . I'll never have to worry about money again."

"Your survival issues will be resolved," he said, then finished off the last of his wine.

"Thank you, Daniel," she said sincerely. "Thank you for coming into my life and for . . . for everything."

"You are welcome, Cristine. But you do know in true reality all your needs had already been met. You were never without the means to survive. That you are here, alive, proves that." He paused, and then grinned. "So what are you going to do with your manifestation?"

She grinned back. "I'm going to celebrate. *We're* going to celebrate!"

"We are?" he asked, surprised.

Cristine nodded. "Absolutely. I mean, you can go out with me, can't you? Outside? To a restaurant? You won't like . . . blink away?"

He laughed. "How long will this celebration last?"

"I don't know, until we're done. A few hours."

"I would very much like to celebrate with you."

She jumped up. "Great! Now I'm going to get ready. I'll meet you back here in an hour? Will that give you time to . . . to recharge, or whatever you do?"

Grinning, he stood up. "Recharge. That's a good way to put it."

"And do you have a suit? I mean, can you get a suit, a man's suit like . . ." She picked up a magazine from the coffee table, flipped through it, and found an advertisement with a male model standing next to a female modeling an Armani dress. "Like that."

He looked at the glossy page. "I believe I can manifest such a garment."

"Goody," she answered with a giggle, and gave him the magazine. "So give me an hour to pull my act together and then, Daniel Burns, you and I are going to paint the town red."

His eyes widened. "I beg your pardon? Paint the town?"

"It's an expression. It means we're going to have some fun."

"But no painting?"

"No painting."

He looked down at the magazine. "This is suitable for painting the town red?"

"Yes, Daniel. It's just right. Now you go and recharge, and so will I.

"Go," she commanded with a big grin. "Go on. I have to get ready the old-fashioned way. And I have to make reservations and wash my hair and—"

He held up his hand. "I'm going."

And with a swirl of tiny white lights, he went.

An hour later, Cristine was dressed in a sapphire-blue dress with simple black heels. It was as though nothing could go wrong today, she thought as she inserted her pearl earrings. Her hair had turned out better than ever before, curling around her face, and her makeup was flawless. She looked at herself in the mirror, adjusted the cap sleeves that rested on the edge of her shoulders, and smiled at her reflection.

"As good as it gets," she murmured, excited by everything.

This was going to be a night to remember.

She was a lottery winner and she was going out for the evening with an angel!

Who'd believe it?

Realizing what she was thinking, she quickly closed her eyes and said, "Delete, delete. *I* believe it! I truly, truly believe it!"

She exhaled loudly and turned to go downstairs.

He was waiting for her in the living room and Cristine had to hold on to the banister to steady herself. Daniel was dressed in the exact Armani suit with the same shirt and tie, with his dark sandy hair combed back, just like the model in the magazine.

"Melt my heart," she murmured, squaring her shoulders and walking toward him.

"You look wonderful, Daniel."

"It is you who looks wonderful," he answered, smiling as he looked at her from head to toe. "I think I am going to enjoy painting the town red with you. What do we do first?"

She grinned. "First, we get my purse and then I'll drive you to dinner."

"Drive? In your vehicle?"

Nodding as she went into the kitchen for her purse, she said, "That's the normal way to get around in this dimension. The restaurant is too far to walk." She picked up her plain black Coach purse and added, "Don't worry. I'm a good driver."

"It will be an adventure," Daniel answered, waiting for her by the door.

She had made reservations at a restaurant, Merimako, that she'd heard had a very good selection of vegetarian meals. The drive took less than ten minutes and Daniel had been fascinated, looking out the window at everything they'd passed. By the time they were seated at their table, Cristine's jaw was beginning to ache from smiling so much.

"Do you like it?" she asked, watching Daniel take everything in, the other diners, the contemporary theme that included Asian art and floral arrangements.

"Yes. Yes, I do," he answered, giving her his attention. "This was a very good suggestion."

"Don't worry about anything. I'll order," she said, opening her leather-bound menu. "They have a variety of vegetarian appetizers and meals."

She ordered wine and soup shots, which turned out to be shot glasses filled with a variety of tortellini soup, butternut squash bisque, and yellow tomato gazpacho. It pleased her to watch Daniel taste each one and see his face light up with culinary delight.

"How does this sound?" she asked, perusing the menu. "We'll start with miniature Parmagiana Frico with fresh herb and pear salad, then for our entrée . . . roasted baby eggplant stuffed with Mediterranean vegetables, pine nuts, raisins, and feta cheese?"

"It sounds . . . very exotic."

She laughed. "It does, doesn't it? This is an adventure for me too, Daniel. I think perhaps I could get used to vegetarian food if someone would prepare these kinds of dishes for me."

"It would be better for you. To eliminate eating animals."

She grimaced. "Please, Daniel, for tonight, don't bring that up again. I *know* you're right, but to prepare these kinds of meals takes time."

"You will have time now, Cristine. You don't have to work so much, or not at all."

She hadn't even thought about that. "I don't think I would stop working. Why should I? Maybe I would just cut back. What would I do with my time?"

"You would evolve."

"But a person can't spend all their time doing that," she protested. "They have to have a life too."

"That is what your life is about, Cristine, why you are here at this time, in this dimension. It's time to figure it out and move on."

"Okay, can we not have this discussion tonight? I promise, tomorrow we can talk all you want, but tonight can we just celebrate?"

His eyes softened and his smile was tender. "Forgive my impatience. Tonight is your night to celebrate."

"It's *our* night to celebrate, Daniel. Give yourself a pat on the back. You're a very good teacher."

He seemed to beam with her compliment. "Thank you."

"Now, let's really celebrate." She held up her wine glass.

"Gulping?" he asked with a grin.

She laughed and shook her head. "No gulping outside the house, or you'll stun everyone here by disappearing and I'll be too drunk to explain."

They were almost through their delicious meal when Cristine heard her name being called. She looked over her shoulder and saw Claire approaching. Her heart sank.

"I thought that was you," Claire said, standing at their table and looking with appreciation at Daniel. "My boss's wife is throwing him an anniversary party and attendance is part of the job description." She looked at Cristine and raised her eyebrows in question.

"Claire, this is Daniel Burns. Daniel, my very good friend Claire Hutchinson."

Claire, looking fabulous as usual in a tiny black dress, put out her hand to Daniel and he smiled while shaking it.

"Nice to meet you," Claire said.

"It is very nice to meet you, Claire," Daniel answered.

"Daniel? Is this the man who finished your kitchen so quickly?" Claire asked, giving Cristine a look that said *why don't I know about this* and *we need to talk*.

Cristine gulped. There was so much she hadn't told Claire, or anyone. Tonight, however, wasn't the time for a full disclosure. "Yes, Daniel is truly gifted."

Claire seemed to take the hint. "Well, I didn't mean to interrupt your dinner. Why don't the two of you come to the party for a drink after you're finished? It's in the back of the restaurant and there's a small band playing."

Cristine shook her head. "I don't think so. We're just—"

"Daniel," Claire interrupted. "Will you please bring my good friend back for one drink? She thinks she'll be intruding, but I really would like to introduce her to some people." She turned to Cristine. "Honey, the networking alone is worth it."

Daniel looked at Cristine.

"I don't know . . . I'm really tired." How could she get out of this gracefully? And with Claire, of all people? "We'll see," she said, not committing herself to anything.

Claire bent down and kissed her cheek while whispering, "Come, or I'm going to show up on your doorstep tonight." She raised her head and smiled brilliantly to both of them. "So I'll see you in a little while. It's directly in the back, a banquet room. Enjoy the rest of your meal."

She walked away and Cristine sighed, her good mood deflated.

"Why don't you want to go?" Daniel asked.

"Because," Cristine said. "How do I explain you? I know Claire, and she's putting two and two together and thinks we're dating. And we're not."

"Dating?"

"Two people seeing each other. For romantic reasons."

"Well, we do see each other, Cristine."

"Yes, as friends. She won't see it like that."

"Do you care? Is it so important what Claire thinks?"

She sighed again and sat back in her chair. "Claire is my best friend, well, one of my best friends, so yes, I do care what Claire thinks. I've kept you a secret and she'll never understand. Even *I* don't understand how you can be real and sitting there across from me like . . . like this is a date, only it's not. My friends are very important to me. They're like my family, the only family I've got."

"So if she is important to you, what harm can there be if we go to her party and have one drink as she said?"

Cristine shrugged. "Fine," she said in defeat. "But one drink and then we're leaving. Do you think you can . . . stay together that long?"

Daniel sipped the rest of his wine and smiled. "I am feeling just wonderful," he stated.

Cristine groaned.

This was going to be another challenge. She could feel it gathering, all the makings of a disaster.

# Chapter
## 16

"Cristine, this is Mark Adams, chief financial officer for Alliance Bank. Cristine is a realtor. She just sold a home to Mamie Pitcairn's mother." Cristine shook the hand of the older man standing next to Claire.

"Well, think of us if you haven't already decided on a mortgage company," the man said good-naturedly.

"It's a cash settlement," Cristine answered with a smile.

"And this is Daniel Burns," Claire said. "A building contractor. I've seen his work and it's fabulous."

Mark Adams shook Daniel's hand. "Are you independent?"

Daniel looked confused. "Are we ever truly independent? Don't we all depend on each other every day?"

Cristine's heart dropped, until Mark burst out laughing.

"Well said, young man. I don't know what I'd do without Claire here giving me advice. I can look about this room and see at least twenty people I'm connected to in business. Do you have a card?"

"A card?"

Cristine stepped in. "Actually, we just stopped in to see Claire. I'll give her the information. If you'll excuse us . . . ?" She pulled on Daniel's sleeve. "Let's dance."

"Dance?"

Did he *have* to repeat everything like that? She continued to pull him toward the dance floor. "It was a pleasure to meet you, Mark. Enjoy your evening, Claire." She left the surprised Claire and her banking friend to stare after them.

When they reached the dance floor, Cristine turned to Daniel. "Do you know how to dance?"

"Were we not rude to those people back there? The man appeared to be interesting, open to new ideas and—"

"And those ideas, Daniel, were about to come flowing. I could feel you warming up. This isn't the time or the place. Mark Adams would never understand you." She could see Claire continuing to stare at them. "Now, do you know how to dance?"

He looked around at the other couples. "It doesn't appear to be too difficult."

"Fine," she answered, holding her purse and moving in closer to him. "Now, just put your arms around my waist."

He did as she asked.

"And now I'll put my arms around you and we sway . . . like this . . ." She moved her hips slightly, leading him to follow. "Nothing difficult. No steps. That's right. Swaying."

"Cristine, why are you so worried? No one suspects anything. You can relax."

No she couldn't. She wouldn't be able to relax until they were out of this place, she thought. And it didn't help that her entire body was beginning to hum or vibrate or *something* just by having Daniel holding her like this.

"Cristine," he whispered. "You are safe with me. Would it make you happy if I disappear?"

"No!" She held him tighter, closer. "You can't do that here!"

He grinned and then looked at the couple next to them. "We are not doing this correctly."

Cristine turned her head to see the man and the woman swaying a little suggestively. "They're probably married."

He seemed to be studying them. "They are, but not to each other."

She couldn't help it. She laughed.

"Good. You released your tension."

And she did feel better, more relaxed, so she moved even closer. "Men and women in this dimension who like each other put their faces close, their heads side by side. Like this . . ."

He seemed to inhale her, and she clutched her purse to his shoulder blades to stay upright. Her breasts seemed to ache as they brushed up against his chest and her entire being felt a sudden urge to . . . to merge, to unite. She exhaled deeply with the effort to control herself.

Daniel pulled back and stopped swaying. "Cristine . . ." His face looked tortured. "Cristine, I cannot dance with you and remain—"

She nodded. "Okay." He didn't have to say any more. She understood completely. "C'mon," she added. "Let's get out of here."

She didn't even say good-bye to Claire as she led Daniel out of the banquet room, out of the restaurant, and onto the street.

"There," she said as they started walking toward her parked car. "Fresh air. Do you feel better?"

"Yes, thank you. Much better. I am sorry I couldn't stay there and dance. I felt you were enjoying it."

She laughed. "Yes, I was, but I understood completely. I remember how you couldn't hold yourself together when I kissed you. I guess I should apologize for—"

She felt a hard bump and then her purse was torn out of her hands. It happened so quickly that she barely had time to register the man running away in a hooded sweatshirt.

"My purse!" she yelled after him and looked at Daniel. "The ticket is inside it!"

And then something happened that later she would question whether her eyes had been playing tricks on her. Daniel disappeared in a trail of light dust and reappeared down the street in front of the man. He held his arm out and the man's neck connected with it and he went down on the sidewalk. She saw Daniel reach for her purse and then place his hand on top of the man's head. A light appeared around his hand and the hooded top seemed to disappear with the brightness. Daniel then helped the man to stand. He spoke to him and the man stumbled away.

Very calmly, Daniel began walking back to her with her purse.

It was only then she noticed Claire at the doorway of the restaurant. Claire's jaw had dropped open.

"Good evening, Claire," Daniel said as pleasantly as if nothing at all had happened. "Your party was very nice, but Cristine is tired and wants to go home."

He continued to walk toward her and Cristine found herself meeting him closer to Claire. Her heart was racing and she could feel her pulse in her fingertips.

"You left," Claire murmured, looking at Cristine and then Daniel. "Without saying a word."

"I . . . I'm sorry, Claire. You were with business contacts and I didn't want to disturb you," Cristine called out. "I'll phone you tomorrow. I promise."

She reached for Daniel's arm and pulled him along the sidewalk. "Don't look back," she whispered to Daniel, feeling her entire body throbbing with a frightening mixture of excitement, dread, and fear.

"I wasn't going to," he replied, calmly walking beside her.

What was she ever going to say to Claire? How much

had her friend seen? How could she ever explain it? They reached her car and when she looked up the street, Claire was no longer at the door of the restaurant. They got in the car and Cristine just sat, staring out the windshield. "She saw you. She saw you stop that man and put your hand on his head. I know she had to have seen that light."

"She would only have seen it if her mind was open to it," Daniel replied, handing her the purse. "Your ticket is safe."

She turned her head and looked at him, her emotions now coming to the surface. "Thank you, Daniel. I should never have brought it with me, but I was scared to leave it at home and—"

"And your fear was manifested by someone trying to take it from you. Cristine, you have to begin controlling your thoughts. You have been given an excellent example tonight of how your thoughts create your reality."

She slowly shook her head. "But it would be like rewiring my brain myself. After a lifetime of worry, how do you stop it?"

"You catch yourself and you immediately realize such thoughts don't serve you. You have to begin to see yourself as a creator, an extraordinary being who, through cultural conditioning, forgot your true identity."

She touched the center of her forehead as she felt the beginning of a headache. "That goes against everything I have been taught, to believe I am extraordinary. It isn't accepted behavior."

"And who taught you not to think of yourself as extraordinary?"

She shrugged. "I didn't have parents, not real parents, but my goal with a foster family was to not make waves, to not speak my mind, and fit in. Then there were the schools and the churches. No one tells you that you are extraordinary."

"Can you not see that the cultural conditioning you, and every other child, were subjected to was intended to control you, to tell you how to think, to not use your imagination, your mind, which is yours alone? No one wanted you to think you were extraordinary, because they didn't believe they were. And so it has been passed down, through each generation, like a virus of the mind. And what makes it all the more curious is that in this time it is most vocal from those who claim to follow a being who specifically told them they were capable of manifestations greater than his own. I tell you, Cristine, if you truly believed in every cell of your being that you could walk on water, you would. That is how powerful your mind is, and why many who are in control don't want you to know that."

"I don't want to walk on water. I just want Claire to forget whatever she saw tonight." She sat behind the steering wheel and crossed her arms over her chest. "I don't know what to say to her tomorrow."

"You can't control another, only yourself. Tell her your truth. That is all anyone can expect."

She turned her head again and stared at him. "Tell her about you?"

He looked at her. "Tell her your truth, but be prepared for rejection."

"I don't want to lose Claire. She's too important to me."

"Cristine, if she loves you, you won't lose her."

She stared into his eyes, trying not to think that eventually she seemed to lose everyone she loved. And she would lose him too. He would go away and she would be left alone. Again. Feeling tears come into her eyes, she tried not to cry.

"Do not be sad. Everything will work out. It always does, doesn't it?'

She shrugged.

"Now I must leave you, as it is becoming more and more difficult to maintain this form. Will you be all right driving your vehicle home?"

She nodded.

He leaned over and kissed the tip of her nose and then he was gone and it felt like all the life had been drained from the car's interior.

She exhaled, feeling her heart pounding, her head throbbing, and suddenly she laughed at herself. She had done it again! She just thought of how he would eventually leave her. And he did, within moments.

She took out her keys and put her purse on the floor in front of her seat. Turning on the ignition, she thought she would have to talk to Claire tomorrow anyway. She had to tell her about the lottery. As a financial adviser, Claire was the perfect person to steer her in the right direction.

That night she signed her name to the back of the ticket, placed it in an envelope, and put it under her pillow. She lay in bed, staring out to the darkness, feeling so alone. She was going to be a millionaire and she had no one, no lover, to share it with, save Daniel, and he wasn't going to hang around forever.

She admitted to herself that she was falling in love with him. Who wouldn't? And how crazy was that? He wasn't even a real man. He was . . . what? Information and energy? That's what he'd said, but it didn't feel like that to her. It felt so *real*. How long did she have? The thought of never seeing him again, of never feeling his presence, made her chest ache and her eyes fill with tears. How was she supposed to go on without him? No ordinary man could ever fill that empty space. She would miss him forever, their conversations, their moments of unity.

"Daniel?" she whispered into the night. "Are you there? Can you hear me?"

Dancing white lights appeared at the foot of her bed.

"Come closer," she murmured, once more in awe of him.

The lights moved around the side of the bed, twirling, coming closer to her. When they began to encircle her, she gasped, "No, wait . . . I want to see you. Please!"

And Daniel, her Daniel, transformed right in front of her, sitting on the bed next to her. She reached out her hand and stroked the side of his face. "You are so beautiful," she whispered. Gathering her courage, she added, "I . . . I want unity with you again, but like this. Can you achieve unity like this?"

"I don't know," he whispered back, staring into her eyes.

"You've never made love, in human form?"

Slowly, he shook his head.

Cristine smiled shyly. "Can we try?"

"We can try anything," he answered, running his finger over her lips.

"It's just that we've had . . . unity your way and I really, really would love to try mine."

Neither of them spoke as Cristine unbuttoned his shirt and slowly pulled it down his arms. She ran her hands ever so softly over his shoulders, down his chest. He inhaled sharply and she stopped, not wanting him to disappear. "Stay with me," she whispered, kneeling in front of him and undoing his jeans. Slowly, she pulled down the zipper.

"Cristine . . ."

"Shh . . ." she murmured. "Let's get these off."

When he was naked, she pulled off her nightgown and held out her hand, bringing him back onto the bed. "Focus on me, Daniel, on my eyes."

He sat against the pillows and she straddled him, gently lowering herself as she held onto his shoulders. Gasping at the naked contact, Daniel said, "I don't know if—"

"Hush," she murmured against his temple, then began kissing his cheek lightly and nibbling his earlobe. "You can do this . . . for me . . . for yourself. Wrap your arms around me. Feel my skin, the way it responds to your touch."

"Something is happening," he gasped, clutching her.

She felt it too. "You're becoming aroused, Daniel."

"It . . . it feels . . ." He was at a loss for words.

Cristine smiled. "Wait till you feel this . . ." And with little effort, she raised herself and took him inside of her.

He groaned with pleasure, closing his eyes and tilting his head back, exposing his neck. Cristine began moving very slowly and his hands slid down to her hips, instinctively guiding her to continue. She watched the surprise, the pleasure, play out in his expression. And then he opened his eyes and she saw something else . . . a light of desire that seemed to burn into her, making her catch her breath.

"I've . . . never felt this," she murmured as her own pleasure began to rise with such ferocity that she stopped moving.

It was as if Daniel drew on a primordial memory, before he had evolved, before he had moved on to another dimension, for without a word he rolled her over onto her back and he was on top of her, following an ancient instinct as he now took control and began moving inside of her.

Cristine wanted to watch him, to see his reaction, to gauge his pleasure, but her own was building as Daniel seemed to come out of her, entice her womanhood to meet him, and then he would thrust back into her warmth. Over and over, she tried to focus on him, but it was hopeless. Her body was betraying her, as her perfect lover, who fit so perfectly, who knew how to please her so well, was rhythmically driving her toward a precipice where she knew she was going to fall hard. And she didn't care. Nothing existed for her but to get there with him.

They gasped. They moaned. They groaned. They pawed each other, clung to each other, and when the moment of exquisite pleasure arrived, Cristine pleaded, "Stay with me, Daniel! Stay!"

He groaned, "Come with me, Cristine!"

And in an instant, as wave after wave of intense joy washed over her, Cristine found herself jerked out of her body . . . clinging to Daniel, soaring into nothingness, and emerging into a divine swirling cloud of celestial light that intensified her pleasure, making it seem endless, a throbbing wave of sheer ecstasy.

She must be dying, for she didn't feel the urge to breathe. She wanted nothing. She thought of nothing, save for the pleasure to continue . . .

And just as suddenly, she heard a voice inside her head commanding her to breathe.

*"Breathe, Cristine!"*

She gasped, sucking air into her lungs, and saw Daniel above her, holding her shoulders. Her heart was pounding furiously as she realized she was lying in bed. She felt him still inside of her and she gasped again.

Daniel withdrew from her and gathered her into his arms as he rolled to lie next to her. "I can't stay like this any longer," he whispered in a shaky voice. "Are you all right?"

"My God, Daniel," she breathed, hearing his heartbeat throbbing against his chest wall. "I don't know what to say."

"Tell me you are all right, Cristine. You worried me."

"I don't know what happened," she murmured, still in awe. "I must have fainted, or . . . or something."

"You left your body. I couldn't hold myself together any longer and your will was to come with me. It was . . . there are no words to describe what you did for me tonight," he added in an emotional voice.

She tightened her hold on him. "Thank you, Daniel. Nothing in my life has ever been so perfect, so exquisite."

"That is a good word, exquisite . . . but even that cannot contain the fullness of what we shared."

"I know you have to go," she said, raising her head. "Just kiss me before you disappear."

He lowered his head and found her lips and, as he devoured her with a new, raw hunger, he transformed and Cristine found herself facedown on the damp sheets.

"I am in so much trouble," she muttered, curling up into a ball to stave off the emptiness at his departure. For she knew, without a shadow of doubt in any of her cells, that she loved Daniel Burns, angel, dimension traveler, whatever he was . . . She wanted him as she had never wanted anyone or anything in her life. Ever. And tonight had just reinforced that in her—

The ringing of the phone interrupted her thoughts and she was so startled that she froze for a moment, unable to move. It kept ringing and she forced herself to drag her arm over to the night table and pick it up. "Hello?" Even to her own ear, her voice sounded out of breath.

"Okay, I don't care how late it is. I was not about to wait until the morning to talk to you."

Cristine closed her eyes. "Hi, Claire."

"I was on my way home and I decided the only way I was going to get any sleep tonight was if I called. I'm two blocks away from your house, so either get up and let me in or I'm going to park in your driveway and start beeping until you do."

Cristine sighed. She couldn't even savor this night. "Claire, can't we do this in the morning? I'm in bed and I promise—"

"Alone?"

"Yes, alone. I promise I'll get up early and we'll have coffee together and I'll explain everything. I'm so tired and . . ." Cristine heard the motor of Claire's BMW in her driveway and saw the headlights race across the front of her house. "And I'll be right there to unlock the door."

Cristine hung up the phone and dragged her body to the edge of the bed. "Oh, dear God," she muttered, wondering if she had the strength to stand up.

She did. Grabbing her nightgown, she pulled it over her head and opened her closet for a robe. She took the stairs slowly, not caring that Claire was probably standing outside her front door, tapping her foot impatiently.

This day had to be the most amazing one of her life, and all she wanted to do was savor it alone before falling into a much-deserved sleep.

Opening the front door, she looked at Claire in her black party dress. Her friend looked annoyed. "Come in," she said.

"Well, thank you. I see you haven't lost all your manners tonight."

She watched Claire stride into her house. "I already apologized for leaving your party. If you remember, I didn't even want to go to it."

"You didn't want me to talk to your new man, is what I'm guessing. The question is why? Why keep him a secret? Why snub me? Why—" Claire paused and her eyes narrowed. "You've just had sex!"

"What?" Cristine asked in shock, touching her face as though it had somehow betrayed her.

"Don't try to deny it. I've seen that look." Her voice lowered. "He's not still here, is he?"

Cristine shook her head. "Claire, can't we do this in the morning?"

Claire was determined and she crossed her arms. "Is it because he's a handyman?"

"Of course not!" Cristine was offended.

"Is it because he's some superhero? 'Cause I'll tell you, Cristine, I didn't have *that* much to drink, and what I saw . . ." She shook her head. "One minute he's stopping some robber and in the next . . . he's doing something to the man that I still can't get a handle on. What the hell happened tonight?"

Cristine sighed and ran her hand through her hair. "Okay, let's go into the kitchen and I'll make some coffee because neither one of us will be getting any sleep."

"Cristine, what's going on?"

She walked past her friend, waving her to follow. "Let me get the coffee started."

"I'm not going to wait until then. Tell me now."

They were in the kitchen when Cristine put her hands on the counter and leaned against it. "First of all, there are two things that are going on right now. One is I've fallen in love. And it'll probably end with me being left again."

Claire's jaw dropped. "You're in love? So fast?"

Cristine hung her head and nodded. "Believe me, Claire, even you, with your strong sense of independence, couldn't have resisted this."

"I'll admit he's good-looking, maybe even great-looking, but—"

Cristine raised her head and held up her hand to interrupt. "Take my word for it. It's got very little to do with his looks."

Claire shrugged. "Well, by the looks of you right now, he must be a good lover."

Cristine half laughed. "He's unbelievable, and I mean that quite literally."

"I don't get it."

"I know."

"So what's the second thing?"

"Okay, here's where it gets truly bizarre."

Claire again crossed her arms and thrust out her hip. "Hit me with your best shot. He's a transsexual? A man in a woman's body?"

Cristine didn't even laugh.

"I won the lottery, Claire. Thirty-six million."

Claire simply blinked.

"Did you hear me? I won the damn lottery!"

# Chapter

## 17

"CLAIRE, SAY SOMETHING."

Her friend visibly swallowed. "You're lying. You're saying that to get me off the Daniel thing."

Cristine grinned. "I'm not lying, Claire. I won. I didn't know until today because I was so busy at Paula's, but I have the ticket upstairs. I won thirty-six million. *Dollars!*"

"You're not lying?"

"I'm not. I swear."

"You won the lottery?"

"I won the lottery."

Claire continued to stare at her. "I don't believe it."

"I know, I know. I don't blame you. I mean, who even knows a lottery winner? But I'm one!" She held her hand over her chest. "I swear to you."

Claire was in such shock that she didn't realize she was holding her breath. She finally exhaled loudly. "If you're pulling my leg, I'll—"

"I'm not pulling your leg!" Cristine interrupted and came around the counter to stand in front of her friend. "Claire Hutchinson, I swear to you I won the lottery, and I'm going to need your help when I collect it."

Eyes wide with shock, Claire grinned widely and

grasped Cristine's shoulders hard. She started jumping up and down with excitement. "Oh, my God! You won the lottery? Oh, my God! *The lottery!*"

Laughing, Cristine jumped with her. "I know!"

They were like two little kids, jumping and laughing, and then Claire stopped and sobered. "That's a lot of money. What are you going to do with it?"

"I don't know. That's where you come in."

"Forget the coffee. I want a drink," Claire said, opening the pantry and bringing out a bottle of Jameson whiskey. "The lottery!" she whispered in awe.

Cristine opened a cabinet and placed a glass on the counter.

"You're not joining me?"

Shaking her head, Cristine said, "I've had enough to drink tonight. Besides, I need to keep a clear head. How do I go about collecting it?"

"Let me research that," Claire said, pouring out the whiskey. And then she shook her head and shivered. "The *lottery!* It hasn't hit me."

Cristine laughed. "I know exactly how you feel."

"All right. Let me think. I'll make a few phone calls tomorrow and get back to you. You know there's going to be publicity. You always see pictures of lottery winners holding that big check and then reporters asking how their lives are going to be changed."

"Okay, I don't want that. Can that be avoided?"

Sipping the whiskey, Claire shrugged. "I don't know. Maybe if you request anonymity? So you're saying you want me to manage this money for you?"

Cristine nodded. "I want to pay off my mortgage and all my bills and then do things for all of you, the gang. Maybe pay off Paula's house and . . . and I know! Send Conor to Coventry Day School and then maybe Paula can finish her thesis and get her master's. And find out what Isabel needs. Is her house paid off? And maybe get her a new wardrobe. Send her to New York and give her a complete makeover. And Tina . . . buy her the house of her dreams, maybe in the islands, so whenever she wants she can chill out on the beach and have her hair braided by little girls."

She was into it now, dreaming of ways to help her friends, and she started pacing back and forth in front of the sink. "What does Kelly need, besides a good man?"

Claire smiled back at her. "All that's very nice, Cristine, but the smartest thing for you to do is to live off the interest and let your money make money for you."

"What would the interest be? I mean, what's the point of having this kind of fantasy money if you can't have some fun with it?"

"So have your fun and then be responsible."

"And I want to do something meaningful, Claire. I don't know what it is yet, but I want this money to help others in some way."

"We can talk about all that once you actually have the money. I promise you won't be one of those winners who's broke in five years. Your money worries in this life are over, Cristine. Will you still work?"

She thought about it. "I don't know. Maybe I'll back off a little. I'm partners with Tina, but she's the brains behind the business. We could hire a few more agents."

Claire raised her glass. "Well, I don't know anyone more worthy of this good fortune. Congratulations, Cristine." She held the glass before her mouth. "Thirty-six million! *Damn!*" Then she gulped and refilled her glass.

"Thanks," Cristine said with a smile of tenderness. It was such a relief to finally tell someone.

Claire sipped her second whiskey and then suddenly put the glass down hard on the counter. Staring at Cristine with wide eyes, she broke into a loud laugh. "Charlie will shit! He'll take to his bed for days when he hears this!

He'll probably have to be hospitalized for a real nervous breakdown!" And she laughed again. "Talk about lousy timing. Serves his cheating ass right!"

Cristine smiled and shook her head. "It never would have happened if I were with Charlie. He was such a passive-aggressive, negative force in my life I never would have even bought the ticket. We're both on very different paths now."

Leaning on the counter, Claire stared at her. "You really are in love, aren't you?"

Cristine simply nodded.

"So tell me about Daniel. How did this start?"

She hesitated. How much could she tell Claire? How much would anyone believe who had not experienced it? "Well, you know he finished my kitchen."

Claire looked around. "And he did a very good job. I wasn't kidding when I told Mark about him." She turned her head toward Cristine. "Which brings me back to why you left like that. It isn't like you to disappear without saying good-bye. Why did you rush Daniel out of there?"

She sighed and ran her hand through her hair. "I felt like . . . like Daniel was on display. You know what a powerful force you can be, Claire. I didn't want to subject him to that just yet. It's so new, almost fragile, and I was being protective."

"What did you think I was going to do? Grill him?"

Cristine laughed. "Yes! That's who you are, Claire. You're like the protector of our little family of friends. Anyone who messes with us, messes with you."

Claire finished her drink and shrugged. "Okay, so I did want to get him aside and tell him if he hurt you I would personally see his life ruined."

Again, Cristine laughed. "Thanks for your love, but if you knew how naïve that statement was, you'd be laughing too. Daniel wouldn't hurt me, not intentionally. Besides, I think he's just passing through."

"Passing through? What does that mean? He's some handyman drifter? I don't think so. Not with that suit he was wearing, unless he charges a fortune for his work."

Cristine didn't say anything.

"Well?" Claire asked. "Does he charge a fortune?"

Shaking her head, Cristine said, "His fee is nothing, compared to what it's worth." So far she hadn't lied.

"So what's his deal? What was that I saw with that guy tonight? I've figured out you had your purse stolen."

"The ticket was inside."

"Oh, my God," Claire breathed in horror.

"I know. Daniel stopped him and got my purse back."

Claire was shaking her head. "But he did something, put his hand on the guy's head and . . . and I swear some weird light appeared. Did you see that?"

Biting the inside of her cheek, Cristine sighed. "I don't know how to explain it. It all happened so quickly. I was just so grateful to him for stopping the man."

"Maybe it was just a reflection from a passing car, or something. It did happen fast, but I could have sworn some kind of weird light was around the man's head. And then he just let him go. Didn't even call the police."

"Daniel got the purse. He wouldn't have wanted to punish the guy. That isn't who he is."

"So who is he?"

Cristine felt her eyes fill with tears. "Someone wonderful. I have to be different this time, Claire. Nothing lasts forever. You and I both know that. I have to be grateful for whatever time I have with him and not try to possess him, make him mine alone."

"Could you really do that?"

Cristine smiled sadly. "I don't think I have a choice with this one."

"Protect your heart then, Cris."

"My heart's already in it, Claire. Deeply and profoundly." She ran her hand over her throat to stop the tears. "I . . . I've never felt like this before, this *connection,* you know?"

Claire smiled and came over to her. She wrapped her arm around Cristine's waist and tilted her head to rest on her shoulder. "This is really something. The lottery *and* being in love. No wonder you've been acting strange."

Cristine snorted with a half-laugh. "You can't even imagine how rattled I've been lately."

Patting Cristine's back, Claire pulled away. "Well, as much as I'd like to stay up all night with a slumber party and hear the rest, I've just added a priority to my morning. I'm going to take off and see if I can manage a few hours of sleep. We'll continue this tomorrow."

"I'm sorry for tonight, Claire," she said, feeling the emotion well up in her again. She hugged her friend and added, "But I'm glad you insisted and came over."

Hugging Cristine back, Claire said, "I am too. And I couldn't be happier for you, for all of it. Not many are blessed like this, Cristine, and you so deserve it all."

She kissed Claire's cheek. "Thanks."

"Okay, I'll call you in the morning when I find out anything. I'll clear my schedule and we'll go claim your money." She pulled back and laughed. "Hey, you've just become my biggest client. My time is yours, lady."

"Then go get some sleep."

When she had closed the door and locked it, Cristine walked back into the kitchen and turned off all the lights. Standing in the darkness, she whispered, "Thank you, Daniel. For everything . . ."

She didn't expect an answer, and none came.

The next few days were consumed by the process of collecting her money. She and Claire went to Harrisburg, met with the lottery commission, had her photograph taken with them, couldn't get out of it, but there was no press conference. Then she and Claire put together her financial plan for the next five years and she found out that she could live, quite nicely, on the interest alone. She instructed Claire to arrange for her gifts to the gang and was planning a dinner to announce her good fortune before it appeared in the newspaper.

She was shopping for the meal in ShopRite, wanting to make it special, when her attention was captured by a woman with three children pulling on her. Cristine watched the woman, dressed in jeans and a stained T-shirt, trying to shop and manage her kids at the same time. She thought of Paula and her heart went out to the woman, who looked like she was barely keeping it together.

Pushing her cart closer, Cristine listened as the woman tried her best to get through the aisle.

"C'mon, put that back. You know we can't afford it. Get the generic cereal, the ShopRite brand."

"Mom! You said I could get the Cap'n Crunch. You promised!"

The woman took the box out of her child's hands, put it back, and picked out the store brand. "That was before your brother broke his arm. You get me health insurance to cover the doctor's bills and you can get Cap'n Crunch. Until then, we have to cut back."

The child, who looked to be around eight years old, sulked. "There's never any money for anything since Dad died."

Cristine could see the woman biting her tongue as another child, around five and sitting in the cart, started to cry. "I want Cap'n Crunch! I want Cap'n Crunch!"

"We have our cereal," the woman pronounced and pushed the cart away. "Let's see if we can possibly get through this shopping trip without everyone falling apart, okay?"

She watched the little family depart and turn the corner to the next aisle. Cristine sighed, only having a tiny idea of how that woman felt. She didn't need to know her story. It was obvious that she was overwhelmed. Making up her mind, she went to the front of the store. Fortunately, food markets now had minibanks in them and this one had hers. She left her cart by the doorway and went up to the counter.

"How much can I get from the ATM?" she asked the clerk.

"Five hundred."

"Then I'd like to cash a check." She took out her checkbook, and when she was finished writing it out, she slid it across the counter.

"A thousand dollars?" the clerk asked. "How would you like that?"

"Can I get it in twenty-dollar bills?"

"Certainly."

"And do you have an envelope? Not a bank envelope, but a plain white one."

The woman gave her one and then turned to her computer.

Cristine grinned as she waited.

Within minutes she had her money. Deciding to leave her cart, which didn't have any perishables in it yet, Cristine walked through the store until she found the woman.

"Excuse me," she said with a smile.

"I'm sorry," the woman answered, "what did they do?"

Shaking her head, Cristine said, "This isn't about your children. This is about you."

"Me?" The woman's shoulders squared, as though she were ready to defend herself. "What did I do?"

Still smiling, Cristine handed her the sealed envelope. "Probably more than you ever thought you would have to. This is for you, an extraordinary woman. Don't open it for a few minutes, okay?"

"What is it?" the woman asked, looking down at the thick envelope.

"Believe in angels." Cristine said, pressing it into her hand. "And when the time comes, pass it on." She turned and hurried down the aisle, past the checkout lanes, and was almost at the door when she heard a loud feminine squeal.

Giggling, Cristine rushed out of the store and to her car. She needed to make a fast getaway, she thought, picking up speed.

As she was driving out of the parking lot, she realized how wonderful she felt and let her giggles come full force. God, it felt great to give! She had such a rush of pleasure that she couldn't stop giggling, imagining the woman telling others about her change of fortune, and those people would tell more to believe in angels, and . . . She would probably never be able to do her grocery shopping at ShopRite again though.

Oh, well, it was worth it. The next time she'd go out of town. And she knew, instinctively, that she wanted to do it again, and again. This was the best high since . . . well, not as good as Daniel, but it was still great.

Driving to another grocery store, Cristine began to think of a plan. It was something she would have to discuss with the gang tonight. Maybe, just maybe, she had found her purpose.

They arrived almost as one, with Tina driving Paula. They were in her kitchen, talking and sharing the latest news on Kelly's daughter, Paula's fight with her insurance company, and Tina's ad that would be appearing in *Philadelphia Magazine,* when Claire came up to her at the sink.

"None of them know? Not even Tina?"

Cristine shook her head. "You didn't tell any of them, did you?"

"My lips have been sealed. I listen to my clients."

"Good. I'm going to tell them at dinner."

"Be prepared for shock."

Cristine grinned. "A good shock, for a change."

"So what can I do to help?"

Cristine looked around her as she prepared the salad. "Check the eggplant in the oven?"

Claire sighed. "Okay, but you'll have to tell me what I'm checking for."

"See if the cheese is browning yet. If not, turn up the heat."

Fifteen minutes later they were seated in the dining room with Cristine at the head of the table. Everyone was still chatting, and Cristine tapped her crystal wine glass with her knife. "Excuse me, ladies, I would like to make a toast."

All stopped their discussions and held up their glasses as they turned their attention to their hostess.

"I am grateful for so much in my life, but most grateful for all of you. You're my family, my only family, so I raise my glass to five extraordinary women who have shown me strength, honor, integrity, intelligence and humor. Thank you for being in my life, and allowing me to be a part of yours." She looked at each one and grinned. "To friendship. To family."

"To friendship and family," they responded.

Cristine sipped her wine, then said, "Now let's eat."

She sat back and watched them resume their discussions while beginning their meals, and Claire raised one eyebrow to her. She shook her head slightly. Now was not the time. If she told them now, they would forget about eating. Waiting until the meal was almost over, Cristine said to no one in general, "Have any of you heard that the lottery was won by someone in Haverton?"

"I heard that," Kelly answered. "People at work were talking about it."

"Whoever it is bought the ticket at the QuickMart," Tina said. "I went in there for coffee the other day and there's signs and balloons. But no one knows who the winner is yet."

"How much was it?" Isabel asked.

"Thirty-two million, before taxes," Claire stated.

"Can you imagine?" Kelly asked. "God, what you could do with that kind of money."

"What would you do, Kelly, if you won?" Cristine asked.

"Well, first I'd pay off every bill I have and then . . . oh, I don't know, something fun. Haven't had fun in way too long."

Cristine nodded to Claire and her friend got up and brought her briefcase back to the table. Opening it up, Claire took out five envelopes and began handing them out.

"What's this?" Tina asked, turning it over to see the sealed back flap.

"I don't get it," Kelly said, looking at the envelope and then back to Claire.

"Do we open it, Claire?" Isabel asked, as puzzled as the others.

"Don't ask me. Ask Cristine."

All their attention focused at the head of the table.

Cristine took a deep breath and smiled. "I have some news and I wanted to tell you all tonight, while we're to-gether."

"What is it?" Kelly asked in a breathless voice. "Do not tell me you're sick."

"Yeah, Cris," Tina added, "what's going on?"

"Okay . . ." Cristine swallowed deeply and then just said it. "I won the lottery."

There was a moment of silence and then a barrage of noise . . .

"You didn't!"

"Oh, my God!"

"*You're* the winner?"

"The lottery! *Oh, my God!*"

She started laughing at their stunned expressions and nodded. "I know! Believe me, I know! It's . . . unbelievable, but it's true."

"Oh, my God, Cristine!" Tina exclaimed. "When did you find out?"

"The day after Paula's accident. I bought the ticket that morning when you called me to get Paula at the hospital and then I forgot about it. It wasn't until I was showing a house and the client mentioned someone in Haverton had won it. That's when I checked and I had the winning ticket."

"This is incredible!" Isabel said with a shocked laugh. "You hear about this happening, but you don't think you'll ever know someone . . ." Her words trailed off as she continued to stare at Cristine with a stunned expression. "Truly, Cristine. You *won the lottery?*"

"Truly. I won."

All of them seemed stunned; she knew the feeling. Deciding to get on with it, she said, "I told Claire and she went with me to Harrisburg to claim the winnings. The announcement is going to be in the paper tomorrow, but I wanted all of you to hear it tonight. Claire's going to handle the money for me." She took a deep breath. "Each one of you has an envelope. Why don't you open them."

As they began opening their envelopes, she added, "Inside you'll find a spreadsheet. Every single bill you have should be entered there, including whoever holds your mortgages. If you don't fill them in, Claire is prepared to use less savory tactics to get the information she needs. And you know Claire. She'll do it."

"But why?" Kelly asked, shaking her head in disbelief.

"I told you why already."

Isabel also shook her head. "Cristine, you can't do this!"

"Issy, all of you at this table are my family. You all know my background."

"She's right, Cristine," Paula said in a stunned voice. "This is uncalled-for. You can't do this!"

"I can and I am. You are the only family I have and it's going to give me great pleasure to know you all aren't going to be worried about survival any longer."

She looked at Tina. "We're partners and I intend to continue that, but from now on I'm not going to draw a salary. Any commissions I make will go back into the company. And since you're the only one of us without a mortgage, in your envelope is a picture of a condo for sale in the Bahamas. If you like it, it's yours. If not, find a place here or in the islands where you can get away like you're always dreaming of and—"

"I can't accept that!" Tina protested. "This is outrageous."

"You can and you will. All of you will, because it's important for the next phase of the Yellow Brick Road Gang."

That produced silence.

Having everyone's attention, Cristine told them the story of the woman in the supermarket. "I can't tell you how happy that made me. I couldn't stop giggling.

Whenever I thought about it, I would start giggling like a little kid. Does anyone remember an old television series called *The Millionaire*?"

"I do," Isabel said. "It was about this man, Michael Anthony, and every week this eccentric man would hand him the name of someone he was giving a million dollars to. The premise of the show was to see how the money changed that person's life, for better or worse."

"Couldn't have explained it better, Issy," Cristine said. "When I was little this foster family I was with only had a black-and-white TV, and maybe four stations came on it. One of them showed *The Millionaire*. I was always fascinated by the program, and so yesterday I thought . . . what if we did that? Not a million dollars, of course, or I'd be broke, but what if we found women, extraordinary women, who are becoming overwhelmed by the circumstances in their lives?" She turned to Paula. "You made me think of this."

"Me?" Paula asked in astonishment.

Cristine nodded. "What would you do if Conor went to Coventry Day School three afternoons a week?"

"I can't afford Coventry. It's out of my league."

"But what would you do? Would you finish your thesis? Would you get your master's degree?"

Paula looked stunned. Again. "I don't know. It's been so long . . ."

"But would you consider it?"

"I . . . sure. I'd . . . consider it."

"And what would you do with your degree? Would you teach? Write a book?"

Paula was shaking her head. "I don't know. I always thought I'd like to write, but who has the time?"

"You will, Paula," Cristine said with a tender smile. She then looked at the rest of them. "And think of what Paula might contribute to the world, when she isn't worried about survival issues. What she could say to women, having lived a life where she put herself last and gave unconditional love to her family. But now it's going to be her time again. Maybe she wasn't ready to write before and maybe it will take her years to do it, but at least she's going to have options now. And that's what I'd like us to do with other women. Find women with potential and see how we can help to nurture that by relieving some of their survival worries."

"Just women?" Isabel asked.

"For now. Just women. Claire has found a way for us to become a foundation. Oprah took the name the Angel Network so I was thinking . . . how about the Yellow Brick Road, and our logo will be glittery red shoes?"

"It's the evolution of the gang," Claire pronounced. "We're simply stepping up a level and expanding. Say, for example, if we find a woman who needs a new washer and dryer, we get them for her—either we pay for them or find a corporate sponsor, like Whirlpool, who would get the tax benefit and local publicity. Corporate sponsorship would be your department, Kelly. You're the ace salesperson."

"I like the idea of it, Claire, but I already have a job. How much time would all this take?"

Claire grinned. "That's the beauty of working for the foundation, Kelly. You would get paid a salary."

"You mean quit my job?"

Claire shrugged. "That's up to you. Cristine is ready to pay you more than you're making now, whatever it is, with full benefits. Or you could do it part-time, whatever you want."

"This is all in the planning stage," Cristine cut in. "Nothing is set in stone. I want us to talk about it, figure it out together. I just know that with everything we've learned, all of us have something to offer others. You see, I think it's time for women to take their proper place on a global scale, but most women are so involved in trying to keep their family together and to make ends meet that they can't even think about themselves and their own dreams. I just want to find a way to empower women, remind them of their potential. I think it's the only way humanity is going to survive on this planet."

"I'm in," Tina pronounced. "Hell, if this thing takes off we could get out of real estate before the bottom drops and sell the business for a tidy bundle. We always knew this was short-term, right?"

Cristine nodded. "Glad to have you aboard, Tina. You're the business brains so you decide when to sell the company. Cristina Realty is now solely in your hands."

She turned to the rest of them. "I know this is overwhelming, so just think about it, okay? I don't have everything figured out. I just know I want to help women in some way. Between us, we should be able to come up with a way to do that with this money to start us off."

"Look," Claire said, "how do you think Oprah got to give away all those cars? Because she gave GM the best product placement and advertisement for a new product they'll ever get. How many people talked about it? On morning talk shows. Late-night television. Worldwide attention. If Oprah can do it, so can we . . . on a smaller scale, of course."

Paula said, "My head's spinning."

"I'd ask if you mixed pills with your wine tonight, but my head's spinning too," Kelly stated. "This . . . all of it . . . it's unbelievable!"

"I know it's a lot to take in at once," Cristine said. "Just think about it while you're going about your daily routine. We've all come across women who look like they're holding it together with a string. These are women who had dreams before life overwhelmed them. Maybe they wanted to be a nurse, but life got in the way. They got married, had kids, had to take a job in the retail market or as an office clerk to make ends meet. I don't know . . . Just try to get their names, or even their license-plate numbers. We'll figure out the rest of it as we go along."

"And I'd like to suggest we keep this to ourselves for

the time being," Claire said. "Paula, you can tell Hank, but the rest of us shouldn't talk about this until we get it up and running. And maybe not even then, or we might just get deluged with requests, and who's got the time to check them all out?"

"Right," Tina said. "If word of this got out Cristine would be flooded with people who want money."

"This is going to be small," Cristine said. "And as uncomplicated as possible. I don't want to spend all my time with this either. I want to enjoy doing it, and I want to have time for myself."

"Speaking of yourself," Isabel threw out. "What are you going to do for you? Surely you must have something you want to treat yourself with now that money isn't an issue."

Cristine slowly shook her head. "I'm just like the rest of you. I want to pay off all my bills and finally own my house, so no one ever again can tell me I have to leave. I want . . ." She paused, knowing she couldn't say what she really wanted. "I guess now that I can have whatever I want, I find I don't really want anything. This money isn't going to change me and, if it even begins to, I'm depending on you guys to give me a swift kick in the arse."

Tina laughed. "Oh, honey, you can depend on me."

"I knew I could," Cristine answered with a laugh then turned to the rest of them. "The foundation is only an idea right now, but those forms in front of you are real. You've got a week to fill them out, and I don't care what you say or how you protest. You are my family and this is what I want to do."

She paused as tears came to her eyes. "And I love you guys. We've always been there for each other and we've shared everything, even the bad times. Now let's share something awesome."

One by one, tears filled their eyes as they looked at each other, knowing it was awesome . . . not just the money, but their circle of love and friendship.

"Hell," Isabel said and sniffled. "When we decided to be women without rules I never thought it would come to this."

Cristine grinned. "We can do whatever we want now. How cool is that?"

# Chapter

## 18

"WHAT A GENEROUS HEART YOU HAVE."

Cristine turned away from the papers in her hand and smiled when she saw him walking out of her kitchen. "Hello, Daniel. I've missed you."

"You haven't called out to me and I know you have been busy."

He was wearing his jeans and the blue shirt and he looked so handsome that Cristine felt a pull in her belly to reach out to him. Eight days felt like eight weeks, and she yearned to have him hold her, touch her, make love to her. Still, not knowing if he had second thoughts about the human side of lovemaking, she felt almost shy to make the first move. "A lot has been going on. The announcement was in the paper and I've been fielding calls from people I haven't talked to in ages." She watched him sit down on the sofa, close to her. "But I guess I don't have to tell you that. You've probably been watching the whole thing."

He grinned. "Being wealthy brings responsibility."

"Yes, it does," she admitted, unable to stop smiling at him. "But I'd rather have this responsibility than worry."

"Your energy has changed," he murmured, looking at her curiously. "It is much brighter, clearer."

"It's probably because I'm happy."

He shook his head slowly. "Perhaps, but I think it's more than that."

"You do? What?"

"I don't know exactly."

She sat beside him and gathered her courage. "Do you mind if we sit closer? Like this?" And she got up and sat down facing him, with her legs curled on the sofa. She leaned over until she was directly in front of him. "Is this all right? You're comfortable like this?"

He was gazing into her eyes with such tenderness that Cristine thought she might be the one not to keep herself together.

"This is very nice."

"You won't disappear?"

His hand reached out and he began to stroke her shoulder, her back. "I don't think so."

She wanted to purr her contentment like a cat. His touch seemed magical, able to take away any shred of stress immediately. "I think I'm most happy because you're here with me," she murmured, closing her eyes to savor the feelings rushing through her body.

"I find it has been difficult to stay away," he whispered. "I didn't want to intrude."

She opened her eyes. "Daniel, you have never been an intrusion."

His eyes widened and he grinned. "Really? I seem to remember several times you asked me to get out of your life."

She shook her head, as though dismissing the notion. "That was in the beginning. Before I knew you were real. Before I . . ." Her words trailed off.

"Finish your thought, Cristine. Before what?"

She swallowed and looked down at the buttons on his shirt. "Before I came to know you." She just couldn't say it to him, not the whole truth. What if it scared him away?

"And now?"

She looked into his incredible blue eyes. "And now every time you come into a room I feel as though I have been blessed with this wondrous gift and . . . and I'm grateful."

He stared deeply into her eyes and his own widened, as though he had seen something that startled him.

"What's wrong, Daniel? You look like someone just hit you in the face."

"I don't know if I should tell you this."

"Tell me what?" He really did look shaken.

He held her shoulders and said, "I believe, Cristine, you are going to have a baby. A new life is beginning inside of you."

She felt her entire body stiffen. "No. You *couldn't* know that. It's only been . . . a week. It's too soon to . . ." She couldn't finish her words. Pushing herself up, Cristine began pacing. "Really, Daniel, you couldn't know such a thing. It isn't possible. Simply not possible. I mean, you . . . *you* aren't even real, not like *real,* you know? And this, a pregnancy, would take a real man and woman to accomplish. It just can't be real."

"You are upset by this news?" he asked, staring up at her.

She stopped her pacing. "Ah, *yeah*?"

"You don't want this?"

She suddenly felt sick to her stomach. Wasn't it only moments ago that she had been happy and fulfilled? "Daniel, you are not human. I can't have . . . the baby of . . . of an extraterrestrial or dimension traveler! I don't know what it would look like! Would it be normal? *I can't be pregnant!*" She paused. "Not now, and . . ." She couldn't finish her sentence.

He did. "And not by me?"

She just stared at him and watched as he slowly disintegrated; this time it was like watching the surf washing away the sand. "Great. Just like a man to leave!"

Cristine knew she had hurt his feelings, if he had feelings . . . okay, he had feelings, but, seriously, how *could* she have his baby? This was not in her plans. Maybe down the road . . . She put her hand on her roiling stomach. The Great Plan was to buy a house, own it completely so she could feel secure, and then have a baby.

She now owned her home completely and had more money than she'd ever dreamed of having, so security was no longer an issue. It was baby time . . . but Daniel's?

"Come back, Daniel!" she called out. "Let's talk about this."

Silence.

"C'mon, it was just such a shock."

Nothing.

She sighed. Now that he had planted this insane idea in her head, she simply had to find the answer. She grabbed her purse and left the house.

Twenty-five minutes later, Cristine was seated on the edge of her tub, holding the kitchen timer in her hands as she waited for the results. Her hands were starting to shake and her stomach felt as if it were twisted into tight knots. Four more minutes. She sat and thought about the possibilities. If she was pregnant, she could continue the pregnancy, or not. Adoption or state care was out of the question. And then she had a sense of her mother facing this same decision.

How horribly ironic was that? she thought as the churning in her stomach increased.

And in that moment she knew that whatever the test result was, if she was pregnant with Daniel's child, she would continue the pregnancy, no matter what. A part of her knew it was a blessing and another part was filled with intense uncertainty. What kind of child would it be? Would it be normal, or gifted, or abnormal, able to disappear right out of her arms?

When the timer bell rang, she was so startled, it fell right out of her hands.

Slowly standing, she leaned toward the sink.

Blue. Bright blue.

"Oh, my God!"

Stunned, she walked out of the bathroom and into her bedroom. As if on autopilot, she pulled down the comforter and slid under it. Lying in bed, she stared out to her bedroom. *How could this have happened?* She *knew* how it had happened; she just didn't think it was *possible* for it to happen with someone from a different dimension. She hadn't even thought of birth control that night.

*That night.*

How many times had she gone over it in her mind? Trying to recapture the feelings, even just in memory? A child conceived like that would have to be extraordinary . . . but was she prepared for an extraordinary child?

She heard the doorbell. Then a loud knocking. She didn't have the energy to get up. Finally, she heard Claire calling out to her.

Damn, she'd left the door unlocked.

Maybe if she just stayed silent Claire would think no one was at home and leave? No. She had left the car in the driveway. And who was Claire talking to down there?

"Claire, up here," she called out, knowing there wasn't any way to avoid her friend. But why was she hearing more than one set of footsteps?

Claire and Isabel came into the bedroom.

"What's wrong?"

"Are you sick?" Isabel asked, sitting on the edge of the mattress.

Cristine shook her head. "I don't know what I am."

"Okay, save that until I pee," Claire pronounced and headed for the bathroom. "We just had lunch and I drank too much water."

Cristine bolted into a sitting position. "Use the one in hallway," she called out.

Claire, standing by the sink, looked back at her. "Why? Is this one broke?" And then she looked around the small room.

Cristine slid back under the covers. She wanted to pull them over her head and not see Claire pick up that stick and stare at it, then at her, then back at the stick.

"Oh, God . . ."

"What are you doing, Claire?" Isabel asked. "What's that you're holding?"

"Here, look for yourself," Claire said, walking out of the bathroom and handing it to Isabel. She then stared at Cristine and said, "I still have to pee. Can I use this bathroom now?"

Cristine shrugged.

Isabel was staring at the pregnancy test in silence. Finally, she asked, "Are you pregnant?"

"Don't answer that until I'm out of here!" Claire yelled from the bathroom.

Cristine looked at Isabel and nodded.

Issy took her hand and squeezed. "It's okay, right?" she whispered.

Again, Cristine shrugged as she heard the toilet flush.

Claire quickly washed her hands and came back into the bedroom drying them.

"So you're pregnant."

It wasn't a question. Cristine swallowed and nodded.

"And this isn't a good thing?" Claire stopped drying her hands. "Oh, no, do not tell me this is Charlie's! You two did not have the infamous breakup sex and now you're pregnant!"

"No!" Cristine protested. "It's not Charlie's, thank God."

"Then who?" Isabel asked softly.

When Cristine didn't immediately answer, Claire said, "Daniel Burns." She looked at Isabel. "The guy who finished her kitchen. The guy who moves on, right, Cristine?"

"It isn't like that, Claire," she said, feeling her throat tighten.

"Calm down, Claire," Isabel instructed. "Cristine, is this Daniel the father?"

She nodded.

"And does he know about this?"

Cristine almost laughed. "Oh, yeah. He was the one who told me, and I took the test to prove him wrong." She pulled her ragged breath into her lungs. "But he was right."

"So you already love him," Claire said. "Get married and have your baby."

"She *loves* him? Who is he?" Isabel demanded. "We don't even know him."

"I'll bring you up to speed later," Claire said, then looked at Cristine. "So marry the guy."

"He can't marry me."

"Why?" Claire demanded. "Of course, we'd require a prenup, so he can't get his hands on your money and—"

"Claire!" Cristine interrupted as tears started to flow. "He isn't like that. He isn't like anyone any of us have ever known!"

"What are you talking about?" Issy asked gently. "Does he love you?"

"I don't know!" Cristine lamented, wiping her face with the palm of her hand. "I think he loves me, but I don't know if he *loves* loves me, you know?"

"Move over," Claire demanded, shucking her high heels and getting in bed next to Cristine. She wrapped her arm around Cristine's shoulders. "Okay, so what's the worst-case scenario? You have this baby without him. You do want to keep it, right? I know a child is part of your plan."

"I guess," Cristine mumbled, and started to hiccup. "I just didn't think"—hiccup—"that it would be like this—" Hiccup. "With *him*."

"Hey, he's a sweet specimen of a man, honey. You should see him, Issy. Tall, lean, dark blond hair. He's got good genes. You can tell." Claire squeezed Cristine's shoulders. "Between the two of you, this child will be gorgeous."

"I'm not worried about a child's"—hiccup—"looks, Claire."

"What does worry you, Cristine?" Isabel asked. "You certainly can provide for the child and give it a loving home."

Cristine shook her head and cried and hiccuped and cried. "You wouldn't understand," she finally was able to get out.

"Try us," Isabel said gently.

"First, Issy, get her a glass of water to stop those hiccups, 'cause it's going to make for a long story this way."

She took the glass from Isabel and gulped, forcing the air down below her diaphragm. Placing the glass on her night table, Cristine sighed and laid her head back against Claire's shoulder. "Thanks," she murmured.

"Okay, now let's hear it," Claire instructed. "What don't we understand?"

"Daniel."

"What don't we understand about Daniel?" Issy asked.

"Who he is. Where he's from."

"Where is he from?

"Not here."

"Then where?"

Cristine waved her arm up to the ceiling. "Out there."

Isabel stared at her. "What do you mean? Out there?"

She didn't know how to tell them, or if she even should. "He's not . . . an ordinary man."

Isabel smiled. "Now you wouldn't have fallen in love

with him if he was, would you? He would have to be outstanding."

"Oh, he's outstanding, all right," Claire chimed in. "I saw him stop a purse snatcher and then—"

Cristine felt Claire's body stiffen.

"Yeah, what do you mean he's not an ordinary man?" Claire asked in a tight voice.

Cristine knew Claire was thinking about that light on the purse snatcher's head, coming from Daniel's hand. Inhaling deeply, Cristine said, "He's . . . gifted. More evolved than us. He knows . . . things."

"What are you talking about?" Claire demanded. "Gifted how? Evolved how?"

Isabel stroked Cristine's arm. "What do you mean? He knows things? What things?"

Sniffling, Cristine closed her eyes with fatigue. This was not going to be easy. "Like the lottery. He told me how to win the lottery."

*"What?"* Claire demanded in shock, sitting up straight as Cristine's head rolled off her shoulder.

"Good heavens," Issy murmured in a worried voice. "How could he tell you how to win the lottery? It isn't possible."

"It is," Cristine asserted, sitting up herself now that Claire had moved away from her, as though putting up a barrier.

"You *cheated*?" Claire demanded in a stunned whisper, as though anyone outside the room could hear her. "Shit!"

"I *didn't* cheat!" Cristine insisted. "Daniel taught me how to manifest what I wanted. And I wanted to win the lottery."

"Cristine," Isabel said in a controlled voice. "How can anyone teach you something like that? Maybe you're having guilt feelings over winning so much money. It isn't unusual for someone in your position to feel unworthy and try to—"

"Hold it, Isabel," Claire interrupted. "Let her explain. I met this guy the other night and I saw something . . ." She looked at Cristine. "Something you obviously didn't want me to see."

"What did you see?" Issy asked, looking genuinely confused.

"Cristine's purse had been snatched and Daniel stopped the guy and then . . . then I saw him put his hand on the guy's head and a light appeared, a strange light, and then it was gone. That fast. I thought my eyes were playing tricks on me, but I was right, wasn't I, Cris?"

She nodded.

"So what's with this Daniel? How did he do that? And how did he fix it so you won the damn lottery?"

Cristine shook her head. "He didn't fix it, Claire. He taught me how to manifest. How to use my mind to create what I wanted in my life. I didn't think it would work, but I kept buying a ticket, day after day, and then worrying it right out of my life by doubt. It wasn't until I had just bought the ticket and Tina called me about Paula's accident that it happened. See, I didn't have time to worry or doubt. I was too busy with Paula. Daniel said I stepped out of my own way and let the universe work for me."

Neither woman said a word. They simply continued to stare at her.

"Look, I know this sounds strange, to say the least, but it worked! I won, though I didn't find out until the next day." She sighed with exasperation. How could she ever get them to understand? "Daniel is a teacher, a . . . a messenger, you could say. He came here to help me reach my potential."

"I thought he was a . . . handyman," Claire muttered, looking as if someone had punched the wind right out of her.

"I let you think that. I couldn't tell you the truth about him."

"What do you mean, Cristine, he came here to help you? *Here?* To this house? This state? This country? What?"

She felt like a little kid as she hunched her shoulders and whispered, "To this dimension?"

Isabel blinked.

Claire, for once, was speechless.

"Look, how do you think he finished my kitchen so quickly? He didn't even use tools. Don't you think I've thought I was going crazy? He's some kind of angel, or dimension traveler, or *something,* and he's saying that if women don't take their rightful place now and bring some sanity back to this planet, the human race may disappear."

Isabel visibly swallowed deeply. "You are saying that . . . that he came to you, to save the planet?"

Cristine chuckled with nervousness. "No. He says the planet will continue. We human beings may disappear. He said they have tried using the males, but they are too predictable in their greed and their chromosomes are dying off, so now they are looking toward the women to turn things around."

"They? *They?*" Claire demanded. "Who the hell are they? Aliens?" she asked with a nervous laugh.

"Not aliens. They, I suppose, are us in another dimension after we have evolved. Daniel says our destructive ways are affecting all dimensions of the universe. We haven't been using our brains to evolve ourselves, but to control our environment, and now we are like children with dangerous toys that, if misused, would have a rippling effect throughout the universe. He says males have had their turn, but something about their dying chromosomes . . . I don't remember what. So now it's the female's turn to bring enlightenment, or something."

Isabel exhaled and crossed her arms over her chest. "How would you do that, Cristine?" she whispered in a worried voice.

"I don't know!" Cristine answered with frustration. "I thought winning this money and starting a foundation would be a start . . . And don't look at me like that, Issy, I am not having a nervous breakdown. I know what I'm saying sounds crazy, but I am not one of your patients. I'm pregnant. This is real!"

Neither Claire nor Isabel said anything; both looking worried.

"And you can't tell anyone what I've just told you," Cristine added. "I wouldn't have told you any of this if you hadn't found out I'm pregnant." She stopped speaking and blinked, not really focusing on anything. "I'm *pregnant.* I'm going to have a *baby,*" she whispered in awe.

"Yes, you are," Claire murmured. "Cristine, you do realize everything you're telling us is . . . well, kinda weird?"

"I know how weird it is! I've been living it since the night I came back from the Bahamas. How do you think my back healed so quickly? I could barely stand, but I was at work the next day without any pain. This is *real,* my friends. Too real, maybe."

Isabel asked in a gentle voice, "Cristine, would you see a friend of mine?"

Cristine stiffened. "Who? A shrink? I'm not crazy, Issy!"

"I didn't say you were crazy. I just think if you talked to a professional you could better make—"

"You're a professional," Cristine interrupted. "If you don't believe me, a stranger certainly isn't going to, right?"

"She needs to see an ob-gyn. She should get checked out immediately," Claire said. "Just to make sure everything is . . . you know, proceeding correctly."

Cristine nodded. "You're right."

Claire looked at Isabel. "Okay, so who do you know,

Issy, that we can call right now and ask for an emergency visit?"

"Kate Abrams is pretty good. She handles women who have babies later in life, women who are at risk," She quickly added, "Not that you are at risk, Cristine."

"I know." Cristine smiled sympathetically. "But I'm also not some twenty-year-old in her prime baby-making years."

"So call, Issy. Hand her the phone, Cristine. Let's do this right away. Then we can make a plan."

Cristine handed the bedside phone to Isabel. "I thought I had a plan," she murmured.

"Yeah, well . . . you know what they say about best-laid plans going astray," Claire said, and wrapped her arm around Cristine's shoulders as Isabel took her address book out of her purse and began looking through it.

"They, whoever they are," Isabel murmured, flipping through pages, "also say we humans make plans and God laughs."

"Considering what we've just heard, there must be great amusement in heaven today," Claire muttered as Isabel began dialing the phone.

They had the last appointment of the day and Cristine was on the examining table with her legs in the stirrups and a stranger between them.

"Everything looks normal. I don't even have to see your test result. You're definitely pregnant," the voice down under stated.

Clutching the sides of the table, Cristine let out her breath. "Okay."

"But you're more like three months pregnant."

Cristine nearly bolted into a sitting position. "That can't be!" Three or four months would mean Charlie! It wasn't possible! They didn't have sex for months at the end. "That's not possible," she declared, as her heart pounded against her chest wall.

Kate Abrams lifted her head. "I'm just telling you what I see by the state of your cervix. You're definitely more than a week pregnant." She rolled her chair away and stripped off her gloves. "You haven't had any symptoms? Tiredness? Nausea? Tender breasts?"

Pushing herself completely into an upright position, Cristine shook her head. "I've been tired, but I've had a lot going on lately. I haven't felt sick."

"Not everyone does," Dr. Abrams said. "Come back next week and I'll do some blood work. Call on Monday for an appointment and I'll leave a note with the receptionist to fit you in."

"Okay," Cristine murmured, feeling as though everything were happening too fast.

"You can get dressed now," the doctor said with a smile. "Don't look so worried. Having a baby is the most natural thing in the world." She stopped at the door. "I'll have some prenatal vitamin samples out at the desk for you. There's instructions on them."

"Thank you, Doctor," Cristine said, sliding off the table, thinking nothing about this was natural. "And thank you for fitting us in today."

Kate Abrams smiled. "When Isabel Calloway calls for a favor, and this is a first for me, you do whatever you can. She's something, isn't she? Lucky you to have her for a friend."

"Yes, Isabel is an extraordinary woman."

"So let me catch up with her while you get dressed." And Kate Abrams closed the door behind her.

Cristine felt as if she were on automatic pilot as she pulled the examining gown off, folded it neatly, and left it on a chair. Then she picked up her underwear and began dressing. She didn't care how good Kate Abrams was supposed to be, she had to have made a mistake. She simply couldn't be three or four months pregnant!

As she pulled up her panties, she noticed a slight

swelling at her lower abdomen. Staring at it in wonder, Cristine could have sworn it wasn't there before. She ran her hand over it lightly and, yes . . . it was protruding a tiny bit.

This can't be happening. Even if she'd had sex with Charlie, which she hadn't, surely she should have noticed her belly swelling. Had she been so preoccupied? But no! Why would she even think it? She needed to talk to Daniel.

Reaching for her bra, Cristine had the strangest sensation that something was taking over her body . . . and she desperately needed to find out exactly *what*.

Forty-five minutes later she had managed to convince Claire and Isabel that she just wanted to get back into bed. She'd promised them both that she would call them later, and she knew as she watched them drive away that they would be discussing her and her crazy explanations. She didn't care. Not then.

Unlocking the front door, she didn't even close it before she called out, "Daniel! Please come now! I need you!"

# Chapter

## 19

She walked into her kitchen, expecting him to appear.

"Daniel?"

Nothing.

"C'mon, I need to talk to you. Don't sulk!"

"I wasn't."

Cristine jumped in fright as she spun around. "You scared me," she breathed, feeling her heart slow down to normal. Why was it every time she saw him she was filled with awe, as if there were this strange gravitational pull toward him? She didn't think she would ever take his appearances for granted.

"You called out to me. I see no reason for you to be frightened."

Cristine knew she had insulted him earlier in the day, and so she smiled. "I am sorry for what I said today, but now we really do need to talk."

He stood on the other side of the island counter. "I am here."

Her shoulders dropped. "Daniel, please! I said I was sorry. Can you even imagine how startling this news is to me? I'm pregnant, and I didn't expect it."

"I didn't either," he replied. "And it wouldn't have happened had we achieved unity in the usual way."

Her jaw dropped. "Hold on a second. This is *my* fault?"

His expression softened. "It is no one's fault, Cristine. A life is growing inside of you. Can you not be happy?"

She threw her hands up in exasperation. "Happy? Maybe after you explain how this happened, and why a doctor today said I am three or four months pregnant when we achieved *unity* in *my* way eight days ago!"

He smiled. "Cristine, you are pregnant with a part of me. The physiology of this baby is not going to be that of a normal human. Though I occupy this body to . . . to commune with you, who I am is so much more. Just as who you are is so much more than you have ever thought."

She started to feel panic well up inside her. "What is going to happen to me?" she demanded. "If this . . . child . . . keeps growing at this rate the body *I* occupy will explode!"

He laughed and shook his head. *Laughed!*

"This is not funny!"

"But it is," he insisted, trying to control his humor. "You will not explode. You will have a normal pregnancy, but much quicker."

"Normal, but much quicker?" She really tried to get her head around what he was saying, but it didn't make sense. "How much quicker? Explain that, because, see, quicker is *not* normal!

"That I cannot tell you, for the baby is growing at its own rate, not mine. Come sit with me. You are upsetting yourself for no good reason."

"No good reason?" Now she laughed, a little crazily, but still *no good reason*? "I am pregnant with a baby, your baby, and . . . and nothing about this is normal!"

He came up to her and took her hand, leading her out of the kitchen. "You must try to understand that what you have always perceived as normal is merely the paradigm you had accepted. Now there is a new normal, a new paradigm, at least for you, because you have raised your vibratory rate. Everything will manifest more quickly for you."

He sat on the sofa and held her in his arms. Running his hand over her arm soothingly, he added, "Also, because this is a part of me that joined with the egg of your body, this child will be different."

"Different?" she whispered against his chest. "How different?" she asked with dread.

"Extraordinary. Like you. Like me. But also unique. This is not something I considered when I first achieved unity with you and made the choice to come into your life, but it has happened. And what a glorious opportunity it can be. This child . . . I will tell you the baby is female . . . she will achieve great things. She will be a light in the face of darkness."

Cristine touched her belly protectively. "I don't know that I could be the mother of such a child. I'm not prepared."

"Of course you are," Daniel said. "All you need is love, and you have so much love to give, Cristine."

She knew she had to ask, even if it meant he disappeared on her, and so she took a deep breath. "Will you be here to help raise her, or will I have to do it alone?"

He didn't answer immediately. Finally, he said, "I will always be with you, Cristine, through our child. But I can't stay here, not like this, not forever."

She pushed him away and sat up straight. "Oh, I get it," she said angrily. "You're going to evolve into another dimension, right? That's what this whole thing has been about since the beginning. It had nothing to do with me, really. This is all about you, what you want for yourself. You get me pregnant and then you're going to leave me with this *extraordinary* child that I have no clue how to raise. You're better equipped than I am to do this. Why didn't you get pregnant? Haven't you evolved yet where it can take over your body, instead of mine?" Okay, so that last part was crazy, but *still*! He was going to leave her with this!

"Calm down, Cristine. I am not going to leave you. I simply cannot stay in this body form."

She tried to calm down, but her throat tightened with emotion and she felt her eyes beginning to burn with tears. "This isn't the way I had it planned. I thought the father of my child would love me and stay with me and we'd make a home and . . . and what's the use?" she said as the tears started to fall down her cheeks. "That's never going to happen now."

He pulled her back into his arms and she felt an immediate wash of love. "I do love you," he whispered into her hair. "Far more than you can comprehend. You are a part of me now, Cristine."

She sniffled and clutched at his shirt. "Then let me come with you. If you can't stay here, take me to your dimension. I can have the baby there, can't I?"

"You would leave everything here?"

"I'd miss my friends, but . . . I'd go with you, Daniel. I don't want to go through this alone."

He kissed the top of her head. "The sacrifice you would make honors me, but in truth you are needed here, in this dimension. And so is our daughter." He held her tighter. "This is how it is unfolding, my love, and we both must respect a power much greater than our own."

She didn't say anything for some time, sniffling as he continued to hold her. Finally, she murmured, "So how long will you be here?"

"That I do not know," he answered gently. "Let us not be worried about the future. Can we not rejoice, Cristine, in our magnificent creation?"

"We're going to have a baby," she whispered.

"Yes, we are, my love," he whispered back, and began stroking her hair. "Now rest, ease your mind and your body."

And with every stroke Cristine felt herself become more and more sleepy.

"I'm so tired . . ."

"I know. You have been through an emotional time. Close your eyes and rest, Cristine. You are safe with me."

And she so wanted to believe him.

The next meeting of the Yellow Brick Road Gang took place at Isabel's graceful Victorian home by the lake. It was rare for them to have a Saturday afternoon meeting, but everyone agreed to take advantage of the warmer weather, and Isabel's backyard would be the perfect setting. Cristine drove up to the white house with long burgundy shutters on each window and noticed Claire's and Tina's cars already parked. She got out of her car and heard voices in the backyard. Following the noise, she saw her friends gathered in the gazebo that had wisteria growing up and on top of the wooden roof.

Waving when she was noticed, Cristine carried the dessert, a lemon pound cake with lemon icing. Homemade. For some reason she was doing a lot of cooking lately.

Probably because she had already gained fifteen pounds, most of it in her belly. The baby ate a lot.

"Hey, you," Paula called out, coming out of the gazebo with bare feet. "Don't you look radiant!"

Cristine chuckled. Radiant? Couldn't be the gauzy flowing coral dress she was wearing to hide her bump? "Hi, Paula. You're looking pretty good yourself. You must be healing well."

"I think it's having less stress in my life," Paula said, kissing Cristine's cheek. "I'll never be able to thank you for what you've done."

"Nonsense. How does Conor like Coventry?"

"Would you believe he's thriving? And so am I. I've looked into what it will take for me to complete my thesis and I think I can do it through the University of Pennsylvania."

"That's fabulous, Paula. Good for you."

Tina yelled out, "Bring that woman up here. I've got news."

"Coming," Cristine called out, and walked with Paula to the big gazebo Isabel's husband had built.

Isabel had put a round table inside and everyone was seated around it.

"This is a terrific idea, Issy. It's so pretty and the weather is perfect," Cristine said with a grin as she took off her wide straw hat and red sparkly heels then began her walk around the table, kissing everyone's cheek. After the greetings were completed, Cristine sat down in the last empty chair next to Isabel and said, "So, Tina. What's your news?"

"I found a woman in need of help."

"What's her story?" Claire asked, picking up her wine glass.

"Let's see . . . she lives in Fort Washington. She's a single mother, and, even though she paid for the used car, her live-in lover of five years put it in his name and then walked out on her and took the car. She's a nurse. Smart enough to go on to medical school. And now she's doing shift work at a hospital and getting there by bus. Like she leaves her house at four in the morning to get into the city."

"How did you hear about her?" Paula asked, using a small triangle of buttered toast to scoop up the artichoke dip.

"A friend of mine lives in her building and told me about her, what a good woman she is and what a lousy deal she got from her partner. I went over to visit my friend and I met her. She must think I'm real nosy, because I kept asking her questions. They really need a car."

Pouring herself a glass of chilled water, Cristine turned to Kelly. "Do you have any time to check in with the local car dealerships?"

"What are we looking for? New or used?"

"Whatever we can get," Claire answered. "The way the foundation is going to be set up is to try first for sponsors and then make up the difference. Say if a dealership would donate a portion of the price of, say, a Hyundai, we would pick up the difference."

"Anybody know any car salesmen?" Tina asked.

"I do," Isabel answered. "The father of one of my clients. I could ask him."

"Great," Cristine exclaimed with a big smile. "See, we can do this!"

"I'll call him on Monday," Isabel said. "Perhaps he can direct us."

"And Claire has news," Cristine announced.

Everyone's attention turned toward Claire.

"I'm in negotiations with a firm in the Bahamas for your condo, Tina. It's looking very good."

Tina's jaw dropped. "No! I can't accept."

Cristine laughed. "I told you if you didn't move on it, Claire would. Face it, Tina, you're gonna be gettin' your groove on soon."

Kelly grinned and started swaying while snapping her fingers. "Ohhhh, Bahama Mama's on the beach with some firm gorgeous island man! Plan on visitors."

"And Cristine has news," Claire pronounced amid the chuckles.

Everyone turned their attention to her and Cristine didn't know whether to glare at Claire or just blurt it out.

The glare wouldn't even faze her friend, so blurting was her only option. "I'm pregnant. I'm going to have a baby."

Tina, Kelly, and Paula looked stunned. Cristine cleared her throat.

"I know it's a shock."

"A baby!" Kelly murmured.

"Who's the father?" Tina asked.

"Charlie?" Paula asked in a voice that sounded troubled.

"First of all," Cristine began, "Charlie is *not* the father."

"Thank God," Tina breathed in relief. "You don't want to pass on those genes."

"Who is?" Kelly asked.

Taking a deep breath, Cristine said, "His name is Daniel Burns."

"The guy who did your kitchen?" Tina asked in surprise.

She nodded. "That's right. And I'm not going to get married and Daniel is not going to move in with me. I'm going to raise this child alone."

"But he'll be a part of the baby's life, right?"

"Yes. He wants that." Cristine smiled. "This is good news, ladies. Somebody ought to be making a toast."

"How do you feel?" Paula asked.

"I feel fine, except that I'm cooking like crazy and gaining weight."

"*That's* why you look radiant," Paula pronounced. "Doesn't she look radiant?"

"Right. Radiant," Claire murmured. "Okay, so let's raise our glasses to the new mommy." She waited for everyone. "To Cristine and the new baby, may you both travel this road with ease, with love, and with good health."

"Here, here."

"To Cristine and the new baby."

"What do you want? A girl or a boy?"

Cristine grinned. "Thanks, everyone. And it's a girl."

"How do you know?" Kelly asked. "Isn't it too soon?"

"I just know."

'Mother's intuition," Paula declared. "It can be very strong. Don't be surprised, Cristine, if your intuitive powers become more sharp during the pregnancy. It's the increase in hormones."

Cristine simply nodded. No need to tell anyone that it was Daniel who named the sex of the baby.

"So you are happy about this?" Isabel asked.

She smiled into her friend's knowing eyes. "Yes, Issy. I'm over the shock and I'm happy."

"Good."

"Now has Paula told everyone her news?" Cristine asked, hoping to take the attention off herself. "About her thesis?"

As Paula became the center of attention, Cristine sat back in her chair. It was then she noticed Claire still looking at her. Cristine raised her eyebrows in question, wondering if Claire was having a problem with this pregnancy and everything surrounding it.

Claire silently mouthed, *You do look radiant,* and smiled.

Cristine smiled back in relief and gratitude. No matter how crazy it all seemed, Claire was on her side. And that's all she needed to know.

On the way home from the meeting, Cristine stopped at the pharmacy to pick up more of the prenatal vitamins Kate Abrams had prescribed. She was waiting for them when she heard a voice behind her.

"Cristine?"

Her stomach seemed to drop below her waistline. She swallowed and turned around. "Charlie. How are you?"

"I thought that was you," he said, smiling.

He looked pale, drawn, and thinner. Somewhere inside of her, she felt sorry for him.

"I'm just stopping in," she said as the pharmacist called out her name. "Excuse me."

She walked up to the counter and brought out her wallet.

"Now there'll be a standing prescription every month for the prenatal vitamins. You won't have to call it in for the next six months."

She cringed, hoping Charlie hadn't heard that. "Thank you. How much is it?"

She paid for the vitamins and turned around to see Charlie staring at her with the oddest expression. He'd heard.

"You're pregnant?" he asked in a stunned voice.

She nodded as his name was called.

He looked frightened, as though not knowing what he should do. "Can you wait a minute? I have to get this new inhaler the doctor ordered."

"Sure." She sighed as he turned to the counter. Why was she not surprised to run into him at his favorite place? The drugstore? Maybe she should switch pharmacies. As Charlie completed his transaction, Cristine studied him from the back, wishing he would move away. Haverton was her home, had been her home before she'd ever met him. She didn't want to run into him, or be dreading that she would.

He came back to her, carrying his little bag of goodies. "Can we go across the street, to the park?"

"All right," she answered, knowing that whatever he had to say to her had been building since that day in her kitchen when Daniel had shown up. She might as well get it over with, she thought, leaving the store and walking next to him across the street.

"You look great," he remarked as they walked toward a bench.

"Thanks." Cristine stopped and sat down. Charlie followed.

They sat for a few moments in silence, then Charlie said, "Is it that guy?"

She grinned. "You mean Daniel, the person you met in my house?"

"Yeah. Him."

She exhaled deeply as she watched the children playing, the people walking dogs. "Yes. Daniel is the father."

Charlie nodded. "I read about you in the paper, about the lottery, but I thought if I contacted you right away you'd think it was because of the money. So I waited. Guess I waited too long."

"Charlie, our time was over. Actually, I wanted to thank you for realizing that before I did. It would have been nice to have talked about it before you found someone else, but I hope you're happy." There. That just about said it all.

"Happy?" His voice sounded strangled. "How can I be happy when you were the best thing that ever happened to me and I . . . I treated you like that? I'm so sorry, Cristine."

"I forgive you, Charlie. I really do."

"Ever since I left you, everything in my life has been falling apart. My car won't pass inspection. That last heavy rain flooded the apartment, ruined her furniture, and created black mold. I can't breathe there, and now I'm going to court to fight her landlord, and I think I'm going to be fired any day now."

He still had his litany of complaints. "You'll get through it. You always do."

He took off his glasses and pinched the bridge of his nose. "I'm too tired this time. I don't see the point when good guys always finish last."

She was silent for a moment. "So now you're thinking of killing yourself?"

"Why get up in the morning when nothing is working out, no matter how hard you try? What kind of world is this when good guys finish last?"

"Okay, hold it right there," she said, turning her head and looking at him. "The best advice I can give you is to look in the Yellow Pages for the county mental health association, and call that number. And this isn't a judgment, but simply an observation: as for good guys finishing last . . . Charlie, you aren't one of the good guys. You're a manipulator. You're doing it right now. Stop feeling sorry for yourself. What you're going through is simply karma. Every single thing that's happening to you is a result of a choice you've made. Accept it and go on, or don't. You have free will."

"God, you've turned cold. Is that what money has done to you?"

She laughed. "I had this figured out before I won the lottery. I didn't realize how much of a manipulator you are until you'd left. And I blame myself. I allowed it. I thought it was love, but it was sick. They call it codependency and I think I could have been the poster child for it with you. I paid more attention to you than to myself. So yes, I do thank you for leaving."

He stood up. "Speaking of leaving. I can't believe what you've turned into."

She grinned. "A healthy human being? If you continue to believe you're weak and sickly, Charlie, you will be. But I'll tell you what I will do for you. I'll buy you a ticket to Denver, if you want to get back to your family. You can stay here and contemplate suicide, or you can begin again closer to the people you love. Let me know." And she glanced at a woman pushing a child in a wheelchair. Now there was someone who was truly sick.

Charlie simply walked away and Cristine, feeling good about speaking her mind, smiled at the woman and the young girl who was wearing a baseball cap to hide her bald head. "Beautiful afternoon, isn't it?" she called out, putting Charlie out of her mind.

"Yes," the woman answered, slowing down in front of her. "We thought we'd take advantage of the nice weather and get out."

"Well, good for you. I'm Cristine Dobbins," she said, holding out her hand.

"Monica Stratford, and this is Casey."

"Hiya, Casey. Like your cap. Think the Phillies have a chance this year?" She held out her hand to the girl, who looked to be about nine years old, pale with dark circles under her eyes.

A thin hand met her own and Cristine gently shook it.

"I don't know," the girl answered with a weak smile.

Cristine's heart broke, as she watched the child's bravery. "Do you live here in Haverton?"

Monica nodded. "How about you?"

"Yes, I've lived here for years and . . ." She stopped speaking and touched her belly. "Oh, I think I just felt the baby move!"

Monica grinned. "Is this your first?"

"Yes, and—" Cristine was startled as the flutter became stronger. "Wow, this is a weird sensation."

"Oh, wait till it starts kicking. I thought Casey was throwing softballs in the womb. Do you mind? Can I touch?"

Cristine was so surprised by the feeling inside of her that she smoothed the material over her bump and exposed it for the woman.

Monica gently put her hand on Cristine and waited.

A strong feeling fluttered inside of her. "Did you feel that?"

"I'm not sure." Monica sat down next to her.

Cristine looked at Casey, staring at her mother's hand. "Do you want to try?" she asked the girl.

"Can I?"

"Sure," Cristine said with a laugh as she moved closer to the edge of the bench. "Why not?"

Cristine watched the girl extend her arm and place her thin hand next to her mother's. Immediately, there was something stronger than a flutter and everyone jumped in surprise and laughed. "What was *that*?" Cristine demanded.

"That was definitely a kick," Monica stated. "How far along are you?"

"Three or four months. We aren't exactly sure yet."

"Really? I would think for a kick that strong you're further along."

"Can I do it again?" Casey asked in a shy voice, seemingly fascinated with the experience.

"Of course," Cristine said, holding Casey's hand and bringing it to her belly. She placed her hand over the child's as they waited.

Soon there was another kick and Cristine stiffened in surprise and then giggled with the young girl. "Did you feel that?"

Casey nodded and grinned broadly.

"Listen, any time you want to make friends, just give me a call. How totally cool for her to have a buddy before she's born." Cristine went into her purse and took out a business card. Handing it to Monica, she said meaningfully, "Seriously, call anytime if you need anything."

"How do you know it's a girl?" Casey asked, interrupting the silent communication between the two women.

Cristine turned her attention back to the child. "Because I've been told it's a girl and now I believe it. She certainly seems to like you."

"Is she kicking again?"

"No, not now."

"Can I try again?"

"Casey, don't be pushy," her mother admonished.

"It's okay." Cristine grinned. "This is so cool, isn't it?"

she asked the child, taking her hand and placing it on her bump. Within moments, another strong kick.

She and Casey giggled together. "See, she *does* like you!"

"Well, we should be going," Monica announced, standing up.

"Me too," Cristine said while rising. She looked at Monica. "I meant that. Please call me. Anything I can do."

Monica smiled her understanding and her thanks. "I will."

Cristine bent down. "And Casey, it was a real pleasure meeting you today. Maybe we can get together again? Your mom has my phone number."

Casey smiled. "What are you going to name her?"

Cristine blinked with surprise. "I haven't thought up a name yet. Why don't we do that? You make a list and I will too, and then we can get together and compare."

"Okay."

She touched Casey's hand. "All right, I'm going to depend on you now. When you have your list, tell your mom to call."

She stood and looked at Monica who mouthed, *Thank you,* and Cristine's heart expanded. How brave of them both.

"Bye, Casey," she said, waving.

Casey waved back as they resumed their walk through the park.

Cristine sighed and held her hand at her bump. Now it was real. Tangibly real. There really was a baby growing within her. "Hello, little one," she breathed as love began to swirl around inside of her. "Hopefully, we just made a new friend." And she prayed Monica would call.

There had to be something she could do for them.

*Chapter*

# 20

CRISTINE PULLED BACK FROM WORK EVEN MORE AS her pregnancy progressed. She stopped trying to hide her state and began wearing clothes that outlined her belly. Everywhere she went people seemed to smile at her. She was happy, truly happy, for the first time in her life. She refused to worry about the future. Daniel said he would be there for them, and he had shown up every time she had called to him. Unfortunately, most of the time was to taste the newest batch of apple cinnamon muffins she'd baked, or the pear tarts or the banana cream pie with chocolate sauce. No wonder she was gaining weight. Today she'd forced herself out of the kitchen and into her garden.

Deadheading a salmon-colored geranium, she looked at the purple and white petunias, the multicolored snapdragons, the daisies, the black-eyed Susans, the vincas, the lilies . . . everywhere she gazed there was an abundance of vibrant color.

Her garden had never looked this good, this alive, and she hadn't done anything different, except give it a little more time and appreciate it more, she thought as the baby kicked and her cell phone rang at the same time. Rubbing her ever-increasing belly, Cristine walked back to the patio and picked up her phone.

"Hello?" she asked, sitting down in a comfortable chair.

"Cristine? Cristine Dobbins?"

She didn't recognize the voice. "Yes," she replied cautiously.

There seemed to be a sigh of relief. "This is Monica Stratford. I met you with my daughter Casey in the park a few weeks ago."

"Yes, of course. How are you, Monica? I'm glad you called."

"I'm sorry it hasn't been sooner, but we've been really busy."

"How is Casey?" Cristine asked, hoping the little girl's condition hadn't worsened.

"She's doing fine. Great, in fact."

"Really?" Cristine asked with relief. "That's wonderful news."

"I was wondering . . . well, Casey has made her list of names . . . I know that you probably were just being nice, but Casey really wants to see you and give them to you."

Cristine had forgotten about the list. "Absolutely. Though I have yet to make up my own. Do you want to meet, or you could come here? I'm just puttering around in the garden."

"You won't mind?"

"I'd love to see you both again. Let me give you directions."

Five minutes later, Cristine brought out chilled juice and a plate of pear tarts and peanut butter cookies. The cookies had been baked that morning and she had never liked peanut butter cookies before. It was a very strange craving, since she'd tasted one and it hadn't done much for her, but she'd had the strongest appetite for them when she'd awakened. So many things about this pregnancy were odd. Like the way she kept getting bigger. When she'd asked Daniel about it, he said he couldn't tell her when the baby would arrive, that the baby would know when to be born. And Cristine couldn't go back to the doctor, for how could she possibly explain what was happening? She couldn't. Daniel said he would be able to tell if anything was wrong and, so far, the baby was thriving.

She sat in the chair, resting her hands on her belly, and looked out on her garden. It really was gorgeous, thriving in a way it never had before. She thought she should take pictures and . . . sheesh, she'd better stop daydreaming and get started with that list before Casey arrived.

Hmm, names . . . She had always liked Gabrielle and Kaelie. Gabrielle Dobbins. Kaelie Dobbins. Sounded all right. And then there was Maureen, such a pretty name, but someone might nickname her Maura and there had been a Sister Maura at one of the catechism schools she'd been forced to attend as a child. The woman wasn't very nice, especially if you dared ask a question, like how did pairs of all the animals in the world fit on one boat. Okay, Maureen was out. This name-picking was harder than she'd thought.

She went into the house to get a piece of paper as the front doorbell rang. That was fast, she thought, anxious to see Casey. When she opened the front door, Cristine's smile froze as she murmured, "Hi . . ."

Monica stood with her daughter at her side. No wheelchair, and Casey looked wonderful in shorts and a T-shirt that said *GIRLS RULE*. The dark circles were gone and her cheeks had color to them. There was even a fuzz of hair peeking out the front of the turned-around baseball cap.

"Are you sure we aren't interrupting?" Monica asked.

Cristine shook her head. "Not at all," she managed to get out. "Casey, you look fabulous!"

The young girl grinned. "Thanks."

Remembering herself, Cristine stepped aside. "I'm sorry. Come in, come in . . ." She looked questioningly at Monica over Casey's head and the girl's mother's eyes widened as she grinned and shrugged.

"Wow, you're blossoming," Monica said, looking at Cristine's stomach. "Are you sure you're only four months along?"

Cristine laughed. "I'm not sure of anything anymore, except I think I'm growing bigger by the minute. C'mon. I have everything set up out back on the patio. We can go out there." She led them through her house, acknowledging Monica's compliments, and opened the back door.

"Oh, it's gorgeous out here," Monica exclaimed. "It looks like a painting. However did you get your flowers to spread so soon? Mine still look like I just planted them."

"I don't know exactly."

"Fertilizer?"

"Just the same planting soil I've used for years," Cristine said, sitting down at the table as Casey put a small book she was carrying on it and then sat in a chair.

Monica joined them and Cristine asked, "Would you like some juice? I made peanut butter cookies this morning. I think they're pretty good."

"They're Casey's favorite," Monica said, and Casey smiled shyly.

"Well, then I must have made them for you," Cristine said, putting two on a small plate and handing them to the girl.

"Thank you," she murmured, looking at Cristine and then at her belly.

"Monica, what can I get for you?"

"Just juice for now, thanks."

After setting back, Cristine looked at Casey and said, "Your mom said you have a list. You're better than I am. I've only come up with two names, and I'm not sure about one of them."

"What are they?" Casey asked.

"Gabrielle and Kaelie."

Casey picked up her book and began leafing through it. "How do you spell them?" she asked her mother.

Monica told her and then turned to Cristine. "She insisted we buy a name book. I'm afraid she took you quite literally."

"Hey, I can use all the help I can get."

"Gabrielle means 'devoted to God' and 'confident.'" Casey read out loud.

"That sounds pretty good and . . . oh, the baby kicked. Maybe she likes it."

"How do you spell the other name?"

Cristine told her and then turned to Monica as Casey began her research. "She looks wonderful," Cristine murmured. "I'm so happy for you both."

Monica looked at her daughter with great love. "I am so grateful. She started feeling better, stronger, and I noticed the color coming back. It's . . . it's like a miracle, isn't it, honey?"

Casey looked up from the book and nodded. "The doctor said my tumor is shrinking. No more chemo."

Cristine's jaw dropped. "My God, that's fantastic! I didn't know what . . . I mean, I thought . . ."

"It's okay, Cristine." Monica grinned. "We're just so happy the CAT scan came back with good results. Fantastic results. First time."

"Kaelie isn't in here," Casey stated. "But Kalea is and it means 'adorned with wreath of flowers.'"

"That's pretty. What about your list, Casey? What did you come up with?" Cristine asked.

Casey went to the back of the book and pulled out a folded piece of paper. Seated next to her, Cristine could see Casey had drawn red hearts all over the page. Her own heart expanded toward this remarkable child.

"I have Chloe. It means 'vibrant one who searches.'"

"Another good name," Cristine said. "What others do you have?"

"Hannah. It means 'gracious and compassionate.'"

"I like that one. Hannah Dobbins."

"Wait. There's more," Casey said, holding her list as though it were an important document.

"Oh, I know," Cristine answered seriously. "I was just trying that one out. What are the rest?"

"Sara means 'beloved princess.'"

"Okay."

"Faith means 'firm believer.'"

"Good one."

"Rachel. It means 'innocent lamb.'"

"Nice."

Casey took a deep breath. "And Angelique. It means 'angel and messenger, a bringer of glad news.' Or you can use Angelea, Angelica, Angelina."

Cristine saw that Casey had drawn tiny hearts all around her last selection. And just then, the baby kicked. "Oh, I do believe she liked that one," she said with a laugh.

Casey looked pleased as she stared at Cristine's belly.

"Do you want to feel her again?"

Casey nodded, looking almost eager.

"Go ahead. Give me your hand."

So Cristine took Casey's hand and placed it on her belly and looked at this dear child who seemed so interested in her own child. The baby kicked and Casey giggled.

"Keep it there. See if she does it again."

They waited a full minute.

"Can I read her the names?" Casey asked shyly.

"Good idea."

Casey kept one hand on Cristine's belly and reached for her paper. "Should we start with yours?"

Cristine shrugged. "Any way you want to do it is fine with me."

"Gabrielle."

A light kick. "Did you feel it?" Cristine asked.

Casey nodded. "She likes it."

"Read yours now."

"Chloe?"

Nothing.

"Hannah?"

Nothing.

"Sara?"

Nothing.

"I think she likes Gabrielle," Casey whispered.

"Read the rest."

"Faith?"

Nothing.

"Rachel?"

Still nothing.

Casey paused and she looked up at Cristine. "This is my favorite."

"I know. Mine too."

The young girl inhaled with great seriousness. "Angelique."

Both Casey and Cristine giggled as they felt a strong kick.

"Wow," Casey breathed, staring at Cristine's belly with fascination. "She hears us."

"I don't know, honey, but she certainly seems to like the name you picked."

"She hears us," Casey said with conviction. "And she understands too."

A shiver ran through Cristine and she wondered if Casey was right.

Monica said, "Casey, why don't you try Cristine's peanut butter cookies? They're your favorite."

Reluctantly, Casey removed her hand. "Okay." She got up, picked up a cookie, and began to walk through the garden, stopping at a lily plant loaded with buds.

"I'm sorry about that," Monica murmured, watching her child. "Ever since she met you, she's been positively fascinated with you and your baby. We had to go out that very afternoon and find the name book and then she pored over names for almost two weeks, and I swear, Cristine, she kept getting stronger and stronger. I thought it was just me, praying for so long, refusing to give up hope, and then I took her back to her oncologist and they did the CAT scan. The doctor was stunned when he saw her and he can't explain it. He can only say it must be the result of the chemo, but it didn't do this last year when she underwent her first treatment. You saw her, Cristine. Except for the lack of hair, she's not the same child."

"The change is remarkable. And in such a short time."

"It's beyond remarkable. It's a miracle. Those doctors were trying to prepare me for losing her, but I refused to listen. You can't give up hope, right?"

"No, no, you can't," Cristine said, unable to imagine what horror Monica had been through. "Your family must be thrilled."

"My mom agrees it must be a miracle. We've all been praying . . ."

"I don't mean to pry, Monica, but you're not alone, are you? Casey's father . . . ?"

The woman smiled sadly. "He blames himself. He was in the first gulf war and he swears they all inhaled depleated uranium from the anti-tank shells. So many have developed diseases since that war . . . and then he started drinking and became depressed. They put him on medication and . . . and he tried to kill himself. He's in Ankcora Hospital now and I'm fighting the government to continue paying for it. They still aren't acknowledging post-traumatic stress syndrome for the first gulf war."

"I don't know what to say . . . you poor woman." Cristine was stunned. "How have you managed?"

Monica grinned and shrugged her shoulders. "I manage because what's the alternative? It's better now. I don't even know how many hours I've spent in the car, going to one hospital for Casey and then another for Mike. I'm just grateful my insurance covered Casey."

Cristine sighed and leaned in, trying to put her elbows on the table. It was too uncomfortable, so she sat back and rested her hands on her belly, like Buddha. "Listen, Monica, you've probably been too busy lately to read the papers, but I won the lottery and some of my friends—"

"Oh, my God! That was *you*?"

Smiling, Cristine held her finger to her lips. "Shh, I'd rather not broadcast it. Way too many strange calls. Anyway, my friends and I are putting together a foundation to help out women, women who are stressed and have given away so much of themselves. What can we do? How can we help?"

Monica shook her head. "That's really kind, but with Casey getting well, that's all I could ask for."

"What about your husband? Isn't Ankcora a state hospital?"

"I know it's like warehousing human beings, but it was the best we could do, and to qualify I had to put my house in my mother's name."

Cristine blew out her breath. "Okay. How about this? What if we do some research to find a private facility that specializes in post-traumatic stress syndrome? Someplace where Mike can get individual help. I'm not saying you'll get your husband back, Monica, but why not try?" She looked at the remarkably strong woman. "Do you want him back?"

Monica's eyes filled with tears. "Oh, don't get me started, Cristine. I put it all in God's hands and—"

"And what if God is using me to help?" Cristine interrupted. "C'mon, all these resources are there to be used. I don't think it was a coincidence meeting you and Casey in the park. I think we were supposed to meet."

Monica wiped away the tears from her cheek. "You want to hear something really crazy?"

"Why not?" Cristine said with a sympathetic laugh. "I'm getting more comfortable with the unexplainable every day."

"Casey says your baby is making her better. Ever since she touched your stomach in the park, she says something happened inside of her. I know . . . believe me, I know. But if she truly believes that and she is getting better than I'm willing to believe anything."

Cristine crossed her arms over her belly. No wonder Casey was fascinated with her baby.

"I didn't mean to make you uncomfortable," Monica said in a low voice.

Cristine shook her head. "I'm not uncomfortable . . . I'm . . . I guess I should feel honored that Casey believes that." She looked at the woman next to her. "I've been doing some research on how powerful the mind is."

"Mind over matter, you mean?"

Nodding, Cristine said, "Exactly. How our thoughts can create our reality. How our state of mind affects what we manifest in our lives. Who knows? If Casey really believes what you've just said, for her it must be true . . . and it's working. Just don't tell anyone else, okay?"

Monica nodded. "All right."

"Look, it may just be what the doctor said, the chemo is finally working, or it may be whatever Casey feels when she touches my belly. I don't know. Nobody knows. I simply want to protect my baby. You can understand that."

"Of course. I only wanted to tell you because it's obvious she's attached to you and your baby. It's the only explanation I have."

"Like I said, I'm honored, Monica, but let's get back to your husband." Cristine wanted to take the attention off her baby. "This isn't charity I'm talking about. These are resources available to women like you who are overwhelmed by life's curveballs. Would you allow me to give your name and phone number to the woman who's direct-ing this foundation? I think we really could help."

Monica swallowed back her emotion. "Sure," she mur-mured. "I just didn't dare allow myself to dream of Mike coming back to us again."

"Dare to dream, Monica," Cristine said, and touched the woman's arm. "And when we get some information that looks like we can make this a reality for your family, then pass on your courage, your belief in hope, to someone else who's taken some tough hits from life. Tell them your ex-perience, your life story."

"But not about the baby."

"No, not about the baby," Cristine said. "I have to pro-tect her. If Casey believes it, then we won't shatter her be-lief, but I don't want this child to become a curiosity. She deserves a normal childhood. You understand that, right?"

"Of course." Monica looked at her watch. "Goodness, we didn't mean to stay so long. I have to get Casey to my mother's and then get ready for work."

"What do you do?"

"Medical billing. And they've been really great about rearranging my schedule to spend the days with Casey."

Cristine smiled. "There are good people in the world."

Monica stood up. "And you're one of them. Thank you for . . . well, for everything, Cristine."

"Let me get your phone number." She stood and walked into the house, hearing Monica tell Casey they had to leave.

They met her in the kitchen and Cristine wrote down the phone number, promising someone would call, then she walked them to the front door. Casey shyly touched her hand.

"Can I say good-bye?"

It took Cristine a moment to realize what the child meant. "Of course."

Casey put her cheek on Cristine's belly.

"Bye, Angelique . . ." she whispered, "and thank you."

Cristine felt her throat tighten with emotion and she placed her hand on Casey's ball cap. "I'm sure she hears you, honey."

"I know she does," Casey said, and kissed Cristine's belly lightly. "She told me."

Cristine looked at Monica, who had tears in her eyes. "She did?"

"I heard her in my head," Casey said with a bright smile as she looked up.

"Okay, Casey, let's get a move on it or I'll be late for work," Monica said with a sniffle.

Cristine bent down and kissed Casey's cheek. "You are an extraordinary young girl, Casey Stratford. Come back and see me soon."

"Okay." She waved as her mother opened the door. "Bye, Cristine."

"Bye, Casey. Bye, Monica."

She watched until they got in the car and then waved again as they backed out of the driveway. Casey waved as they drove away, and when Cristine closed the door, she shook her head at the unusual visit. Casey believed that her baby was making her better?

Walking through her house, Cristine touched her belly and said, "Honey, it looks like you've made your first friend." She opened the back door to clean up the patio table and her attention was immediately directed to her garden.

It was too early, her rational mind told her. The buds were just beginning to grow larger. How could this have happened?

The lilies Casey had been standing in front of were now in glorious full bloom.

# Chapter

# 21

"Daniel," she called out. "We need to talk."

"Do you realize most of our discussions begin in your kitchen?"

She was getting comfortable with him suddenly appearing and no longer jumped in surprise, but when she heard his voice and turned her head, her heart tightened with emotion. "Why don't you come on your own? Don't you ever just want to be with me?" Even to her own ears she sounded clingy and needy and she mentally cringed. "I just mean that it might be nice if you wanted to be with me." That sounded as bad.

He came to stand behind her and wrapped his arms around her, stroking her belly. "I always want to be with you, Cristine. You are a part of me now." He kissed her earlobe. "Our daughter grows big," he whispered.

She shivered as his breath ignited desire. Wasn't she not supposed to feel sexy when she was as big as a house? "Yes, our daughter grows big and I'm beginning to resemble a beached whale when I lie down. Honestly, Daniel, it's not even five months and I look like I'm ready to pop. People are starting to ask questions."

"Do you have to answer their questions?"

She shook her head. "You don't understand. How do I

explain this? It's bad enough I can't go to a doctor every month for a regular checkup, but what happens when I deliver this baby sooner than nine months? It's got to be sooner, or I won't be able to get out of bed, let alone breathe."

"Shh, let me check," he whispered and held his hands again over her belly. "Yes, she is progressing well. It won't be long."

Cristine turned around to face him. "Daniel, I'm scared. I can't deliver this baby at home without a doctor. What if something goes wrong?"

"Why do you even entertain such thoughts? You know how powerful your mind is. I promise you everything will be fine. You must believe that."

"And you'll be with me?"

"I promised I would."

She sighed. "We have to talk about Casey, the little girl who came over here. What's happening to her?"

Daniel smiled and pushed a tendril of hair behind her ear. "She is healing."

"I know that. I can see that. But how? She's told her mother she thinks it's because of the baby."

"There was a transference of energy."

Cristine pulled out of his embrace and held her stomach protectively. "You mean our baby *did* heal her?"

"I mean our baby transferred energy to Casey and Casey was receptive to a higher vibration."

"That's how she did that with the lilies? Casey now has some of my baby's energy?"

"Casey's energy needed a boost, you might say, and once she had received that, her own frequency kicked in, but at a high vibration. She will be an extraordinary healer herself."

"Daniel, I don't want people to think our baby can heal them. I want to protect her so she can grow up normally . . . as normal as possible," she added, envisioning lines of people wanting to touch her child. "This can't turn into a circus!"

"Circus? Why would you use that word?"

"I mean that I don't want people to look on our baby as some miracle healer and want to touch her or be near her. I'm not being selfish. If it happens like with Casey, okay, but it could be dangerous if the wrong people heard about"—Cristine's voice lowered—"her power."

"You mean the government?"

"Or if pharmaceutical companies think it's something in her and they might want to study it. You just don't know."

Daniel reached out and took her hand. "Then you must stop these thoughts. Immediately. Haven't you experienced that what you fear you will manifest in some way? Stop worrying."

She pulled her hand away. "Well, that's easy for you to say. You're not the one who's pregnant, who'll be the child's only parent, who'll raise her and protect her and—"

"And you think I am going to desert you?" he interrupted. "Have we not already had this discussion?"

"Well, I'm scared!" she protested and broke into tears. "All this responsibility is on me!"

Daniel pulled her into his arms again. "It's all right. It is the chemicals, the hormones in your body."

"Oh, that's right!" she blubbered, grabbing a dishtowel to wipe her face. "Blame it on hormones." She left his embrace again and began pacing in front of the sink. "Which brings me to another question. If men have been screwing up, playing *Lord of the Flies* for thousands of years, and women are hormonal, then how can women be the answer to saving the world?"

"Not saving the world, Cristine," he answered with that now maddeningly patient smile. "Saving humanity. And more than likely, it will be women who are . . . how would you say it . . . ah, yes, postmenopausal women who will assume positions of power."

"Old women?"

"Not old. Wise women."

She stopped and stared at him. "So you're saying that we'll have to wait until this baby is over fifty years old before we see any changes?"

"I never said that. You're seeing changes already. Look at Casey. Look at your garden. Do not think you are alone in this, Cristine. There are others."

"What do you mean, *others*?"

"Just what the word implies. I am not the only one who has chosen this way to evolve, and I am not the first."

"There are other women who are pregnant? Other babies?"

He nodded. "And there will be more."

She held on to the counter to steady herself. "From you?" She had to ask, even though the thought made her feel ill.

"From me?" He looked puzzled.

"Yes! Will you be the father of these . . . children?"

He laughed and shook his head. "You give me too much credit, my love. For me, you are quite enough. I am not evolved to handle anything more."

She felt the tension leave her body and the baby kicked as if in protest to the emotional turmoil taking place. Cristine gently rubbed a tight knot on her side. A knee? A foot? She mentally apologized for being so irrational.

"So I test your limits, huh?" she asked with a reluctant grin.

He leaned on the counter and grinned back at her. "Yes, you do. And I shall admit to you that I miss our times of unity. Do you?"

She laughed. "God, yes! When you whispered in my ear earlier I wanted to tear your clothes off. I didn't think big pregnant women got this horny."

"Horny?"

"Aroused." She walked up to him and stroked his hair. "Sexually excited."

"Yes . . ." he murmured, his eyes becoming darker with desire.

"But we can't."

"We can't?"

"Can we?"

He blinked, pulling her into his arms as far as he could with a big belly separating them. "We can my way."

"Really?"

His smile deepened and he nodded.

"The baby will be okay?"

"I think she will be fine."

Cristine pulled away and took his hand. "But not here," she said eagerly. "I can't fall down. Let's go upstairs to bed. We can make love my way until . . . unity."

Once upstairs they began to undress. Cristine was shy because of her body and Daniel must have sensed it.

"Why are you hiding yourself?" he asked, taking her hand away from her breasts.

"Daniel, please, I'm just not comfortable with the way I look now." She tried to take her hand back and get under the sheets.

Instead, he held her tighter and brought her closer to him. He pulled the cotton panties down and she stepped out of them. Rising, he said, "Please let me look at you. You're beautiful."

"I'm not," she protested. "I've gained so much weight and I feel clumsy and ungraceful and—"

"Stop," he gently commanded, turning her around until her back was against his bare chest. "Don't be afraid of this . . ."

"What? What are you going to do?"

The bathroom door closed by itself and the full-length door mirror exposed her naked body.

"Oh, God, Daniel . . . don't."

"Shh . . . look at yourself the way I see you."

"I can't!" she protested, closing her eyes.

"Open your eyes. Please . . ."

"This is so embarrassing, Daniel."

"Open your eyes, Cristine, and see who you are."

Reluctantly, she did as he asked, and tried not to cringe at the sight of her bloated body. It was one thing to observe herself getting out of the shower. Quite another to have the man you love standing behind you ready to do a critique.

"Shh, stop your chaotic thought process and listen to me," he asked.

She tried to clear her mind. Maybe if she concentrated on him, his hard naked body behind her, his hands on her . . .

"This is how I see you. You are everything a woman is meant to be, Cristine," he whispered against her hair, staring into her eyes through the mirror. "Your breasts . . ." And he cupped them in his hands. "So full and beautiful." He ran his hands over them until her nipples were tight and erect. Then he moved his hands slowly to her belly. "We did this, Cristine," he whispered, and she was mesmerized watching his hands. "We did this to express ourselves and created this miracle we call our daughter. How wondrous are you that your body expands to cradle our child? You are a magnificent woman. A goddess. This is your destiny, Cristine, and you radiate your beauty to all who see you." He bent his head and began kissing her shoulder while she watched in the mirror as his hand lowered even more. He cradled her and murmured against her skin, "And your womanhood is warm and moist to the touch, fertile, ripe, waiting . . ."

"I'm gonna fall down," she moaned. "My legs aren't going to hold me up."

"I will hold you up, my love," he said, straightening

and supporting her. "But look at yourself, your real self now, and see your beauty."

And she did as he asked, seeing herself as he said . . . fertile, ripe, whole.

"You're beautiful, Cristine, more beautiful than you have ever been."

She looked at her reflection and believed what he was saying and she began to notice a light, an aura of soft, hazy colors swirling around them both. "I am beautiful," she whispered in surprised awe as tears of gratitude sprang from her eyes.

"Yes, you are. And I love you, every cell that makes you the goddess you are."

And then he took her, carried her to the bed and beyond. Far beyond.

There were certain aspects to having Daniel around that were proving to be extremely handy, Cristine thought as she observed the guest bedroom turning into a nursery. She'd paid to have the walls painted a soft creamy buttercup yellow and the wooden floors refinished in a white wash, but Daniel insisted that he assist her in making a sanctuary for their child. She had shown him several pictures from magazines and, together, they had picked their favorite selections.

"Now, it will be much more efficient if I do not keep this form," he said, looking at all the pieces of the crib on the floor. He scanned the instructions one more time and then disintegrated into swirling lights.

Cristine held her hands on her belly as she watched the crib being assembled in a matter of minutes. When the mattress floated in the air and landed in the standing crib, she said, "It needs to be higher. Bring the metal spring thing to the first position."

And the mattress hovered in the air as Daniel did as she requested. When it was in position, she grinned. Perfect. The creamy white Jenny Lind crib might be old-fashioned, but it was exactly what she had wanted. And it matched the white dresser and the changing table that had been delivered the day before.

Standing at the doorway, she watched as the white curtains with a yellow satin trim that she had ironed in the morning and slipped onto the curtain rods were taken from the top of the dresser and placed into position. Next, the round yellow rug was rolled out in the center of the room. The lights swirled around the rocking chair Daniel had chosen and it came to rest next to one window. Cristine picked up the cream-colored cashmere throw she had ordered and she carefully placed it over the back of the rocker while pictures they had chosen together were placed on the walls.

And then, unexpectedly, from out of nowhere, something began appearing in the center of the rug. Cristine stared in amazement as first a green pedestal formed, adorned with leaves, to be topped by something that resembled a large open white flower with a yellow center.

"What is it?" she asked, coming closer. And then she saw that it was a little bed of some sort. She touched the center and it felt like foam, but not really. It was firm, yet unbelievably soft, and left the imprint of her fingers when she lifted her hand. "It's a bed for the baby?"

The lights swirled around the bed and her and she inhaled with pleasure as she watched it sway gently back and forth. How ingenious, she thought, for a newborn baby. She almost wished he'd make another for her, imagining being cradled within the soft petals of a flower and the gentle swaying putting her to sleep. "I love it!" she proclaimed. "And so will Angelique."

They had agreed on Angelique. Daniel thought it appropriate for his daughter, yet Cristine felt the baby had already picked it with Casey. "Thank you, Daniel. All I have to do is make up the crib and we're done."

She watched the lights dance around the ceiling and then he was gone. Cristine opened the dresser, filled with tiny clothes, and brought out the soft fitted sheet she had already washed. Putting it on the mattress, she smiled with happiness. It didn't matter that she was as big as a house at six months. Daniel couldn't stop touching her, making her feel beautiful. It didn't matter that she hadn't seen a doctor since Kate Abrams. Daniel checked in with the baby every few days and said she was fine. Nothing mattered anymore, except that her home was filled with love. There were no worries any longer. It would all work out. Daniel said it would and she believed him.

When she heard the doorbell ring, she was slightly annoyed because the best part was about to begin, putting out all the stuffed animals and toys. She dropped a cuddly teddy bear into the crib and went downstairs. In the foyer, she looked at herself in the mirror and shrugged. She was dressed in maternity Capris and a stretchy form-fitting top, and her hair which had grown so fast was pulled back into a short ponytail, with the sides escaping. She blew up on her bangs to get them out of her eyes and opened the door.

"Charlie!" She was stunned to see him standing there. It didn't register that he had lived in the house with her for almost seven years. It was like staring at a distant cousin, one she didn't care to see again.

He seemed stunned himself as he stared at her belly. "You're so big!" he muttered.

"Well, hello to you too."

He seemed to recover slightly. "I . . . I just came by to talk to you," he stammered. "But you can't be—"

"Can't be what?" she asked.

He straightened his shoulders. "You can't be a few months pregnant. When is this baby due?"

"I don't think that's any of your business." Cristine intuitively knew where he was heading and she wanted to stop him. "This is Daniel's child."

"It can't be!" he insisted, looking agitated as he ran his fingers through his hair.

"I'm not having this discussion on my front porch. Come in . . . for a few minutes."

Charlie walked into the house and Cristine closed the door. No point in inviting him in any farther.

"This is my baby, isn't it?"

"No, Charlie, it is not."

"You look like you're ready to deliver any minute."

"I'm just big, that's all."

"Cristine, it makes no sense. How could you be this pregnant by someone you only met a few months ago? It *has* to be mine!"

She exhaled. "Charlie, if you will recall, we didn't have sex there at the end. It would make even less sense to say I'm pregnant by you."

"But we did. The night I made you dinner on the patio. It adds up . . ."

She sucked in air between her teeth and shook her head. "We drank too much wine, remember? We never completed the . . . act." She wouldn't call it making love, not after what she'd experienced with Daniel.

"I don't remember, and that's the problem. We *could* have. I want a paternity test."

*"What?"*

"A paternity test, to determine who the father is."

"Don't be absurd. I am not pregnant with your child." Cristine was insulted and also scared. She didn't want the law brought into her pregnancy. "Charlie, I promise you, this isn't your child."

"How do I know that?" He stuck his hands into the

pockets of his jeans. "And if it is, I have a right to know." He looked at her imploringly and started speaking quickly. "Cristine, I've changed. I realize what a fool I've been, what I've put you through. I guess I was having a nervous breakdown, or something. I know you can't trust me right away, and I wouldn't expect it. I'd have to earn your trust. But this baby . . . it needs a father, and together we could raise it . . . just like your plan."

"Hold it right there," she said with one hand on her hip and the other protectively covering her belly. "First of all, this child already *has* a father. Daniel Burns."

"And who is this guy? He comes out of nowhere. I've asked around and no one's ever heard of him. What if he just wants to get to your money through this baby? Have you even thought of that, Cristine? You know you can be naïve."

The breath left her body in a rush. "Wow, you really are desperate, aren't you? I may have been naïve where you were concerned because I actually believed in your integrity, but you blew that. So why don't you just tell me how much money you need. That *is* the reason you came here today, isn't it?"

She knew she had him when he couldn't look her in the eye any longer.

"That was before I saw how far along you are. This has to be my baby."

"And you actually think I would even have your baby? You, the neurotic hypochondriac who should be living in a sanitized bubble?" She took a deep breath to calm down. "I'm sorry for that last remark, but allow me now to tell *you* something. I don't hate you. I'm not even upset with you any longer, haven't been for many months now, and I don't blame you for anything anymore. I always was an adult and what happened was a result of my choices too. But it's over. I'm not saying this to hurt you, but I am thrilled you are out of my life and Daniel is in it.

You gave me a gift when you took off because it forced me to look at myself and my own life, what I wanted in my life . . . and what I didn't. It took me a while, but I finally got it. I'm an extraordinary woman, Charlie, and you don't deserve me. You never did."

"I want the paternity test," he said, as though he hadn't even heard her words.

She stared at him and felt sick. "How much money do you want?"

He didn't say anything for a few moments. "I was going to ask for enough to get me back to Denver, but now—"

"Now, what? You aren't the father. I can't explain why I'm so big so just tell me how much you want and then get out of my life."

"I'm not going to say anything until there's a paternity test."

"You're delusional. *Daniel!*" She wasn't going to get through to him and she couldn't allow him to make trouble. Not now. Not when everything was working out so well.

"You called, my love."

She breathed a sigh of relief as Daniel came toward them from the kitchen. "Yes. Charlie thinks he's the father of our child. I've tried getting through to him, but he refuses to listen."

Daniel walked past Charlie and put his arm around Cristine's shoulders. "Hello, Charlie."

Charlie simply nodded, looking unsure now that he realized another man was in the house.

"Cristine is carrying our child, not yours."

"And how do I know that? Look at her, she's too big to be having your child."

Daniel smiled patiently. "Yes, she is blossoming quite well, but the child she is having carries no genes of yours."

"A paternity test will put that question to rest."

"There will be no test," Daniel said firmly. "Cristine's honor is not to be questioned."

"You may have moved in on her, but you can't control me. I'm getting a lawyer."

"Why, Charlie?" Cristine asked. "Because of the money? You think you're entitled to some of it?"

"I did help restore this house, and I was never paid anything for that."

She almost laughed. "Charlie, you *lived* here. I didn't charge you rent and, quite frankly, for most of that time I supported you."

"What do you really want?" Daniel asked in a quiet voice. "It isn't the baby, so why don't you just tell us?"

"How do you know?" Charlie challenged. "If she's carrying my child I would want at least partial custody, visiting rights, something."

"Explain the something," Daniel said, "because that's what you originally came here for."

"I don't have to talk about it with you."

Daniel moved so quickly that Cristine sucked in her breath in surprise to find Daniel's hand on Charlie's head. A light appeared, almost like a halo, and Daniel murmured, "Charlie, you know you are not the father of Cristine's child. Stop fighting for what you are not entitled to any longer. Tell Cristine what you came here to say."

"I need fifty thousand dollars to buy a new car and move to Denver."

Daniel looked at Cristine and she nodded. "I'll give it to him."

"And you will move to Denver in one week, and forget about Christine and our child?"

"Yes." Charlie seemed almost in a trance.

"Very good," Daniel replied. "And as an added gift your immune system will now function fully. You will no longer be dependent on chemicals to breathe normally. You will be a healthy human being." He took his hand away and put his arm back around Cristine.

Together they watched Charlie blink a few times and stare at them.

"Claire will have your check ready for you tomorrow. Call her. She's handling all my financial affairs." Cristine pulled out of Daniel's embrace and opened the front door.

Charlie moved toward it.

"Good luck in Denver. I wish you well," she added.

Charlie, looking shaken, nodded as he walked out. "And good luck to you both with the baby."

"Good-bye, Charlie." She shut the front door and turned back to Daniel.

"Better?" he asked with a grin.

She sighed with relief. "Much better. Small price to pay to get him out of our lives for good. I'm sorry I had to call for help. He wasn't listening to me."

Daniel wrapped her in his arms. "And I'm sorry I had to intervene, but you are right . . . he would have contacted a lawyer to get to you and your money. He really wasn't interested in the baby."

Cristine nodded. "I'd guessed that."

Daniel kissed the top of her head.

"He's really going to go?"

"He has no reason to stay now. He will make a new beginning as a healthy human being and find his own destiny."

Standing sideways, Cristine laid her head against Daniel's chest. "I think I'm going to have Claire give him twenty thousand for the car and deposit the rest in an account in Denver, just to be sure he actually leaves."

"He'll leave. He's drawn there for a reason."

"His family," she said, rubbing her cheek against the soft fabric of his shirt.

"And someone else."

She lifted her head. "Really?"

Daniel nodded. "His destiny awaits him."

Cristine smiled. "Good. I really hope he gets his act together."

"Now show me what you've done to Angelique's room and I will show you what I have done to the ceiling." He led her to the stairs.

"The ceiling?" she asked, not remembering having planned anything.

"Yes. When the sun goes down and the moon takes over, our child's ceiling will illuminate her part of the Milky Way . . . so she knows her home in the universe."

Cristine climbed the stairs with effort. "She's going to be one loved little girl," she murmured. "I hope she likes what we've done."

"She's most anxious to see it herself."

"What does that mean?"

"It means it is a very good thing that Charlie will be leaving quickly."

At the top of the steps, Cristine turned to him. "Are you saying I'm about to have this baby?"

"I am saying, my love, that our daughter is going to determine the time, not me. But I believe it will be soon."

Great, she thought. She had better contact a midwife, or someone to help her out, 'cause she wasn't doing this alone, no matter what Daniel said or thought.

She wanted a real person, someone with some experience in birthing.

But who could she trust?

# Chapter

## 22

"PLEASE TELL MRS. BROOKER THAT IT'S CRISTINE Dobbins, her realtor."

She watched the guard go back into his booth and pick up the telephone. He spoke for a few moments and then the tall iron gates began to slowly open.

"Have a good day," the man called out.

"Thanks. You too," she answered as she drove into the gated community. This visit was long overdue, she thought, passing an older couple walking their brown spaniels. She should have brought the housewarming present weeks ago. Her life had just been so busy that she had put things off. She hadn't even been into the office in weeks, though she kept in touch with Tina, who had hired two more agents and was thrilled with the response to her ad in *Philadelphia Magazine*. Still, something in Cristine was urging her to take care of details, wrap up loose ends, and this visit was at the top of her list.

She pulled into the wide driveway and parked her car. It took more effort to get out of it than the last time she was at this house and Cristine knew if she got much bigger she soon wouldn't fit behind the wheel. The seat only went back so far and her legs were only so long. Straightening, she rubbed her lower back and then pulled her gauzy dress into place before opening the rear door of the car. She reached in and lifted the colorfully wrapped present and the bouquet of flowers she had picked from her garden.

Walking up to the house, she saw the front door open and Maxine stood there, waiting to greet her. "Hi," she called out.

Maxine slowly waved back and Cristine could see the shock written on her face. As she came closer Cristine said, "I know. I'm huge, right?"

"I didn't even know you were pregnant," Maxine said with a confused expression.

Cristine was trying hard not to lie, and so she gave her stock answer. "I just started blossoming and it feels like the baby is growing by leaps every minute." That was the truth.

"Come in, come in," Maxine said. "Let me take that from you."

Cristine handed over the gift. "I'm sorry it's taken me this long to bring you your housewarming present."

"I can see why you've been busy. I've never known a pregnant woman to go from not showing to . . . to . . ."

Remembering Maxine was a nurse, Cristine laughed. "Go ahead, say it. To huge in so short a time."

"You look full-term, and that can't be possible."

Shrugging, Cristine asked, "How is Lillian? Does she enjoy your new space here?" She simply had to divert Maxine's attention from asking questions when there were no logical answers. Cristine looked into the living room, decorated with antique pieces. "It's lovely," she murmured.

"Oh, most of those are Mamie's castoffs," she said, carrying the present down the hallway.

Cristine followed with her flowers. "But Lillian does like her new home, your new home?" she corrected.

"Lillian has her good days and her bad ones now."

Cristine stopped walking. "Is Lillian sick?"

Maxine turned, her lined face looking worried. "It's her heart. She started falling, blacking out. The doctor said they want to go back in and do more surgery, but Lillian refuses. She says at her age, she could die on the table and she wants to at least know when she's going."

"I'm so sorry, Maxine." Cristine's heart felt heavy. Lillian had seemed so full of life at the settlement and excited to move in. She saw the fear in Maxine's eyes.

"But she was happy to hear you were coming for a visit. You don't mind that the visit will take place in the bedroom, do you?"

"Not at all," Cristine answered as they continued down the hallway.

"Now wait until you see Cristine," Maxine called out. "You're not going to believe it, Lilly."

Walking into the large bedroom, Cristine clutched the flowers in her hands and pasted a big smile on her face. Nothing could have prepared her for the shock of seeing the once-feisty woman dwarfed in the king-sized bed, devoid of makeup, her hair down lying on her thin shoulders like a spiderweb. She was wearing a pink bed jacket, but the color only accentuated the woman's pale face.

"Hello, Lillian," Cristine called out, coming up to the bed. "I'm so sorry it's taken me this long to bring you your housewarming present."

Maxine put the wrapped present on the satin comforter.

"Sit," Lillian whispered, motioning to a nearby chair that Maxine must have been using. She then looked at Maxine. "Did I black out again? Or was I in a coma?"

Maxine laughed. "Nah, hon. You're seeing things right. Cristine is very much pregnant."

Cristine sat down, still holding the flowers. "These are from my garden," she said, trying to keep her emotions under control. "For some reason, this year my garden is spectacular."

"Lovely," Lillian murmured, then narrowed her gaze. "You look different. Not just the pregnancy. You look . . . radiant."

Cristine smiled, seeing Lillian's eyes still held the light of intelligence. "Why, thank you, Lillian. Being pregnant agrees with me. Of course, I can't wait until I can get out of bed without feeling like a manatee, but that will come soon enough."

Lillian grinned. "And when is that?"

"Not soon enough," Cristine replied with a laugh. "Why don't you open your present?" she asked, to divert attention away from herself.

Lillian looked at the box wrapped in a pastel floral paper, tied with a wide white satin ribbon, and topped with a cluster of fresh white rosebuds Cristine had picked only minutes before leaving her house. "Maxine, you do it . . ."

Cristine watched as Maxine sat on the other side of the mattress and pulled the present to her. "Look how pretty it's wrapped, Lilly."

"I see." Lillian smiled weakly. "From your garden?"

Cristine nodded.

They waited as Maxine carefully removed the flowers, the ribbon, and the paper. She was methodical and Cristine imagined that it was Maxine who had kept Lillian's life near the center of the road, which was funny since now Maxine had trouble driving and doing that for herself.

Maxine brought out the dark gray box with *Lalique* printed in gold. "Do you want to open it?" she asked Lillian.

The other woman shook her head. "Go ahead."

Maxine lifted the lid and exposed a crystal figurine of two swans with their long necks intertwined. "Oh, it's beautiful." She reached across the mattress and put it in front of Lillian.

The other woman raised a shaky hand with age spots,

papery skin, and blue veins to touch the crystal. "How thoughtful of you, Cristine," she whispered, and her eyes became glassy with emotion.

"I saw it and thought of you two. Like the swans, mated for life."

Lillian sniffled. "Put it over there on the dresser, Maxie, so I can see it."

The other woman placed it by a double silver frame showing much younger versions of Lillian and Maxine in individual pictures, the old kind with pastel painting highlighting skin color and hair. Each was facing the other with happy smiles.

"Now, how about a cup of tea or a glass of juice?" Maxine asked Cristine. "And let me put those flowers in water."

"Herbal tea if you have it, if not, juice will be fine," Cristine said, handing the flowers over.

"How about you, hon? Doesn't a cup of tea sound good?"

"Sure," Lillian murmured with a smile, watching Maxine leave the room. She turned her head back to Cristine. "She'll be gone for a few minutes. I need to ask you a favor."

"Of course," Cristine said, leaning in as much as her belly would allow.

"I'm not doing too good. I'm not asking for pity, but I do need something from you."

"What is it?"

"I've already drawn up a new will, leaving the house to Maxine. Mamie isn't going to like that one bit and will give Maxine a hard time of it."

"Don't talk that way, Lillian. I'm sure you'll—"

"Let me talk," Lillian interrupted, taking a deep breath, at least as deep as she could. "Look, I don't think I've got much time left and Maxine . . . her family disowned her thirty years ago . . . she's going to need someone, a friend to talk to, to keep on going. It's always hardest on the one . . . left behind. I know she pretends to be the strong one, but she's just mush inside." Lillian narrowed her eyes. "I'm the only one that knows that about her, and now you, so you can't let her know. Understood?"

Cristine nodded.

"Can I count on you to be her friend? It would give me such peace to know she won't be all alone facing that daughter of mine."

Cristine reached out and took Lillian's hand. Squeezing it, she said, "You have my word on it."

The tears came back to Lillian's eyes. "Thank you. First time I saw you, I knew you were a good person."

Still holding the older woman's hand, Cristine pushed herself up from the chair and sat on the edge of the mattress to be closer. "First time I saw you, I thought you were a character . . . all done up, lookin' pretty good for an older dame."

Lillian chuckled and coughed. "I never let myself go, no matter what." She chuckled again. "'Cept dying. Just don't have the energy for it anymore."

The baby kicked hard, surprising Cristine, and she grinned as she touched her belly. "She's a strong one."

"Kicking?"

"Want to feel?" Cristine asked, taking Lillian's hand and holding it over her stomach. Sighing, she looked over her shoulder to the pictures of the two women. "How did you and Maxine meet? If you don't mind me asking."

Lillian looked at the pictures and smiled. "That was so long ago. I was married, you know, and I was a good wife." She paused and drew in her breath. "I loved Mamie's father as best I could and he loved me. I'm sure of that. He fought in the Battle of the Bulge over there in World War Two and stayed in the army and made a career out of it." She caught her breath. "Mamie came nine months almost to the day after he came back from Germany and I named her after Eisenhower's wife. That's how army I was in those days. We had a pretty good life, I guess, save for the moving around, but then he went to Korea." Again, Lillian paused while drawing in her breath, and Cristine wondered if it was only her imagination, or was color coming into Lillian's cheeks?

"He came home in a casket from that war. And there I was with a nine-year-old child, no longer an army wife, and I had to make a life for us, so we moved to Philadelphia and . . . that's when I met Maxine. She was something when she was younger and . . . Oh! I just felt the baby kick!"

Cristine grinned, keeping Lillian's hand on her belly. If it could work for Casey, it could work for this remarkable woman. "So you met Maxine in Philly . . ." she said, encouraging Lillian to continue.

She nodded. "Right. She was so independent then and women weren't encouraged to be independent. Not then. We were supposed to stay home and take care of our husbands and make life easier for everyone. I was pretty good at that myself, until my husband died. I just wasn't prepared to be a woman alone."

Her breathing seemed easier as she continued. "Maxine had a nice home, was a registered nurse, making decent money with two jobs, one for a private doctor and the other at the hospital. We became friends and talked a lot. It was Maxine who told me I could do it alone, who encouraged me to go to nursing school while Mamie was in school. Of course, I only became a practical nurse, but Maxine helped me to study and then we both worked at the same hospital. I so admired Maxine. She was my best friend, closer than a sister, and I could tell her anything. And she made me laugh again, at myself, at the world. She talked to me about all sorts of things, like politics, and wanted my opinions." She sighed deeply.

"You wouldn't have recognized me then. I was so quiet and shy."

"Not you, Lillian," Cristine chided with a grin, enjoying listening to Lillian's story and noticing that the old woman's voice was becoming stronger and color was coming back into her nails.

"Yes, me. I was such a conformist then. I wanted to belong and I cared about what other people thought. I really cared. If I wasn't in my nurse's uniform, I was in a Girl Scout troop leader's uniform, doing what I thought I should to keep up appearances . . . but I was falling in love, real love, for the first time in my life. And it terrified me."

"It must have been so different then," Cristine said. "Today it's more acceptable."

"It's funny when you get to be old like this. You see things differently, I guess. It was hard then. There were laws, stupid laws, about two people of the same gender loving one another . . . as if the politicians or religions could tell you who to fall in love with, like they're trying to do again today. Taboos, they were called back then. The love that dare not speak its name. But I've come to see it's what we don't understand that we fear. And I was filled with fear. You know that I waited until Mamie went off to college before finding a house with Maxine."

"Wow," Cristine murmured. "You were a devoted mother."

Lillian laughed. "I was a terrified mother. I didn't want Mamie to find out. How could she understand what I couldn't? Nothing romantic happened for years, but when it did . . . well, then I knew why nothing earth-shattering happened to me with Mamie's father, why it always felt so . . . so awkward. I thought something was wrong with me. With Maxine it was all so natural. But you see, I had so many years of ignorance, of accepting others' views. Loving another woman like that, or any way, seemed wrong and I spent years feeling guilty, that something was wrong with me again, that I would be punished in hell and . . . all that rubbish I accepted into my head. But I couldn't kill off this love I had for her. And she waited through all my anguish, all my fears."

She looked at the pictures on the dresser again and shook her head. "What I put that woman through. When we finally moved in together I insisted we each have our own bedroom so if anyone came over it would look proper. Mamie thought I was moving in with my best friend to save money to put her through college, so she went along with it . . . didn't she, Maxine?"

Cristine turned her head to see Maxine walking into the bedroom with a heavy tray. She got up. "Let me help you."

Shaking her head to Cristine, Maxine asked, "Didn't who do what?" She put the tray at the foot of the bed. "What are you talking about?"

"I was telling Cristine that Mamie thought I moved in with you to save money for her college tuition."

"Oh, don't be boring the woman with ancient history," Maxine said, handing Cristine a cup of tea as she sat back in the chair.

"But it *is* our history, Maxine, and it should be told."

"Here, drink some tea," Maxine said, moving to sit on the edge of the mattress and holding the teacup for Lillian. "You have some color in your cheeks again. Maybe this visit was just what you needed."

Cristine smiled, praying that whatever gifts her child possessed were working.

"I was just at the part where we moved in together."

"So you didn't get to the rallies, the marches for civil rights, the endless telephone calls, or standing on street corners handing out pamphlets while people spat on us?"

"Oh, no," Cristine murmured. "How ignorant."

Maxine turned her head and smiled, transforming her

stern expression. "That's the word for it. Ignorance. Lack of knowledge or understanding. And fear. Do you know that most of the men at gay bars who are interested in one-night stands are married men?"

"No, I didn't," Cristine said with surprise.

"Well, it's a fact. And fear of being discovered leads people to irrational behavior."

"Like Mamie's current husband," Lillian murmured, sipping her tea.

"Now, Lillian," Maxine cautioned.

"Well, he's such a hypocrite."

Maxine turned back to Cristine. She tilted her head toward Lillian. "When she finally came out of the closet, she didn't give a damn about what anyone thought."

"It was about time too! When *was* it going to be a good time to just live my life as who I am?"

"Mamie didn't take it well, as was expected."

"She was on her first husband, a doctor, who thought I should have electric shock treatments."

"It was the times, Lillian," Maxine said, stroking her partner's arm.

"What we've been through, Max . . ."

"But we're still here, after thirty-two years." Maxine leaned in and kissed the tip of Lillian's nose. "And we still have a few good years left."

"Amen to that," Cristine said with a smile. "You know, you two have had a profound effect on me."

They both looked at her. "Oh, don't tell me Lillian has turned you?" Maxine asked with a laugh.

Lillian shook her head and playfully slapped Maxine's hand. "Are you now totally blind, or can't you see how radiant Cristine is? She's happy."

"Yes, I am, but I admire you both so much. When I first met you I watched you walk through the garden together, do you remember?"

They nodded.

"And I saw the love you two shared over the years and I was envious. In my relationships, I had never been able to maintain what you have. The bumps became fatal crashes, until I met the father of my child. We won't be married, but he will be in our lives, and I'm okay with it, with being me finally, with the way my life is unfolding. It isn't storybook perfect. It isn't what I've read or seen in movies about traditional happily-ever-afters. But it's real. And the love I feel is real. It doesn't have to fit into someone else's picture of what should be . . . it just *is,* and it's more than good enough."

"Congratulations, Cristine. You've grown up," Maxine said with a wide grin. "You've realized what you think of yourself is far more important than anyone else's opinion. You're being true to you."

"I like that saying I heard once," Lillian said. " 'What you think of me is none of my business.' "

"Well, I think you two are terrific. Not that it matters," Cristine added with a laugh. "And I should be going so you, Lillian, can rest."

"Oh, I feel so much better. It's as if you walked into the room like a breath of fresh air."

"You do look better," Maxine again remarked, holding Lillian's wrist. After a few moments, she said, "And your pulse is much stronger. No longer thready."

"See?" Lillian said with a grin. "She's good medicine for me."

"I'll come back. I promise," Cristine said, getting up. Maxine began to stand and Cristine put her hand on the woman's shoulder. "Stay with Lillian. I'll show myself out."

"Thank you so much for coming," Maxine said. "You've worked wonders with this woman."

"Mind if I kiss you both good-bye?"

Lillian held out her arms.

Cristine held on to the night table as she bent over Lillian. "Thanks for taking a stroll back in time for me. It was fascinating."

Lillian kissed her cheek. "I'll tell you the only things I know for sure after spending over eighty years on this planet. Love is what matters in the end, not how much you've accumulated or how many toys you've got. It's how many moments of genuine love you've been given. That's your final treasure. And the other thing is, there is no going back in time, or even forward. Life is the continual present. All the rest is the story we tell ourselves to keep ourselves sane."

Cristine smiled as she straightened. "Life is the continual present," she repeated. "That's so true. I'll try to remember that if I ever tell my story."

"Better yet, Cristine, just make sure your story is about *you,* the real you, not the person someone else wants you to be. Otherwise, it won't be your story you've spent a lifetime living, will it? It will theirs."

"Too many of us are living other people's stories," Maxine said. "So afraid to be different."

"It takes courage, Maxine," Lillian murmured. "You taught me that."

In that moment, Cristine realized how much she had in common with these women. It takes courage to love differently.

And loving Daniel Burns, a being who popped in and out of dimensions, was most certainly different.

But it was worth it. Oh, yes . . . so worth it.

# Chapter

## 23

"DAMN, WOMAN, YOU *ARE* BIG! NOT JUST BIG, *huge!*"

"Thanks, Claire, as if I needed you to tell me that. Why don't you just attach strings to me and I can be in Macy's Thanksgiving parade this year? Big Fat Momma balloon. Best form of birth control around. I'll scare Manhattan into celibacy."

Claire laughed as she came into the house. "Honey, if you last until Thanksgiving, I just might do that." She turned around and kissed Cristine's cheek. "It's mostly the big belly," she added, as if that might make a difference. "And the boobs. There are women who would kill to be that size. What are you now, a D cup? More?"

"Who knows," Cristine muttered, trying not to be miserable and failing. "How far up the alphabet do I have to go?" she demanded, holding her breasts like huge cantaloupes. "F? G? Do they even make bras in a G cup? Do you realize I actually sweat under my breasts now? And just forget sleeping. There aren't enough pillows in this house to get comfortable. Pretty soon I'm going to need a hoist just to get out of bed. Oh, and how many times a night do I have to heave myself up to use the bathroom? Don't ask." She held up her hand in frustration.

"When *are* you due?"

"Now that's the million-dollar question. When are the others arriving?"

"Any minute. Are you telling me you don't know when you're going to have this baby?"

The doorbell rang and saved Cristine from answering Claire. She waddled to the door.

"Welcome, welcome, and Claire's already taken care of the fat jokes so we can dispense with any more."

One by one they entered the house, each with a look of bewilderment, amazement, or shock.

"I don't know what to say," Tina remarked, kissing her cheek.

"Well, that's a first for you," Cristine said with a laugh.

When they were all inside, staring at her, Cristine shut the front door and announced, "Yes, I am huge and my feet are swollen, which is why I am asking for a special dispensation." She bent down to the staircase with great effort and picked up her sparkly red heels. "I can't get my feet into them," she added, feeling a tight pull in her lower back when she straightened. Great, another ache to add to the backache she'd had since she had gotten out of bed in the morning. She dropped her heels to the floor.

"Sure, we'll all take off our shoes," Paula said, and the others began slipping out of their heels while murmuring their agreement.

"Cristine," Isabel said, while staring at her, "I have to ask . . . when are you due? I've . . . never seen anything like this."

Sighing, Cristine held a hand to her lower back as she walked into the living room. "I'm not really sure."

"What do you mean, you're not sure?" Isabel demanded as they all followed her. "What did Kate Abrams say?"

Cristine sighed again. She was doing a lot of sighing lately, or maybe it was just too damn hard to carry around all this weight and breathe! She had known this interrogation was coming. In fact, it was the reason she had called them together—to get it over with. Sooner or later they were going to see and—

"Well?" Paula asked, interrupting her thoughts. "What did your doctor tell you about a due date?"

She might as well just say it and get it over with . . . no point in delaying the storm that was going to erupt. "I haven't seen Kate Abrams since that first time."

"Who's your doctor then?" Tina asked.

"I don't have one."

*"What?"*

"She's kidding," Kelly said. "She has to be."

"I don't think she is," Claire said, coming to stand in front of Cristine. "Are you saying you haven't been to the doctor since . . . we took you?"

"Calm down, everyone," Cristine pleaded. "I'm an intelligent woman. I haven't put myself or the baby at risk. I'm taking my prenatal vitamins and watching what I eat and—"

Claire laughed sarcastically. "Oh, it looks like you're watching what you eat. Is that why you haven't seen a doctor, because you've gained so much weight so fast?"

For Cristine it felt as if Claire had just stabbed her in the belly, and her abdominal muscles seemed to tighten in defense.

"Back off, Claire," Isabel directed as she came closer. "Most of the weight she's gained is the baby . . . which brings me to ask a delicate question, Cristine. Exactly how far along are you?"

Cristine felt Isabel's maternal energy closing around her. "I don't know . . . exactly."

"You don't know when you're going to have this baby?" Paula asked in an incredulous voice. "You look like you could deliver any minute."

"I don't get it," Kelly said, crossing her arms over her chest. "You said this is Daniel's baby and he . . . he hasn't been here but what? Four months now, maybe five . . ."

Isabel touched Cristine's arm. "Honey, how could this be Daniel's baby?"

"It *is*!" she insisted, and watched as everyone looked at her and then at Isabel, the one they all turned to when it came to matters of the mind and soul. "I'm not crazy," Cristine declared. "I don't care if you believe me or not."

"Isn't it possible," Paula began in a placating voice, "that it just might be Charlie's?"

"No! Absolutely not! Look, I know none of this makes sense, but if you love me, you'll believe me. This is Daniel's child."

"Cristine, you're not four months pregnant," Isabel said, putting her hand gently on Cristine's belly. "You're hard as a rock, like you're ready to deliver any day now. Daniel wasn't here nine months ago."

"Or was he?" Claire asked in a low voice. "Did you have an affair with him before Charlie left?"

Cristine stared at Claire and felt tears come into her eyes. "I love you, Claire, so do not make me call you a bitch while I'm carrying an innocent child."

"I'm just asking, because nothing since this Daniel character arrived has made any sense."

Cristine felt such a heaviness in her heart that she murmured, "I have to sit down."

Paula immediately sat next to her. "Listen, if it is Charlie's, no one in this room will ever tell and—"

"It's not Charlie's!" she cried. "It's Daniel's child."

Claire knelt down in front of her and put her hands on Cristine's knees, which was the only part of her legs visible as her belly rested on her upper thighs. "Sweetie, we all love you, but you have to admit to yourself you are not four months pregnant."

Cristine dropped her head and her shoulders with defeat. They were never going to understand. She'd known it was going to be difficult, but she was so weary, so tired . . . "I know I'm farther along than four months, Claire. I'm not stupid."

"So then how can it be Daniel's?"

"I can't explain how. He's different. This baby is different. You're just going to have to accept that."

"Hello, ladies. So this is the Yellow Brick Road Gang . . ."

Daniel came into the room carrying a large silver tray with a tall crystal pitcher of some colorful drink and seven glasses. Everyone turned their heads and stared as he placed the tray on the coffee table.

He straightened and looked at Cristine and her heart lightened, for instinctively, he knew she needed help and he came to be at her side. With difficulty, Cristine pushed herself upright, using Paula's hand and Claire's head for support. Just to touch him; he'd give her the strength she needed.

And that's when it happened . . .

Right there, in front of everyone, her water broke, all over Claire's beige designer suit.

Cristine, along with everyone else, just stared as the carpet became darker along with Claire's suit.

"Ohmygod!" Paula whispered. "Her water . . ."

"Right," Claire said, slowly standing and holding her arms out and her legs apart. "Thanks for the news bulletin, Paula."

"I'm sorry, Claire," Cristine whispered in shock "Go upstairs and find something else to wear . . ."

Kelly was clutching Isabel's arm as the two of them closed the distance. Isabel, prying Kelly's fingers open, looked at Cristine and said, "You'd better get to the hospital."

"Actually, Issy, we were thinking about a home birth." Cristine reached out for Daniel's arm, truly scared now that the time had come.

Claire, on her way to the stairs, spun around like an ice skater. "Oh, she did not just say that! *A home birth!* Have you lost your fucking mind? Both of you?"

"Cristine will be fine," Daniel said calmly, wrapping his arm around her.

Claire marched back to him and stood not five inches away. "Now you listen here, Mr. Daniel Burns, Starman, or whoever you are . . . this is women's business. Not men's. Everything about this pregnancy has been crazy from the beginning, but now it's time for the baby, and the craziest thing she could do is have it here in this house. She needs to get to a hospital. Either we go, or I'm calling an ambulance right now."

"Daniel," Cristine murmured, clutching the front of his denim shirt. "I want to go to a hospital. Claire's right. Please come with me."

"Are you sure?" he asked.

She nodded, feeling a tightness start in her lower back and wrap around the front of her. "I want the baby born in a hospital."

He smiled and tenderly kissed her temple. "Whatever you desire, my love."

"Good," Isabel declared. "Claire, you and I will go upstairs. You get changed and I'll get Cristine new clothes. Tina—you call Mercy and tell them we're bringing in a woman ready to deliver. Be sure to mention her water broke."

"What should we do?" Kelly asked, her eyes wide with concern.

"We'll clean up this," Paula said, standing.

Cristine felt another spasm begin and this time it was harder, so hard she caught her breath and clutched Daniel's waist so tightly that he straightened with pain.

"What's wrong?" he demanded, looking concerned for the first time.

"I think it's a contraction," she muttered between clenched teeth.

"Okay, that's it!" Isabel called out. "She's having contractions. You time them, Daniel, and we'll take care of the rest." She turned to everyone. "Let's move."

"Yes . . . time them . . . I will do that."

Claire and Isabel hurried up the stairs. Tina went into the kitchen to use the phone for information and get Mercy General's number. Paula and Kelly followed her to get sponges and carpet cleaner.

Daniel turned to Cristine. "What did she mean, 'time them'? How long they last?"

"How long in between them," Cristine mumbled, rubbing her lower back now that the contraction had eased. "I'm scared, Daniel. None of us has ever done this, except for Paula and Kelly and they're cleaning the rug. I need to get to some professionals. What if something goes wrong?"

"Nothing is going to go wrong. Our child is coming. This is a time for celebration."

"Yeah, well, we'll celebrate when she gets here. In the meantime I should be breathing or something."

"You are breathing."

"No. I mean like Lamaze. We never even practiced anything. Look how unprepared we are!" Cristine started crying.

Daniel tried to wrap his arms around her, but she caught one of his wrists and gasped with pain. "Oh, God, it's so much stronger this time!"

"Hurry!" Daniel called out to the women, sounding more than a little unnerved as Cristine's nails dug into his skin. "What can I do, Cristine?"

"Noth . . . ing," she gasped, doubling over in pain. "This is the way babies are . . . born. In . . . pain."

Kelly and Paula came back into the room and began cleaning up her water.

"Hold on, Cris . . ." Paula said, putting a mass of paper towels down on the rug.

"Can we do anything?" Kelly asked, gritting as though she were feeling Cristine's pain. "Yell out if you want. I did with Colleen."

Cristine just shook her head.

Daniel supported her. "Should I make the pain go away?"

"Can you?" Cristine would take any relief she could get. Dear God, women went through *hours* of this? She'd never make it.

"I'll try," Daniel murmured, placing his hand on her belly. Within seconds he lifted it. "I can't interfere. You and the baby are working together."

"Great!" Cristine muttered as the contraction began to ease and she slowly stood straight again, or at least as straight as she could. "Okay, baby," she whispered, running her hands over her hard belly. "It's you and me now." She looked at Daniel. "I've got to sit down. I can't keep standing up like this."

"Before you sit," Isabel called out from the stairs, "I've got new panties for you and I say we just wrap this bath sheet around your bottom. No sense in trying to get into and then out of these." And she held up a pair of Lycra maternity Capris. "That's all I could find."

Cristine looked at her choices. For a split second she imagined trying to get the pants on and she shook her head. "You're right. Let's just use the towel."

"Mercy's ready and waiting for you," Tina declared. "They said to come to the emergency entrance and they'll have a wheelchair ready."

"Great, let's go," Claire called out, coming into the room wearing a pair of jeans and a white T-shirt with the sleeves rolled up.

"At least let her get fresh underwear on," Isabel demanded, kneeling in front of Cristine. "I'm just going to roll everything down and you step out of it, okay?"

"Okay," Cristine murmured, not feeling well at all and not caring that she was going to be nude from the waist down as everyone watched. She managed to get her feet free just as the next contraction started. "Hurry, Issy . . . please."

"I'm hurrying, honey." Isabel threw the rolled mass of maternity jeans and underwear off the rug and held the underpants wide for Cristine to put her feet into. They were halfway up to her knees when the contraction got stronger.

"Just pull them up, Isabel!" Tina commanded in a panicked voice.

"She's not going to pop the baby out this second," Paula said. "We can wait until the contraction is over."

"Okay, so who's driving?" Claire demanded. "Paula? You have your SUV?"

She nodded.

"Good, you drive Cristine and Daniel and we'll follow."

"It's too high for her to get into," Paula said. "You'd better drive them."

"Fine. And I swear if you pop this baby in the back seat of my BMW, Cristine, you're not only buying me a new one, but you're naming this kid after me."

"Don't . . . make . . . me . . . laugh . . ." Cristine gasped, clutching Daniel's shoulders as she bent over. "Her name . . . is . . . Angelique . . . Oh, Goooooooodddddd!"

"Angelique. What a pretty name," Paula said soothingly while gently rubbing circles on Cristine's back.

Tina was wringing her hands together. "We've got to get her to the hospital so they can give her something. Some drugs. Something to stop this."

"This is birth, Tina," Kelly said. "It's supposed to be painful. The baby is coming down her birth canal."

"Ah, geez," Claire moaned. "Get those big underpants on her and let's get out of here."

"She can't walk like this," Isabel said. "Maybe we should call the ambulance."

"No," Cristine gasped. "It's easing up now. I . . . I'll walk."

Isabel quickly pulled the pants up, not bothering to make sure they covered Cristine's hips. "Now the towel. We'll just wrap it around like this and—"

"And I'll carry you," Daniel interrupted, leaning down and lifting Cristine into his arms.

"Wow, he's strong," Kelly whispered, helping Isabel to stand.

"Okay, *now* can we go?" Claire demanded.

Everyone began to pick up their purses when Paula called out, "Oh, and don't forget to put on your red shoes! Remember, we did that for Conor?"

"It's not like we have much of a choice, is it?" Tina asked. "We wore them here."

"Everybody get out of the way," Claire commanded as Daniel carried Cristine to the door. She was acting like a cop at a crime scene, pushing back the crowd.

Cristine clung to Daniel's shoulders as he easily carried her outside. Claire ran ahead of them to open the back door of her car and Cristine smiled as she saw the Yellow Brick Road Gang with their sparkly red shoes.

"Wait, wait," Paula yelled, carrying Cristine's heels. "You forgot these."

"She can't fit into them," Claire shot back.

"She has to wear them. It's tradition, for good luck."

Claire ran back, took the heels and stuck them on the tops of Cristine's feet, where they hung. "There? Satisfied?"

"Thank you, Paula," Cristine murmured as Daniel brought her to Claire's car.

Dear God, she was wrapped in a towel with red glittery

high heels hanging from her toes and surrounded by nutty women and a man who seemed to have superman's strength.

What were they going to think at the hospital?

Fifteen minutes and five contractions later, they were all following Cristine in a wheelchair, who was holding Daniel's hand as they left the elevator and walked onto the delivery floor. The orderly wheeled her up to the nurse's station.

"Her water broke and contractions are three minutes apart," the young man said. "We've done no paperwork on her yet."

An older woman smiled at Cristine. "Now if we could just have some information and then—"

"The woman is in labor," Claire interrupted. "Can we do your paperwork later? It's not like she's about to run out of here, is it?"

"Claire . . ." Isabel warned, pulling on the sleeve of her T-shirt to get her away from the counter. "Let Cristine handle this."

"Fine. Anybody think to bring her purse?"

"I did," Kelly said, holding up the black Coach bag.

"Thanks," Cristine murmured. "My wallet's inside, Kelly, with my insurance card."

"And who is your OB?" the nurse asked, pen in hand.

Cristine blinked.

"Your doctor's name?" the nurse repeated.

Cristine looked at Isabel.

Isabel cleared her throat. "Who's on duty tonight?"

"Dr. Ramsey, but—"

"He'll do," Paula said. "I've heard of him."

"How could you have heard of him? He's doing his residency," the nurse protested. "He's not her doctor."

"She's doesn't have a doctor. She's been . . . traveling," Tina said, coming up with a cover story. "That's right. She's the lottery winner, you know. The one from

Haverton. She's been traveling and . . . and went into labor and . . . well, here we are, so tell Dr. Ramsey to get scrubbed or whatever he does to deliver a baby."

"Here's your insurance card," Kelly announced, proudly placing it on the counter.

"*Now* can we get her into a room?" Claire asked, as Cristine began to feel another contraction.

She clutched Daniel's hand and the arm of the wheelchair as she moaned in pain.

"See?" Claire asked in an impatient voice. "While we're standing here debating doctors and insurance cards, she's having this baby!"

"She's not having the baby this moment if her contractions are three minutes apart. There is time to get her prepped." The nurse obviously didn't like Claire's attitude and Claire didn't care.

Daniel cleared his throat as he tried to speak, with Cristine's grip taking the feeling out of his hand. "Please, can you help her? She's in pain."

The nurse looked at Daniel and her expression melted. "Well, we're so busy tonight, the only labor room left is the family room."

"We'll take it," Claire announced, scrambling through her purse. "How much is it?" She brought out her platinum American Express.

"This isn't a hotel!" Kelly muttered, and Claire shrugged while shoving her credit card back into her purse.

"The family room, that's where families can be with the mother as she delivers?" Paula asked in a sweet voice.

"That's right, but it has to be cleared with the department head first and—"

"We're family!" Isabel interrupted. "Sisters. All of us."

The nurse looked at the women before her. "*All* of you are sisters?" she asked in disbelief.

Isabel blinked.

"She's adopted," Paula said, nudging Tina.

"Right. Right. I'm adopted," Tina stated.

"Do you have something against interracial adoption?" Isabel asked, pretending to be insulted.

"No," the nurse answered defensively. "Of course not!"

"Okay, while all of you are debating family history, may I remind you that Cristine is having a baby here?" Claire asked.

Cristine looked up pleadingly. "Daniel?"

He reached across the counter and touched the woman's arm. "May we please all go into this family room? The woman I love is not going to have our baby out here."

"Yes. Absolutely," the nurse answered with a silly smile, as though enamored by Daniel's touch. "Just follow me."

"Finally," Cristine breathed as the contraction lessened.

Daniel pushed the wheelchair around the counter while Tina said to the others, "Did you see *that*?"

"A . . . a light . . . on the nurse's arm?" Kelly asked.

"Must be the fluorescent lights in this place," Paula murmured, as they all walked behind Daniel to the family labor room.

"*Sistahs,*" Claire called out as she joined them and put her arm over Tina's shoulders, "I believe we are in for one hell of a night."

Angelique Isabel Claire Tina Kelly Paula Dobbins-Burns was born at exactly three minutes past eight o'clock. She weighed eight pounds, fifteen ounces, and was twenty-five inches long. After a short, but intense, transition

labor, she emerged into the world through the hands of
Dr. Louis Ramsey, who placed the calm, wet child into
the combined cradle of five women's gloved hands. They
held her in awe as Daniel severed the cord . . . and then
she was placed at her mother's breast. She was only minutes old when already she and her family were the talk of
the delivery floor . . . the strange sisters/aunts who all
wore tacky red high heels, the dreamy, good-looking father whom every nurse wanted to get a look at, and the
lucky mother who had given birth to such a big healthy
baby in so short a time. And what was even more juicy
was the talk about Dr. Ramsey, the good-looking, shy resident who seemed quite taken with the adopted sister.
One nurse claimed she saw Louis Ramsey write down his
phone number and give it to the sister named Tina before
he left the happy family.

There seemed to be a jovial mood on the floor and
none of the nurses could figure it out. They didn't know
why they were so happy. They just were, and when the
mother was wheeled down to the maternity floor, everyone was sorry to see the small crowd leave, even though
the one named Claire called out that a crate of Godiva
chocolates was going to arrive by special delivery that
night at the nurses' station.

Everyone agreed something . . . different . . . had happened that night, though no one could put their finger on
exactly what it was. But it felt like joy was in the air.

# Chapter

# 24

THEY STOOD AROUND HER BED, LIKE GUARDIAN AN-
gels or fairy godmothers, serene and protective.

"Isn't she just beautiful?"

"She looks like Cristine with all that dark hair, but she
has Daniel's eyes."

"Definitely Daniel's eyes."

"And look at the way she looks at you, like she understands everything already."

"Oh, I just love their hands, perfect baby hands, with
perfect baby nails."

"And she doesn't cry. I haven't heard her cry yet."

"Oh, you're lucky, Cristine. Looks like you've got a
good baby. Maybe she'll let you sleep through the night."

"I'm not lucky, Paula," Cristine murmured, smiling
down at the absolute perfection in her arms. "I'm
blessed."

"Amen to that," Tina said.

"Looks like you're blessed too," Claire claimed, reluctantly pulling her attention away from the bed. "Louis
Ramsey seemed quite enamored with my adopted sister.
A doctor! *And* a gynecologist! That's like hitting a grand
slam, girl."

Tina shook her head as though dismissing the idea. "He was just being nice. Probably felt sorry for me, thinking I grew up with all of you crazy white women."

Isabel laughed. "We did act a little crazy up there on the delivery floor, didn't we?"

"Yes, you did," Cristine said with a grin. "And I treasure every bit of your combined craziness, starting at my house."

"Claire . . ." Kelly said with a laugh. "You should have seen your face when Cristine's water broke all over you! It was priceless!"

They all laughed and then Daniel came back into the private room carrying a big bouquet of flowers in a glass vase and a small gift wrapped in white with a big pink bow.

"Presents!" Paula announced. "This is the best part . . . being showered with attention."

"These are for you, my love," Daniel said, bending down and kissing Cristine's forehead. He placed the flowers on the small table next to the bed. Holding the present, he added, "And this is for our daughter and for all of you . . ." He paused and swallowed down emotion as he looked at the women. "I will always be grateful to the Yellow Brick Road Gang for loving Cristine and my daughter. Thank you for all you've done today."

"So open it," Tina said.

Cristine shifted the baby higher on her arm and freed her left hand. She tore off the bow and paper and opened the small white box. "Oh, Daniel . . ."

"What is it?" Paula demanded.

Cristine held up a tiny pair of red sparkly shoes.

"How adorable!"

"I love them!"

"They're perfect."

"How did you ever find them?"

Daniel smiled. "They seemed to find me," he said as Claire walked up to him.

She looked him in the eye and said, "Okay, Daniel Burns, I want you to promise me you won't ever hurt her. That you'll love her and protect her."

"I vow to always love her and protect her, and our daughter."

"Because if you don't, you'll answer to me. I'll hunt you down like a rabid dog and—"

"Claire," Isabel interrupted. "He just vowed. I think you can leave it be now."

Claire exhaled and nodded. "Okay, so you seem all right, but I'm going to be watching you."

Cristine laughed. "Good luck with that, Claire. Now will you just give him a hug and a kiss and be done with it?"

Claire looked up at Daniel and shrugged. "C'mere . . ."

After the hug, Claire straightened her T-shirt and sighed. "I can see why you're crazy about this guy, Cristine. He's a good hugger."

"Yes, he is."

Embarrassed, Claire announced, "Okay, so maybe we should give the new parents a little time together? Let's all go to dinner and celebrate. My treat."

"Good idea," Isabel said.

Everyone stood in line to kiss the new family. Promising to return in the morning, the gang left and silence enveloped the room.

"I am glad you have them," Daniel whispered, coming to sit on the edge of the hospital bed. "They certainly took over when I was helpless."

"You were wonderful in delivery, Daniel. If I hadn't had you to keep me focused I don't know how I could have done it."

"You were magnificent," he said, placing the box with the red shoes on the night table. He faced Cristine and said, "I didn't know a miracle could be so . . . so painful. I am sorry you had to go through that."

"But look at the miracle," Cristine whispered.

He sat closer and touched his daughter's hair. "She is lovely, isn't she?"

"She is."

"Thank you," he murmured, his voice sounding emotional. "Thank you for her, for us."

"I love our little family."

"Even though it is not going to be what is considered normal?"

"I'm not going to try for normal anymore, Daniel. This is my version of normal, and I don't care what anyone thinks."

He leaned in and kissed her, deeply and profoundly. "She is gifted, you know," he said when the kiss ended.

"Oh, I know. I've seen what she can do while in the womb. I don't know what to expect now that she's out here in the world. I'm sure I'm going to have to home-school her."

"She isn't alone, Cristine. I want you to know that."

"What do you mean? That she has us, and the gang?"

"Tonight there is an unusual alignment of stars. Many gifted ones are entering this planet on this night."

"What do you mean?"

"Babies, like our Angelique . . . messengers of hope and—"

"Time to bring that little angel to the nursery so you can get some rest," a nurse announced as she entered the room pushing a rolling crib.

"I'm fine," Cristine protested. "Can't I hold her for a little while longer?"

"Rules, my dear," the nurse said, coming to the bed and holding out her arms. "Besides, you should spend some time with her daddy while you can. Won't be much of that from here on out."

Cristine kissed Angelique's cheek and reluctantly handed over her daughter.

"If she cries, or anything, you'll bring her back?"

"If she cries, she won't be alone. There's a nursery full of crying babies and she can make friends." The nurse placed Angelique in the crib and pushed it out of the room.

"I miss her already," Cristine whispered as tears came into her eyes.

"But now I can hold you," Daniel whispered, turning around to lie next to Cristine and envelop her in his arms. "You will heal quickly. I will take care of that."

"Good, because I'm really sore. She's a big baby, but beautiful, so beautiful. And she has your eyes. They seem so intelligent, like they're looking right into my soul."

"They are," he whispered, kissing Cristine's temple.

"They are?" she asked. "Really?"

"Really."

"Oh, God, I hope she likes me."

"And I will answer and say she has loved you always."

Cristine stiffened. "What do you mean? Loved me always?"

"Her love is eternal. It knows no limits."

Cristine took a deep breath. "What are you trying to say to me, Daniel?"

He held her even more tenderly. "The time has come to help you better understand who our daughter is, who I am, who you are."

Cristine felt her heart beating faster. "I'm not going to like this, am I?

Daniel laughed. "You're simply going to remember."

"Who are you? Really? An angel?"

He didn't say anything and she could feel her pulse in her fingertips as she tried to stay calm. "You are, aren't you? Then why don't you have wings?"

"That's a myth to explain appearing in one place and

then instantly appearing in another. Would you like to me have wings? I can, you know."

And in a sparkle of light they were enclosed in soft feathers.

"Don't!" Cristine protested. "Someone will see!"

The wings disappeared.

"Oh, God, I'm in love with an angel. My baby's father is an angel!" Cristine started to cry.

"Hush, my love. It's simply part of the plan."

"The *plan*? What plan? I *had* a plan, and it wasn't *this*!"

"Besides, I wouldn't exactly say I am an angel. Your myths have attached too much superstition to that label. Everything in this universe, along with those universes that your scientists have yet to find, and every dimension contained within them, comes from the Source of all creativity and intelligence. You, me, our daughter, your friends, everyone in this hospital, those that live in grand houses and also those who live on your streets. Everyone is related to everyone through the Source by simply existing. They just have to wake up and remember it. Our daughter and others born this night will help them."

"It's too big a job for anyone," Cristine said and sniffled. "Can't she just have a nice, normal childhood?"

"Wipe your tears, my love," Daniel said, using his thumb to absorb the wetness on her face. "Angelique will have a wondrous experience. She knows why she is here."

"I'm scared. I so want to protect her . . ."

"You must now understand something, Cristine. She and the others like her already know they are the light of the world. They will help all those they encounter to remember they are too. And they do not need the world's permission to shine their light upon the darkness. So release your fear, for it cannot exist if you decide not to entertain it. Haven't you learned that yet?"

"So I can't be worried?"

"It's a waste of your energy and will work against you and our daughter. May I make another suggestion?"

"Please, anything . . ."

"Allow me to heal you."

Cristine felt a surge of sexual energy rush through her body. "Daniel . . . you can't. Not now. Not here. Not when I'm . . . like this!"

"Come with me," he whispered. "We'll be back before anyone notices."

"See, you are just like a man," she accused with a laugh. "At a time like this and all you have on your mind is sex."

He held her face in his hands and smiled into her eyes. "Not sex. Come with me, Cristine. Come dance with me amid the stars."

Cristine smiled back. "Oh, you are tough to resist, Daniel Burns."

"I'm counting on that." he whispered, mischief appearing in his expression.

"You realize I just gave birth to your daughter two hours ago."

"Let the light heal you."

"Just the light, right?"

"My love, I would never harm you."

"Okay. I trust you." She looked at the closed door to the room. "But make it quick."

*What a life I'm going to have,* she thought, right before she surrendered and they merged into a swirling cloud of exquisite, dancing white light.

## Epilogue

THE HOSPITAL NURSERY WAS QUIET, SAVE FOR THE hum of electrical equipment. None of the babies were crying, which was unusual, for it was only minutes before the last evening feeding with the mothers.

"They should be howling," one nurse said to another, as three of them checked the rows of babies.

"They're all okay, though. Most of them are awake."

"You know what's really weird," the most experienced one said. "It's the girls. Look at them. They follow you with their eyes and I swear it feels like they know what you're saying."

"Did you notice," the youngest asked, "when you brought in the Dobbins girl, the rest of them quieted down?"

"I didn't notice. I was just relieved to have some peace."

The three women surrounded the small crib with Angelique Dobbins-Burns's name on it.

"She is a pretty baby."

"Yeah, you'd think her head wouldn't be so perfect being so big. I heard she was natural."

"Ouch. Practically nine pounds."

"See the way she's looking at each of us. Isn't that something?"

"God, she is adorable. I thought I was immune to falling in love with them after all these years." And the nurse reached in and placed her finger by the baby's hand.

Tiny fingers closed around the bigger one.

"Look at her!" the nurse exclaimed. "She's smiling!"

"That's gas. You should know better."

"Yeah? So who cares? Suddenly my headache's gone and . . . and I swear my feet don't hurt. I'm telling you, she's smiling at me."

"It's gas," another nurse declared and walked away. "We'd better get them ready for their mommies."

"I guess," the nurse said with a sigh, disengaging from the baby. "It was probably just gas."

Angelique continued to smile.

*This is such a fun place to be.*

*I must never forget that.*

## *Author's Note*

*Best Laid Plans* is the first book of a trilogy called the Guardian Series.

The idea came a few years ago. I so wanted to write a book about a circle of close women friends, having several wonderful friends of my own who have seen me through thick and thin. I know how supportive and nurturing these relationships can be, and I suppose my close friends are going to see characteristics of themselves in this book. It was written with great love.

*Twice in a Lifetime* will be Isabel's book, and I am beyond thrilled to be writing about an older heroine, someone who has had a great love and doesn't believe it could ever come again.

The last book will be *Old Friends,* Claire's story of giving up on love. Down deep, buried under years of cynicism, is the romantic in her still alive and struggling to resurface? I can't wait to write it.

And writing is exactly what I'll be doing, as this trilogy is to be published within one year. I do so hope you have enjoyed meeting the Yellow Brick Road Gang, and will look for the next two books to hit your bookstore.

Kindest regards,
Constance O'Day-Flannery

# *Acknowledgments*

**Richard Curtis**, who listened to my idea for a trilogy and then sold it so quickly

**Anna Genoese**, my editor, and all those at Tor, for all their efforts and their support

**Mike and Tom**, dear friends who rescued me from humidity and showed me a wonderful time in the desert

**Victoria O'Day**, my sister-in-law, for being there and helping to read over galleys

**Jennifer and Mitch Prensky**, of **the Global Dish Caterers**, Philadelphia, for their creatively mouthwatering menus

**Joe Dispenza, D.C.; John Hagelin, Ph.D.; Candance Pert, Ph.D.; Jeffery Santinover, M.D.; M.S.; William Tiller, Ph.D.; Fred Allen Wolf, Ph.D.; J. Z. Knight**, for their amazing explorations into the mind. Their intelligence and work inspired me, and I ask their indulgence if it appears I have oversimplified their efforts in this work of fiction.

**Randy Folgestrom, aka Amala**, for allowing me to use the lyrics of his song, "Strong"

**Mark**, for the fun and laughter as I tried to stay focused

**Kristen and Ryan**, as always, the bright shining lights of my life. Thanks for the traditional throwing of frozen veggies!

*Continued from Front Flap*

the present book, he had become a master stylist in the English language. This is perhaps the best introduction to Zen that he has written. He is concrete, as Zen itself is concrete. By means of a direct and succinct description of the training that a Zen Buddhist monk undergoes, he has given us the most precise picture possible of Zen in life.

The forty-three illustrations give a unique value to the book. The artist, Zenchu Sato, has depicted here the record of his own experiences in going through all the disciplinary measures pertaining to the life of Zen.

Zen is still a living spiritual force in Japan. The Zendo (Meditation Hall) is by no means an institution exclusively meant for the monks. It is visited by youths of character and intelligence; many devoted followers can be found among businessmen, statesmen and intellectuals. The sale of books on Zen is substantial and grows.

"Zen ought to be studied not only in its theoretical aspects as a unique product of the Oriental mind, but in its practical aspect as it is to be seen in the Zendo life. This is the chief motive for my writing this book."

*The*
# TRAINING
*of the* ZEN
# buddhist
# MONK

# The TRAINING

禪

UNIVERSITY BOOKS

by DAISETZ TEITARO SUZUKI

of the ZEN

buddhist

monk

Illustrated by Zenchu Sato

New York

monasticism and religious orders, Buddhist
Buddha and Buddhism - Japan
Zen Buddhism

This is a facsimile edition of the work originally published
in Kyoto by The Eastern Buddhist Society in 1934,
with the addition of a new Introduction by
Dr. Suzuki, written in 1964

D. T. SUZUKI, HIS LATE WIFE, BEATRICE LANE SUZUKI,
AND THEIR ADOPTED SON (ABOUT 1925)

D. T. SUZUKI AND MISS MIHOKO OKAMURA (1964). DR. SUZUKI IS NOW 95

# CONTENTS

# LIST OF ILLUSTRATIONS

# EARLY MEMORIES*

## DAISETZ TEITARO SUZUKI

MY FAMILY had been physicians for several generations in the town of Kanazawa.[1] My father, grandfather and great-grandfather were all physicians and strangely enough they all died young. Of course, it was no very unusual thing in those days to die young, but in the case of a physician under the old feudal regime it was doubly unfortunate, since the stipend his family received from his feudal lord was cut down. So my family, although of samurai rank, was already poverty stricken by my father's time, and after his death when I was only six years old we became even poorer owing to all the economic troubles which befell the samurai class after the abolition of the feudal system.

To lose one's father in those days was perhaps an even greater loss than it is now, for so much depended on him as head of the family — all the important steps in life such as education and finding a position in life afterwards. All this I lost, and by the time I was about seventeen or eighteen these misfortunes made me start thinking about my karma. Why should I have these disadvantages at the very start of life?

*At the age of 94, in 1964, Dr. Suzuki permitted Miss Mihoko Okamura and Dr. Carmen Blacker to prepare this article from notes taken at repeated interviews. The article was published in the November 1964 issue of *The Middle Way* and is here reprinted by the kind permission of Mr. Christmas Humphreys, President of The Buddhist Society of London. The article is unique in Dr. Suzuki's many writings: he has always answered requests to speak of his early life with, in effect, a refusal, in the spirit of humility. His own experiences as a monk, which he now gives us, provides us with a new key to our understanding of this book. The two together show us that he writes at all times with the spiritual authority of his own experience. In the more than thirty years since this book itself appeared, Dr. Suzuki has published more than twenty works in English in the field of Buddhist scholarship. Now we can ground his scholarship in his own spiritual experience. — The Publisher.

1 Kanazawa is the capital of the Ishikawa Prefecture in the middle of the West coast. For 300 years it was under the jurisdiction of the feudal clan of Maeda, and Dr. Suzuki's ancestors were physicians to the Lord Maeda's court.

My thoughts then started to turn to philosophy and religion, and as my family belonged to the Rinzai sect of Zen it
was natural that I should look to Zen for some of the answers
to my problems. I remember going to the Rinzai temple where
my family was registered — it was the smallest Rinzai temple
in Kanazawa — and asking the priest there about Zen. Like
many Zen priests in country temples in those days he did not
know very much. In fact he had never even read the *Hekiganroku*,[2] so that my interview with him did not last very long.

I often used to discuss questions of philosophy and religion
with the other students of my own age, and I remember that
something which always puzzled me was, what makes it rain?
Why was it necessary for rain to fall? When I look back now I
realise that there may have been in my mind something similar
to the Christian teaching of the rain falling on both the just
and the unjust. Incidentally, I had several contacts with Christian missionaries about this time. When I was about fifteen
there was a missionary from the Orthodox Church[3] in Kanazawa, and I remember him giving me a copy of the Japanese
translation of Genesis in a Japanese style binding, and telling
me to take it home and read it. I read it, but it seemed to make
no sense at all. In the beginning there was God — but why
should God create the world? That puzzled me very much.

The same year a friend of mine was converted to Protestant
Christianity. He wanted me to become a Christian, too, and was
urging me to be baptised, but I told him that I could not be
baptised unless I was convinced of the truth of Christianity,
and I was still puzzled by the question of why God should have
created the world. I went to another missionary, a Protestant
this time, and asked him this same question. He told me that
everything must have a creator in order to come into existence,
and hence the world must have a creator, too. Then who created
God, I asked. God created himself, he replied. He is not a

---

[2] Hekiganroku, usually translated "The Blue Cliff Records." One of the most
important text-books of Zen. See "The Blue Cliff Records," trans. Dr. R. D. M.
Shaw. Michael Joseph. 1961.
[3] The Greek Orthodox Church.

creature. This was not at all a satisfactory answer to me, and always this same question has remained a stumbling block to my becoming a Christian.

I remember, too, that this missionary always carried a big bunch of keys about with him, and this struck me as very strange. In those days no one in Japan ever locked anything, so when I saw him with so many keys I wondered why he needed to lock so many things.

About that time a new teacher came to my school. He taught mathematics, and taught it so well that I began to take an interest in the subject under his guidance. But he was also very interested in Zen, and had been a pupil of Kōsen Rōshi,[4] one of the great Zen masters of that time. He did his best to make his students interested in Zen, too, and distributed printed copies of Hakuin Zenshi's work *Orategama*[5] among them. I could not understand much of it, but somehow it interested me so much that in order to find out more about it I decided to visit a Zen master, Setsumon Rōshi, who lived in a temple called Kokutaiji near Takaoka in the province of Etchū. I set off from home not really knowing how to get to the temple at all, except that it was somewhere near Takaoka. I remember travelling in an old horse-drawn omnibus, only big enough to hold five or six people, over the Kurikara Pass through the mountains. Both the road and the carriage were terrible, and my head was always bumping against the ceiling. From Takaoka I suppose I must have walked the rest of the way to the temple.

I arrived without any introduction, but the monks were quite willing to take me in. They told me the Rōshi[6] was away, but that I could do *zazen* in a room in the temple if I liked. They told me how to sit and how to breathe and then left me alone in a little room telling me to go on like that. After a day

---

[4] Imagita Kōsen Rōshi was the predecessor of Soen Shaku Rōshi at Engakuji, Kamakura, where he is buried. Dr. Suzuki has written a biography in Japanese.

[5] *Orategama*, "my little iron kettle," is a collection of letters written by Hakuin Zenji (1685-1769) to his disciples. See *The Embossed Tea-kettle* trans. Dr. R. D. M. Shaw. Allen and Unwin. 1963.

[6] The Rōshi is the master of the Zen monastery who takes pupils in *sanzen*, personal interviews and supervises their *zazen* meditation.

or two of this the Rōshi came back and I was taken to see him. Of course at that time I really knew nothing of Zen and had no idea of the correct etiquette in *sanzen*. I was just told to come and see the Rōshi, so I went, holding my copy of the *Orategama*.

Most of the *Orategama* is written in fairly easy language, but there are some difficult Zen terms in it which I could not understand, so I asked the Rōshi the meaning of these words. He turned on me angrily and said, "Why do you ask me a stupid question like that?" I was sent back to my room without any instruction and told simply to go on sitting cross-legged. I was left quite alone. No one told me anything. Even the monks who brought me my meals never spoke to me. It was the first time I had ever been away from home and soon I grew very lonely and homesick, and missed my mother very much. So after four or five days I left the temple and went back to my mother again. I remember nothing about my leave-taking with the Rōshi, but I do remember how glad I was to be home again. A most ignoble retreat.

Then I started teaching English in a little village called Takojima on the Noto peninsula — that peninsula protruding into the Japan Sea. There was a Shin temple there with a learned priest who showed me a text book of the Yuishiki school called *Hyappo Mondō*, "Questions and Answers about the Hundred Dharmas." But it was so remote and abstruse that, though I was eager to learn, I could not understand it at all well.

Then I got another position, teaching in Mikawa, a town about five *ri* (15 miles) from our home in Kanazawa. Again I missed my mother very much and every weekend I used to walk all the way back to see her. It took about five hours and it meant my leaving the house at about 1 a.m. on Monday morning in order to be at the school on time. But I always stayed at home until the last minute as I wanted to see my mother as much as possible.

I might add, by the way, that the English I taught in those days was very strange — so strange that later when I first went to America nobody understood anything I said. We always

translated everything absolutely literally, and I remember being very puzzled by the way one says in English "a dog *has* four legs," "a cat *has* a tail." In Japanese the verb to have is not used in this way. If you said "I *have* two hands" it would sound as though you were holding two extra hands in your own. Sometime afterwards I developed the idea that this stress in western thought on possession means a stress on power, dualism, rivalry which is lacking in eastern thought.

During the six months I spent in Mikawa my Zen study stopped. But then I moved to Kobe, where my brother was working as a lawyer, and soon afterwards he sent me to Tokyo to study, with an allowance of six yen a month. In those days a student's board and lodging for a month cost about three yen fifty sen. The university I chose to study at was Waseda, but one of the first things I did on arriving in Tokyo was to walk down to Kamakura to study Zen under Kōsen Rōshi, who was Abbott of Engakuji at that time. I remember that I walked all the way from Tokyo to Kamakura, leaving Tokyo in the evening and arriving in Kamakura early the next morning.[7]

The *shika* monk, the guestmaster, took me to have my first introduction to the Rōshi with ten sen "incense money" wrapped in paper and offered to him on a tray. The guestmaster impressed me very much. He looked just like the pictures of Daruma[8] I had seen, and had very much a Zen air. The Rōshi was 76 years old when I first met him. He was a very big man, both in stature and personality, but owing to a recent stroke he had difficulty in walking. He asked me where I came from, and when I told him that I was born in Kanazawa he was pleased and encouraged me to go on with my Zen practice. This was probably because people from the Hokuriku district round Kanazawa were supposed to be particularly patient and steady.

The second time I met him, in a special interview, he gave

---

[7] From Tokyo to Kamakura is thirty miles.
[8] Daruma is the Japanese name for Bodhidharma (Sk). or Tamo (Chin.), the first Patriarch of Ch'an or Zen Buddhism who arrived in China from India in 520 A.D.

me the kōan[9] *Sekishu*, "the sound of one hand." I was not at all prepared to receive a kōan at that time. In fact as regards Zen my mind was like a piece of blank paper. Anything could be written on it. Each time I went to *sanzen* he just put out his left hand towards me without speaking, which puzzled me very much. I remember trying to find reasonable answers to the kōan of the sound of one hand, but all these Kōsen Rōshi naturally rejected, and after going to *sanzen* a few times I got into a kind of blind alley.

One interview with him impressed me particularly. He was having breakfast on a veranda overlooking a pond, sitting at a table on a rather rough little chair and eating rice gruel which he kept ladling out of an earthenware pot into his bowl. After I had made my three bows to him he told me to sit opposite him on another chair. I remember nothing that was said at that time, but every movement he made — the way he motioned me to sit on the chair, and the way he helped himself to the rice gruel from the pot — struck me with great force. Yes, that is exactly the way a Zen monk must behave, I thought. Everything about him had a directness and simplicity and sincerity and, of course, something more which cannot be specifically described.

The first time I attended his *teisho* lecture was also unforgettable. It was a solemn business, starting with the monks reciting the Heart Sutra and Musō Kokushi's last words[10] — "I have three kinds of disciples" and so on — while the Rōshi prostrated himself in front of the statue of the Buddha, and then got up on his chair facing the altar, as though he were addressing the Buddha himself rather than the audience. His attendant brought him the reading stand, and by the time the chanting was finished he was about ready to start his lecture.

It was on the 42nd chapter of the *Hekiganroku*, the one

---

[9] A kōan is a word or phrase which cannot be "solved" by the intellect. It is given by a Rōshi to his pupil to help him gain insight into reality, which lies beyond the reach of dualistic thought.

[10] Musō Kokushi's Last Words may be found, see Suzuki, *Manual of Zen Buddhism* at page 182 of the first edition.

where Hō-koji visits Yakusan, and after the interview Yakusan tells ten monks to see him off down the mountain to the temple gate. On the way the following conversation takes place: "Fine snow falling flake by flake. Each flake falls in its own proper place."

This struck me as a strange subject for Zen monks to talk about, but the Rōshi just read the passage without a word of explanation, reading as though he were entranced and absorbed by the words of the text. I was so impressed by this reading, even though I did not understand a word, that I can still see him sitting in his chair with the text in front of him reading "Fine snow falling flake by flake."

All this happened in 1891, when he was 76 and I was 21.

I remember that year, too, attending the ceremony of Toji at the winter solstice, when the monks all pound rice to make rice cakes and have a general carousal which goes on all night. The first of these rice cakes was always offered to the Buddha, and the second to the Rōshi. Kōsen Rōshi ws very fond of rice cakes dipped in grated daikon[11] sauce, and in fact he would eat any amount of them. On that occasion he demanded a second helping, which his attendant monk refused to give him, saying that it was not good for him to eat so much. The Rōshi replied, "I shall be quite all right if I take some digestive medicine."

On 16th January of the following year, 1892, the Rōshi suddenly died, and as it happened I was present at his death. I was in the anteroom next door to his with his attendant monks, when suddenly we heard the sound of something heavy falling in the Rōshi's room. The attendant monk rushed in and found him lying unconscious on the floor. Apparently just as he was coming out of the washroom he had a stroke, fell and hit his head on the chest of drawers. That large body falling on the floor made a big noise. A physician was immediately summoned, but when he arrived and felt the Rōshi's pulse he said it was too late. The Rōshi was already dead.

Kōsen Rōshi's successor as Abbot of Engakuji was Shaku

11 A daikon is a very long and large white radish. A popular vegetable in Japan.

Sōen.[12] At the time when Kōsen Rōshi died he had just come back from a visit to Ceylon to study Theravada Buddhism and was already a rising personality. He was not only very brilliant intellectually, but had also received his *inka-shōmei*, or certificate to become a Rōshi, while he was still quite young – an unusual thing in those days when it took about fifteen years to reach so advanced a stage. After receiving his *inka* he went to Keio University to study western subjects, which was again an unusual thing for a Zen priest to do. Many people criticized him for this step, including Kōsen Rōshi, who told him that western studies would be of no use to him at all. But Shaku Sōen never took any notice of other people's criticisms, and just went quietly on in his own way. So altogether he was a remarkable person, with rather unconventional tendencies.

At Kōsen Rōshi's funeral he was the chief mourner and performed all the ceremonies, and in the spring of 1892 he was installed as the new Abbot and I started to go to *sanzen* with him.

He changed my kōan to *Mu*, as I was not getting on very well with the sound of one hand, and he thought I might have my *kenshō* quicker and earlier with *Mu*. He gave me no help at all with the kōan, and after a few *sanzen* with him I had nothing to say.

There followed for me four years of struggle, a struggle mental, physical, moral and intellectual. I felt it must be ultimately quite simple to understand *Mu*, but how was I to take hold of this simple thing? It might be in a book, so I read all the books on Zen that I could lay my hands on. The temple where I was living at the time, Butsunichi, had a shrine attached to it dedicated to Hōjō Tokimune,[13] and in a room in that shrine

---

[12] Shaku Sōen is known to the west by the name of Soyen Shaku as the author of Sermons of a Buddhist Abbot, Chicago, 1906. He was the favorite disciple of Imagite Kosen (see Note 4), and was only twenty-five when he received his master's "seal" (inka... In 1893 he attended the World's Parliament of Religions in Chicago. He later travelled in Europe.

[13] Hōjō Tokimune was the Regent who in 1282 founded Engakuji, the Zen monastery north of Kamakura where Dr. Suzuki lived for many years in the sub-temple building, Shoden-an.

all the books and documents belonging to the temple were kept. During the summer I spent nearly all my time in that room reading all the books I could find. My knowledge of Chinese was still limited, so many of the texts I could not understand, but I did my best to find out everything I could about *Mu* intellectually.

One of the books which interested me particularly was the *Zenkan Sakushin*, "Whips to drive you through the Zen Barrier," compiled by a Chinese master of the Ming dynasty called Shuko. It was a collection of writings on Zen discipline and of advice given by various masters on how to deal with the koan. One of the examples I found in this book I thought I must try to follow. It said, "When you have enough faith, then you have enough doubt. And when you have enough doubt, then you have enough satori. All the knowledge and experience and wonderful phrases and feelings of pride which you accumulated before your study of Zen — all these things you must throw out. Pour all your mental force on to solving the koan. Sit up straight regardless of day and night, concentrating your mind on the koan. When you have been doing this for some time you will find yourself in timelessness and spacelessness like a dead man. When you reach that state something starts up within yourself and suddenly it is as though your skull were broken in pieces. The experience that you gain then has not come from outside, but from within yourself."

Then in the way of moral effort I used to spend many nights in a cave at the back of the Shariden building[14] where the Buddha's tooth is enshrined. But there was always a weakness of willpower in me, so that often I failed to sit up all night in the cave, finding some excuse to leave, such as the mosquitoes.

I was busy during these four years with various writings, including translating Dr. Carus's *Gospel of Buddha* into Japanese, but all the time the koan was worrying at the back of

[14] The Shariden building in Engakuji (see Note 13) is the only surviving example of Sung dynasty temple architecture. It is quite small and severely plain. Although damaged in the great earthquake of 1923, it was later restored.

my mind. It was, without any doubt, my chief preoccupation and I remember sitting in a field leaning against a rice stack and thinking that if I could not understand *Mu* life had no meaning for me. Nishida Kitarō[15] wrote somewhere in his diary that I often talked about committing suicide at this period, though I have no recollection of doing so myself. After finding that I had nothing more to say about *Mu* I stopped going to *sanzen* with Shaku Sōen, except for the *sōsan* or compulsory *sanzen* during a *sesshin*.[16] And then all that usually happened was that the Rōshi hit me.

It often happens that some kind of crisis is necessary in one's life to make one put forth all one's strength in solving the kōan. This is well illustrated by a story in the book *Keik-yoku Sōden*, "Stories of Brambles and Thistles," compiled by one of Hakuin Zenshi's disciples, telling of various prickly experiences in practising Zen.

A monk came from Okinawa to study Zen under Suiō, one of Hakuin's great disciples and a rough and strong-minded fellow. It was he who taught Hakuin how to paint. The monk stayed with Suiō for three years working on the kōan of the sound of one hand. Eventually, when the time for him to go back to Okinawa was fast approaching and he had still not solved his kōan, he got very distressed and came to Suiō in tears. The Master consoled him, saying, "Don't worry. Postpone your departure for another week and go on sitting with all your might." Seven days passed, but still the kōan remained unsolved. Again the monk came to Suiō, who counselled him to postpone his departure for yet another week. When that week was up and he still had not solved the kōan, the Master said, "There are many ancient examples of people who have attained satori after three weeks, so try a third week." But the third week passed and still the kōan was not solved, so the Master said, "Now try five more days." But the five days passed, and the

---

[15] Nishida Kitaro (1870-1945). The great modern Japanese philosopher and an intimate friend of Dr. Suzuki's since early youth. See *A Study of Good,* trans. by V. G. Viglielmo, Tokyo: Japanese National Commission for UNESCO, 1960.
[16] Sesshin. A period of intense meditation lasting one week.

monk was no nearer solving the kōan, so finally the Master said, "This time try three more days and if after three days you have still not solved the kōan, then you must die."

Then, for the first time, the monk decided to devote the whole of whatever life was left to him to solving the kōan. And after three days he solved it.

The moral of this story is that one must decide to throw absolutely everything one has into the effort. "Man's extremity is God's opportunity." It often happens that just as one reaches the depths of despair and decides to take one's life then and there that satori comes. I imagine that with many people satori may have come when it was just too late. They were already on their way to death.

Ordinarily there are so many choices one can make, or excuses one can make to oneself. To solve a kōan one must be standing at an extremity, with no possibility of choice confronting one. There is just one thing which one must do.

This crisis or extremity came for me when it was finally settled that I should go to America to help Dr. Carus with his translation of the *Tao Te Ching*. I realized that the *rōhatsu-sesshin*[17] that winter[18] might be my last chance to go to sesshin and that if I did not solve my kōan then I might never be able to do so. I must have put all my spiritual strength into that *sesshin*.

Up till then I had always been conscious that *Mu* was in my mind. But so long as *I* was conscious of *Mu* it meant that I was somehow separate from *Mu*, and that is not a true *samādhi*. But towards the end of that sesshin, about the fifth day, I ceased to be conscious of *Mu*. I was one with *Mu*, identified with *Mu*, so that there was no longer the separateness implied by being conscious of *Mu*. This is the real state of *samādhi*.

[17] *Rōhatsu sesshin. Rō* refers to the month of December, and *hatsu* or *hachi* means the eighth. 8th December is tratditionally regarded as the date of Buddha's enlightenment. Everyone makes a special effort at this sesshin, which begins 1st December and ends early at dawn on the 8th, to become enlightened. Usually they go without sleep the whole time long in their earnest endeavor.
[18] This would be the Rōhatsu sesshin of 1896.

But this *samādhi* alone is not enough. You must come out of that state, be awakened from it, and that awakening is *Prajñā*. That moment of coming out of the samādhi and seeing it for what it is — that is satori. When I came out of that state of *samādhi* during that *sesshin* I said, "I see. This is it."

I have no idea how long I was in that state of Samādhi, but I was awakened from it by the sound of the bell. I went to *sanzen* with the Rōshi, and he asked me some of the *sassho* or test questions about *Mu*. I answered all of them except one, which I hesitated over, and at once he sent me out. But the next morning early I went to *sanzen* again, and this time I could answer it. I remember that night as I walked back from the monastery to my quarters in the Kigenin temple, seeing the trees in the moonlight. They looked transparent and I was transparent too.

I would like to stress the importance of becoming conscious of what it is that one has experienced. After *kenshō*[19] I was still not fully conscious of my experience. I was still in a kind of dream. This greater depth of realization came later while I was in America, when suddenly the Zen phrase *hiji soto ni magarazu*, "the elbow does not bend outwards," became clear to me. "The elbow does not bend outwards" might seem to express a kind of necessity, but suddenly I saw that this restriction was really freedom, the true freedom, and I felt that the whole question of free will had been solved for me.

After that I did not find passing kōans at all difficult. Of course other kōans are needed to clarify *kensho*, the first experience, but it is the first experience which is the most important. The others simply serve to make it more complete and to enable one to understand it more deeply and clearly.

---

[19] *Kensho.* "Seeing into the Self-nature." Can be described as the first glimpse of satori or enlightenment.

# PREFACE

For those who have not read my previous works on Zen Buddhism[1] it may be necessary to say a few words about what Zen is.

Zen (ch'an in Chinese) is the Japanese word for Sanskrit dhyāna, which is usually translated in English by such terms as "meditation," "contemplation," "tranquillisation," "concentration of mind," etc. Buddhism offers for its followers a triple form of discipline: Śīla (morality), Dhyāna (meditation), and Prajñā (intuitive knowledge). Of these, the Dhyāna achieved a special development in China when Buddhism passed through the crucible of Chinese psychology. As the result, we can say that Zen has become practically the Chinese modus operandi of Buddhism, especially for the intelligentsia. The philosophy of Zen is, of course, that of Buddhism, especially of the Prajñā-pāramitā[2] highly coloured with the mysticism of the Avataṁsaka.[3] As Zen is a discipline and not a philosophy, it directly deals with life; and this is where Zen has developed its most characteristic features. It may be described as a form of mysticism, but the way it handles its experience is altogether unique. Hence the special designation "Zen Buddhism."

The beginning of Zen in China is traditionally ascribed to the coming of Bodhidharma (Bodai Daruma) from Southern India in the year 520. It took, however, about one hundred and fifty years before Zen was acclimatised as the product of the Chinese genius; for it was about the time of Hui-nêng (Yenō)[4] and his followers that what is

---

[1] *Essays in Zen Buddhism*, First Series, published 1927; Second Series, 1933; Third Series, 1934. Luzac and Company, London.
[2] See my *Zen Essays*, Third Series, p. 207 ff.
[3] *Ibid.*, p. 1 ff. and p. 55 ff.
[4] 慧能, 639–713.

now known as Zen took definite shape to be distinguished from the Indian type of Buddhist mysticism. What are then the specific features of Zen, which have gradually emerged in the history of Buddhist thought in China?

Zen means, as I have said, Dhyāna, but in the course of its development in China it has come to identify itself more with Prajñā (*hannya*) than with Dhyāna (*zenjō*). Prajñā is intuitive knowledge as well as intuitive power itself. The power grows out of Dhyāna, but Dhyāna in itself does not constitute Prajñā, and what Zen aims to realise is Prajñā and not Dhyāna. Zen tells us to grasp the truth of Śūnyatā, Absolute Emptiness, and this without the mediacy of the intellect or logic. It is to be done by intuition or immediate perception. Hui-nêng and Shên-hui (Jinne)[1] emphasised this aspect of Zen, calling it the "abrupt teaching" in contrast to the "gradual teaching" which emphasises Dhyāna rather than Prajñā. Zen, therefore, practically means the living of the Prajñāpāramitā.

The teaching of the Prajñāpāramitā is no other than the doctrine of Śūnyatā, and this is to be briefly explained. Śūnyatā which is here translated "emptiness" does not mean nothingness or vacuity or contentlessness. It has an absolute sense and refuses to be expressed in terms of relativity and of formal logic. It is expressible only in terms of contradiction. It cannot be grasped by means of concepts. The only way to understand it is to experience it in oneself. In this respect, therefore, the term *śūnyatā* belongs more to psychology than to anything else, especially as it is treated in Zen Buddhism. When the masters declare: "Turn south and look at the polar star"; "The bridge flows but the water does not"; "The willow-leaves are not green, the flowers are not red"; etc., they are speaking in terms of their inner experience, and by this inner experience is meant the one which comes to us when mind and body dissolve, and by which all our ordinary ways of looking at the

---

[1]  神會, 686–760. One of Hui-nêng's principal disciples.

so-called world undergo some fundamental transformation. Naturally, statements issuing out of this sort of experience are full of contradictions and even appear altogether nonsensical. This is inevitable, but Zen finds its peculiar mission here.

What Indian Mahayana sutras state in abstract terms Zen does in concrete terms. Therefore, concrete individual images abound in Zen; in other words, Zen makes use, to a great extent, of poetical expressions; Zen is wedded to poetry.

In the beginning of Zen history, there was no specified method of studying Zen. Those who wished to understand it came to the master, but the latter had no stereotyped instruction to give, for this was impossible in the nature of things. He simply expressed in his own way either by gestures or in words his disapproval of whatever view his disciples might present to him, until he was fully satisfied with them. His dealing with his disciples was quite unique in the annals of spiritual exercises. He struck them with a stick, slapped them in the face, kicked them down to the ground; he gave an incoherent ejaculation, he laughed at them, made sometimes scornful, sometimes satirical, sometimes even abusive remarks, which will surely stagger those who are not used to the ways of a Zen master. This was not due to the irascible character of particular masters; it rather came out of the peculiar nature of the Zen experience, which, with all the means verbal and gesticulatory at his command, the master endeavours to communicate to his truth-seeking disciples. It was no easy task for them to understand this sort of communication. The point was, however, not to understand what came to them from the outside, but to awaken what lies within themselves. The master could not do anything further than indicate the way to it. In consequence of all this, there were not many who could readily grasp the teaching of Zen.

This difficulty, though inherent in the nature of Zen,

was relieved a great deal by the development of the koan exercise in the eleventh century. This exercise has now become the special feature of Zen in Japan. Koan, literally meaning "official document," is a kind of problem given to Zen students for solution, which leads to the realisation of the truth of Zen. The koans are principally taken from the old masters' utterances. Now with a koan before the mind, the student knows where to fix his attention and to find the way to a realisation. Before this, he had to grope altogether in the dark, not knowing where to lay his hand in his search of a light.

The koan exercise is no doubt a great help to the understanding of Zen, but at the same time it is liable to lower the spiritual quality of the students who come to study Zen. Systematisation in one sense means popularisation, for things become easier to comprehend by being put in order. But this democratic diffusion tends to kill the chance for originality and creativeness, and these are the characteristics of the religious genius. System does not permit irregularities, they are generally excluded from it. But in Zen these irregular leapings are the thing most needed, although the koan exercise is a very flexible system and by the judicious use of it the master is able to educate his students in full accordance with the real spirit of Zen.

Zen came to Japan in the thirteenth century when the Kamakura government under the Hōjō family was having its heyday. It was at once embraced by the military class. Being direct and not requiring much learning, it was the very thing for the Hōjō warriors. Japanese culture under the Hōjō regime is noted for its austere simplicity, and for its vigorous creativeness, especially in religious thought: great Buddhist leaders were produced, who founded new schools of Buddhism; most Zen monasteries of the first importance were established; and the rise of Bushidō—the Warrior's Way—is co-incident with the spread of Zen among the warrior class. The art of fencing too owes a

great deal to the teaching of Zen, for it is deeply imbued with its mystic spirit. That the Japanese sword is to be used with both hands and that the Japanese warrior never carries a shield, always bending on attack, show how well the samurai appreciates the practice of Zen, in which the idea of "going-straight-ahead-ness"[1] is strongly emphasised.

Zen has had far more in Japan than in China to do with the moulding of the character of her people and the development of her culture. That is perhaps one of the reasons why Zen is still a living spiritual force in Japan, while in China it has almost ceased to be so. The Zendo (Meditation Hall) in Japan is visited by youths of character and intelligence, and that Zen tradition is very much a living fact is shown by the sale of books on Zen. Many devoted followers of Zen can be found among business men, statesmen, and other people of social importance. The Zendo is thus by no means an institution exclusively meant for the monks.

There are at present over twenty such institutions in Japan which belong to the Rinzai branch of Zen. In the Sōtō branch too there must be many, of which, however, I am not so well informed, and what is described in the following pages is principally applicable to the Rinzai. While both the Rinzai and the Sōtō belong to Zen, they have been differentiated from each other in the course of their history in China, but much more emphatically in Japan.

It is impossible, as I maintain, in the study of the Orient, especially in the study of Japanese character and culture, to neglect—much less to ignore—the influence of Zen. Zen ought to be studied not only in its theoretical aspect as a unique product of the Oriental mind, but in its practical aspect as is to be seen in the Zendo life. This is the chief motive for my writing this book, which is fully illustrated by Reverend Zenchū Satō, of Tōkeiji, Kamakura.

---

[1] 驀直去 (mo chih ch'u).

He is not a professional painter, but being one of those who have gone through all the disciplinary measures pertaining to the Zendo life, he is thoroughly imbued with its spirit, and what he has depicted here is the record of his own experience.

I have added many Zen "interviews" or "dialogues" or "stories" of the ancient masters culled somewhat at random from a work entitled *Zen-rin Rui-shū* (禪林類聚) in twenty fascicules. It is quite a handy book, giving Zen stories under classified headings; unfortunately, it is now a rare book.

DAISETZ TEITARO SUZUKI

Kamakura, January, 1934

# I. INITIATION

# I. INITIATION

## 1

The training of the Zen monk takes place at the Semmon Dōjō which is the "seat of perfect wisdom" (*bodhimaṇḍa*) specifically built for the purpose. While Dōjō has lost its original meaning and is nowadays used to designate any place of training, it still retains its primary connotation when it is applied to the Zen monastery. Attached generally to all the principal Zen temples in Japan we find such a training station for the monks. A Zen monk is no Zen monk unless he goes through at least a few years of severe discipline at this institute. All the monks, therefore, who are ordained after the rite of the Zen school of Buddhism are supposed once in their life to enter here; with all their higher modern college education, no monks can have any ecclesiastical standing in their own circles if they were not once students of Zen here. They have thus every reason to come to the Semmon Dōjō and to submit themselves to its disciplinary curriculum.

As the writer at this moment of writing is living in the grounds of Engakuji, Kamakura, which is one of the main Zen monasteries in Japan, let him describe the Dōjō here. The monastery is surrounded by hills, and in one of the valleys along which one walks up to the higher and inner part of the grounds there is a temple called Shōzoku-in. The Semmon Dōjō is inside the gate of this temple, which comprises, as we have it at present, the tomb of the founder of Engakuji, the hall dedicated to him, the hall enshrining the Buddha's Śarīra (in the classical style of Sung architecture), the Zendo (i.e., meditation hall), the Shōzoku-in itself (constituting the Jōjū part of the monastery), the belfry, and the residential quarters of the Master known as Zempanryō or Inryō. Most buildings here are reconstructions since

3

the earthquake of 1923. Let us imagine that all the scenes to be depicted in the following pages are with more or less exactitude referred to a Semmon Dōjō somewhat resembling the one in the Engakuji monastery, while the pictures themselves may often remind the reader of one of the Kyoto Semmon Dōjō if he has ever been resident there.

The life at the Semmon Dōjō, which, by way of abbreviation, will be later spoken of as the Zendo life, is something altogether out of keeping with modern life. We can almost say that anything modern and many things ordinarily regarded as symbolic of a pious life are absent here. Instead of labour-saving machinery, what may appear as labour-wasting is encouraged. Commercialism and self-advertisement are banned. Scientific, intellectual education is interdicted. Comfort, luxury, and womanly kindness are conspicuous for their absence. There is, however, a spirit of grim earnestness, with which higher truths are sought; there is determined devotion to the attainment of superior wisdom, which will help to put an end to all the woes and ailments of human life, and also to the acquirement of the fundamental social virtues, which quietly pave the way to world-peace and the promotion of the general welfare of all humankind. The Zen life thus aims, besides maturing the monk's spiritual development, at turning out good citizens as social members as well as individuals.

The Zendo life may be roughly analysed into (1) life of humility, (2) life of labour, (3) life of service, (4) life of prayer and gratitude, and (5) life of meditation. After his initiation to the Brotherhood, the monk is to be trained along these lines.

By "initiation" is meant a monk's being taken into the communal body of a Zen Brotherhood connected with a given monastery. This presenting himself as a noviciate requires some preliminary steps. He must first be provided with a certificate as a regularly ordained disciple of a Zen priest, and then he is to be equipped with all the articles

which belong to the make-up of a monk travelling for the study of Zen. The articles a monk needs are very few in number, and easily carried by him over the shoulders. With a bamboo hat, deep and large, over his head and a pair of straw-sandals and cotton leggings securely protecting his legs and feet, the monk appears before the porch of the Dōjō.

This travelling or pilgriming[1] which is technically known as *angya* (*hsing-chiao*, "going on foot")[2] has a special significance for the monk, and even when every form of modern transportation is available, he has to dress himself in the complete travelling attire as in ancient days and thus to present himself before the Dōjō authorities. (Plate 1.) Here is the "Song of *Angya*" composed by Shan-chao of Fên-yang, (Funnyo Zenshō 汾陽善昭), one of the noted Chinese Zen masters of the early Sung:

"Determined to leave his parents, what does he want to
    accomplish?
He is a Buddhist, a homeless monk now, and no more
    a man of the world;
His mind is ever intent on the mastery of the Dharma.

"His conduct is to be as transparent as ice or a crystal,
His is not to seek fame and wealth,
He is to rid himself of defilements of all sorts.

"He has no other way open to him but to go about and
    inquire;
Let him be trained in mind and body by walking over
    the mountains and fording the rivers;
Let him befriend wise men in the Dharma and pay them
    respect wherever he may accost them;
Let him brave the snow, tread on the frosty roads, not
    minding the severity of the weather;
Let him cross the waves and penetrate the clouds,
    chasing away dragons and evil spirits.

---

[1] It is possible that the usage originally started from Sudhana's visits, as related in the *Gaṇḍavyūha*, to more than fifty masters in various walks of life.   [2] 行脚.

"His iron staff accompanies him wherever he travels and
   his copper pitcher is well filled,
Let him not then be annoyed with the longs and shorts
   of worldly affairs,
His friends are those in the monastery with whom he
   may weigh the Dharma,
Trimming off once for all the four propositions and one
   hundred negations.

"Beware of being led astray by others to no purpose
   whatever;
Now that you are in the monastery your business is to
   walk the great path,
And not to get attached to the world, but to be empty
   of all trivialities;
Holding fast on to the ultimate truth do not refuse
   hard working in any form;
Cutting yourself away from noise and crowds, stop all
   your toiling and craving.

"Thinking of the one who threw himself down the precipice, and the one who stood all night in the snow,
   gather up all your fortitude,
So that you may keep the glory of your Dharma-king
   manifested all the time;
Be ever studious in the pursuit of the Truth, be ever
   reverential towards the Elders;
You are asked to stand the cold and the heat and priva-
   tions,
Because you have not yet come to the abode of peace;
Cherish no envious thoughts for worldly prosperity,
   be not depressed just because you are slighted;
But endeavour to see directly into your own nature, not
   depending on others.

"Over the five lakes and the four seas you pilgrim from
   monastery to monastery;
To walk thousands of miles over hundreds of mountains
   is indeed no easy task;
May you finally intimately interview the master in the
   Dharma and be led to see into your own nature,
When you will no more take weeds for the medicinal
   plants."

Travelling nowadays is done by railways or air-line, and all the charm, all the experience, and all the education one gets from travelling on foot as in ancient days are entirely lost—which is one of the great moral losses we moderns sustain in this mechanical age. When mountain-climbing is made too easy, the spiritual effect the mountain exercises vanishes into the air. The moral benefit the modern monk thus forgoes together with the picturesqueness of his life is to be greatly regretted. We must somehow find ways—the sooner the better—to compensate all such losses inevitably arising from science, machine, and capitalism.

2

In whichever way we may travel, on foot or by train, life itself is a form of *angya*: "Whence?" is the name of our starting station and "Whither?" is that of the arrival. Hence this admonition by Ta-hui[1] given to one of his lay-disciples:

"Whence is birth? Whither is death? He who knows this 'Whence and Whither' is said to be the true Buddhist. But who is the one that knows birth and death? Who is the one that suffers birth and death? Who is the one that does not know whence birth is and whither death is? Who is the one that suddenly comes to the realisation of this 'Whence and Whither'? When this is not thoroughly understood, the eyes rove, the heart palpitates, the viscera writhe, as if a fire-ball were rolling up and down inside the body. And who is the one, again, that undergoes this torture? If you want to know who this one is, dive down into the depths of your being, where no intellection is possible to reach; and when you know it, you know that there is a place where neither birth nor death can touch."

The object of the Zen monk's pilgrimage as well as that of our life-*angya*, is to come to the understanding of all these questions set up by Ta-hui; for this is "seeing into

[1] Ta-hui (大慧) was one of the greatest characters in the Sung history of Zen.

one's own nature." Mere visiting one holy sight after another is not in the programme of the Zen travelling, *angya*.

As Life carries its own bundle in the form of the body, so does the monk carry a travelling bundle over his shoulders. How happy we might be—so we imagine quite frequently indeed—if we were freed from this inevitable "bundle" known as the body or the flesh! As this is impossible, all we could do is perhaps to reduce the amount and weight of the bundle to a minimum. The less the bundle the freer will be our movement. For this reason, the monk limits his luggage to the contents of a papier-mâché box about $13 \times 10 \times 3\frac{1}{2}$ inches called *kesa-bunko*. In it we find a priestly robe (*kesa*=*kashāya*), a razor, the home address, some money (which is to be used for burial in case of his unexpected death), a book or two, a set of bowls (which are tied outside to the box), and other little miscellaneous things.

The worst passion we mortals cherish is the desire to possess. Even when we know that our final destination is a hole not more than three feet square, we have the strongest craving for accumulation, which we cannot ourselves make any use of after death. The monk mutely protests against this human passion by limiting his possessions to the last degree.


3

In ancient days when there was yet no railway travelling, the monk had to pass many nights on his way to the monastery where he decided to study Zen. Since he had no money, those nights were to be spent under any shelter he would come across, generally in a Buddhist temple where hospitality was most generously extended, but, if such was not available, in the open field or in a lonely roadside shrine. This was indeed a good practical education for the young monk who has now decided to give final solution to the

questions, as were formulated by Ta-hui, but which, really, have been stirred deep in his own heart. For the questions are to be solved, if they are at all solved, by keeping a close contact with life. When this contact is lost, the questions become subjects of intellection. The young monk must, therefore, experience life in its hardest and toughest aspects; unless he suffers he cannot probe into the depths of his own being. Travelling teaches this, and it was well for him to be prepared for all that might be coming to him in his monkish pilgrimage.

He has now arrived at his destination. The picture (Plate 2) shows the entrance to the temple which is attached to the Zendo. One of the monk-officials has come out to see the new applicant. The latter respectfully presents his letter of introduction and a certificate from his master by whom he was ordained. But he is politely but firmly refused acceptance to the Brotherhood. The plea is conventional these days: the Zendo is too full, or the temple is too poor, and no more admittance is possible. If the monk-novice accepts this quietly and tries another monastery, there will be no Zendo where he can find entrance; for he will everywhere meet this form of refusal.

The refusal is given once and the official withdraws. Being left alone, the monk has now nothing else to do but to continue his supplication in the same attitude as was assumed in the beginning: he leans over his baggage with his head down. He is fortunate if he is left to himself thus undisturbed. For he is sometimes forcibly ejected as an obstinate monk who refuses to accept the decision given out to him by the Brotherhood.

4

When the Zen monks want to be rude, they can be so. The new persistent applicant is now rejected by force from the entrance and pushed outside the gate which is closed behind him. He will not, however, be dismayed; he spreads

his seat, lets down his bundle, and begins to sit cross-legged; before long he may be found apparently deeply absorbed in meditation. The night advances, and the moon is seen going down between the branches of a tree. (Plate 3.)

It seems as if no soft spots were left in the heart of the Zen master. What he generally doles out to his monks is "hot invective and angry fist-shaking." For the Zen truth is something which must be snatched away from the hands of the master; he will never be too ready to bestow it mildly on those who beg. He is to be made willy-nilly to hand it to them. This is where the Zen discipline differs from other religious trainings. We will have further occasions to see how this is.

## 5

As is mostly the case, the "new arrival" (*shin-tō*) will be invited in when the evening comes. He is then at least for one night assured of being sheltered from exposure; but if he expects to sleep under a warm bedding, he will be terribly disappointed. No such accommodations are waiting him, and he is ready to stand all trials. He has been informed of all these inconveniences before he started on this pilgrimage. Zen monks are not supposed to pass their nights lying comfortably in bed; when the questions baffling all intellectual attempts at solution are still harassing them, how can they hope to have any kind of rest? There were many examples in the annals of Zen, which they may follow if they really want to be enlightened. Tzu-ming (Jimyō, 慈明) of the Sung pierced his thigh with a drill when he felt sleepy while meditating. The new arrival passes his nights facing the wall in the posture of meditation. (Plate 4.) When the morning comes, he puts on his straw-sandals, goes out, and nods his head over his own baggage as he did on the previous day.

This period of probation, otherwise called *niwa-dzume*, "occupying the entrance court," may last at least two or

three days—which formerly extended even to a week. This spending all day with the head down on the bundle is, to say the least, a most tiresome and trying procedure. How high his ideal and how exalted his aspirations, the Zen monk without the sense of humility and self-abnegation is not expected to attain the highest degree of purification. This *niwa-dzume* is the first practical lesson given to him as soon as he arrives at the Zendo.

After the *niwa-dzume* comes what is known as *tangwa-dzume*. *Tangwa* literally means "to leave in the morning" and is the name given to the room where travelling monks are given a night's lodging; they are not allowed to stay for a second night, hence the name. The monk-novice is now allowed to come inside and pass another three days' probation period in this room. Thus left in solitary confinement, as it were, he passes all day in meditation.

6

When about five days are passed since the arrival at the monastery, the novice monk gets a notice from the office known as *Shika-ryō*, which is the directing centre of the whole Brotherhood. According to the notice, he is to be at last permitted into the Zendo. He is told about the regulations, and good sound advice is given to him by the head-monk. In the following morning after breakfast he is transferred from the lodging room to the Zendo. He puts on his *kesa*, which is the formal ceremonial robe for all the Buddhist priesthood. He is ushered by one of the monks in charge of the Zendo, first to pay respect to Mañjuśrī the Bodhisattva, who is enshrined near the front entrance. Spreading his *zagu* which is a square piece of silk with a design, he prostrates himself three times before him. (Plate 5.) When this is done, he is led to his own seat where he finds his humble baggage leaning against the window. As he takes it, the usher-monk in a loud voice announces the admission of a new member into the Brotherhood. A tea-

ceremony follows, and the novice monk begins his Zendo life.

The novice has not yet been presented to the master himself—this takes place a few days later. One morning he is told to have his "interview incense" in readiness, which is to be offered to the Rōshi, that is, the master. Incense is used for various purposes in the monastery. In this case, incense-offering is a kind of pledge that this newly-admitted one takes in good faith the present master for his instructor in Zen. At the threshold of the master's room, the monk spreads his "seat-cloth" (zagu) and on it bows three times. In the meantime the master folds his hands before him. (Plate 6.) "Tea-ceremony" is partaken by both, which consists in just drinking tea each out of his cup. The Rōshi is likely to ask the monk concerning his name, native place, education, etc.

The first interview may end with this kind of conversation, since the monk is a perfect novice in Zen. Anciently, however, even the initial interview between a new arrival and the master went directly into the heart of the matter, and something like the following took place:

Hsüeh-fêng (Seppo 雪峰) asked a monk, "What is your name?"

Monk: "My name is Hsüan-chi" (玄機, "mysterious loom").

Seppo: "How much cloth do you weave everyday?"

Monk: "Not a piece of cloth I have on me."

Seppo: "Go back to your Zendo."

Before the monk took a few steps to leave the master's presence, the latter called out: "Your kesa (priestly robe) is dropping on the ground!"

The monk turned his head, whereupon Seppo said: "Fine that you have not a piece of cloth over you!"

Han-chu (Ganshu, 含珠) asked a monk: "Wang and Huang, Li and Chao—these are not your original family names; what is your original one?"

Monk: "Same as yours."

Ganshu: "Let alone being of the same family; I want to know your original family name."

Monk: "When the River Han reverses its downward course, I will tell you."

Ganshu: "Why not now?"

Monk: "Has the River reversed its course, or not?"

Ganshu was satisfied with the monk.

Wên of Chên-ching (Shinjō Bun, 眞淨文) asked a monk: "Where do you come from?"

Monk: "From Ta-yang (Daigyo)."

Bun: "Where did you pass your last summer sojourn?"

Monk: "Ta-kuei (Dai-yi)."

Bun: "Where is your native place?"

Monk: "Hsing-yüan Fu (Kōgenfu)."

Extending his hand now, Bun said: "How is it that my hand is so much like the Buddha's hand?"

The monk did not know how to take it. Said the master: "So far your answers have been splendidly natural and easy; and what obstructions do you feel now that I ask about my hand resembling the Buddha's?"

Monk: "I fail to perceive the point."

Master: "All is perfectly open to you, and there is nothing specially for you to perceive."

Thus commented on, the monk at once had his obstructions removed.

Our novice-monk has not yet had his koan, and we must wait until he has solved his first one when he will be able to understand these "dialogues." At the time of the evening *sanzen,* he is told to come to the Rōshi with the rest, and then he will have his koan, which means the real beginning of his Zendo life.

**Monk Starting on Pilgrimage**  *Plate 1*

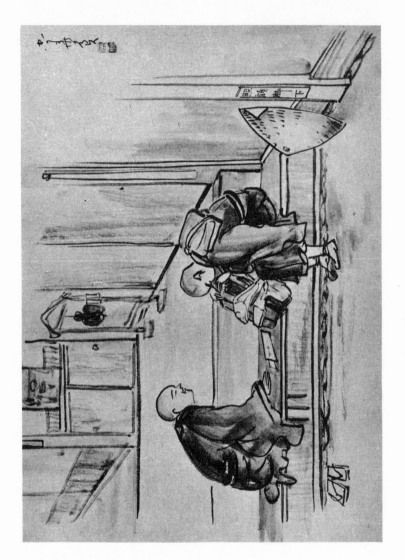

Asking for Admittance  *Plate 2*

Admittance Refused  *Plate 3*

16

Night in the Lodging Room  *Plate 4*

Initiated to the Zendo *Plate 5*

Introduced to Rōshi  *Plate 6*

# II.  LIFE OF HUMILITY

# II.  LIFE OF HUMILITY

While there is no doubt that the chief means of supporting the Zendo life is begging, as was in the ancient days of the Buddha, begging has, besides its economic value, a two-fold moral signification: the one is to teach the beggar humility and the other is to make the donor accumulate the merit of self-denial. Both have a great social value when they are understood in their proper bearings, and what is most strongly emphasised in the monk's life is this social meaning, and not necessarily its economic importance. For if it were necessary to support themselves by some other means, the monastery authorities would soon have found the way for it. But on account of its educative value begging has been selected for the monks to be the chief method of maintaining themselves physically. On certain days the monks all go out forming a long line and walk slowly in the streets, crying "Hō." (Plate 7.) Each of them carries a bowl, in which he receives money or rice. The offering is thanked for with a short recitation. Generally, however, the monks go out in a small company of four or five. They all wear deep broad hats which permit the wearer to see only three or four feet ahead. They cannot even notice the face of the donor who may drop a cent in their bowl. This is purposely done. The donor is not to know who the beggar is, nor does the beggar observe who the donor is. The deed of charity is to be practised altogether free from personal relationships. When the latter are present, the deed is apt to lose its spiritual sense. It is just an act of favouritism, that is, it harbours in it on the one side the feeling of personal superiority and on the other the degrading consciousness of subserviency.

The bowl the monks carry has figured very much in

23

the history of Zen.   Together with the "robe" it symbolises priestly authority.   When Hui-nêng (Yenō, 慧能) had an insight into the truth of Zen, his master, Hung-jên (Gunin, 弘忍) is said to have handed his own robe and bowl[1] over to Hui-nêng in order to testify that his disciple had the correct understanding of Zen.   Later, one of Hung-jên's disciples wanted to carry the bowl away from Hui-nêng. Hui-nêng made no special efforts to resist the intruder, but for some mysterious reason the latter could not lift the bowl. Later the Emperor Tai-tsung of Sung held up a monk's bowl in his hands, and asked Wang Sui, his minister: "Once at Tai-yu Ling the bowl was not to be lifted up, and how is it that it is now securely in my hands?"   The minister failed to answer the Imperial question.

When Nan-ch'üan (Nansen, 南泉) saw one of his monks washing a bowl, he took it away from him.   The monk stood empty-handed.   Thereupon Ch'üan remarked: "The bowl is in my hands, and what is the use of making so much talk about it?"

While Hsüeh-fêng (Seppo, 雪峰) was staying at the Kuo-ch'ing monastery, he held up his bowl and said to a Buddhist scholar: "When you understand the Truth, this will be given to you."

Scholar: "Such transaction is the business of a Transformation-Buddha."

Fêng: "You are not worthy even of being a servant to a Buddhist scholar."

Scholar: "I fail to understand."

Fêng: "You ask me then, and I will give you the answer."

When the scholar was about to make a bow, Fêng kicked him down to the ground.

Later, the Buddhist scholar came to Yün-mên (Ummon,

---

[1] What was really handed to Hui-nêng was the robe only, but later somehow the bowl came to be mentioned along with the robe.

雲門) and said: "It took me seven years to see into the meaning."

Mên: "Did it really?"

Scholar: "Yes, indeed."

Mên: "Another seven years may have to elapse before it fully becomes yours."

To see into the meaning of Zen is not enough; it must be thoroughly assimilated into every fibre of one's existence; and to do this fourteen years' constant application cannot be said to be too arduous a task. In fact, the Zen monk has to pass about that length of time in the Zendo before he is fully qualified as a Zen master.

Attached to a Zendo there are generally many householders who regularly contribute so much rice towards the maintenance of the institution. To collect such offerings, the monks are detailed to go out once a month. Each carries a bag over his shoulders, and visits the donors' houses one after another; when the bag is filled with rice, it proves to be quite a heavy load, especially when he has to walk along the muddy or pebbly country road in a storm back to his monastery.

Anciently, there was a monk, who, thus equipped, visited a householder. The monk was bitten by a dog. The householder said, "When a dragon puts on even a piece of cloth over him, it is said that no Garuda will ever dare attack him. You are wrapped up in the monk's robe, and yet you have been hurt by a dog: why is this so?"

It is not mentioned what reply was given by the monk-mendicant.

Wang the court-official once asked a monk: "All beings are endowed with the Buddha-nature; is it really so?"

Monk: "Yes, it is."

Wang pointed at the picture of a dog on the wall and said: "Is this, too, supplied with the Buddha-nature?"

The monk did not know what to say. Whereupon the official gave the answer for him:

"Look out, the dog bites!"

The monk and the dog have been associated in a strange way from the early days of Zen history in China. The koan "Mu!" or "Wu!" which is the "iron bull" given to all the Zen monks to chew thoroughly, is no other than Chao-chou's (趙州, Jōshū) answer to the question: "Is the dog endowed with the Buddha-nature?" Even when out in the collecting tour, the monk is accosted by the dog. (Plate 8.)

In the autumn the monks go out in the country when the farmers are ready to gather up pumpkins, daikons, potatoes, turnips, and other vegetables. They ask for such as are rejected by the farmers as unfit for the market. When they have enough collected they pile them on a hand-cart which is pulled by them as far as the foot of the hill where the monastery is situated. After that, the load will be carried on their backs up to the kitchen, and then some will be made ready for immediate consumption while others will be used for pickles or preserved for winter supply. (Plate 9.)

Takuhatsu-ing in the Streets  *Plate* 7

27

**Monthly Collection of Rice** *Plate 8*

28

Takuhatsu-ing for Daikon *Plate 9*

29

III. LIFE OF LABOUR

# III.  LIFE OF LABOUR

"A day of no work is a day of no eating" is the literal rendering of the first rule of the monastery life.  Pai-chang (百丈, 720–814), who was the founder of the Zendo institution, was always found together with his monks engaged in some manual work.  The monks wanted to keep him away because they did not wish to see their old master working as hard as themselves.  But he insisted, "I have accumulated no merit to deserve service by others; if I do not work, I have no right to take my meal."  His motive of work evidently came from his feeling of humility, but in fact manual labour forms one of the most essential features of the Zen life.  In India, the monks simply begged for their food and were not inclined to work hard.  But things were different in China.  Life meant to the Chinese monks to be engaged in physical labour, to move their hands and feet, to handle tools, in order to accomplish some visible and tangible ends.  This practicalness of the Chinese mind saved Buddhism from sinking into a state of lethargy and a life of mere contemplation, as we see this fact emphatically verified in the life of the Zen monastery.

However high and soaring to the sky our ideas may be, we are firmly fixed to the earth; there is no way of escaping this physical existence.  Whatever thoughts we may have, they must definitely be related to our body, if they are to have the power to influence life in any way.  The Zen monk is asked to solve highly abstract metaphysical problems; and to do this he devotes himself to meditation.  But as long as this meditation remains identified with abstractions, there will be no practical solution of the problems.  The Yogin may think he has clearly seen into this meaning.  But when this does not go beyond his hours of meditation, that is, when it is not actually put to experi-

ments in his daily life, the solution is merely ideational, it bears no fruits, and therefore it dies out before long. Zen masters have, therefore, always been anxious to see their monks work hard on the farm, in the woods, or in the mountains. (Plates 10, 11, 12.) In fact, they themselves would lead the labouring party, taking up the spade, the scissors, or the axe, or carrying water, or pulling the cart.

There was also a democratic spirit here in action. The term *pu-ch'ing*, "all-invited" (普請), means to have every member of the Brotherhood on the field. No distinctions are made, no exemptions are allowed; for the high as well as the low in the hierarchy are engaged in the same kind of work. There is a division of labour, naturally, but no social class-idea inimical to the general welfare of the community.

The history of Zen abounds with allusions to the master actually in the midst of some physical labour when a monk comes and asks him a question.

A monk caught Chao-chou (趙州) in the act of sweeping when he proposed this question: "You are a great Zen master free from the dust of evil thoughts, and why this busy sweeping?" "The dust comes from outside!"—came quickly from the master.

Chao-chou was once keeper of fire (*huo t'ou*) at a certain monastery. One day closing up the gate, he made a fire and filled the house with smoke. He went on loudly crying, "Fire! Fire!" The entire Brotherhood was astir and rushed up to the gate which they found closed, and there was no way of getting inside. Chao-chou said, "If you can say a word, the gate will be opened." The monks were taken aback and no words were forthcoming. Nan-ch'üan (南泉) who was among the crowd, however, took out the key and passed it over to Chao-chou through the window. With it Chao-chou opened the gate.

Chih-chang, of Kuei-tsung, (Kisu Chijō, 歸宗智常), one

day went out to the monastery farm to pick some vegetables. He drew a circle around some herbs, and said to the monks not to disturb them. The monks were careful not to touch them. After a while the master came out again in the yard, and seeing the herbs untouched he chased all the monks with a stick and said, "O this company of fools! Not one of them has enough intelligence!"

Hsüeh-fêng (雪峰) once asked Chang-ch'ing (Chōkei, 長慶) who came up to see the master in his room, "What is that?" Said Chang, "Fine weather, just the day for general outdoor work (pu-ch'ing)."

Another time seeing a monk pass by, Hsüeh-fêng beckoned him to approach and asked, "Where are you going?" The monk answered, "I am going to join the 'general work' (pu-ch'ing)." Said the master, "Then, go!"

Yüeh-an (Gettan, 月庵) once asked Lien, of Yü-ch'üan (玉泉璉), about Yün-mên's excusing Tung-shan (Dōzan) for thirty blows which Shan deserved.[1] But Lien failed to give An a satisfactory answer. One day he joined a general work party (pu-ch'ing). When he came up to the Mi-t'o Ling with a load of rice on his back, he was thoroughly exhausted. He set the load down on the ground, drawing a long breath. This unexpectedly opened his mind to the meaning of the koan previously challenged. He exclaimed, "How happy I am!" Later when he saw Yüeh-an, An said, "You now believe that I never deceived you."

Yüeh-shan (Yakusan, 藥山) one day seeing the monk-gardener planting vegetables said to him:
"Very well with your planting, but don't let the roots grow."
The monk protested, "If the roots fail to grow, what has our Brotherhood to eat?"

[1] *Zen Essays*, III. Pp. 135-6.

"Have you a mouth to eat?" queried the master.
No answer came from the gardener.

When Yün, of Shih-mên (石門蘊), was working as head-gardener at Ch'ing-lin (青林), Lin the master asked: "What are you going to do today?"

Yün: "I am going to plant vegetables."

Lin: "The Buddha-body fills the entire universe and where do you find a patch of ground to plant your seeds?"

Yün: "No sooner the golden spade moves than the holy plants begin to grow everywhere."

The following day Lin came out on the farm and called to Yün the gardener. The latter replied, "Yes, master." Lin suggested: "Let us plant a shadowless tree for the sake of posterity."

Yün: "If it is a shadowless one, it will never suffer our plantation."

Lin: "We won't talk about whether it suffers our plantation, or not; have you ever seen its branches, its leaves?"

Yün: "No, never yet!"

Lin: "If you have never seen them, how can you know that it will not suffer our plantation?"

Yün: "Just because I have never seen them, I say that it will not suffer our plantation."

Lin: "Yes, so it is, so it is."

While Hsüeh-fêng was at Tung-shan (洞山) he was carrying a bundle of kindlings which he set down before Shan. Shan asked: "How heavy is it?"

Fêng: "Even when all the people of the world try to lift it, they cannot."

Shan: "How then has it come up so far?"

Hsüan-sha Pei (Gensha Shibi, 玄沙師備) said to his monks, who were all employed with him in carrying fuel: "You are all sharing my power." One of the monks said,

"If we are all sharing your power, what need is there for us to be engaged thus in this general work?" The master gave him a scolding, saying, "If not for this general work, how can we come home all loaded with fuel?"

Chang, of Hsi-shan (䔸山章), used to be the head wood-chopper at T'ou-tzŭ-shan (投子山), and later came to Hsüeh-fêng. Fêng said, "Are you not Chang the wood-chopper?" Chang at once raised his arms and swung them as if chopping wood with an axe. Fêng nodded his head.

Ch'êng, of Ti-t'sang (地藏琛), was found one day working on the paddy-field. Seeing a novice-monk coming his way, he asked, "Where do you come from?"
Monk: "From the south."
Ch'ên: "How is Buddhism faring in the south?"
Monk: "Discussions on the spiritual subjects are going on fine."
Ch'ên: "With all their discussions on Zen, there is nothing there comparable to our cultivating the field, gathering crops, and eating boiled rice."
Monk: "What about the triple world?"
Ch'ên: "What do you mean by the triple world?"
The monk had no words to say.

When Mi, of Shên-shan (神山密), was working with Tung-shan on the tea-garden, Tung let down his hoe, saying, "I am all tired out, no energy whatever is left in me."
Mi: "If there were no energy left, how could you even say that?"
Tung: "You thought there was one with enough energy, did you not?"
Mi did not pursue him any further.

Shêng, of Yün-yên (雲巖晟), was hoeing on the ginger farm, when Tao-wu (道吾) came up to him and asked: "You are just hoeing this one, but can you hoe the other one?" Shêng retorted, "Bring me the other one."

As we may see from these Zen dialogues, the masters as well as the monks were equally employed in all kinds of manual labour, which were needed in their monastery life. Nothing was regarded as mean and below their dignity, for they were perfectly aware of the deep meaning in everything they did, whether with their hands or with their minds. There was no dualistic discrimination in their way of thinking and feeling. Otherwise, all these dialogues could not have taken place while they were thus working in the field or inside the monastery buildings. The dialogues or discussions were most intimately connected with life itself. Each pulsation of the heart, the lifting of the hands and feet—all evoked considerations of a most serious character. For this is the only way to study Zen and to live it. Nothing can ever really be learned until it works through the nerves and muscles. Pai-chang was a great Zen master who had a wonderful insight into the working of human psychology. If not for him, Zen as we have it might never have come into existence. In this respect we owe a great deal to the Chinese genius.

The monks are not always hard-working farmers and labourers; they often have free energy left for physical sports. When they are exempt from the daily routine work, they entertain themselves by planning wrestling matches, which is one of the great national sports of Japan. (Plate 13.) It goes without saying that in this the principle of fair play is most scrupulously observed.

Wood-gathering  *Plate 10*

Sweeping *Plate 11*

40

Gardening *Plate 12*

Wrestling   *Plate 13*

# IV.  LIFE OF SERVICE

# IV.  LIFE OF SERVICE

The government of the Zendo life is entrusted to the hands of the senior members of the Brotherhood. Their offices are generally: Tenzo-ryō which looks after food supplies and prepares them for the monks: Densu-ryō which attends to all the affairs connected with the Buddha shrine; Shika-ryō which is a kind of general directing office; Fūsu-ryō which keeps accounts; Yinji-ryō which attends on the master known as Rōshi; Jisha-ryō which looks after the Holy Monk as well as the Zendo; etc.  Generally the offices change twice a year.

1

To serve as a cook in the Zendo life means that the monk has attained some understanding about Zen, for it is one of the positions highly honoured in the monastery, and may be filled only by one of those who have passed a number of years here.  The work is quite an irksome one, and, besides, a kind of underground service which is not very much noticed by superficial observers. (Plate 14.)  Just because of this, to be the cook in the monastery affords the monks a good opportunity "to accumulate merit" which is turned over to their own attainment of Sarvajñatā as well as its universal realisation.  The meaning of service is to do the work assigned ungrudgingly and without thought of personal reward material or moral.  The only desire the worker cherishes in the execution of his service is to turn its merit to the general treasure-house of All-knowledge (*sarvajñatā*).

The main problem with the cook will then be to make the best possible use of the food material given to him for the maintenance of health among the members of the Brotherhood.  There is naturally nothing very appealing to the sense of a gourmand in the Zendo pantry, but cooking

47

may to a great extent be improved by a judicious use of *shōyu* or *miso*. The high-browed ones are generally apt to despise this kind of work as below their dignity whatever the term may mean. But with the monks there is nothing low or high in their work. If they could have chances to do good to others in any way they might come across, they should be willing to avail themselves of them and do the work assigned to them to the best of their abilities. The training at the Zendo is not only for the development of a man's inner psychic powers but for that of his moral character as a social being.

K'ai, of Ch'ing-yin (淨因楷), was a cook at T'ou-tzŭ (投子). The master of T'ou-tzŭ said, "It is no easy task to work as a cook like this."

K'ai: "It is very kind of you."

Master: "Is your office to boil gruel, or to steam rice?"

K'ai: "The one helper rinses rice and starts the fire, while the other boils gruel and steams rice."

Master: "What is your work then?"

K'ai: "Through your kindness I have nothing to do but idle away my time."

Had K'ai really no work to do as a cook? Was he just passing his time idly? How then could he be detailed as cook? In the Zendo life deep problems for solution are lying everywhere, and the master is ever ready to pick them up and make the monks face them.

One of the principles governing the life at Zendo, as was elsewhere alluded to, is not to waste. This applies with special emphasis to cookery where the vegetables or grains of rice and barley are always liable to be thoughtlessly thrown away. Chu, of Shih Shuang (石霜諸), who acted as keeper of the granary at Kuei-shan (溈山), was one day found putting rice through a sieve, when the master of the Kuei-shan monastery appeared and said: "Don't scatter the grains for they come from our kind-hearted donors."

Chu: "No, master, I won't scatter them about."

The master looked around and picked up a grain of rice from the ground and said: "You say you don't scatter them about; if so, where does this grain come from?"

Chu remained silent; the master continued: "Be careful not to think slightingly of this one grain of rice, for hundreds of thousands of grains all come out of it."

Chu: "May I ask where this one grain comes from?"

The master made no special answer to this, but laughing heartily went back to his own quarters. In the evening he came out into the Hall and said: "O monks, there is a worm in our rice."

### 2

Eating is a solemn affair in the Zendo life, though there is not much to eat. The best meal called *saiza* or *otoki* which takes place about ten o'clock in the morning consists of rice mixed with barley, *miso* soup, and pickles. The breakfast is gruel and pickles, while the supper is what is left of the *saiza*. Properly speaking, the Zen monks are supposed to eat only twice a day after the fashion set up by the Buddha in India. The evening meal is, therefore, called *yaku-seki*, "medicinal food." The modes of living are to be adjusted to climatic conditions.

When they are all seated, the *Prajñāpāramitā-hṛidaya-sūtra* (*Shingyō*) is recited, the ten Buddha-names are invoked: Vairochana Buddha as the Dharmakāya pure and undefiled; Lochana Buddha as the perfected Sambhogakāya; Śākyamuni Buddha as one of the innumerable Nirmāṇa-kāyas; Maitreya Buddha who will descend among us in the time to come; all the Buddhas of the past, present, and future, in all the ten quarters; Mañjuśrī the Bodhisattva of Great Wisdom; Samantabhadra the Bodhisattva of Great Deed; Avalokiteśvara the Bodhisattva of Great Love; all the venerable Bodhisattva-Mahāsattvas; and Mahāprajñā-pāramitā. After this, if it is breakfast, the virtues of rice

gruel are recounted; if it is dinner, the prayer is offered
that the meal be equally shared by all sentient beings including the denizens of the spiritual worlds.  The five subjects of
meditation are then repeated: (1) Do we really merit this
offering? (2) We are seriously made to think about our
own virtues; (3) The object is to detach ourselves from
the fault of greed and other defects; (4) Meal is to be
taken as medicine in order to keep the body healthy and
strong; (5) We accept this meal so as to make ourselves fit
receptacles for the truth.  The Five Meditations are followed by these vows: The first morsel is for destroying all evils;
the second morsel is for practising all deeds of goodness;
the third morsel is for delivering all beings so that we all
finally attain Buddhahood.[1] (Plate 15.)

No words are uttered during the course of eating, everything goes on silently and in the most orderly sequence.
The waiters are monks themselves taking their turn.  When
finished, the head-monk claps the wooden blocks.  The bowls
are quietly washed at the table and wiped and put up in a
piece of cloth which is carried by each monk.  While this is
going on, some verses are recited.  When the hand-bell is
struck, the diners all stand and walk back to their Hall in
perfect order.

3

When a monk is sick and cannot stand the Zendo life,
he is taken into a separate room called *Enjudo* ("life-prolonging room") where he is nursed by a fellow-monk.  It
is thus that the young novitiate begins to learn how to serve
his fellow-monks. (Plate 16.)  In graver cases the patient
will of course be sent to a hospital where he is with due care
looked after.

Even while sick, the monk is not to release himself from
spiritual exertion; he is always made to think of the masters

---

[1]  These recitations with many others are given, more literally
rendered, towards the end of this book.

and their ways of dealing with the problem—the problem of human ills which befall us most annoyingly in multitude of forms.

Why was Vimalakīrti (Yuima, 維摩) sick? To the inquiry made by Mañjuśrī he said, ''He was sick because of all beings, who were constantly suffering from ignorance and anger and passion.'' But, according to the *Prajñā-pāramitā,* the Bodhisattva is not to become frightened about sickness because there is no such thing as sickness in the realm of Sarvajñatā. Why is this? Let us see how the ancient Zen masters handled the problem.

The most noted case recorded in the history of Zen is that of Ma-tsu (Baso, 馬祖) the great teacher of Zen. When he was ill, the keeper of the temple asked: ''How do you feel these days?'' He answered: ''Oh, the Sun-faced Buddha! The Moon-faced Buddha!''

Yün-mên (Ummon, 雲門) asked a monk: ''What is your business now?''

Monk: ''Nursing the sick.''

Master: ''Do you know that there is one who never gets sick?''

Monk: ''I do not understand.''

Master: ''Whether you say 'yes,' or whether you say 'no,' it is all the same—'I do not understand.' ''

The monk was silent.

Master: ''You ask me.''

Monk: ''Who is it that never becomes sick?''

The master pointed at a monk who happened to be near him.

Shun, of Pai-yang (白楊順), was out of sorts for some time and gave out the following to his monks:

''Afflicted with illness I have not been able to lift my head from the wooden pillow.

Visitors are many and varied, asking me how I am;
In response to inquiries, various in nature and form,
    I have given my answers,
While the nightingale before my window more busily
    chatters away its praise of the spring.

"Let those of you who are able to answer as regards the source of my illness come forward and point out for me where in this body seven *ch'ih* long lies this trouble of mine."

The monks tried to answer the question, but none were found satisfactory. Thereupon, the master himself gave this for answer: He stroked the palm of his hand and opening his mouth made the movement as if to vomit. Another answer of his was: "What a fine pillow this!"

Hsin, of Huang-lung (黄龍新), one day noticed his head-monk laid up with a cold. He sent his attendant to his sick-chamber with this question: "Has your cold come from within, or from without? If it has entered from without, you have no pain inside; if it has come out of yourself, you are not hurt anywhere outwardly. Where does it come from, anyway?" The sick monk's reply was: "The monk finds his night-lodging at the monastery; the robber does not break into the poor man's house." Hsin, however, refused to approve of it, and gave his own answer: "See how the nose flows!" Or, "The head aches and the eyes are watery."

4

Certain dates are set apart for the purpose of washing soiled clothes, patching underwears, and curing the aching body by moxa-burning. The latter is one of the ancient Oriental methods of healing the tired body. After working hard on the farm, or walking to the distant villages to beg for rice, or sitting for a long time cross-legged on the cushion, intently meditating on a koan, the monk is sure to ache all over the body, perhaps particularly in the legs. In

such cases the burning of the moxa herb on some definitely specified spots of the body is considered quite effective to cure the pain or strain. The cauterisation of the skin seems in some unknown way to help the even circulation of the blood. The choosing of the spots where the treatment is most beneficial is left to the experts. But some of the spots are known generally to us, and the monk is quite an adept in this. (Plate 17.)

As the monk washes and mends his own clothes, he becomes a great expert in this after one or two years' stay at the Zendo. He also knows how to shave his own head, though in regard to this he will generally be helped by his friends. But since the introduction of the safety razor, the art of shaving has greatly been simplified. (Plate 18.)

The Brotherhood is a community of men pursuing one common object, and the spirit of mutual help and service is everywhere evident in its life. Democracy is also made, as was already stated, one of the principles governing this social body. Each monk, therefore, endeavours, on the one hand, to give others the least trouble for his own sake, while on the other he will do his utmost to do the most good he can for the general welfare of the community. This is known technically as "accumulating a stock of merit." It is natural that those who have successfully graduated from the Zendo life are some of the most efficiently trained and the most thoroughly equipped members of society.

To do service does not always mean to do something for others. If it is done with the thought of a reward or without the sense of gratitude and humility, it is not at all service, it is a deed of mean commercialism. The Zen monk ought to be above that. A life of service is closely related to that of humility and gratitude.

In the use of the materials, natural or artificial, which are the common possessions of the Brotherhood, the monks are taught to be scrupulously careful about not wasting or abusing them. Water is everywhere obtainable in this part

of the earth, especially in the mountain monastery; but they are strictly instructed not to use it too freely, that is, beyond absolute necessity. An attendant monk to a Zen master was one day told to change water in the wash-basin as it had stood too long in it. The attendant carelessly threw it out on the ground. The master was indignant and said, "Don't you know how to make it work usefully?" The monk confessed ignorance, whereupon the master advised him to pour the water around the root of a tree which was evidently in need of moisture. (Plate 19.)

I said "usefully," but the correct rendering is "livingly," and there is in it a note peculiar to Zen. "To make the living use of a thing" and not "to make the dead use of it," means, economically speaking, to develop its efficiency to the highest possible degree in consideration of circumstances. But the Zen point of view is not to look at the matter economically or dynamically: rather, if I could say so, "livingly" or "creatively." Merit, virtue, benefit, service, and other terms belonging to this category are conventionally religious. The way Zen handles so-called truths is satisfyingly fresh and stimulating; and there is at the same time a certain reverential attitude towards nature and her resources. In this machine age I have a strong desire to see this feeling of reverence towards nature restored and also the "living" use of things generally more properly appreciated by us.

This attitude of reverence towards nature, together with the idea that a man should not eat his meal unless he had something accomplished for the community to which he belongs, forms the foundation of the Zendo life. While the monk's mind is intensely occupied with the solving of the koan, which is more or less inevitably on the intellectual plane, he is liable to pay not so much attention to the social and practical aspect of his life. The doctrine of Emptiness (śūnyatā), as we have seen elsewhere, tends to divert the thought of the Buddhist away from the world of particulars,

though this is never the case with those who have truly grasped the doctrine. The two wings of the Buddhist life, therefore, are to be kept well balanced in power and activity, inasmuch as the monk is to develop this side of his life as a good student of Zen.

Modern life seems to recede further and further away from nature, and closely connected with this fact we seem to be losing the feeling of reverence towards nature. It is probably inevitable when science and machinery, capitalism and materialism go hand in hand—so far in a most remarkably successful manner. Mysticism, which is the life of religion in whatever sense we understand it, has come to be relegated altogether to the background. Without a certain amount of mysticism there is no appreciation for the feeling of reverence, and, along with it, for the spiritual significance of humility. Science and scientific technique have done a great deal for humanity; but as far as our really spiritual welfare is concerned we have not made any advance over that attained by our forefathers. In fact we are suffering at present the worst kind of unrest all over the world. The question is thus how to get us back to the appreciation of the Incomprehensible (*acintya*). This is no doubt the gravest and most fundamental of all the problems that are harassing people of modern times.

To come back to Zen. Ying, of Ting-shan (定山英), seeing his head-monk washing his clothes, asked him: "What are you doing?" The monk held up the clothes. The master said: "What kind of clothes are those you are washing?" The monk answered, "I spent some money for them while at Fu-chou." The master told the overseer of the monastery to degrade the rank of this monk.

In the Zendo life a monk cannot even have his own laundry thoughtlessly done!

Shi, of Yang-shan (仰山寂), was washing his robe when Tan-yüan (耽源) came along and asked: "Where is your

thought at this very moment?'' Shi at once retorted: ''At this very moment what thought do you want me to have?''

5

In Mahayana Buddhism various saints are worshipped. The bath room has a shrine dedicated to a Bodhisattva called Bhadrapāla, to whom the monks pay their respect before they take a bath. (Plate 20.)    Anciently, it is said that this Bodhisattva had his *satori* when he was about to bathe, and that the Buddha gave him this certificate: ''The mysterious feeling of touch which you have now illuminatingly testified entitles you to the stage of Bodhisattvahood.''    This is one of the one hundred ''cases'' commented on by Hsüeh-t'ou (Seccho 雪竇) in his *Pi-yen Chi* (*Hekiganshu*, 碧岩集). His comment in verse reads when freely translated:

''At last here is one who has successfully attained to the state of Emptiness;

Stretching his legs in full length, he can now peacefully sleep on his long couch:

But if you say that he has understood something to be discriminated as 'perfectly thoroughgoing,' I'll declare you to be still dreaming;

However much you are washed in perfumed water your face remains forever bespotted, so long as your mind is not free from discrimination.''

The monks are thus requested to wash off all the dirt of conceptualism as they are engaged in their daily work.    But one may ask, ''Where does this dirt come from, when we are told all the time by Mahayanists that we are from the first thoroughly clean and there are no defilements anywhere in us?    Why then this constant bathing?''    A master gives this answer: ''Even the idea of cleanliness is to be done away with.''    Another master has: ''Just a dip, and no why.''

The following episode is of a different trend. Nan-ch'üan (南泉) happened to pass by the bath-room, and seeing the monk attending to it said to him: "What are you doing?"

Monk: "I am heating the bath-water."

Ch'üan: "Don't forget, when ready, to give a bath to the bull."

The monk said, "No, master," and towards the evening he came up to the Abbot's quarters. Ch'üan asked: "What are you doing here?"

Monk: "I want to get the bull and give him a bath."

Ch'üan: "Have you got a tether?"

The monk failed to answer. When Chao-chou came up to see Nan-ch'üan, the latter told Chou about this incident. Chao-chou said: "I know what answer to make." Where-upon Nan-ch'üan repeated: "Have you got a tether?" Chao-chou stepped forward and straightway took hold of Ch'üan's nose and gave it a hard pull. Ch'üan said: "It is quite proper, but how rough you are!"

To give another episode in connection with bathing. Tsan, of Ku-ling (古靈贊), came back, after some time of the Zen peregrination, to his own temple where he was ordained. His old master while taking a bath told him to scrub his back. Gently stroking the back of his old master who had yet no knowledge of Zen, Tsan said: "What a fine Buddha-hall! But there is no Buddha enshrined here." The master was angry at this remark and said: "O this lunatic, how could you be so rude?" Tsan made another remark: "Though there is yet no Buddha enshrined here, he knows just the same how to emit his rays."

The monks take their turn to be the bath-boy whose work in the bath-room is to scrub the back of the bather. As the back is hard to be thoroughly washed by oneself, the bath-houses in Japan are generally provided with back-washers who are ready to serve you for a few extra sen.

When a monk is helped by his brother in this capacity, he folds his hands before him, expressive of his grateful acknowledgment of the service.

As we read in the bath-room regulations attached to this book, the material used for heating the bath-water is the dead-leaves and other refuse gathered in the monastery yards.

## 6

Not to let your left hand know what your right hand does—this is known in the Zendo life as practising "secret virtue." It is also the spirit of service. Secret virtue is the deed done for its own sake, not looking for any form of compensation anywhere, neither in heaven nor on earth. The trouble with our social life is that we are always seeking for a reward, and more frequently for one enormously out of proportion to the merit of the deed itself. When this is not forthcoming, we are dissatisfied, and this dissatisfaction causes all sorts of trouble in our daily walk of life.

Human life is not always governed by economic principles: there is something more in it, and the peace and happiness we all are seeking is attained only when this "something more" is understood. It is most unfortunate that our modern life is systematically moving away from this thought, in fact deliberately trying to stifle the inner voice.

Buddhist teachers, therefore, earnestly urge to make us grasp the doctrine of Śūnyatā not only philosophically but in the most practical way. Unless this is done, the practice of secret virtue will be something artificial and, therefore, hypocritical.

How do we understand the doctrine? Ying-an T'an-hua, of T'ien-t'ung (天童應庵曇華), gives the following sermon: "Students of Zen should by all means avoid wrong applications of mind. To attain enlightenment or to see into one's own inner nature—this is a wrong application

of mind; to attain Buddhahood or to become a master—
this is a wrong application of mind; to recite the sutras or
to discourse on the philosophy—this is a wrong application
of mind; walking, staying, sitting, and lying—this is a
wrong application of mind; putting on the dress and taking
meals—this is a wrong application of mind; to attend to the
calls of nature—this is a wrong application of mind; in fact,
every movement you make, whether turning this way or
that, or whether walking on this side or that—all this is a
wrong application of mind. Kuei-tsung has never given
you a discourse on the Dharma. Why? Because 'when one
word passes in through the gate of the government office,
even nine bulls are unable to get it out.' "

What is the ultimate signification of such a discourse
as this? From the so-called common-sense point of view it
looks like sheer nonsense. If we, following the literal meaning of the sermon, try to avoid "wrong applications of
mind," where do we finally land? This very trying to
follow the master—is this not also a wrong application of
mind? He evidently teaches us not to awaken a thought,
but to realise a state of *acittatā*, "no-mind-ness"; but this
is again a faulty attitude of mind. A monk asked Yün-
mên: "Is there any fault when not one thought is raised,
or not?" Mên answered: "Mt Sumeru!" If so, what is
required of us to do in this *impasse*? Everything is taken
away from us; the earth itself fails to support us. But
this is the very situation into which all Zen masters contrive
to drive us. A light flashes out of the darkness when the
latter reaches its limits. Then we realise the truth of the
following dialogue:

A monk asked Ch'ê, of Shih-mên (石門徹); "How shall
we make an advance when no thoughts are cherished of
anything?" The master's reply was: "The wooden man
sits on the loom and the stone-man at night throws in the
shuttle."

When this is understood, Śūnyatā becomes facts of our

daily life, and the practice of secret virtue is no more Pharisaism. Any work, however offensive or repulsive in the ordinary sense, ceases to be so and is willingly undertaken. Cleaning the lavatory, for instance, especially the one constructed in primitive style, is generally relegated to people whose profession is to do that kind of work. In the monastery, however, monks are disciplined to take up whatever work that is assigned to them without a murmur and to do it in the best possible manner. Apart from its moral or social value, this attitude of mind is cultivated, as we have already seen, from the point of view which may be called specifically Zen or Mahayanistic. The Christian idea of attending on unfortunate patients suffering from disgusting diseases, which is specially considered by the Christians to be pious or meritorious, shows a great similarity to the Buddhist motive. The thought at the back of the deed admits of variations, but the same feeling which may be called religious underlies here both the Christian and the Buddhist mind.

Ucchushma is the name of the god enshrined at the lavatory, who is supposed to swallow up all the impurities discoverable here. His business does not seem to be a very pleasant one; but as long as we are not beings thoroughly purgated of impurities inside as well as outside, there must be some who will take care of them; and this one no doubt is he who has reached the state of mind to which no "wrong applications" are possible. (Plate 21.)

Cooking  *Plate 14*

Dining Room *Plate 15*

Nursing the Sick  *Plate 16*

Sewing and Moxa-burning  *Plate 17*

64

Shaving  *Plate 18*

65

Washing  *Plate 19*

Bath-room  *Plate 20*

67

# V. LIFE OF PRAYER AND GRATITUDE

# V. LIFE OF PRAYER AND GRATITUDE

## 1

The life of prayer begins with confession; for prayer, in whatever sense it may be taken, is the expression of an earnest desire which is raised when the devotee feels something lacking in himself and seeks to complete himself either through an outside power or by digging deeper into his own being; and the confession consists in frankly recognising this fact which is in some cases felt as sinfulness. In Buddhist terminology, this means to grow conscious of the heaviness of one's own karma-hindrances which have been raised in the past by means of body, mouth, and mind. When the devotee is innerly impelled to become conscious of this, he prays. He may not have any definitive knowledge as regards the objective body to which his prayer is offered. This knowledge is not generally essential, because his prayer is the uncontrollable outburst of an intensely intimate desire. In Zen Buddhism prayers are offered to all the Buddhas and Bodhisattvas of the past, present, and future in the ten quarters and also to Mahāprajñāpāramitā.

The confession formula is:
"All the evil deeds I have committed in the past are
    due to greed, anger, and folly cherished since
    the time beyond calculation,
And have been produced by means of my body,
    mouth, and mind—
All these I now confess without reservation."

With Zen Buddhists prayer is more in the form of self-reflection and vow or determined will than asking for an outside help in the execution of desires. The following is what is known as "the Bodhisattva's Vow and Deed":

"When I reflect upon the true character of all things I perceive that it is mysteriously expressive of the virtue of the Tathagata and that the entire universe down to

73

its smallest particles is a ray issuing from him in the most incomprehensible manner. For this reason the ancient masters have cherished a kindly and reverential attitude towards all beings inclusive of birds and beasts. In all the foods and clothes wherewith our body is kept warm and nourished through the twelve divisions of the day we recognise the flesh and blood of our masters; for even these inanimate objects reflect their love and compassion, for which we all feel the deep sense of reverence and gratitude. This being the case, we ought to think most tenderly and kindly towards those who are not sufficiently endowed with intelligence. Even when enemies vilify us or torment us in one way or another, let us consider them Bodhisattvas in disguise, whose loving hearts endeavour by this means to efface the effects of all our evil deeds and thoughts which we have been constantly committing because of our egotism and prejudiced views since the immeasurable past. Let us thus thinking cultivate the virtue of humility in words and deeds and raise with single-mindedness thoughts of devotion. The very moment when thus pure faith is awakened from the depths of our being, a lotus of enlightenment will open up in bloom. Each lotus flower carries a Buddha in it, and wherever there is the Buddha, there is a pure land in full array, and its glory will follow every step of ours. May this way of feeling be shared by all sentient beings and they together with us equally attain to the realisation of Sarvajñatā!''

Ta-hui's (大慧) prayer which is recited daily in the Zen monastery may be said to sum up all that is stirred in the heart of the monk:
''My only prayer is to be firm in my determination to pursue the study of Truth, so that I may not feel weary however long I have to apply myself to it; to be light and easy in the four parts of my body; to be strong and undismayed in body and mind, to be free from illnesses, and

to drive out both depressed feelings and light-heartedness; to escape every form of calamity, misfortune, evil influence, and obstruction, so that I may instantly enter upon the right way and not be led astray into the path of evil; to efface all the evil passions, to make grow the Prajñā, to have an immediate enlightenment on the matter that most concerns me, and thereby to continue the spiritual life of the Buddhas, and further to help all sentient beings, to cross the ocean of birth and death, whereby I may requite all that I owe to the loving thoughts of the Buddhas and Patriarchs. My further prayer is not to be too ill, or to be too suffering at the time of my departure, to know its coming beforehand, say, seven days ahead, so that my thoughts may dwell peacefully and properly on Truth; abandoning this body, unattached to any tie at the last moment, to be reborn without delay in the land of the Buddhas, and seeing them face to face to receive from them the final testimony of supreme enlightenment, and thereby enabled to divide myself infinitely in the Dharmadhātu to help universally all sentient beings in their fording the ocean of birth and death. These prayers are offered to all the Buddhas and Bodhisattva-Mahasattvas of the past, present, and future in the ten quarters, and to Mahāprajñāpāramitā.''

Besides these prayers, the monk recites the ''Inscriptions on the Right-hand Side of the Seat'' written by Chung-fêng the National Teacher (中峰國師坐右銘):
''The Bhikshus in these latter days resemble in form those homeless ones but at heart have no feelings of shame and remorse.
''Their bodies are covered with the priestly robe but their minds are tainted with worldly defilements.
''They recite with their mouths the sacred scriptures, but they harbour in their minds greed and lust.
''During the day they are addicted to the pursuit of fame and wealth, while at night they are drunk with impure attachments.
''Outwardly they observe the moral precepts, whereas inwardly they are secret violators of the rules.

"Forever busy with worldly affairs, they are neglectful of disciplining themselves for deliverance.

"They are devoted so much to the cherishing of idle thoughts that they have already thrown away right knowledge.

"1.   Have the desire for Truth firmly set up in order to be able to see into your own nature.

"2.   Cherish deep doubt in regard to the koan you have and be as if biting at an iron ball.

"3.   Keeping up your erect posture on the seat, never lie down in bed.

"4.   Cultivate the sense of humility and remorse by reading books and sayings left by the Buddha and the Patriarchs.

"5.   Keeping the body pure in accordance with the Precepts, never get it tainted, and the same is to be said of the mind.

"6.   Behave . yourselves on all occasions with quiet dignity and be in no circumstances rash and boisterous.

"7.   Talk softly and in a low tone, do not be given up to idle jokings.

"8.   There may be people who do not believe you, but do not let them deride you.

"9.   Be always ready to use your dusters and brooms in order to keep the monastery buildings and courts free from dust.

"10.   Untiringly pursuing the course of Truth, never be addicted to excessive eating and drinking.

"Birth and death is the grave event,
Every moment of this life is to be begrudged,
Impermanency will be here too soon,
Time waits for no one.

"A rare event it is to be born as human beings,
And we are now born as such;
It is not easy to be able to listen to the Buddha's teaching,
And we have now listened to it.

"This being so, if we do not attain emancipation in this life,
In what life do we expect to emancipate ourselves?"

2

Besides these prayers and admonitions, the sutras are also daily recited in the early morning and in the afternoon. In Japanese and Chinese Buddhism sutra-reading performs a double function; primarily as getting in touch with the thought of the founder, and secondarily as creating spiritual merit. The first may better be called sutra-study whereas the latter is properly sutra-reading or reciting, for the object is just to recite it, not necessarily accompanied by an intellectual understanding of its content. The recitation itself is regarded as meritorious as it is so stated in the sutras. Not only reciting or reading but copying is also merit-producing. The sutra-reading in the Buddhist monasteries can thus be reckoned as a sort of prayer. The reading, even when its full meaning is not grasped, detaches one's mind from worldly concerns and self-centered interests. Though negative, the merit herewith gained tends to direct the mind towards the attainment of Sarvajñatā.

The sutra-reading is also an expression of gratitude towards one's teachers, ancestors, and other beings generally. To be grateful in Buddhism means that Sarvajñatā has gained so much towards its realisation in the world. In this feeling there is nothing personal, that is, egotistic. The monks, therefore, in their daily exercises which consist in sutra-reading, prayer-recitation, incense-offering, bowing, and so on, express their appreciation of what the Buddhas, Bodhisattvas, patriarchs, teachers, and other personages have done for the Buddhist cause.

The sutras most commonly used in the Zen monastery are (1) The *Prajñāpāramitā-hṛidaya Sūtra*, known as *Shingyō*, (2) The *Samantamukha-parivarta* known as *Kwannongyō*, which forms a chapter of the *Puṇḍarīka Sūtra*, and (3) The *Vajracchedikā Sūtra* or *Kongōkyō* in Japanese. Of these three, the *Shingyō* being the simplest is recited almost on all occasions. Besides these Chinese translations, the original Sanskrit texts in Chinese transliteration which

is pronounced in the Japanese way are also used; they belong more or less to the Dhārani class of Buddhist literature and are altogether unintelligible, even when they are translated.

On some special occasions the *Mahā-prajñā-pāramitā Sūtras* in six hundred fascicules are read in the way known as *ten-doku* (*chuan-tu* in Chinese). *Ten-doku* means "to read revolving." As the sutras are of such a bulk, they cannot be finished within a prescribed period. The six hundred volumes are divided among the monks and each monk reads two or three pages in the beginning and at the end of each volume while the middle part is read by turning over the entire volume for a few times; hence the phrase "read by revolving." Each volume consisting of one long sheet of strong paper is folded up to so many folios, and when the monks read them "by revolving" the sutras look as if they were so many long narrow pieces of yellow cloth flying in the air. (Plate 22.) And especially because they recite them at the top of their voices, the whole scene is quite a lively one. The reading of the sutras is full of spiritual benefits not only for readers themselves but for all to whom the merit is dedicated. The first three early mornings of the New Year are devoted to this ceremony at all the Zen monasteries, when not only the welfare of the nation but the peace of the entire world is most earnestly prayed for.

An old lady once sent a messenger with money to Chao-chou, requesting him to "revolve" the whole Tripitaka. Chao-chou came down from his seat, and, walking around the chair once, said: "The revolving is finished." The messenger went back to the old lady and reported the proceeding as it happened. The old lady said: "I asked him to 'revolve' the entire Tripitaka but his 'revolving' covers only a half of the Tripitaka."

On this, Ta-hui (大慧), one of the great Zen masters

of Sung, commented: "Some ask, 'What is the other half?'
others say, 'Make another round'; or 'Snap your fingers';
still others say, 'Give a cough'; or 'Utter a *kwatz*!' or 'Clap
the hands!' Those who make these remarks do not know
what shame means. As regards 'the other half,' do never
make such a remark as this: 'Make another round'! Even
when hundreds of thousands of kotis of rounds are made,
they are, from the point of view of the old lady, no more
than a half Tripitaka. Even when Mount Sumeru is gone
round for hundreds of thousands of kotis of times, they
are, from the point of view of the old lady, no more than
a half Tripitaka. Even when the great Zen masters of the
whole empire walk round the mountain for hundreds of
thousands of kotis of times, they are, from the point of view
of the old lady, no more than a half Tripitaka. Even when
all the mountains and rivers and the great earth and everything that makes up this universe of multiplicities, including
every plant and every blade of grass, each endowed with a
long broad tongue, unanimously revolve the Tripitaka from
this day on to the end of time, they are, from the point of
view of the old lady, no more than a half Tripitaka."
Ta-hui remained silent for a while and continued:

" 'The beautiful pair of ducks, embroidered in the finest
    style, is there for you to see as much as you like;
But take care not to deliver up the gold needle that
    did the work!' "

After these references, another Zen master gave his own
idea saying: "The old lady claims that Chao-chou has only
finished revolving a half of the Tripitaka. This is replacing
the genuine by the spurious. The only thing that was needed at the time to say was this: Why not take the whole
thing in even before Chao-chou started to walk round the
chair?"

3

How the hungry ghosts came to find their place in the

scheme of the Zen conception of the world is a subject of special research in the institutional history of Zen in China. Zen in its pure form has the tendency to become acosmistic, but in its "affirmative aspect" it accepts everything that is going on in the world of multiplicities. Even all the polytheistic gods including denizens of the air, of the earth, and of the heavens, and any other beings, who are living only in the realm of superstitional and traditional beliefs, are indiscriminately taken into the system of Zen. Each of them is permitted to have his or her place in Zen according to values given by the popular religions; and this is the reason why Zen has come to harbour so much of what I should call the Chinese Shingon element. The Dhāranī-sutras are recited; ancestors are worshipped; the prosperity of the ruling powers of the time is prayed for,—although "to whom!" is the question still to be settled; the protection of the local gods is earnestly sought after; all the rituals in connection with the "departed spirits" are strictly observed; and all forms of exorcism are to a certain extent also practised. The Feeding of the Hungry Ghosts (*segaki*), which is observed at least twice a year during the Higan Season ("other shore") is thus one of the excrescences added from the outside; but at the same time the idea of a communion may be said to be noticed here, which is recognised to exist between all living beings and those who are supposed to have passed away. The form is to feed the hungry ghosts, but, as we can glean from the prayer-formula, the feeding is in reality sharing food, participating in the same staff of life, which symbolises the idea of one grand community comprising all the spirits seen and unseen.

The hungry ghosts, *preta* in Sanskrit, find their place in the six paths (*gati*) of existence. They are departed spirits, but as they seem to be eternally desiring something to eat because they are hungry, they are known as "hungry ghosts." Perhaps they betoken the human desire to have, which never knows satiation. If all the greed in the world

expressing itself in infinite varieties of form is appeased by the performance of the *Segaki* ritual, the Pure Land will in no time be an actuality here with us. We are all then hungry ghosts, though not necessarily departed spirits. By feeding the supposedly departed we are feeding ourselves; when they are filled we are filled; no real distinction is to be made between the dead and the living. The living so called are living on the dead, that is, the dead so called are living most lively in the living. Prayer is then for being abundantly fed with Enlightenment, and gratitude is for enjoying this opportunity of realising Enlightenment together with the "departed spirits."

A tablet dedicated to "all the departed spirits of the triple world" is set up at the centre of the altar. Flowers, candles, and incense, together with food, are as usual offered to it. The holy enclosure is protected by the banners bearing the names of the Tathagatas, Bodhisattvas, Arhats, gods, demigods, and other non-human beings. They are supposed, thus invited, to be present at the ceremony and participating in the erection of the mystic effects over the unhappy denizens of Limbo. (Plate 23.)

When the *dramatis personae*—Buddhas, gods, and hungry ones—are invited, the Dhāranīs are read and a prayer is recited to this effect:

"It is desired that all the hungry ghosts inhabiting every corner of the worlds filling the ten quarters come to this place and partake of the pure food offered to them. You be filled with it, and when you are fully satisfied, you come here, and see to it that all sentient beings in turn are fed by you. It is also desired that by virtue of this magic food you shall be delivered from the pain you are suffering and be born in the heavens and visit as you will all the Pure Lands in the ten quarters; that you come to cherish the desire for Enlightenment, practise the life of Enlightenment, and in the life to come attain Buddhahood. It is again desired that you protect us days and nights so

as to let us attain without hindrances the object of our lives. Whatever merit that is productive of this deed of feeding the hungry ones—let it be dedicated to the universal realisation of the Supreme Enlightenment and let every sentient being come speedily to the attainment of Buddhahood. This prayer is offered to all the Buddhas and Bodhisattvas of the past, present, and future in all the ten quarters, and to Mahāprajñāpāramitā.''

In fact, this feeding of the hungry ghosts and other spiritual beings is practised daily at the meal time. Before the monks begin to take up their bowls of rice, they pick out about seven grains of it called *saba* and offer them to those non-human beings. The idea is perhaps partly thanksgiving and partly sharing good things with others.

Do those departed ones really come and hover about us?

When Tao-wu (道吾) had a feast prepared in commemoration of his late master Yüeh-shan (藥山), a monk asked: "Why do you have this feast for your late master? Does he really come to take it?" Said Tao-wu, "How is it that you monks have the feast prepared?"

When Tan-yüan (耽源) set up a feast for Chu the National Teacher (忠國師) on his death-day, a monk asked, "Will the Teacher come, or not?"

Yüan said, "I have not yet attained the art of mind-reading."

"What is then the use of setting up the feast?"

"I don't wish to discontinue the doings of the world."

When a similar question asked of Jên of Pai-shui (白水仁), he said, "Have another offering ready." Did the master take the questioner for one of the hungry ghosts?

These statements by the masters do not seem to be very illuminating from our worldly relative point of view. Let us see what they say at the time of their departure about their own destination. Or, when we observe the manner in

which they take leave of their earthly existence, it is perhaps possible for us to gain something of an insight into the whereabouts of the departed.

On the twenty-fifth of December, P'u, of Ho-shan, (禾山普), said to his attendants: "When a master dies it is customary for his Zendo followers to put up a special meal for him; but in my opinion this is altogether unnecessary. When I am to die, let me have your offerings before and not after my departure." The monks thought he did not quit his joking even in his old days. They asked, "When will you pass away?" "I pass away when you all have had your offerings made to me."

A curtain was set up in his bed-room, behind which he sat; all the ceremonial vessels were placed before him, the eulogies were read, and food was offered him in due reverence. P'u the master had a good appetite and consumed all the food offerings, showing no symptoms of an early departure. The ceremony continued for some days until everybody in the monastery, including his immediate disciples down to all the coolies, duly paid his respect to the master who was thus treated as one really passed away. On New Year's day all the ceremony in connection with a death came to an end. The master said to the monks, "The time is come; tomorrow when it ceases to snow I will go." On the following day the weather was fair, but it began to snow, and when this stopped he passed away, quietly sitting and with incense burning.

When Hsiu, of Cho-chou, (琢州秀), was about to die, he had a bath, and afterwards ordered to have a cup of tea brought to him. When he finished the tea, the attendant proceeded to carry the tea-tray away; but the master withdrew the tray and said; "Do you know where I am bound for?" "No, master, I do not know." Whereupon the master handed the tray over to the attendant-monk, saying, "Go on, you do not know where I am bound for." When

the monk came back after putting away his tray, he saw the master already passed out.

When Jên, of Su-shan, (疎山仁), was asked where he was bound for after his death, he said, "Lying on his back in the heather, his four limbs point to the sky."

Mo, of Wu-hsieh, (五洩默), before his death, had a bath and incense burned. Quietly sitting in his seat, he said to the monks: "The Dharmakāya remains forever perfectly serene, and yet shows that there are comings and goings; all the sages of the past come from the same source, and all the souls of the world return to the One. My being like a foam is now broken up; you have no reason to grieve over the fact. Do not needlessly put your nerves to task, but keep up your quiet thought. If you observe this injunction of mine, you are requiting me for all that I did for you; but if you go against my words, you are not to be known as my disciples." A monk came out and asked, "Where would you depart?" "No-where." "Why cannot I see this 'no-where'?" "It is beyond your senses." This said, the master peacefully passed out.

The Zen master's end was not always so peaceful; sometimes there were some who struggled hard to drop this "begging bag" (鉢囊子). When Chên, of Ts'ui-yên (翠巖眞), was at the point of death, he suffered terribly, rolling on the straw matting which was spread over the ground. Chê (喆) the attendant was in tears as a witness of this agonising scene and said to the master, "While yet strong, you made all kinds of defamatory remarks on the Buddha, on the Fathers; and what do we see now?" The master gazed for a while at the attendant and scolded, "You too make this remark?" He now got up, and assumed a cross-legged posture, and, ordering the attendant to burn incense, quietly gave up the ghost.[1]

[1] For another example like this, see my *Zen Essays*, III, p. 35.

The Revolving of the Prajñāpāramitā Sutra  *Plate 22*

The Feeding of the Hungry Ghosts  *Plate 23*

# VI.  LIFE OF MEDITATION

# VI. LIFE OF MEDITATION

## 1

Now we come to the central facts of the Zendo life, which constitute the characteristic training given to the Zen monk. The term meditation does not quite express the idea prevailing here, and what it really means when it is used in connection with the life of the Zen monk will become intelligible as we go on with its description below. Before going further, let me acquaint you with the construction of the Zendo.

The Meditation Hall (*zendo* in Japanese and *ch'an-t'ang* in Chinese), as it is built in Japan, is generally a rectangular building of variable size according to the number of monks to be accommodated. As this number however does not as a rule exceed one hundred, the size of the Zendo is to that extent limited. The one at Engakuji, Kamakura, which was reconstructed after the earthquake of 1923, measures about 36 feet by 65 feet, which can contain fifty or more monks.

It has two entrances. The front one is shown in the Plate 24 and the rear one in the Plate 25. The tablet at the top of the entrance (Pl. 24) reads *Shō-bō-gen Dō* meaning "The Hall of the Eye of the Right Dharma," because the hall is intended for opening the Dharma-eye of the occupants who with it can see into the secrets of life and the world. The square board of wood which the monk is about to strike is used for various purposes: to call the monks to meals, lectures, services, etc., or to tell them that the meditation hour has begun or ended. The characters on the board read:

> "Birth and death is a grave event;
> How transient is life!
> Every minute is to be grudged,
> Time waits for nobody."

The shrine behind the half-opened door contains generally the image of Mañjuśrī, who represents Wisdom (*prajñā*). The opening of the Dharma-eye means acquiring this Prajñā, and the Bodhisattva is the fit object of worship in the Meditation Hall.

The rear entrance (Pl. 25) is used by the monks for their private purposes such as washing, going on errands, etc. Observe those foot-gears in perfect order. They are of the simplest kind, but very well taken care of; and when the monks leave them at the door to enter into the Hall, they see to it that the *getas* are not scattered about in confusion. The wooden tablet over the entrance contains the regulations of the Hall, a translation of which is given below.

The interior of the Hall is furnished with raised platforms called *tan* which runs along the longer sides of the Hall. The *tan* is about eight feet wide and about three feet high. At one end of the empty floor oblong in shape, which occupies the centre of the building between the *tan*, there stands the shrine for Mañjuśrī the Bodhisattva, which opens towards the front entrance. This centre-floor is used for an exercise called *kinhin* (*ching-hsing* in Chinese), which consists in circulating in Indian file along the *tan*. (Plate 26.) This is practised at definite intervals during the meditation hours. This walking helps to keep the monks' minds from falling into a state of torpidity.

The *tan* has a *tatami* floor, and a space of one *tatami*, about three by six feet, is allowed to each monk. This little space is for each monk his "heaven and earth," for here he sleeps, sits, meditates, and does all other things permitted in the Hall. Whatever little belongings he has are kept at the window-end of the *tan*, where a low closet-like arrangement is provided along the whole length of the *tan*. The bedding is put away on the spacious shelf constructed overhead and concealed with a curtain (Plate 27).

When the hour to sleep comes which is ordinarily about 9 p.m., the monks recite *The Shingyō* (*Prajñāpāramitā-*

*hridaya-sūtra*) and bow three times to Mañjuśrī. They lie down in one row (Plate 28). The *jikijitsu* (*chih-jih* in Chinese), who directs every movement of the monks in the Hall—the most important office in the Zendo, seeing them all quiet under the *futon*, offers his last incense to the Bodhisattva and puts away his *keisaku* ("staff of admonition," 警策 *ching-ts'e* in Chinese). (Plate 28.) When this is all done, he himself goes under a scanty *futon*. The one who sits on the opposite *tan* is called *tantō*, meaning the "head of the *tan*." His office is nowadays more or less honorary.

The bedding given to each monk is one broad *futon* or quilt wadded with cotton-wool, which is about six feet square in size. He wraps himself in this only, even in the midst of the cold winter, and sleeps from 9 p.m. till about 3.30 in the morning. For the pillow he uses a pair of small cushions, each about two feet square, on which during the daytime he sits and keeps up his meditation. As soon as he wakes, the bedding is put up to the common shelf overhead (Plate 27). He then goes out from the rear door to what may be called a general wash-stand. The stand holds one big basin filled with fresh water and supplied with a number of small bamboo dippers. The dipper does not hold much water. This is purposive, for, according to Zen philosophy, as was stated before, it is an act of impiety to use the gifts of nature too lavishly or more than is actually needed. (Plate 29.)

When Hsüeh-fêng (Seppo), Yen-t'ou (Gantō) and Chin-shan (Kinzan) were travelling together on their Zen pilgrimage they lost their way in the mountains. It was growing dark and there was no monastery to ask for the night's lodging. At the time they happened to notice a green vegetable leaf flowing down along the stream. By this they naturally inferred that there was somebody living further up in the mountains. But one of the monk-pilgrims argued; "That is quite probable, but a man who does not

mind letting go the precious vegetable leaf is not worth our consideration.'' Before he finished saying this, they saw a man with a long-handed hook, running down after the lost leaf. This may be an extreme case, but the legend beautifully illustrates what profound respect Zen feels towards the gifts of nature as well as the offerings of its pious devotees.

Humility, self-discipline, aspiration for the higher objects of life, etc. are at the bottom of the philosophy of asceticism. Asceticism is not always negativistic, nor does it issue from an unhealthy state of mind or from a perverted view of life generally. There is something positive, manly, and self-asserting behind the mask of a dry abnegation. To regard Zen as a form of asceticism and nothing more will be a grievous mistake. What Zen aims at is to reduce the claims of the body to a minimum in order to divert their course to a higher realm of activities. To torture the body is not its object, nor is it its object to gain merit and thereby to lay one's fortune in heaven. When a man sees higher values which he desires to realise in his own life not only for himself but for all his fellow-beings, he is always required to rise above the considerations of his merely physical welfare. The physical welfare of course is not to be altogether ignored so long as it is the vehicle for things higher than itself; but when it is given too much consideration it is bound to overstep the sphere properly belonging to it. This is one of the weaknesses inherent to human nature. Especially, when Zen sometimes appears to teach the gospel of antinomianism or latitudinarianism, it is well for Zen to emphasise the practice of self-discipline in the life of the Meditation Hall. Even in trying to become an expert athlete, daily training involving a great deal of self-denial and asceticism is absolutely needed. If he indulges in any of his natural weaknesses, he is barred from entering into the arena. With those who aspire to denote themselves to the attainment and realisation of things of the highest value

in life, how can they think of shrinking before a certain measure of discipline?

How much sleep is needed for a man to keep himself healthy, strong, and always capable for work is a great problem; it cannot be decided without considering various incidental circumstances besides his own hereditary constitution. But sleep seems to be something that permits much latitude, and discipline or habit can do much to reduce it to its lowest terms. Perhaps this is one of the reasons why the Buddha and many other great spiritual leaders severely denounce those indulgent in sleep. But from another point of view, sleep is indicative of peace and contentment; those who are always wakeful and look about with an unsteady gaze, or those who are startled at every little incident or mishap of life, and unable to fall asleep being so miserably nerve-racked, are those whose spirits are somehow maladjusted to the general scheme of the universe. In these modern times when environment by artificial means changes so rapidly, the very author of these changes finds it extremely difficult to adapt himself to them, and the result is the manifest growth of all kinds of neurotics. Is it not indeed refreshing then to find such examples as follows in the history of Zen?

Yen-t'ou Ch'üan-kuo (嚴頭豁, Ganto Kwatsu), a great Zen master of late T'ang, seeing Su-shan (Sōzan) approach, fell soundly asleep. Shan came up to the master and stood by him, who, however, paid him no attention whatever. Shan gave one stroke to his chair. The master turned his head about and said, "What do you want?" Shan replied, "O master, have a good sleep!" So saying, he went off. The master laughed heartily: "I have for these thirty years fooled with so many horses, and today I find myself kicked down by an ass!"

While Tou-tzŭ I-ch'ing (投子義青) was in the monastery presided over by Yüan-t'ung Hsiu (圓通秀), he never came up before the master to make inquiries about Zen, but

went on all the time dozing. The chief director appealed to the master, saying: "There is a monk in our Zendo who passes his time sleeping and doing nothing. He ought to be dealt with in accordance with the Regulations."

Hsiu: "Who is that?"

Director: "Brother I-ch'ing (義青)."

Hsiu: "Don't be hasty. Wait till I try him."

The master now took up his staff and went into the Hall. Seeing the said monk dozing, he struck the floor with his staff and scolded him, saying: "You cannot go on like this while consuming our rice."

Ch'ing: "What do you want me to do then, O master?"

Hsiu: "Why do you not study Zen?"

Ch'ing: "When a man's stomach is already filled up, to what fine meal are you going to treat me?"

Hsiu: "Unfortunately, there is one who does not fully endorse you."

Ch'ing: "What is the use of waiting for such endorsement?"

Hsiu: "Whom did you see before coming here?"

Ch'ing: "Fu-shan."

Hsiu: "I was wondering how you came to be so stubbornly self-assuring."

So saying, the master took the hand of the sleepy monk, and smilingly left the Hall.

To reach this stage of understanding, however, is no easy task and will require an enormous amount of energy. Hence the following admonition by T'ui-yin (退隱) in his *Mirror for Zen Students* (禪家龜鑑): "Unless you reflect within and strive hard to realise the truth of it, the mere learning of so many sutras will be of no real avail to your spiritual welfare. It is like the birds chirruping in the springtime and the insects singing in the autumn nights— they all have no meaning beyond mere making noise. The sutra-reading ought not to be like this. When your study

is not yet in complete tune with the truth, it may add to your reputation as a learned scholar or an eloquent speaker. However much you may excel in this, it is like painting your dirt-carrier in vermillion.

"The Buddhist monks ought not to be induced to study worldly or mere scholarly literature. It is like cutting a lump of clay with a sword: the clay itself does not gain anything in the way of its usefulness, while the sword is damaged beyond repairs. It is not a small matter—this abandoning the householder's life and becoming a monk. It is not to enjoy an easy comfortable life, it is not to gain worldly glory or to amass wealth; it is for the sake of becoming free from the bondage of birth and death, it is to subjugate the tyranny of the passions; it is to continue the Prajñā-life of the Buddha; it is to deliver all beings from their transmigration in the triple world.

"The fire of transiency burns everything in the world, and the robbers of the passions are stealthily looking for every chance to take hold of your inner treasure. Those monks who are ever after wealth and reputation are worse off than the simple-minded peasants on the farm. Says the Buddha: 'Those who wearing my dress disparage the Tathagata and amass all kinds of evil karma—they are my enemies.'

"O monks, you are all sons of the Buddha; every thread of the dress you wear comes from the loom of the hard-working weaver, and every grain of rice you consume is indicative of the sweat of the farmer's brow. If your Prajñā-eye is not yet opened, what claim can you ever have on those precious gifts from your fellow-beings? Do you wish to know what animals they are who are covered with fur and carry a pair of horns on their heads? They are no other than those monks who accept shamelessly all the pious offerings from their devotees. Monks are not to eat while not hungry, they are not to wear anything more than they actually need. Instead of accepting from their pious-mind-

ed devotees fine raiment, a bowl of rice, or a hut, let monks wear a dress of red-hot steel, make a meal of molten metal, and live in a blazing kiln, if their hearts have not yet burned with the desire to save themselves as well as all beings from the despotism of birth-and-death, and if they are not straining all their spiritual energy towards the attainment of this end.

"Monks ought to behave like a grinding stone: Chang-san comes to sharpen his knife, Li-szŭ comes to grind his axe, everybody and anybody who wants to have his metal improved in anyway comes and makes use of the stone. Each time the stone is rubbed, it wears out, but it makes no complaint, nor does it boast of its usefulness. And those who come to it go home fully benefitted; some of them may not be quite appreciative of the stone; but the stone itself remains ever contented......"

This may be called non-resistance, or non-injury (*ahimsa*), but in Zen Buddhism it is known as cultivating "secret virtue," or practising "deeds of effortlessness" (*anābhogacaryā*).

2

What properly constitutes the study of Zen in the Zendo life is to study on the one hand the writings or sayings or in some cases the doings of the ancient masters and on the other to practise meditation. This practising is called in Japanese to do *zazen*, while the studying of the masters consists in attending the discourses given by the teacher of the Zendo known as *rōshi*. *Rōshi* means literally "an old teacher," but in this case "old" means "venerable," and has no reference to the age of the master. The discoursing is technically called *teishō* or *kōza*. To give a *teishō* or *kōza* does not mean "lecturing on the textbook," it means to manifest the inner meaning of it. The master (*rōshi*) does not explain anything, for he refuses to appeal to the intellect of his audience in his discourse; what he tries to do is rather

to re-awaken in the minds of his monks the psychology of the ancient master that directed the course of the Zen interview in question. This being the case, the monks whose Prajñā-eye still remains closed will not be any wiser after attending so many discourses given by the Rōshi.

The *teishō* is a solemn affair. When the hour approaches, the monk on duty strikes the board hung at the front entrance to the Zendo (Pl. 24). The occupants make themselves ready by putting on a special cloth called *kesa* (*kashāya* in Sanskrit). When the drum or the bell is heard at the lecture hall, the monks filing themselves in due order leave the Zendo and walk in a most dignified manner to the room where the *teishō* takes place (Plate 30). When they finish sitting, the Rōshi comes out of his own quarters, accompanied by two attendant-monks (*jisha*).

As soon as he comes in, he walks towards the inner shrine where the Buddha is. A stick of incense is offered to him, to the founder of the monastery, to the succeeding abbots, and to the master of the Rōshi himself if he happens to be already dead. Each time an incense-offering is made, the Rōshi bows and prostrates himself three times on the floor. While this goes on, the monks recite three times a short Dhāraṇī-sutra dedicated to Kwannon Bosatsu (Avalokiteśvara), and then once the spiritual admonition left by the founder of the monastery or by one of the great ancient masters, or the "Song of Meditation" (*Zazen Wasan*) by Hakuin. The recitation is punctuated by the *mokugyo*,[1] which is a large spherical wooden implement with the inside hollowed out and a fish pattern carved on the outside. It is struck with a short stick, one end of which is wrapped with a stuffed piece of leather. The sound helps to make the minds of the audience receptive for the ensuing discourse.

Now the Rōshi mounts the high chair facing the Buddha-shrine; one of the attendants sets a reading table before

[1] The illustrations of the various sound instruments used in the Zen monastery are given below.

him, and the other a cup of tea. (Plate 31 ` If the text-book is *Lin-chi Lu* ("Sayings of Rinzai" 臨済錄), the Rōshi will begin like this:

"Wō Jōji, Governor of this district, together with his officers asked the master (Rinzai) to take his seat. The Master mounted the platform and said: It was inevitable for me today not to accept the kindness of the Governor and others; I could not but yield to humanly feelings and find myself now in this pulpit. If I were to expound the great experience in accordance with the tradition of our ancient Fathers, there would absolutely be no need for opening my mouth at all; for here is no room for anybody to put in his feet. But, to respect the persistent request of the Governor, I will not today hide anything from you in my treatment of the truth of Zen. Are there some in this congregation, who, like great generals, dispose the army in battle array and hoist their banners for the good fight? I will testify to them before the congregation.

"A monk asked: 'What is the ultimate truth of Bud-dhism?'

"The Master gave a '*Kwatz*!'

"The monk bowed.

"The Master said [sarcastically?]: 'The venerable brother can hold his point in controversy.'

"The monk asked: 'Whose tune do you play? and to what school do you belong?'

"The Master said: 'When I was at Huang-po, I asked him a question three times and was struck by him three times.'

"The monk hesitated.

"Thereupon, the Master gave a '*Kwatz*!' which was immediately followed by a blow and this: 'Impossible it is to fix nails onto vacuity of space.'

"A monk scholar came forward and asked: 'The Triple Vehicle and the Twelve Divisions—do they not all elucidate the Buddha-nature?'

"The Master said: 'The rampantly-growing weeds have never yet been mown down.'

"The scholar said: 'The Buddha cannot be a trickster.'

"The Master pursued: 'Where is the Buddha?'

"The scholar remained silent.

"The Master said: 'There is no use of trying to confound me before the Governor. Be expeditious enough to give up your seat, for others may be following.'

"The Master then continued: 'We are gathered here today for the sake of the one great event. Anyone wishing to ask me questions, come forward, don't delay. But the moment you try to say something, you slip off the board. Why is this so? Do you not know the Buddha say that the Dharma is beyond words, because it is not to be sought where causation rules? It is all due to your not having enough faith that I have appeared here today to make the matter worse confounded than ever. I am afraid that I have done enough to hinder the Governor together with his officers from having a clear insight into the Buddha-nature. It is best for me now to retire.'

"The Master now gave a '*Kwatz*!' and said: 'O you, people of little faith! There is no end of work for you. ......I have kept you standing too long. Farewell.' "

In case of the text-book being the *Hekigan Roku* (碧巖 錄), the Rōshi's discourse will be something like this:[1]

"*Preliminary Comment*—When smoke is seen on the other side of the hill, one knows at once that there is a fire burning. When a pair of horns is noticed on the other side of the fence, one knows that a cow is grazing there. It is an everyday affair for a monk with any amount of intelligence to take in the whole situation even when he is allowed to have a glimpse only of its one corner. When all the streams

---

[1] The following is the Case I of the *Hekigan*, omitting all the commentary insertions by Yengo and also his general remarks on the Case I as well as on Seccho's verse.

are cut off, i.e., when the state of absolute Emptiness is realised, a man is capable of moving in every possible direction, beyond all the conceptual limitations imposed upon us by reason of our imagination and discrimination.[1] Whose behaviour can this be if such is ever attainable? Let us see what Hsüeh-tou (Seccho, 雪竇) gives us as an instance of such a master.

"*The Case*—The Emperor Wu, of the Liang Dynasty, asked Bodhidharma the Great Teacher: 'What is the first principle of the Sacred Doctrine?'

"Bodhidharma answered: 'In Vast Emptiness there is nothing to be designated "Sacred".'

"The Emperor asked again: 'Who is he then who now confronts me?'

"Bodhidharma said: 'I know not.'

"The Emperor failed to grasp the meaning, and finally Bodhidharma crossed the River and went off to the Kingdom of Wei. Later, the Emperor asked Chih-kung (Shiko 誌公) about this interview with Bodhidharma. Said Chih-kung: "Do you know this man?' The Emperor confessed his ignorance, saying: 'I really do not know him.'

"Chih-kung said: 'He is a Kwannon Bosatsu attempting to transmit the seal of the Buddha-mind.'

"The Emperor was grieved and tried to hasten an envoy after Bodhidharma. But Chih-kung said: 'It is of no use for your Majesty to try to send for him. Even when all the people in this land run after him, he will never turn back.'

"*The poetical comment*—
   "The sacred truth is Vast Emptiness itself,
   And where can one point out its marks?
   'Who is he who confronts me?'
   'I know not'—his answer this.

---

[1] Literally: one may rise in the east and sink in the west; one may walk against or in accord with; one may go straight ahead or crosswise; whether to give up or to take away from, one is in perfect freedom.

Thereby in the dark he crossed the River;
But what thorny brambles that have grown after
    him!
Pursued even by the entire populace of the land,
    there is no turning back for him.
For all the time to come we vainly think of him;
No, let us no more think of him;
A refreshing breeze sweeps all over the earth to
    its remotest ends.

"Seccho now turned his head, and, looking around him, said: 'Is there a patriarch among us here?' The answer came from himself: 'Yes, here he is. If so, let him come over here, for I want him to wash my feet.'"

When the *kōza* is over which lasts about an hour, the entire audience recites the "Four Great Vows," and the monks go back in the same orderly manner as before to their own quarters. The Vows are:

"However innumerable sentient beings are,
    I vow to save them;
However inexhaustible the passions are,
    I vow to extinguish them;
However immeasurable the Dharmas are,
    I vow to study them;
However incomparable the Buddha-truth is,
    I vow to attain it."

### 3

The object of *zazen* or meditation in the life of the Zen monk is to open the Prajñā-eye. As we read in the *Prajñā-pāramitā Sūtra,* without the Prajñā all the other virtues are incapable of accomplishing anything, for they lack 'the eye which sees into the meaning of things generally. The monk, therefore, must by all means have the scale cleared off by means of his koan, which is a kind of question given him for solution. When one koan is successfully solved, another is given until the master is thoroughly satisfied with the

understanding of his monk. There is a large number of such questions available for the purpose. But in fact when one koan is grasped in a most penetrating fashion, all the remaining ones present no substantial hindrances to the final Zen realisation. The koan exercise is the most important feature in the Zendo life.

A special posture is recommended, though the koan exercise can be carried on in whatever work one may be engaged and in whatever bodily position one may assume; for Zen has nothing to do with the form the body may take, sitting or lying, walking or standing still. But for practical reasons the following posture is considered conducive to the acquirement of the mental attitude which is favourable to the Zen experience (Plate 32) :

When a man wishes to practise meditation, let him retire into a quiet room where he prepares a thickly wadded cushion for his seat, with his dress and belt loosely adjusted about his body. He then assumes his proper formal posture. That is to say, he sits with his legs fully crossed by placing the right foot over the left thigh and the left foot over the right thigh. Sometimes the half-cross-legged posture is permitted, in which case simply let the left leg rest over the right thigh. Next, he places the right hand over the left leg with its palm up and over this rests the left hand, while the thumbs press against each other over the palm. He now raises the whole body slowly and quietly, moves it repeatedly to the left and to the right, backward and forward, until the proper seat and straight posture is assured. He will take care not to lean too much to one side, either left or right, forward or backward; his spinal column stands erect with his head, shoulders, back, and loins each properly supporting the others like a *chaitya*. But he is advised to be cautious not to sit too upright or rigidly, for he will then begin to feel uneasy before long. The main point for the sitter is to have his ears and shoulders, nose and navel stand to each other in one vertical plane, while his tongue rests

against his upper palate and his lips and teeth are firmly closed. Let his eyes be slightly opened in order to avoid falling asleep. When meditation advances the wisdom of this practice will grow apparent. Great masters of meditation from of old have their eyes kept open. When the position is steadied and the breathing regular .the sitter may now assume a somewhat relaxed attitude. Let him not be concerned with ideas good or bad. Let him concentrate himself on the koan, which is to think the unthinkable by going beyond the realm of thought. When the exercise is kept up persistently for a sufficient space of time, disturbing thoughts will naturally cease to assert themselves and there will prevail a state of oneness, which is however not to be understood conceptually.

In the Zendo all the monks sit facing one another along the *tan*. The practice of the Sōtō School, however, is just the opposite: instead of facing one another the monks of one *tan* sit with their backs turned against those of the opposite *tan*. When they are not actually engaged in outdoor work, or when they are permitted to look after their personal affairs, they are invariably found sitting in meditation in their Zendo.

There is a special period generally once a month during the "stay-at-home" season, which is May-August and November-February. The period called "Great Sesshin" lasts one week. *Sesshin* means "to collect thoughts," and during this period the monks are exempt from work and practise *zazen* from early morning (3.30 a.m.) till evening (9.30 or 10 p.m.), except when they eat and when they attend the *kōza* which now takes place once every day.

Without doing what is known as *sanzen*, *zazen* does not bear fruit. [*Sanzen* means the monk's seeing the master and presenting his views on the koan.] Ordinarily, this takes place as a rule twice a day, but during the great *sesshin* the monks have to see the master at least four times a day. But if they have no special views to present for

the master's examination it is not necessary for them to do
*sanzen*. This kind of *sanzen* is called *dokusan*, individual
or voluntary *sanzen*. At the *sōsan*, however, no monks are
allowed to stay away from seeing the master. (Plate 33.)
*Sōsan* means "general *sanzen*." This is enforced three times
while the *sesshin* is going on.

When the bell rings at the master's quarters, those
monks who have prepared an answer, go out each singly
by the front door. The Zen interview with the master takes
place in his own room. Before a monk invades the latter,
he strikes the bell and announces his coming. (Plate 33.)
He may meet the one who preceded him and is now on his
way back. He bows at the entrance to the room where the
master sits quietly like a crouching lion and awaits the
monk. Once in this room and all the preliminary bowings
over, the monk is ready to behave himself in the way best
expressive of his view. No conventionalism will restrain
his giving the master a slap or a kick. On his part the
master may strike the prejudiced monk and most violently
chase him out of the room. The confusion thus ensuing
may be heard even in the waiting room where the monks
congregate, each biding the time for his turn. (Plate 34.)

In the meantime another kind of confusion may be
proceeding in the Zendo. On the occasion of *sōsan*, or when
the senior monks deem the time maturing, they will urge
those brother-monks to go to *sanzen*, who stay away too frequently from it. It is one of the most trying experiences
in the life of a young monk to be thus urged by his seniors.
He is not deliberately shunning the interview with the
master; he really wants to see him and get his koan satis-
factorily disposed of; he has almost exhausted all his energy
in the endeavour to come to this happy conclusion. But
he has now nothing to say; he knows no way to get out of
the *impasse*; he stands at the end of a pole—no way to go
ahead, and no way to beat a retreat; he feels, again, as if
walking deeply enveloped in a dense fog. In the psychology

of Zen this is the critical moment, and unless something desperate is not decided upon by the perplexed monk, there will be no further opening for him. To help him in this, his seniors will use physical force to pull him down from the *tan*, or to tear him away from the post or the door to which he clings with might and main. A scene of regular wrestling matches will be enacted in the midst of the quiet solemn atmosphere of the meditation hall. (Plate 35.)

That, in the breaking-through of the psychological crisis which is experienced in the study of Zen, an emotional excitement of the highest order is frequently needed, is quite evident. Zen is full of such instances, and the masters are never weary of advising their followers to exert their psychic energies to the utmost.

Suiwo was one of the great disciples of Hakuin. He had a monk from Ryūkū who wished to solve the koan of "One Hand." He stayed with the master for three years, but no enlightenment came over him. He was greatly disturbed because he could not possibly stay with his master beyond the period of three years. His disappointment knew no bounds. He could not think of going back with no new spiritual outlook to his native island which lies over beyond the south-western end of Japan. Suiwo comforted him saying, "Don't be grieved, but go back to your seat and devote the coming week exclusively to the mastery of the koan." When the week was over, the monk appeared before Suiwo with nothing to show to him. Said the master, "Never mind; but go on with your *zazen* for another week, and you will surely have an insight this time." The monk faithfully followed the advice. But at the end of the week he was the same old monk with no experience whatever. The master was not, however, discouraged, for he told him again to try for another week reciting examples of some ancient masters. The monk went back to his quarters with a renewed courage. The third week passed, but no result. He was then the most miserable man in the world. Utterly dejected in spirit

and body, he came to the master for some means to help him out of the inextricable difficulties which were glaring at him. The master was apparently not yet at the end of his resources; he told the monk to try a *sesshin* of five days this time instead of seven.

The five days went on like the preceding seven days, and the monk was naturally almost at his last grasp. Beyond this, there was nothing left for him but to yield his breath, either out of despair or out of despondency. The master now said to him: "If you cannot come to any result after so many weeks of meditation, limit your time now to three days, apply yourself most intensely with all the psychic power there is in you to the solution of the koan, and if you still fail death is the only way now left to you." The monk made up his mind as was told by the master. On the third day sure enough a light dawned on him and he finally penetrated into the meaning of the "One Hand." Perhaps the master was a happy man no less than the monk himself.

The Christian theologians may have their own doctrine to explain this kind of experience and also their own way of bringing it about. But psychologically the process is well known, and the Zen masters out of their own experience give advices purporting to create what may be called the Zen state of consciousness. The master Pan-jo (Hannya, 般若) has this for his monks: "When your mind is steadily and intensely and without interruptions on the koan, you will begin to be unconscious of your bodily existence, while the koan occupies the centre of your consciousness. At this stage, however, you have to be careful not to give up yourself to unconsciousness, for you are sometimes apt to go astray as in a dream and induce a state of insanity. Do never let your hold go off the koan, let the latter be present all the time in your consciousness. The time will come when together with the koan everything vanishes out of your mind including the mind itself. At this very instant, as when a

bean pops out of the cold ashes, you realise that while Chang is drinking Li becomes tipsy.''

Ku-mei Yu's (Kyōzan Kobai Yu 仰山古梅友) advice is: ''What is needed in the beginning of your exercise is to stir up your spunky spirits and be most resolutely determined to go on with your task. Summarily making a bundle of all you have hitherto understood or learned, together with your Buddhist knowledge, your literary accomplishments, and your clever manipulation of words, sweep it off once for all into the great ocean; and never think of it again. Gathering up eighty-four thousand thoughts into a seat, which enter into every hidden corner of your consciousness, squat on it, and strive to keep your koan all the time before your mind. Once lifted up before the mind, never let it slip off; try to see with all the persistence you find in yourself into the meaning of the koan given to you, and never once waver in your determination to get into the very bottom of the matter. Keep this up until a state of *satori* breaks upon your consciousness. Do not make a guess-work of your koan; do not search for its meaning in the literature you have learned; go straight at it without leaning on any kind of intermediary help; for it is in this way only that you can make for your own home......''

According to P'u-yen Tuan-an (Fugan Dangan, 普巖斷岸), the following is the method to reach one's own final abode: ''All things are reducible to the One, and where is this One reducible? Keep this koan in your mind and never allow yourself to think that quietude or a state of unconsciousness is the *sine qua non* in your koan exercise. When you feel confused in your mind so that your power of attention refuses to work its own way, do not try to gather it up again by means of a thought, but mustering your spirits keep up your koan by all means before you. Courage and determination are most in need of at this juncture.

''But if you still feel dull and confused and unable to bring the thought to a focus, get down from the *tan* and

walk for a while somewhat briskly. After a while you will find yourself much refreshed; you will then come back on your cushion and continue your exercise. Suddenly there prevails a state of consciousness in which your koan rises on its own accord before the mind, asking for its own solution and refusing to vanish away from the centre of your attention. You do not then know whether you are walking or sitting, your 'spirit of inquiry' alone occupies the whole field. This is called the stage of passionlessness or egolessness, but this is not yet an ultimate state; another strong whipping is needed, and you must double the effort to see where after all the One is to be reduced.

"At this stage you do not feel any definite advance made in the 'lifting-up' of the koan. 'The spirit of inquiry' so intensely working out its own way, there is no conscious effort on your part to continue the koan exercise. After a while even this is swept away, and you attain a state of unconsciousness in which there is neither the koan nor the one who holds it. This is what is known as the stage of objectlessness. Is it a final one? No, by no means. Says an ancient master: 'Don't think the state of unconsciousness is the truth itself, for there is still another frontier-gate which is now to be broken through.'

"While you are in this state of mind, you happen to hear a sound or to see an object, and the whole thing comes to a sudden end; you have at last touched the ultimate reality. Nothing is left to you at this moment but to burst out into a loud laugh. You have accomplished a final turning and in very truth know that 'when the Kuai-chou cow grazes the herbage, the I-chou horse finds its stomach filled.'

From all these advices which are at the same time records of the experience lived through by the Zen masters, we can see what the koan exercise means and where the Zendo life leads us. The monks are not idling away their precious time in the monastery. They are trained here in a peculiar way to develop their moral and spiritual energies

and also to see into the mysteries of their being. When all this is appraised in the proper light, we can appreciate the real significance of the Zendo life, which goes on in a.way so contrary to modern trends of thought and actual living.

4

While a great *sesshin* is going on, there is a general tension of nerves all around. Though the wisdom of such an institution is sometimes problematical there is no doubt about its doing immense good to those who have first entered upon the Zendo life. The development of the koan exercise is inevitably followed by the institution of the *sesshin*. However this may be, the nervous strain periodically experienced is a good practical discipline for all young men whether they are Zen followers or not.

That the so-called meditation practised in connection with the koan exercise is not the same mental training as is generally understood in the West, will now be plain to all who have studied the preceding pages. That is to say, to practise *zazen* is not the same as practising meditation. As so much psychic energy is concentrated on the "lifting-up" of the koan, the physical side of our existence also undergoes great pressure; and the result is that the muscles become cramped and the nerves too taut. To relieve the monk of this kind of discomfort, his shoulders are frequently slapped with a stick called *keisaku*, which means "staff of admonition." The staff is also used to prevent a monk from falling asleep while sitting in meditation. While the *zazen* hours are on, a monk with the *keisaku* stands at the end of either *tan*, keeping a close watch on his brother-monks. (Plate 36.)

The monks who are desperate with their koans often quietly slip out of the Zendo and pass the night outdoors, sometimes on a flat rock which is found near the Zendo, or sometimes on the porch of a building, or in the cave which was probably once the favourite retreat of the founder of the monastery. (Plate 37.)

In the Zendo no books are allowed except when they are absolutely needed, for instance, when the monks have to look up a passage expressive of their understanding of a koan. This is required of them by the master when they successfully solve a koan. A book called *Kuzōshi* or *Zenrin Kushū* (禪林句集) contains various kinds of passages relating to Zen. It is one of the vade-mecums to be carried along by all Zen students—monks and lay-disciples. This practice of regularly looking up the passages culled from ancient literature helps the monks very much to become acquainted with the literary and cultural phase of the Zen life. In olden days, it was a part of the liberal education for the monks, who were taught to despise book-learning and who thus came to be too one-sided and prejudicial of the ancient lore bequeathed by their predecessors. When they have to wade through the *Kuzōshi* or some other books, they go out of the Zendo and turn their pages hurriedly under the dark light near the lavatory. (Plate 38.) In any event even to-day the Zen monks are unreasonably disposed against books and the culture based on their study. This is surely the outcome of their Zendo training.

Zen may sometimes go too far in its discouragement of the study of Buddhist literature or in its depreciation of scholarly attainment, but this discouragement or depreciation has been the traditional policy of its masters. There is no doubt that the policy, in spite of its sometimes untoward consequence, has imparted a refreshing atmosphere to the conventionalised Buddhist life.

A keeper of the Tripitaka once noticed a monk sitting quietly for some time in his library building. Asked the librarian: "Why don't you read the sutras?" "I don't know letters," was the monk's reply. "If so, why don't you ask people to teach you?" So advised, the monk stood up respectfully holding up his hands before his chest, and said: "Pray tell me what character this is." The librarian failed to enlighten him.

Wang, one of the government officers, visited the monastery under Lin-chi (Rinzai). As they entered the grounds Wang asked, "Do the monks here read the sutras?"

"No, they do not," replied Rinzai.

"Do they then study Zen?"

"No, they do not."

"If they neither read the sutras nor study Zen, what do they do here?"

"They are all going to be made Buddhas and Fathers."

"Even precious particles of gold dust prove to be disastrous when they get into one's eyes. What do you say to that?"

"I thought you were a mere layman," was Rinzai's comment.

A monk came up to Yu of T'ien-kai (天蓋幽), and asked, "I wish to read the sutras, and what would you advise me to do about it?" The master remarked, "Do you think a great merchant would bother himself about making a few cents?"

A monk asked Yeh-hsien (葉縣), "Is it advisable to read the sutras, or not?" Said the master, "There are no byroads, no cross-roads here; the mountains are all the year round fresh and green; east or west, in whichever direction you may have a fine walk." The monk said, "I wish to learn something more definite from you." "It is not the sun's fault if the blind cannot see their way," concluded the master.

P'ang (龐居士), the great layman of Zen, once attended the lecture given by a Buddhist scholar on the *Vajracchedikā*. When the scholar began discoursing on the Prajñā philosophy of "no-ego and no-personality," P'ang queried, "If there is neither ego nor personality, who is lecturing now? and who is the audience?" The scholar made no reply, whereupon P'ang said, "Though I am a mere layman,

I know a thing or two about the ultimate truth of the Buddhist teaching.'' Urged to express himself, he continued:
"No-ego, and again no-personality,
There is neither subject nor object;
I advise you: Cease further lecturing,
And seek the truth without any intermediary;
In the Prajñā itself which is known as Vajra,
There is not a particle of dust defiling it;
From the beginning to the very last,
The whole sutra is no more than words.''

The koan exercises which are the prevailing method at present of mastering Zen involves many years of close application.  Naturally, there are not many graduates of the Zendo life, and this is indeed in the very nature of Zen; for Zen is meant for the *élite*, for specially gifted minds, and not for the masses.  This has been the case since olden days, but especially it is true in this modern age when democracy is the ruling spirit in all the departments of human life.  Standardisation so called goes on everywhere, which means the levelling-down or the averaging-up of inequalities and "class-distinctions.''  Unless aristocracy in one form or another is admitted and to a certain extent encouraged, the artistic impulses are suppressed and no religious geniuses will be forthcoming.  Institutions like the Zendo are becoming anachronistic and obsolete; its tradition is wearing out, and the spirit that has been controlling the discipline of the monks for so many hundred years is no more holding itself against the onslaught of modernism.  Of course, there are still monks and masters in the monasteries all over Japan, and yet how many of them are able effectively to respond to the spiritual needs of modern youth and to adjust themselves to the ever-changing environment created by science and machine?  When the vessels are broken, the contents too will be spilt out.  The truth of Zen must somehow be preserved in the midst of the prosaic flatness and shallow sensationalism of present-day life.

The Zendo life is considered finished not only when the truth of Sūnyatā is intuitively grasped, but when this truth is demonstrated in every phase of practical life with its multitudinous trials, duties, and complications, and also when a great heart of Karuṇā (love) is awakened in the way rain falls on the unjust as well as on the just, or in the way Chao-chou's stone bridge is trodden on by all sorts of beings,—by horses, donkeys, tigers, jackals, tortoises, hares, human beings, etc. This is the greatest accomplishment man can achieve on earth, and every one of us cannot be expected to be capable of this; but there is no harm in our doing the utmost to approach the ideal of Bodhisattvahood, if not in one life, then in lives to come through kotis of kalpas. When something of this ideal is firmly grasped, the monk takes leave of the Zendo (Plate 39) and begins his real life among his fellow-beings, as a member of the great community known as the world. As we observe in the picture, the whole Brotherhood comes out to see such a graduating senior monk off from the monastery gate. The scene is quite different now. When he first applied for admittance into the community, he was regarded almost as *persona non grata,* and all harsh treatment was accorded to him. But he has successfully buffetted the waves, ridden the storm finally to the harbour of safety, and he is ready for his mission among his fellow-beings which he will perform in whatever form he deems most expedient. Such ones are, indeed, to be also most enthusiastically greeted by the outside world.

5

Having been nourished among nature-mystics and born metaphysicians, Zen may seem to be lacking in religious feeling or in the emotional aspect of the religious life. At least as far as its literary expressions go, Zen abounds in allusions to objects of nature and statements indicative of philosophical aloofness.

"The birds fly high in the air, the fish swim and dance in the water."

"The clouds are peacefully floating over the mountains, the stream is hurriedly running below the porch."

"The bamboos are growing thick, the pines are towering high, and how refreshingly green the mountains are!"

"Look at the steaming clouds about to leave the mountain-peaks, and listen to the murmuring stream which flows dancing over the rocks."

"The moon, bright and serene, shines over the peaks after peaks; the wind blows rustling through branches of trees ten thousand years old." (Plate 40.)

If I begin to cite such passages as these, there will be no end to them. Most Zen masters have passed their lives in the mountain monasteries, and it is natural for them to make references to the surrounding views when they are asked about Zen. Besides this fact, nature is to the Oriental mind something most intimate and appealing. She speaks her inmost yearnings directly to our hearts. In the waving of a blade of grass the intelligent eye detects a power transcending the vicissitudes of human life. The moon is not a mere heavenly body—an object of telescopic investigation or spectrum analysis; but in it there shines a light which makes us see into the eternity of things. Is this the imagination of the poet, or no more than the fantasy of a dreaming mind? Even so, there are many souls who perceive in this dream things of a very much higher value than so-called scientific knowledge. I would loathe to see this type of mind wiped away before the on-coming tide of modern rationalism.

In Zen literature there is an expressive term called *kafū* (家風) or *kyōgai* (境涯). *Kafū* literally means "household air," or "house atmosphere;" or "family tradition." *Kyō-gai* is "a sphere," or "a realm," that is, "an area enclosed within boundaries." *Kyōgai* and *kafū* express practically the same idea: *kyōgai* has a more subjective and psycholog-

ical connotation while *kafū* is historical and may be conceived as a kind of atmosphere prevailing in a given community. In the history of Zen, questions frequently concern this "spiritual atmosphere" in which the master is moving, or the general psychological attitude or reaction characterising a Zen master as such. These questions amount to asking about the fundamental teaching of Zen, for when we know where the master's abode is, we know also where Zen finally purports to lead us. In the sutras, such words as *gocara*, *vihara*, or *sthāna* are used to denote the same conception. The following answers given by various masters as culled at random from the annals of Zen will help us to surmise where is the final destination of the Zendo life and of the koan exercise:

"The garden is terribly dry; have the spinach well watered."

"The moon is rising from the ocean and its rays reach far and wide."

"The blue sky and the broad daylight."

"The spring breeze is still blowing cold against my face; I wonder for whom is this brightly shining moonlight."

"Each time it is held up it is a new thing."

"I belong to one of the despised classes, whose forehead is broad."

"I am the standard of all the world."

"A simple meal of rice and soup."

"A silver bag of perfume behind the brocade screen makes the whole avenue odorous as it blows."

"With one bowl and one staff, I make my home wherever I go."

"Harvesting in autumn and garnering in winter."

"One word out of the mouth and even a team of four horses cannot overtake it."

"A rootless plant at the top of the mountain; no wind is blowing, but see how the leaves sway."

"Even a fist angrily lifted would not strike the smiling baby."

"This body from head to toe is not worth five cents."

"The body is lying on the vast expanse of waves; see the man carrying a torch in the broad daylight.

"A dish of gruel in the morning and rice for noon."

"There is in the kitchen no extra meal for a visitor."

"The cock made of mud, the dog made of brick."

"However lovingly cherished flowers soon wither away; however despised and down-trodden weeds never cease to grow."

"The sleeves being too short, the arms are bare."

"Tumbling over again and again."

"The three-legged toad carries an enormous elephant on its back."

The above quotations are enough to show where is the abode of the Zen master, that is, in what "household air" he is living. However enigmatically these passages may appear, their fundamental keynote is what is technically called "deeds of no purpose" or "a life of effortlessness," or in Sanskrit *anābhogacaryā*. All the Mahayana sutras give the greatest significance to the attainment of this "life of no-purposiveness." The lilies of the field are living it, so are all the greatest spiritual leaders of the world. And all the "Great Vows" of the Bodhisattva grow out of it; his vows are no vows in the ordinary sense of the word.

### 6

Among the few incidents in connection with the Zendo life we must not forget mentioning are the tea-ceremony which takes place twice a month on the first and on the fifteenth, a sort of examination which takes place at the end of a term, and the bell the ringing of which is so expressive of the spirit of Buddhism which is found moving in the depths of its followers and also of Oriental people generally.

The tea-ceremony is a simple affair but the fact that all

the monks together with the Rōshi partake of the tea from one teapot is indicative of the democratic and brotherly feeling which is at the bottom of the Zendo life. Sometimes the Rōshi may give them a little talk about the study of Zen or the doings of the ancient masters and shake them up to new redoubled efforts. Simplicity and orderliness is the one prevailing and most noticeable spirit in all the aspects of Zendo life, but there is no military austerity here. (Plate 41.)

At the end of each sojourn, the summer and the winter, each monk is taken to task to render account for his behaviour during the term. He is then free to leave the monastery where he has spent his term and go somewhere else. Each is summoned before the chief monk-official and asked what he is going to do now that the *angya* season has set in and he is at liberty to take advantage of it. If he expresses the desire to leave for one reason or another, he is so registered in the book. But if he wishes to continue his Zendo life here, the chief monk may have something to say about his conduct during the period that has just past. If the monk behaved properly, he will pass without much comment. When otherwise, he will quite severely be reprimanded for his misdemeanour, and in some extreme cases even a refusal to renew his term will be the verdict. This is fatal to the career of the monk, because the stain clings to him wherever he goes, and all the Zendo doors may be found closed to him. This term-end examination is therefore quite a nerve-racking event in the life of the Zendo monk. (Plate 42.)

There are several kinds of bell[1] used in the monastery for different purposes; the one shown here in the picture is the largest. It rings regularly at least four or five times a day; in the morning it reports the time for the monks to wake up, which is about half past three, and in the evening to start their evening meditation, and at night to keep up

[1] See the Appendix.

their exercise in a reclining position, which is about nine or half past nine.

The spirit of Buddhism is most intimately connected with the big bell, apart from which we cannot think of the monastery life. The meaning of the bell is revealed in a most significant way: when the dusk approaches, the clouds grow chillier, the air is perfectly still, the pale and almost indistinguishable new moon is about to set, and the birds quite tired after a day's labour seek their nests for the night among the mountain trees, then the bell begins to ring its evening mission. As the solid body of metal hollowed out is struck with a heavy piece of wood, a soft, resonant, soul-pacifying sound issues from it, which fills and reverberates through the entire valley. If we are near enough, we shall hear the monk recite the *Kwannon-gyō*—a fitting accompaniment to the booming bell.

Yün-mên (Ummon) once had a bell made; when it reached his monastery, the monks asked the master to strike it to celebrate the occasion. He gave it the first stroke, and the monks followed him. The master asked: "What do you want to do by striking the bell?" The monks: "To invite the master to a feast." Yün-mên was not satisfied with the answer and gave his own: "To stop suffering, to put an end to sorrow."

On another occasion, seeing a monk strike the bell, Yün-mên asked: "Who made this bell?" The monk gave no answer, whereupon the master said: "You ask me and I will give you an answer." The monk asked, and the master said: "The monks." Another response given by the master was that he struck the bell once by himself saying "Mahā-prajñā-pāramitā!"

Yün-mên once announced that "True emptiness does not destroy existence as it is (*astitva*); true emptiness does not differ from form (*rūpam*)." The monk asked: "What

is true emptiness?'' The master said, "Do you hear the bell?" The monk answered: "That is the sound of the bell." Yün-mên concluded, "You wouldn't understand even when you wait for an ass year to come."[1]

The following poem on the bell was composed by Sōyen Shaku (died 1919), of Kamakura:

"In early morning it wakes one from a long night's slumber, enveloped in clouds of ignorance;
At close of day it makes one turn towards the perfect moon of Truth, shining in the sky of vast emptiness;
Where there is nothing heard, nothing taught, nothing done and doing,
The booming bell goes on filling the air and shaking up the entire Brahma heaven."

The following is by Ju-ching (如淨) on a little hanging bell under the eaves; he was the teacher of Dōgen while the latter was studying Zen in China between 1223–1228:

"The whole body is the mouth, hanging in the air;
It is unconcerned which way the wind blows; East or West, North or South;
Without distinction it gives out its own sermon on the Prajñā:
*Ti ting tung, ti ting tung,* and again *ti ting tung.*"

---

[1] The ass is not found among the twelve animals figuring in the Chinese calendar.

**The Front Door of the Zendo** *Plate 24*

The Rear Door of the Zendo  *Plate 25*

123

Kinhin (Walking Exercise)  *Plate 26*

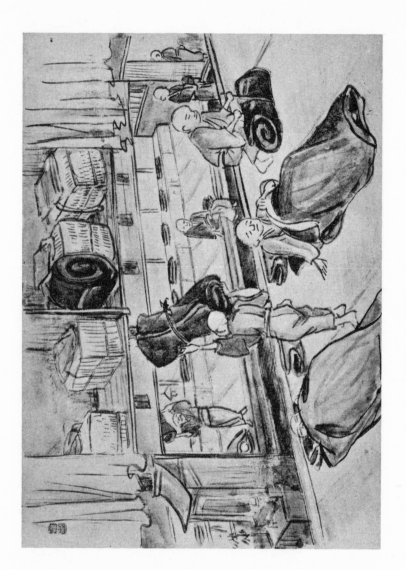

Bedding Put up  *Plate 27*

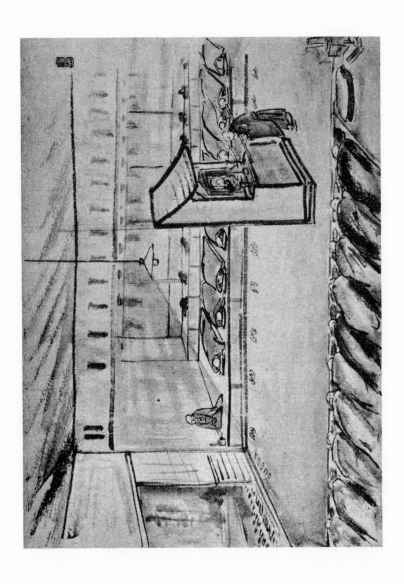

Good Night to the Holy Monk   *Plate 28*

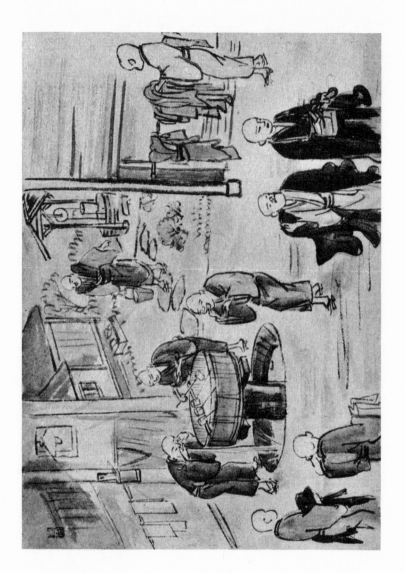

Morning Wash *Plate 29*

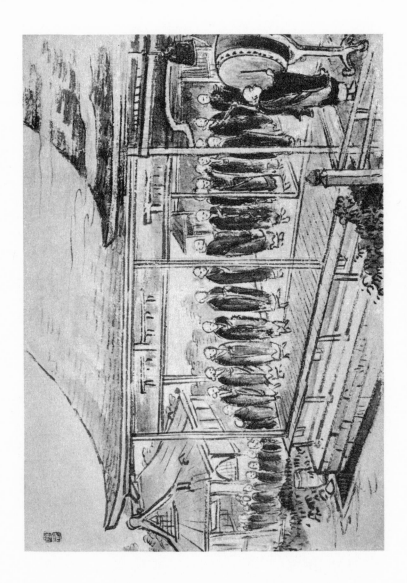

Monks Filing up *Plate 30*

Rōshi Ready for a Koza  *Plate 31*

Meditation Posture  *Plate 32*

130

Ready for a Zen Interview  *Plate 33*

Interview with Rōshi  *Plate 34*

Deeds of the Utmost Kindness  *Plate 35*

The Warning Staff  *Plate 36*

Deeply Absorbed in Meditation  *Plate 37*

135

Monks Looking for Zen Passages   *Plate 38*

136

Seeing Off a Senior Monk  *Plate 39*

137

Zen Monks on Pilgrimage  *Plate 40*

Tea-ceremony with Rōshi  *Plate 41*

139

Term-end Examination *Plate 42*

**Monks Striking the Large Bell**  *Plate 43*

141

# VII.  APPENDICES

# NAMES OF THE TEN BUDDHAS

1. Vairochana Buddha as the Dharmakāya, Pure and Undefiled;

2. Lochana Buddha[1] as the Sambhogakāya, Perfect and Full;

3. Śākyamuni Buddha as the Nirmāṇakāya, Whose Forms are Manifested in Hundreds of Thousands of Kotis;

4. Maitreya the Venerable Buddha, Who is to be Born Here in Time to Come;

5. All the Buddhas of the Past, Present, and Future in All the Ten Quarters;

6. Mañjuśrī the Bodhisattva of Great Wisdom;

7. Samantabhadra the Bodhisattva of Great Deeds;

8. Avalokiteśvara the Bodhisattva of Great Love;

9. All the Venerable Bodhisattva-Mahāsattvas;

10. Mahāprajñāpāramitā.[2]

---

## VERSE OF THE MORNING GRUEL-MEAL

The gruel-meal has ten advantages
Whereby the Yogins are benefitted;
The results accruing from it are boundless,
Finally leading them to eternal happiness.

---

## VERSE AFTER THE MORNING GRUEL-MEAL

Having finished the morning gruel-meal,
Let us pray that all beings
Accomplish whatever task they are engaged in
And be furnished with all the Buddha-dharmas.

[1] Notice the distinction made between Vairochana Buddha and Lochana Buddha, while practically they are the same.

[2] The presence of Mahāprajñāpāramitā in the list of the ten Buddhas is significant. In fact, whenever prayers are offered, "Mahāprajñāpāramitā" is always mentioned together with "all the Buddhas and Venerable Bodhisattva-mahāsattvas" as if it were something quite personal.

## VERSE OF THE MIDDAY MEAL

The meal has three virtues and six tastes,
Offered to the Buddha and the Brotherhood;
Let all sentient beings in the Dharmadhātu,
Universally share alike the offering.

---

## VERSE OF THE SABA

O you of the spiritual worlds,
I now offer this to you;
Let this food fill the ten quarters
And all the spirits enjoy it.

---

## THE FIVE REFLECTIONS

First, let us reflect on our own work, let us see whence this comes;

Secondly, let us reflect how imperfect our virtue is, whether we deserve this offering;

Thirdly, What is most essential is to hold our minds in control and be detached from the various faults, greed, etc.

Fourthly, That this is taken as medicinal is to keep our bodies in good health;

Fifthly, In order to accomplish the task of enlightenment, we accept this food.

---

## VERSE OF THE THREE MORSELS OF FOOD

The first morsel is to destroy all evils,
The second morsel is to practise all good deeds,
The third morsel is to save all sentient beings—
May we all attain the path of Buddhahood.

---

## VERSE OF THE WASTE WATER

This water wherewith the bowls were cleansed,
Has the taste of heavenly nectar;
I offer it to you hosts of the spiritual realms,
May you all be filled and satisfied!
Om, Ma-ku-la-sai Svāhā!

---

## VERSE AFTER THE MIDDAY MEAL

Having finished the rice-meal, my bodily strength is fully
restored,
My power extends over the ten quarters and through the
three periods of time, and I am a strong man;
As to reversing the wheel of cause and effect, no thought is
to be wasted over it;
May all beings attain miraculous powers!

---

## THE MIRROR OF ADVICE

The most important thing to do for the Zen monks of
our school is to understand the koans left by the ancient
masters. There are recently, however, some ill-advised fel-
lows who are quite ignorant of the meaning of the thoughtful contrivance bequeathed by wise men of the past; they
despise the ancient wisdom, not allowing [their pupils] to
study it with due care. Our own monk-students, failing to
weigh properly the merit of such a misguided attitude of
those ignorant critics, bury themselves in the den of the
ghostly beings; they make light of the ancient koans and
are vainly proud of this fact before well-seasoned followers
of Zen. They are truly to be pitied, and also to be laughed
at.

Those who come to study Zen under my guidance should
cherish a grave doubt, each according to his capacities, as
to the meaning of the ancient koans as if his head were
set on fire. Let them keep on, without interruption, doubt-

ing the koans until they come to realise a state of great fixation. When this state of fixation is broken through, they are able to leap out of the cave of birth and death. Then they can penetratingly understand what was in the hearts of the wise men of old. This is the time when they feel at ease with themselves and are able to requite all the kindly feelings the Buddhas and Fathers have cherished for them. Why then should they waste this precious life of theirs by not doing anything serious or of enough importance?

---

## RULES REGULATING THE DAILY LIFE[1]

The most urgent task is to study and master Zen. Therefore, whenever you have a view to discuss with the master, consult with the directing monk (*jikijitsu*) and try to see the master regardless of the hours of the day.

1. When entering the Zendo, fold your hands, palm to palm, before your chest; when going out of it, hold your hands, the right over the left, in front of the chest. Let your walking and standing be duly decorous. Do not walk across the front of the Mañjuśrī shrine; be not in a flurry or swaggering when walking the floor.

2. During the meditation hours, no one is permitted to leave the Hall except for interviewing the master. To other necessary movements, the intermission hours are to be devoted. While outside, no whispering, no tarrying is allowed.

3. When the *kinhin* (walking) goes on, do not remain in your seats; when walking do not shuffle your sandals. If you are, on account of disease, prevented from taking part in the *kinhin*, with the consent of the directing monk (*jikijitsu*) stand on the floor at your seat.

4. The *keisaku* (warning-stick) is to be used with discrimination on the monks, whether they are dozing or

---

[1] This applies to the *Dōnai*, i.e., Zendō proper where the monks observe their meditation hours. As to the distinction between *Dōnai* and *Jyōjū*, see below, where the *Jyōjū* regulations are given.

not. When submitting to the warning stick, courteously fold your hands and bow; do not permit any egoistic thoughts to assert themselves and cherish anger.

5. At the time of tea-ceremony (*sarei*) taking place twice a day, no one shall be absent; no left-overs are to be thrown on the floor.

6. No sundry articles are to be scattered about your seats (*tan*). No writing materials are allowed. Do not take off your upper garment at your seats when going out of the back door.

7. Even when the Zendo is not in regular session, you are not to pass your time dozing, sitting against the back-wall.

8. No one is allowed on his own accord to use the warning-stick (*keisaku*) although he may be suffering from the stiffness of his shoulder-muscles.

9. Going out to town or visiting the *jōjū* quarters is not permitted: if absolutely necessary, transact the business through the attendants (*jisha*) of the Zendo; otherwise, all private affairs are to be settled on the "needle and moxa" days (*hashin kyūji*).

10. On ordinary days the monks are not allowed at the attendants' quarters (*jisharyo*); if necessary, the *jikijitsu* (directing monk) is to be notified.

11. At the time of morning service, the dozing ones are to be severely dealt with the *keisaku* (warning-stick).

12. At meal-time the monks are to conduct themselves quietly and to make no noise in the handling of the bowls; the waiting monks should move about quietly and in due decorum.

13. When the meditation hours are over at night, go right to bed; do not disturb others by sutra-reading, or bowings, or whispering with the neighbouring monks.

14. During the term, the monks are not allowed to leave the monastery unless their teachers or parents are critically ill or dead.

15. When a monk is newly admitted into the Brotherhood, the fact is announced and he takes the seat assigned to him; but before this is done, he must first make bows to the Holy Monk (i.e., Mañjuśrī), and then pay his respect to the head of the *tan* and to the *jikijitsu* (directing monk).

16. When the monks go out for their begging round, they are not to swing their arms, or put their hands inside the dress, or walk the streets staggeringly, or whisper to one another; for such behaviours are damaging to the dignity of monkhood. If they meet horses, carriages, etc., in the streets, be careful to avoid walking against them. In all their movements, the monks ought to be orderly.

17. The days bearing the numbers four and nine, are the days for general sweeping, shaving, bathing, working outdoors, etc.; sewing, moxa-burning, etc. may also take place on these days. The monks are then not supposed to visit one another and pass their time in talking idly, cracking jokes, and laughing nonsensically.

18. As to fixing bath days for the Brotherhood, the monks entrusted with the task are requested to consult the *shikaryo* (head of the general office) and act according to his directions.

19. When any one is indisposed, the matter is to be reported to the *jikijitsu* and the attendant-monk (*jisha*), and the sick one will be removed from the Zendo. While being nursed, he is neither to read books, nor to be engaged in literary work, nor to pass his time in idle talk. If he comes back after five days, he is expected to perform the rite of "returning to the Zendo."

The above regulations are to be carefully taken notice of. Those who violate belong to the family of the Evil One and interfere with the welfare of the community. They are to be expelled speedily after holding a council. The reason is to preserve as long as possible the life of the community.

---

## REGULATIONS OF THE SICK-ROOM

Anyone who happens to be the occupant of this room because of ill health, is not to forget practising *zazen* silently along with taking medicine, even with his head on the pillow. Never neglect exercising himself in the cultivation of the right thought. When this is not done, the disease may be aggravated and the medicine cease to be effective. Three doses of medicine are to be taken daily; each basketful of charcoal costs three sen.[1]

1. Fire of all kind is to be carefully kept under control.

2. Neither *sake* nor herbs of the onion family are allowed even as medicine. According to the nature of the disease, special cooking is allowed after reporting to the office. Other things are prohibited.

3. Be careful not to soil the bedding, etc.

4. While in sick-bed, a monk is not allowed to read books, to engage in literary work, or to idle away his time in trivial talk. If he comes out of the sick-room after staying away for five days, he is expected to perform the rite of "returning to the Zendo."

---

## REGULATIONS OF THE OFFICIAL QUARTERS (JYŌJŪ)[2]

The most essential business of monkhood is to study Zen, and you are expected to exert yourselves in this. After the daily work, keep your evening meditation as in the Zendo.

---

[1] These regulations were compiled many years ago before prices began to go up after the Great War.

[2] Literally meaning "eternally abiding." The monastery where Zen is studied is divided into two sections: *jyōjū* and *dōnai*. The *jyōjū* section is the official or business quarters where affairs connected with the Zendo life are carried out, such as cooking meals for the monks, taking care of the Buddha-hall, planning for daily work, getting provisions, seeing visitors, paying bills, receiving donations, etc. For these offices, elder monks of some experience are chosen, and change of per-

Says an ancient master, "The exercise while working is hundreds of thousands of times more valuable than the one practised while in quietude." Keeping this in mind, exert yourselves to the best of your abilities.

1. Take the best care of all kinds of fire and light.

2. At the morning and the evening service and on other occasions requiring attendance, the monk-officials are not to fall behind the others.

3. At meal-times try by all means to attend a second sitting if you are detained by your work. In handling the bowls, in sipping soup, you are not to make a noise. The waiting-monks must behave orderly and with decorum.

4. In going the begging rounds or in performing outdoor work, you are also expected to join the others; if you are prevented from this, do not neglect reporting the fact at the *shikaryo*.

5. Do not visit other official rooms and spend the time in gossipping and talking trivialities whereby interrupting their hours of meditation. When business requires visits, do not prolong them beyond absolute necessity.

6. Going out in town is strictly forbidden. If it is necessary to go out of the gate, the *shikaryo* is to be notified. When out in town the mannerly behaviour of monkhood is expected.

7. When sick and not able to attend the service, etc., the fact is to be reported at the *shikaryo*; such monks are not to visit other official rooms.

8. When the evening meditation hours are over, each monk is to retire at once to his own bed. No wastage of the light is allowed by sitting up late and talking nonsense. The bedding and other articles are to be kept clean.

9. All the articles and pieces of furniture belonging to the *jyōjū* quarters are to be used with the utmost care. After use, take note to return them where they are kept.

sonnel takes place every few months. They have their own separate rooms outside the Zendo. The *dōnai* means "within the Zendo, or *Sōdō*." This is where the monks generally have their seats of meditation.

Says an ancient master: "All the belongings of the *jyōjū* are to be used as a man does his own eyes."

10. The sandals are not to be left carelessly on the floor. While stepping up and down the hall, do not make rustling sounds. Do not make light of the trivial deeds of daily life, for great virtues are born of them. Pray, be mindful of all that has been stated above.

## REGULATIONS OF THE LODGING ROOM

Monks intently bent on the mastery of Zen go on a pilgrimage in search of an able master and superior friends. When the evening comes, they find out a monastery where they may pass the night. Being permitted to the lodging room, they release themselves of the travelling outfit, and sit in the meditation posture facing the wall. It is to be most regretted that recently there are some travelling monks who have no desire to conduct themselves in accordance with old usage. The main point for the monks, however, is to devote their entire energy to the settlement of the gravest business they can have in this life in whatever surroundings they may find themselves. The meaning of the pilgrimage in Zen lies nowhere else but here, as was anciently seen in the company of Seppo, Ganto, and Kinzan. O monks, be ever diligent!

1. After the evening bell is struck, no travelling monks are admitted.

2. Do not ask for a second night's lodging however stormy and windy the day may be. In case of sickness this rule is waved.

3. No dozing against the travelling bag is allowed. The lodging monk is not to go to bed until the evening meditation hours are over or until a notice to that effect is given to him.

4. Attend the morning service when the bell in the Hall is heard; the *kesa* may be omitted.

5. The morning gruel is served when the *umpan* ("cloud-board") is struck.

6. No light is to be burned in the night.

---

## REGULATIONS OF THE BATH-ROOM

While taking a bath, the "exquisite touch" of warmth must be made to lead to the "realisation of the nature of water."[1] No idle talking is allowed here. Before and after the bath, proper respect is to be paid to the venerable Bhadra.

1. The best care must be taken of fire.

2. The bath-room work is attended in turn by the monks from the Zendo. Otherwise, orders are issued from the *shikaryo*.

3. When the master takes his bath, have his attendants notified. In case of other respectable personages, special attention will be given to the cleanliness and orderliness of the bath-room.

4. When the bath is ready, the wooden blocks are clapped according to the regulations, and the monks led in rotation to the room by the Zendo attendants.

5. For the fuel, dead leaves gathered from the woods and other waste materials are to be used.

6. When the bathing is all over, be thorough in scraping all the embers and hot ashes out from under the bathing pot and have them completely extinguished.

7. On the day following, the bath-tub will be thoroughly scrubbed, and the entire room nicely cleansed, while the vessels are properly arranged.

The above articles are to be observed at all points. No random use of the bath-room is permitted, which may interrupt the speedy execution of the public office.

---

[1] See the seventy-eighth case of the *Hekigan* (*Pi-yen-chi*). Cf. p. 40, of the present work.

## THE SOUND INSTRUMENTS IN THE
## ZEN MONASTERY

In the Zendo life, the movements of the monks on various occasions are directed by the use of different kinds of sound-producing instruments. No oral orders are given; but when a certain instrument is sounded, the monks know what it means at that particular time. The accompanying pictures[1] illustrate such instruments.

The *Ōgane* (1)[2] is the largest bell used in the monastery, It hangs underneath a specially-designed structure as illustrated in Plate 43. The heavy swinging beam (2, *shumoku*) is used to strike the bell. It is this bell which reflects the spirit of the Buddhist temple. The ring has a peculiarly soul-pacifying effect. Lafcadio Hearn in his *Unfamiliar Japan*, Vol. I refers to the "big bell of Engakuji" and most beautifully describes its "sweet billowing of tone" when it is struck and the "eddying of waves of echoes" which rolls over the surrounding hills. As a work of art the bell occupies an important position, and there are many old bells now in Japan which are classed as "national treasures" of the country.[3]

*Denshō* or *Hanshō* (3) is a much smaller one and generally found hanging under the eaves. It is struck with a mallet (4). When a gathering takes place in the Buddha-hall, this calls out the monks from the Zendo.

*Umpan* (5) is "cloud-plate" made of bronze. When this rings, it means that the dining room is open.

*Han* (7) is a heavy solid board of wood hung by the front door of the Zendo. When this is struck, the monks know that the time is come for them to get up or to retire to bed or that a *teishō* is to take place, etc. The characters read:

[1] See p. 108.
[2] The figures in parentheses refer to the illustrations on p. 108.
[3] Soyen Shaku's poem on p. 91 of this book refers to this *Ogane*, while Ju-ching's is what is known as wind-bell (*fêng-ling*).

"Birth-and-death is the grave event,
Transiency will soon be here,
Let each wake up [to this fact],
And, being ever reverend, do not give
yourselves up to dissipation."

The last two lines sometimes read differently in different Zendos. The board is taken hold of, when struck, by means of the strings hanging below in a loop.

*Kin* or *Keisu* (9) is a high, somewhat large, metal gong in the Buddha-hall. Its rim is struck with a stick (10) to punctuate the sutra-reading. The smaller one, *Rin* or *Shōkei* (16), is also used in this connection.

Two kinds of bells (*suzu* or *rei*) used by Rōshi are shown in (11). The choice is individual. Other kinds are also used, one of which is given in (15).

*Inkin* (12) is always carried in the hand and struck with a metal stick attached to it with a string. When the head-monk strikes it in the Zendo, it means the beginning or the end of the meditation hours. When he does so at the head of a procession it means that all the monks joining it are to stand still and then sit, or that they have to rise from the sitting position and walk back to the Zendo.

*Kanshō* (13) is used when the monks want to interview the Rōshi on Zen. When the *sanzen* hour comes, the Rōshi's attendant strikes this bell with the hammer (14). The monks come out of the Zendo, one by one if it is a *dokusan,* and in file if it is a *sōsan;* they sit before the bell in the order of arrival. The master interviews one monk at a time. Being ready, he rings his hand-bell (11) to which the monk responds by striking his bell (13), once for *sōsan* and twice for *dokusan.*

*Rei* (15), also called *Rin,* is a hand-bell which rings by shaking. It is used by Rōshi, and also by a monk when he reads the sutras while standing, for instance, before Idaten, the kitchen god, at meal-time.

The big drum, *Hokku* (18), is generally set up on a

high stand in a corner of the Buddha-hall. When a general gathering takes place, it is beaten with two sticks (19) alternately with a peculiar rhythm.

The big wooden fish (20) called *Hō* is used principally in the Sōtō monastery and not in the Rinzai. The inside is hollowed out. It is used to announce the midday meal. How the fish came to function in the Buddhist temple is unknown. Some think the fish is a symbol of immortality, and for this reason it is frequently found in Christian symbolism. But Buddhism is the teaching in which rebirth and not individual immortality is emphasised.

*Mokugyo* (24), literally "a wooden fish" is said to be the modification of the *Hō* (20). It is a peculiarly-shaped roundish solid block of wood with the inside hollowed out, and obtainable in all sizes, the smallest being as small as one inch on its longer side while the larger ones may measure even more than three feet. It has a fish-scale pattern on its body and where it tapers off into the form of a handle, a pair of eyes is carved. It is beaten with a stick, the top part of which is stuffed and wrapped with leather (25). The sound thus emitted has a strange hypnotic effect on the hearer. When it accompanies the sutra-reading, for example, before a *teishō*, it makes the minds of the audience properly receptive for what is to come.

There are two kinds of clappers, *Hyōshigi* (22 and 23) in use in the monastery. They are solid pieces of hard wood: the larger ones may be somewhat longer than one foot in length and the smaller ones about half a foot. The latter are used in the Zendo while the former are used outside, for instance, when the monks are about to eat, when the bath is ready, and on other occasions.

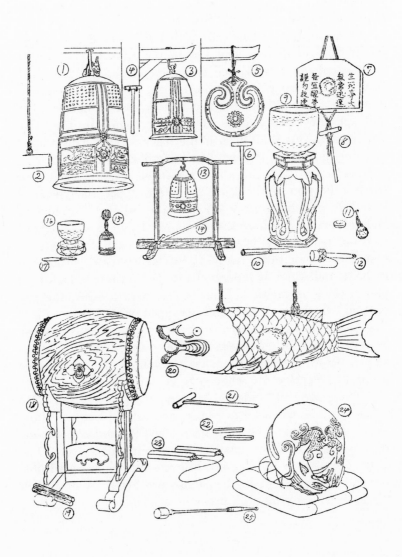

## GLOSSARY OF THE JAPANESE TERMS

Angya, "going on foot," Zen pilgrimage.

Densuryō, office in charge of the Buddha Hall.

Dokusan, individual *sanzen* voluntarily done.

Dōnai, another name for Zendo, as distinguished from the office quarters called *Jōju*.

Enjudō, "life-prolonging room," where the sick are taken care of.

Fūsuryō, office where all accounts regarding the Zendo life are kept.

Futon, quilt filled with cotton-wool.

Geta, foot-gear made of wood.

Hashin kyūji, "taking-up needles and treating with moxa."

Higan, "the other side," *pāramitā*; the *higan* season is March 18–24 and September 21–27, when people visit the temples and decorate the graves.

Hōjō, "ten feet square," abbot's quarters.

Inryō, "retreat-room" for Rōshi (master of the Zendo).

Jikijitsu, head-monk and director of the Zendo.

Jisha, attendant.

Jisharyō, attendants' office attached to the Zendo.

Jōju, official quarters, where the business side of the Zendo life is carried on.

Kafū, "household air."

Keisaku, warning staff.

Kesa, *kashāya* in Sanskrit, the official or ceremonial dress worn by Buddhist priests and monks.

Kesa-bunko, a box in which *kesa* is kept and carried.

Kinhin, walking exercise in the Zendo.

Koan, to be pronounced *kō-an*; a problem given by the master for solution.

Kōza, discourse on a Zen textbook.

Kwatz!, an ejaculation given by the Zen masters, especially connected with Rinzai, originator of the Rinzai school of Zen Buddhism.

Kyōgai, *gocara* in Sanskrit, general mental attitude, the basic tone of one's inner life.

Mokugyo, a wooden sound-producing implement used in accompaniment with the sutra-reading.

Niwa-dzume, "occupying the court," one of the experiences a novice-monk has to go through before his admittance into the monastery.

Otoki, dinner.

Rōshi, master, "old teacher."

Saiza, dinner

Saké, intoxicant made from rice.

Sanzen, studying Zen.

Sarei, tea-drinking ceremony.

Satori, understanding the truth of Zen.

Segaki, feeding the hungry ghosts; *gaki=preta* in Sanskrit.

Semmon Dōjō, Zen institute.

Sesshin, a special period devoted to the study of Zen.

Shikaryō, originally, office entertaining visitors, but nowadays in combination with Fūsuryō, a general directing office.

Tan, raised tatami floor in the Zendo.

Tangwa-dzume, "occupying the lodging room," where the novice-monk has to stay for a few days before he is admitted into the Zendo.

Tan-to, head of the *tan*.

Tatami, a straw matting about $3 \times 6$ feet.

Teishō, same as *kōza*, Rōshi's talk on a Zen textbook.

Tendoku, "reading by revolving."

Tenzoryō, office in charge of provisions and cooking.

Umpan, bronze board with cloud-design, used to call monks to meal.

Yakuseki, evening meal taken as a "medicine."

Zagu, a piece of cloth carried by the Zen monk on which his bowing is done.

Zazen, sitting in Zen meditation.

Zempanryō, quarters reserved for Rōshi.

Zendo, the building where monks live apart from the *jōju* quarters.

# Library of the Mystic Arts

## A LIBRARY OF ANCIENT AND MODERN CLASSICS

**BARTON, R. F.** Autobiographies of Three Pagans in the Philippines. intro. by Dr. Nancy Oestreich Lurie. ill. index bibliog. 320 pp. 5½" x 8¼" 62-19195. $7.50                        ANTHROP
"It is difficult to realize that the people in these autobiographies, two men and a woman live on the same planet that we do. Head-hunting and spearing your enemy are everyday occurrences. Anyone who knows your kin is an enemy, unless he is your kin. It is the savage eye for an eye and tooth for a tooth of Biblical times, even though coming of the Americans has discouraged some of the practices. R. F. Barton was among the Ifugaos long enough to select three representatives of the tribe. In the autobiographies he gives their life history before marriage, including many of their ceremonies and customs. It is an interesting and informative anthropological study." — WICHITA EAGLE & BEACON

**BERNHEIM, H.** Hypnosis and Suggestion in Psychotherapy: The Nature and Uses of Hypnotism. intro. by Ernest R. Hilgard. index. 428 pp. 6⅛" x 9¼" 63-22664. $10.00                        PSYCH
Hypnosis has had a checkered career over a period of centuries, going through cycle after cycle of general approval and total eclipse. The fate of this book indicates how fragile the reputation of hypnosis has been; written almost eighty years ago, and translated into English a few years later, it has always been acknowledged as a great classic. Yet it has been out of print for some seventy years. It was not obsolete; nor was it suppressed. It has simply been neglected — as has hypnotism itself. It was the Second World War that reintroduced hypnosis in psychotherapy, and the widespread contemporary interest dates from that time. Today its potential is recognized by practically all medical societies over the world, and courses in hypnotism are appearing in medical school curricula and in training programs for psychiatric residents. Numerous psychologists are also turning to hypnosis as a fertile field for research and therapy.

**BULLOUGH, Vern L.** The History of Prostitution. index. 320 pp. 6⅛" x 9¼" 64-16619. $7.50   HIST
Prostitution, like the weather, has often been talked about, but very rarely has any scholar bothered to do any research on the topic. Few serious studies on prostitution have been undertaken by social scientists over the past fifty years. Although an occasional sociologist, psychologist, psychiatrist, or anthropologist has concerned himself, the historian has totally neglected the subject. As a result this book is the first attempt at a serious history of prostitution in English in this century.
The author, Dr. Vern L. Bullough, is a historian who has specialized in the history of medicine and science. He has published numerous articles, primarily on medical history, in various learned journals. He was assisted in his researches by his wife, Bonnie L. Bullough.

**COOMARASWAMY, Ananda Kentish.** Buddha and the Gospel of Buddhism. intro. by John C. Wilson. ill. index. bibliog. glossary. 370 pp. 6⅛" x 9¼" 64-16160. $10.00                        REL
A classic introduction to Buddhism, Coomaraswamy's book was originally published in England in 1916. It was reprinted without change in 1927, and it is now finally available in its original form in an American edition. The author was revered both in the East and the West for his unique contributions to art

and philosophy as well as religion. An ardent Indian nationalist, his life work became the preservation of India's heritage and the monumental task of teaching the West to respect and revere the great civilization of India.

When Coomaraswamy died, Aldous Huxley spoke of his "unique importance as a mediator between East and West."

The author was fond of calling himself a traditionalist and often emphasized the virtues of orthodoxy. He was always suspicious of the Western fashionable interest in Buddhism and frequently spoke with considerable irony of the contemporary offbeat Zen enthusiasts. "The suspicious popularity of 'Buddhism' in Europe," he wrote in 1938, "has rested upon a very thorough misunderstanding of what Buddhism really means. The essential doctrines of Buddhism, like those of all orthodox relgions, are in radical opposition to our modern individualism."

The book continues to be a solid exposition of Buddhistic thought and its reissue should be timely in view of current rapprochment between the West and Eastern religious systems. Some twenty plates add interest and value.—VIRGINIA KIRKUS SERVICE.

**FEILDING, Everard.** Sittings with Eusapia Palladino and other Studies. intro. by E. J. Dingwall. 324 pp. 6⅛" x 9¼" 63-18682. $10.00　　　　　　　　　　　　　　PARAPSYCH

"The author, well known as an objective observer of psychical phenomena, presents primarily a detailed report of 13 seances with the noted Italian medium of the 20th Century. There are included accounts of other mediums and of the stigmata of a French abbe. Facts are given; conclusions are left for the reader."
— JOURNAL OF THE AMERICAN MEDICAL ASSOCIATION

"William James deplored the cheating and the vulgarity connected with the mediumship of Eusapia Palladino, but he believed that there was a residuum of phenomena in her performances which could not be explained. So did Everard Feilding of the Society for Psychic Research. He put her through the most rigid tests possible early in this century and concluded that she possessed some inexplicable power which caused tables to levitate, bells to ring, and lights to flash. In this most interesting collection of Feilding's writings we find that although he was a serious researcher, he always retained a sense of humor and a healthy skepticism. Eric Dingwall, who was his friend, has contributed a witty and appreciative introduction which reinforces the impression one gets from these papers that Feilding was a "most acute and well-balanced investigator" of ESP. Recommended for all libraries interested in this field of research." — LIBRARY JOURNAL

**GUIGNEBERT, Charles.** Jesus fwd. by Joel Carmichael. index. bibliog. xv + 560 pp. 6⅛" x 9¼" 56-7837. $10.00　　　　　　　　　　　　　　　　　　　　　　　REL

This historical study of the life of Jesus and the origins of Christianity has received the highest possible praise from biblical scholars of the status of Niebuhr, Barth and Pfeiffer. Its author, Charles Guignebert, is generally considered one of the finest examples of European scholarship. He spent a lifetime of research into the genesis of all forms of religious belief; toward the end of his life he held the chair of the History of Christianity at the Sorbonne.

REINHOLD NIEBUHR: "The virtue of Professor Guignebert's venture lies in his comprehensive analysis of the scholarship of the past decades in this field. The specialists are acquainted with all the evidence which he analyzes. But there is no book of recent years which will give the interested layman a more comprehensive account of what has been written and said about the life of Jesus and a fairer estimate of conflicting evidence. Naturally the author has a position of his own to maintain, but the reader is permitted to see how he arrived at it, and with what cogency and plausibility he defends it against contrasting views."

ROBERT H. PFEIFFER: "Aside from Guignebert's JESUS, only Goguel's LIFE may be regarded as a serious attempt to write a critical and objective historical work.

Guignebert furnishes an excellent introduction to the subject, a reliable guide to beginners, and an informing manual for scholars. We need to be reminded again by Guignebert of the strict and sober discipline required of the true historian."

**JAFFE, Aniela.** Apparitions and Precognitions: A study from the Point of View of C. G. Jung's Analytical Psychology. intro. by C. G. Jung. index. 224 pp. 6⅛" x 9¼". 63-19744. $7.50  PSYCH
The author, well known for her valuable contributions to the literature of analytical psychology, was specifically selected by Dr. Jung to write this book. The book represents a psychological evaluation of more than 1500 personal accounts elicited in response to a series of articles by Dr. Jung, dealing with prophetic dreams, coincidences, premonitions, apparitions. The articles appeared in the popular Swiss magazine, *Schweizerische Beobachter,* and the astonishing response to it came from all social classes — farmers, workmen, tradesmen, office employees and various professions.
One of the notable things to come to light in Dr. Jaffe's book is the fact that among the Swiss, who are commonly regarded as stolid, unimaginative, rationalistic and materialistic, there are just as many ghost stories and strange tales as is likely to be found in any other land; bewitching, sorcery, magic spells, as practiced in the Middle Ages and remoter times have by no means died out, but presently flourish among the Swiss as rampantly as they did centuries ago.
The author leaves aside the questioner of ultimate truth; instead she tries to inquire into the psychological questions: Exactly who is it that sees a ghost? Under what psychic conditions does he see it? What does a ghost signify when examined for its content as a symbol?

**KING, C. Daly.** The States of Human Consciousness. fwd. by Roy Finch. index. v-xiii + 176 pp. 6⅛" x 9¼" 63-10385. $7.50  PSYCH
The crucial thesis of this book is that in addition to the forms of consciousness known to all human beings (Sleep and Waking) there exist two further forms not yet widely known (Awakeness and Objective Consciousness).
What led such an extremely skeptical man as Dr. King to accept the unorthodox idea that additional states of human consciousness are possible? There were four main lines of evidence which convinced him: These were: 1) the neurological and physiological teachings of the Guardjieff Institute; 2) his personal psychological experiments and experiences; 3) his historical studies of ancient civilizations; 4) his studies in behavioral patterns.

**LEARY, Timothy; ALPERT, Richard; Metzner, Ralph.** A Guide to Psychedelic Experience. 150 pp. 8" x 9" 64-19705. $5.00  PSYCH
During the past few years newspapers and magazines have poured out unrestrained criticism on the subject of psychedelic drugs. Meanwhile certain technical journals have simultaneously dealt out unrestrained praise. Whom are we to believe?
Perhaps the most objective evidence available on these important new drugs comes from recent studies made by four scientific research groups, which administered LSD and psilocybin to 462 persons — among them physicians, lawyers, writers, ministers, psychologists, artists, musicians, engineers and housewives. The percentage of these persons reporting it was a pleasant experience was 73%; the percentage reporting they wished to try it again was 82%; a total of 67% reported the experience brought them greater regard for other human beings; 67% felt a sense of relaxation and freedom from anxiety and tension; 65% felt it was of lasting benefit; 38% said it increased their interest in nature, art, music; and 64% felt the experience had changed their lives.
Drs. Leary, Alpert and Metzner have for years been among the most prominent names in the research of psychedelics.

Date Due

| | | | |
|---|---|---|---|
| MAY 2 6 1967 | MAY 1 1 | DEC 2 9 1995 | |
| | OCT 6 | DEC 1 8 1997 | |
| APR 3 0 1971 | 1971 | | |
| NOV 5 | REC'D | | |
| NOV 8 | | | |
| MAR 1 7 1972 | | | |
| FEB 2 6 1974 | | | |
| APR 2 1 1981 | 1981 | | |
| MAY 4 | 1984 | | |
| FEB 2 4 1984 | | | |
| OCT. 2 6 1984 | DEC | | |
| 9 1986 | | | |
| MAR. 2 5 1987 | | | |
| DEC 2 1988 | | | |
| DEC 0 8 1992 | | | |

Demco 293-5